SPIRITS OF THE EARTH BOOK ONE

AFTER THE SKY

MILO JAMES FOWLER

www.aethonbooks.com

AFTER THE SKY
©2020 MILO JAMES FOWLER

This book is protected under the copyright laws of the United States of America. No part of this publication may be reproduced, stored in a retrieval system, or transmitted, in any form or by any means, without the prior permission in writing of the publisher, nor be otherwise circulated in any form of binding or cover other than that in which it is published and without a similar condition including this condition being imposed on the subsequent purchaser. Any reproduction or unauthorized use of the material or artwork contained herein is prohibited without the express written permission of the authors.

Aethon Books supports the right to free expression and the value of copyright. The purpose of copyright is to encourage writers and artists to produce the creative works that enrich our culture.

The scanning, uploading, and distribution of this book without permission is a theft of the author's intellectual property. If you would like to use material from the book (other than for review purposes), please contact editor@aethonbooks.com. Thank you for your support of the author's rights.

Aethon Books
PO Box 121515
Fort Worth TX, 76108
www.aethonbooks.com

Print and eBook formatting, and cover design by Steve Beaulieu.

Published by Aethon Books LLC.

Aethon Books is not responsible for websites (or their content) that are not owned by the publisher.

This book is a work of fiction. Names, characters, places, and incidents are the product of the author's imagination or are used fictitiously. Any resemblance to actual events, locales, or persons, living or dead is coincidental.

All rights reserved.

ALSO IN THE SERIES

*You're reading: **After the Sky***
Tomorrow's Children
City of Glass

For Sara

All come from dust, and to dust all return.
Who knows if the human spirit rises upward
and if the spirit of the animal goes down into the
    earth?
Ecclesiastes 3:20-21

PART I
BEGINNINGS

1. MILTON

NINE MONTHS AFTER ALL-CLEAR

"You'll be sorry!"

Jackson spits blood and drags his beard across the sleeve of his blue jumpsuit, leaving a trail of crimson. He stands over me with big fists clenched, knuckles spattered.

"You knew it could be any one of us, Milton."

I pull myself away from him, my battered body sliding across the slick concrete of the storeroom floor. My mouth works to speak, slurring.

"Why?"

"It's a random draw, Milton. Always is."

I wish it was. It should have been.

"Why her?" I manage, shaking my head to clear the flashing pinpoints of light.

"It was her turn." Jackson shrugs like it's just that simple.

I sob like a child, impotent rage dissolving into whimpers. The coppery tang of my own blood oozes thick from both nostrils, mixing with the sand and ash—

I jerk upright with a start, spitting to clear my mouth. For a moment, I don't know where I am. I look for Jackson, for Julia— they were right there with me in the bunker.

Not anymore.

I'm the only one here now. Outside. Free.

I'll never get used to the silence.

Dawn's golden fire breaks across the eastern horizon and crawls along a massive ridge of mountains in the distance. They look like sleeping giants, lying on their backs. Dark, with only their profiles aflame, they wait with craggy jaws and protruding bellies for the full light of day to awaken them from their slumber. Part of me wishes they'd rise up and greet me with a yawn. I speak to them sometimes, but I know they won't respond.

I'm not crazy. Not yet.

"Time to wake up, boys. It's a new day." I grab one of my hydropacks and take a swig, swish the stuff around. It's enough like water to do the trick. I wipe my mouth with a sleeve, watch the ash trickle out of my beard. I curse quietly. I must have rolled onto my face in my sleep. Probably would have smothered myself if I hadn't woken up in time.

Not a bad way to go out, I guess. Considering the alternatives. Starvation. Loneliness.

I bend down to tie up my bedroll. The thermal blanket is showing serious wear. Maybe I'll get lucky in the next ghost town I pass through, find an actual sleeping bag among the rubble.

"Any chance you guys can point me in the right direction?" I glance at the mountains, jutting upward from kilometers of desolate hardpan stretching out in every direction, parched and cracked, interrupted only by occasional wounded hills—shadows of what they once were in both size and shape.

Silence answers me. A slight breeze whisks across the ground, stirring the dust. The only sound, my own voice. And my noisy thoughts.

The mountains don't look as much like my giants now with the sun climbing over, burning across the scorched earth as far as my groggy eyes can see. For the past week or so, I've headed straight for that ridge, the only thing separating me and this barren wasteland from whatever lies on the other side.

"Just more of the same, right?" I sure hope not.

I still have *hope*? Now that sure is something. Maybe I am crazy, after all.

The sun cooks my face a little before I pull on my hood and tinted face shield. I guess I could sleep under some kind of makeshift shelter at night, but I like breathing the cold air. It chills my lungs, reminds me I'm still alive. Sometimes I breathe in a little too much of the ash and wake up coughing and spitting like this morning—but it's worth it. Being out under the stars makes me forget, sometimes.

Then I remember: So long without fresh air in the bunker—just the recycled variety they said was perfectly fine for us.

Never again. I'd sooner die.

And that might happen a whole lot sooner than I'd planned. I count my packs: three hydro, two vitamineral, four protein. The last bit of ingenuity from those United World scientists before they were blown away. These packs were issued by the ton to every bunker in the sector. They'll last me two days, no more.

That's how long I have to scale those sleeping giants and see what's on the other side. I'm counting on a city—ruins with leftovers where I can re-stock my supplies. Maybe there will be people. Survivors, like me.

It's been two months since I came across my last neighbor. But I probably shouldn't count him. There wasn't much left. Bones, mostly, and what looked like organic matter baked into the broken concrete nearby. I called him *Adam*, since he was the first person I saw after All-Clear. I knew he wasn't *Eve* because his pelvis wasn't the right shape.

I like people. I miss them.

I am so, so sorry for what I did.

Packs counted, bedroll slung across my back, every centimeter of my body covered by my jumpsuit, face shield, hood, gloves, and boots, I make my way down the rocky hillside where I spent the night. As I reach a level stretch of gravel below, I settle into an easy walking pace. There's no rush. Not anymore. Life has slowed to barely a crawl, and I'm the only one out here doing the crawling.

I check my gloves again. Habit. A few weeks ago, I forgot to zip them to my sleeves. As I climbed down a knoll, the sand shifted and I lost my footing. My left glove snagged on a piece of shale and almost slipped off. The instant sunburn across my wrist was excruciating. Haven't forgotten since. And now I have this delightfully compulsive little habit of checking them every few minutes. Just a tug every now and then to be sure.

All I can hear now are the dull thuds my boots make across the dusty ground and the echo of my breath against the face shield. Every morning it hits me like this: how alone we are now.

We?

Humankind. I can't be the only one left. That would be too depressing. There have to be others like me somewhere out there. The bunkers were designed to safeguard the continuation of our species. I survived, so others must have as well. They all couldn't have lost their minds and killed each other—or eaten each other.

"Cannibalism is not an option." Jackson's voice echoes clearly through my mind.

A smirk creeps across my face. He didn't say anything about murder.

It was one way to keep the rations coming.

Before the end, back when we had more restaurants and grocery stores than we needed, when they used to throw away extra food into dumpsters in back alleys, I'd fantasize about my favorite meals. My mouth became a wellspring of hot saliva at the thought of a large, extra cheesy pizza loaded with toppings; nachos smothered with salsa and jalapeños; lasagna with piles of garlic bread on the side... Then there were the desserts: ice cream sundaes, cheesecake –

"Cheesecake," I murmur out loud. I shake my head.

Why am I torturing myself?

Because you deserve it.

Those years in the bunker may not have erased my memories of the way life used to be, but they did train me for the life to come. I learned to eat ration packs not because of their taste (they were designed by the government geniuses to have no flavor) or because I was hungry. I ate them to survive. They nourished me and kept me alive. That was their only purpose, and they did it well enough.

So now when my stomach growls, when I feel that sharp hunger pang knifing me, I don't even think about what I want to eat. That part of the equation doesn't exist anymore. Things are simpler. My hunger is relieved by a ration pack. No use reminiscing on the flavors of a past life.

It's too soon to eat. With only a handful of packs left, I need to be careful. Hydration is no problem with this jumpsuit the scientists designed. The cooling system recycles my piss. Used to gross me out, but not anymore. I've learned to appreciate it. So even under the hot sun, three hydropacks will see me all the way to the top of those mountains. But I need to make the other rations last. Once I start climbing, I'll need my strength.

I hum while my footsteps keep the beat. I don't recognize the tune. Something original? Improvised and improved, one bar at a time. I have to do something in the silence, or it'll get to me. The overwhelming enormity of it. The finality. And me, all alone, swallowed whole by it.

I really don't want to go crazy.

Spending time hiking the great outdoors was never really my thing before the end of the world. I liked to swim or run in the Preserve on occasion when I could get the time off. It was great to see the wild life. I was in their world, visiting. The earth belonged to the animals, and we took it from them. We took it, and we destroyed it. We destroyed them. In the past few months, I don't know how many kilometers I've covered. But I've done more than enough hiking to last a lifetime.

The earth is so quiet now, I can't help but wonder if it's sleeping. Should I walk on tip-toe to keep from waking it? No birds with morning calls. No snakes to slither, no lizards to blink in the sun. This land was a desert once, full of life.

Now it's an ash-scape, blown to hell. Like the rest of the planet.

I glance over at the road, asphalt rippled and twisted like a frozen river. The InterSector highway at one time, with vehicles rushing in both directions. As long as it heads east, I'll keep it nearby; but if it decides to change direction, it'll be on its own. We've traveled together for a long stretch, linking each other to a past when life was good and gas cost seven bucks a gallon.

"*We should've seen the end coming,*" Jackson would often say. "*There were signs. Good God, there were signs.*"

He was a big man, and the way he told it, his father had been a professional ball player back in the day. I didn't doubt it. Jackson carried the genes of a bull. Years in the bunker had dulled his features, and his beard covered most of his face, but you could still see it in the way he carried himself. He was made to be a leader.

He would have killed us all.

I whirl around at a sudden noise behind me. A rock, tumbling down the hillside. Maybe I disturbed it as I passed by. It eventually finds a resting place and lies still.

Well, that's the most action I've seen in weeks. I almost smile.

I resume my trek. The mountains look as far away as they did when I woke up. I fight off the weight of defeat that's always lurking for an opportune moment to strike.

"There's no better direction to go." My voice is loud, hollow-sounding against the face shield. It's pretty clear what's on this side of these mountains—the spawn of Mars and the Sahara. It can't be like this everywhere. Somewhere out there, a tree is still growing. Grass, green and lush. A cool stream of fresh water. And people.

I just have to find them.

Defeat sulks back to the sidelines to wait. It will have another chance to play in this game. If I counted my nourishment packs right, this is only the first quarter.

Another rock moves on its own, skidding down the slope at my right. It falls against a boulder and lies flat.

I stop and face it. Stare at it.

Hope is a funny thing. I've been longing for months to find another living soul—human, animal, or otherwise. Hell, even a cactus would have sufficed. Every morning, I awake with that hope burning in my gut.

But now I stand staring at the second rock that's moved in as many minutes, and I'm feeling a bit disquieted, I have to admit.

"Hello?" I call out. I should take off my face shield if I really want to be heard. I look up to my right, then turn and check behind me.

It's only logical to assume I'm not alone. Before the end, there were more than nine billion people on the earth. Figure a few billion were lost on the surface thanks to the bombs and toxins and nuclear winter that followed. And a few billion more probably didn't make it underground, couldn't hack it. Lost their minds and killed each other in the bunkers. Or their airlocks malfunctioned, infecting everyone inside. Worst case scenarios. But that would still leave a whole lot of survivors to make the breach after All-Clear.

And what about animals? Any left on the surface couldn't have made it, obviously, and most of the ones taken below were eaten. But some could have survived. And hadn't those government geniuses collected two of every species, male and female, up in the Preserve? They were looking ahead. Planning, always planning.

"Hello?" My boots shift, scraping across the dusty hardpan.

Maybe it's a dog. Starving, most likely. Nothing out here to eat, not even weeds. Bare as the moon. I wouldn't mind sharing a protein pack or two. The company would be worth it. I'd have someone to talk to, and he'd listen to me, and I wouldn't have to consider the prospect of losing my mind anymore. We'd be in this together, the two of us.

I shake my head. Not thinking clearly. The scientists didn't design doggy jumpsuits, as far as I know. There can't be a dog out here—or any kind of animal. Unprotected under the sun, the poor fur ball wouldn't last a minute before it was charred head to toe. Dog burger.

Yum.

The longer I stand in the silence, the more certain I become that it was just another rock deciding to migrate on its own. Bored with its life halfway up the hill, hoping to start over at a lower altitude. Or maybe it wanted to come with me.

Join the half-crazy human, see what's left of the world!

Deriding my own foolishness, yet unable to stop myself, I clamber up to where the rock landed and retrieve it, hefting it in my hand.

"I shall dub thee...*Rocky*." I hold it in front of my face shield and turn it over, noting how well it fits into the palm of my glove. I won't be able to touch it, run my fingertips along its smooth edges, not until sundown. Or until I find some shade. "Thou shalt be my pet, Rocky."

I unzip a pocket in my pant leg and drop it inside.

Then I jump out of my skin as another rock—much bigger this time—clatters down the hill, bounding and spiraling toward me. I have to lunge sideways to keep from getting hit by the thing.

"What the—?" My voice sounds like it's coming from someone else.

Rocks tumble toward me from all sides. Innumerable, they roll and leap, catapulting themselves in a sudden avalanche. The ground shifts at my feet. Dust rushes out from under me, sucked by an invisible vacuum.

Earthquake? Shouldn't the ground be shaking?

A basic survival instinct kicks in, and I run. Faster than I've ever run in my life. I leap over the mid-size boulders tumbling across my path. My feet are swift, my boots barely making contact. The ashen world around me melts away as my jumpsuit presses flat against me. I should be gasping, fighting for breath, but I'm not. I'm in good enough shape, but not for a long-distance sprint like this.

I run faster, carried by a strength that's not my own. I look down at my legs, pumping effortlessly in a bizarre blur of speed.

This is incredible!

I glance over my shoulder. The rocks hurtle after me now, skipping across each other as if they too are propelled by some unseen force of nature.

What the hell is going on? Maybe it's all in my head. I've finally lost it.

A sharp pain jabs my calf muscle as a stone slams into it. I stifle a short cry.

Yep. This is really happening.

I leap over another boulder, then across a yawning ditch. My vision is consumed by the eastern mountains. They loom closer, growing as I approach. At the speed I'm running—as insane as it sounds—I'll reach them within minutes.

Thirty kilometers? Forty? How fast am I moving?

A heavy stone hits me as hard as a fastball, square in the back. I cry out, but I can't hear my own voice above the rumble of the avalanche rampaging after me, gaining ground. Have I offended Mother Earth somehow? I've been minding my own business out here, trying to survive one day at a time, leaving her to her beauty sleep, doing my best not to disturb her.

Rocky.

Cursing, I reach into my pocket mid-stride and dump my erstwhile pet into the rushing dust below.

"Take it!" I yell, hoping the stampede will be appeased by my offering.

Rocky hits the ground and bounces back, striking me in the shin. I howl and stagger, losing some of my momentum. Then gravel launches upward from all sides. I run through sheets of dust and sand swirling up from the ground, obscuring my vision. My face shield is instantly caked with the stuff. I should wipe it off so I can see where I'm going, but I can't slow down to do so. I run faster than ever, carried blindly by a superhuman speed I'm unable to fathom.

I don't bother trying to comprehend. It's the only thing keeping me alive right now.

Gravel pings against the reflective polymer of my face shield. Did those scientists design it to withstand an attack like this? Unlikely.

Another rock hits me in the back, followed by another. They're catching up—or I'm slowing down. One good shot to the head, and all of this will be over.

I should have worn that suit with the helmet. Thought it was overkill at the time. As soon as the bunker doors opened, I couldn't get out of there fast enough. Didn't care what was waiting for me on the other side. Couldn't stay another second.

Not with all that mess down there.

The gravel—thicker now—pelts my face shield. It's going to crack—only a matter of time. Then I'll meet my end. I will have survived a nuclear holocaust only to be pulverized by killer rocks.

Some kind of sedimentary mutation? There have to be all kinds of side effects the government scientists never could have foreseen. You don't nuke a planet and expect everything to stay the same—or ever be the same again. And with all those toxins and bioweapons released during the early stages of the war, maybe there was a bizarre chemical reaction, and the rocks and dust became sentient in some kind of freak molecular interaction.

Ridiculous maybe, but didn't the ancient Hebrews believe we all originally came from dust?

Tears trickle down my cheeks, an involuntary response to the pain as one rock after another slams into my back.

Didn't *stoning* also originate with the ancient Hebrews?

My legs keep running, but I've dissociated myself from them. They're connected through bones, ligaments, and muscles to my back, which is racked with pain right now. I want to be as far away from this insane situation as possible. I want to hover above it and watch from the outside-in.

I've always wanted to fly...

The sudden silence is peaceful but deafening in contrast to a moment ago. The gravel around me has hit the ground and now lies still. The rocks and boulders have done the same. I imagine the sand and dust clearing, wafting away slowly, settling. I stand swaying in the breeze. My breath is steady and unlabored, as though I haven't just run over thirty kilometers in a matter of minutes. I can't see a thing—other than the crack in my face shield from my brow to my chin. Blindly, I wipe at it with my gloves, succeeding only in smearing the dust around the imbedded gravel.

Eventually I see light. Shapes.

I catch my breath. I've reached the foot of the mountains—my sleeping giants. They're even more massive up close. It would have taken me all day to travel this far. Can't quite believe my eyes. It's like a weird dream, not possible, yet there they are, and here I am.

I wipe the remaining layer of dust from my face shield.

You're not alone.

Stumbling backward in surprise, I stare at the human form on the north ridge. He stands twenty meters above me, as high as a five or six-story building, and wears loose sand-colored garments unlike my standard-issue jumpsuit. Every centimeter of his skin is covered, but instead of a hood and tinted face shield, he wears strips of the cloth wrapped around his head, leaving room only for black goggles over his eyes.

I raise my hand as hope swells within me. I wave, giddy like an idiot.

"Hello, friend," I call. Can he hear me?

A gust of wind ripples his outer garment as his goggles seem to study me. His gloved hands remain firmly planted on his hips.

"Hello?" Heart racing, I struggle to unlatch my face shield, opening it just enough to be sure I'm heard. My hood will provide enough protection from the sun at this angle. "Hello!" I take an unfiltered breath of the dry, dusty air. It smells like an old ash tray filled to the brim. "Good to see you!" I can't contain the smile taking over my face. "It's been so long. Started thinking I was the only one out here..."

My awkward laugh echoes, fading until silence reclaims the moment. My smile dims. As still as a statue, the figure watches me. I try to quell the uneasiness clenching at my stomach. It's only natural that the first meeting between two members of the human race after the end of the world might be a little strange. Particularly so if this person assumed he was the last living survivor. I never truly believed that to be the case, but I suppose if you've resigned yourself to that fact, it might come as a shock to see another *homo sapiens* running around.

Or maybe it was the running itself. That was pretty weird, I have to admit, along with the attack from Mother Earth. This guy's probably just wondering what kind of freak I am.

Or how I might taste. That would really stink. The first person I meet after All-Clear turns out to be a freaking cannibal! Is that why he's regarding me so carefully? Sizing up his next meal?

"Do you have a name?" The feeling in the pit of my stomach is turning cold and heavy. "I'm Milton, from Sector 43. I—we got out a few months ago." I'm making an effort at congeniality here, but if I'm dealing with a cannibal, I don't want it to be common knowledge that I'm traveling alone. "Where-uh... Where are you from?" I take a few steps back, hoping I still have the strength to run for my life if I need to.

The figure launches himself from the ridge and seems to hang in mid-air for a moment before landing on all-fours before me.

"Holy—!" I gasp, nearly tripping over my feet. To jump from such a height and land with ease—he can't be human. Not a normal human, anyway.

The figure stands facing me, arms down at his sides. "You said you were alone," he says in the even cadence of a young woman's voice.

So *he*'s really a *she*. Maybe it wouldn't be so bad getting eaten by a female cannibal. Even so, I keep my distance.

"So you can speak." I attempt another smile. My mouth is the only part of me visible beneath my open face shield. Will the size of my teeth determine dominance?

"First you said you were the only one out here. But just now, you said *we* got out. So which is it?" Her head cocks slightly to one side. "Are you alone, or are there others with you?"

Judging by my reflection in her goggles, I can tell why she's being cautious—if she isn't a cannibal, that is. I look like a freak, a filthy survivalist who gnaws on bones in his spare time.

Maybe she thinks *I'm* a cannibal.

I really need to think about something else.

"I am. Alone, I mean. Not a..." For some reason, I go with the truth. "I've been alone since All-Clear."

Her shoulders seem to relax, so I go on.

"I never gave up hope, though. I knew there had to be others. And there are, right? You're not the only one out here, are you?" Playful thoughts of Adam and Eve pass through my mind. I wish I could see her face.

"Come with me." She turns away and leaps onto an outcropping of rock, pulling herself upward in a single movement.

Does she expect me to do that? Not happening. I might be able to super-run or whatever that was before, but rock climbing has never been my thing. I've never had the grip strength for it.

"Why should I? I don't even know who you are."

She half-turns, and her goggles stare down at me. "Remember what you were running from?"

How could I forget? It was the weirdest thing that's ever happened to me...outside the bunker. "You saw that, huh?"

She resumes her climb. "You're not safe here."

Me? What about her? Shaking my head, I drop my face shield into place and start up after her. "At least tell me who you are."

Strange. With all that's happened in the last half hour, the only thing I want to know right now is the name of my newfound companion. Who cares about killer rocks when after months of solitude, I finally have someone besides my imaginary giants and an ill-conceived pet to talk to.

I'm not alone anymore. There are others like me out here. And as I climb after my new friend, the only thing I know for sure is that I would follow her anywhere.

"You have a name, right?" I watch her swing one-handed from a crevice in the rock and grab hold of another. Amazing, really. So agile—

"Climb." Her tone is firm, making it clear that conversation won't be part of this journey, wherever we're going.

I do my best to keep up, lagging five meters behind her at all times—but not due to any lack of effort. "Where are we going?"

"Higher."

Well, that much is obvious. She reaches the ridge where I first saw her and stands there, waiting for me.

"How far?" I grunt, pulling myself upward.

"Not very."

I pause to catch my breath. "You're not going to eat me, are you?" I half-smile, but my charm is lost now behind my face shield. "Because—if you are—then there's really no point in me going much farther. Right?"

"You need to hurry." Her tone is flat. "We don't have much time."

"About that." Straining every muscle in my fingers and forearms, I manage to reach the ledge at her feet. With as much grace as I can muster, I heave myself up and crawl toward her dusty boots. "The whole *attack of the killer rocks* thing. Is that commonplace around here? I mean, have you seen anything like that before? Because it kind of freaked me out."

Her goggles are fixed on me as I stand. Wish I could see her eyes. I like her voice—even-toned and calm, albeit humorless.

I've really been alone too long.

"We go up and over from here." She points. "Follow me, and stay close."

"Yes ma'am." I salute.

She watches me for a moment, then takes a running leap from the ridge, upward and to the left, landing with both hands jammed in the crevice of a sheer rock wall. She dangles for a moment, then swings single-handedly across to another outcropping, her movements effortless.

"Stay close, huh." I shake my head.

This must be some sort of initiation into her clan. She's from a cave-dwelling, mountain-climbing bunch of survivors, and this is their rite of passage in order to join the tribe. If so, then I should consider my current humiliation an honor. Maybe she'll look past my grunting and gasping and slug's pace and see the effort I'm making here. That's got to be worth something. If I make the cut, I'll be part of a community again. No more going it alone.

As long as there isn't anybody like Jackson in the mix, count me in.

"Hungry?" I call up to her and reach into my pocket for a protein pack.

"We'll eat when we get there."

"Anybody I know?" I chuckle as I tear open the pack and take a bite.

"You've got to hurry." Her tone has changed. There's an urgency to it now. She looks below us, past me, as if something may be following.

"Okay." I lose my contagious sense of humor for the moment and drop the pack into my pocket, doubling my efforts at keeping up.

I've never had a fear of heights, and I'm glad of it now. Between my boots, there's a good twenty-five meters or more that we've climbed already, and who knows how much farther we have to go. One thing's for certain: my companion knows the way. Her familiarity with every crevice and outcropping proves that she's made this trip many times before.

She must be fairly muscular underneath all those loose, billowing garments. She moves with such ease and grace. My arms are already sore and trembling, and I've tried to keep in shape over the years with hundreds of push-ups every day. But

I'm using different muscles now—pulling instead of pushing. Guess I trained for the wrong Olympic event.

Thoughts of Adam and Eve cross my mind again, but I have to dismiss them. Even if she is the most perfect, beautiful woman I've ever seen (and after these past months of solitude, I know she would be), I have a feeling she's not alone. She didn't seem shocked to find me. There will be others waiting for us, maybe all from the same bunker. They weren't all like Sector 43. They couldn't be. And for all I know, she might be married to a polygamist—some kind of mountain tribe living off their stockpile of nourishment packs. Or maybe they're all women who outlived the men from their sector and set off on their own to live out their days in peace. If that's the case, then I'm sure I'll be very popular. We'll have this entire continent to repopulate, and we'll need to get started on that right away. Good things definitely come to those who wait.

Don't tell them you're sterile.

Everyone in Sector 43 was. Jackson said he wasn't, but I never believed him. We were a labor sector, and the government geniuses didn't want us reproducing while underground—consuming carefully planned resources, space, and oxygen. Sterilization was mandatory unless you were one of the sectors' best and brightest. Rumor had it that there were bunkers designated for all-male and all-female populations. Carefully selected based on the results of genetic and intelligence tests, they were the hand-picked gene pool of the future. Of course they weren't sterilized. They had one purpose in life: making plenty of whoopee. And babies, too, when the time was right.

My companion could hail from an entire enclave of prime female specimens, all eagerly awaiting the arrival of a virile young male to get our species back on the road to recovery...

Dream on.

I reach a rock ledge and pull with my left hand curled into a crevice. I throw my right forearm over the top to brace myself. Strong hands take hold of my shoulder and the back of my dusty jumpsuit, helping me onto a level sheet of rock. Gasping from the effort, I roll onto my back.

"Thanks," I manage.

My companion stands over me, and I see myself in her goggles again. I look pathetic lying there with my lungs heaving.

"We're here," her voice comes through the material wrapped around her face, but her tone is difficult to interpret.

Behind her, the yawning mouth of a cave opens into the side of the mountain. The first few meters in there look safe enough, shielded from the sun's rays but with sufficient light. Farther back it's pitch black, and I can't tell where it leads or what could be lurking inside. I try to quell my overactive imagination.

"By *here* you mean..." I leave the blank for her to fill in.

She turns away and enters the cave. "Follow me." Her voice echoes against the earthen walls.

Except for the sound of my slightly labored breathing, silence reigns supreme. I listen to it, remembering all too well what it's been like to live completely alone. Not a single living thing since All-Clear. No vehicles passing me by on the InterSector, no planes flying overhead, no animals, not even insects to prey upon me. One thought has kept me sane all along: the hope of finding life.

So that's why I struggle to my feet and follow this stranger into the cave. I have no idea what awaits me, but I can honestly say I feel no fear, no dread. I may be walking to my death, but at least I won't die alone.

I find my companion seated on a large rock inside the cave, her goggles already off as she works to remove the wrappings from her head. I disconnect my face shield and throw back my hood, letting it fall to my shoulders. I take a seat on a rock across from her.

"You're one hell of a climber," I thoughtfully articulate.

Her eyes dart to me briefly—long enough for me to see they're a pair of dark chocolates with matching eyelashes. They focus on the ground as she frees the rest of her head from the cloth strips binding it.

I catch my breath and run a hand through my shaggy mop of hair, damp with perspiration. The jumpsuit absorbed most of my sweat—thanks to the ingenuity of those scientists who designed it—and used the moisture to cool off the rest of me. I turn my face shield over in my hands as I watch her.

"Any reason why you don't wear a suit?"

"They sicken me." Her lips and chin are free now—perfect, beautiful—as well as her cute little nose. The area above her eyes is still covered. I like her face. Her skin looks soft.

"But you can't argue with the results. They were definitely looking ahead, you know. They knew what we'd need out here with no water and this savage sun. It's ingenious, really. The packs keep us hydrated, and the suits regulate our temperature." Am I rambling? Have I destroyed whatever potential existed for our first conversation?

She's bald. There isn't a single hair on her head, not even the stubble from a day-old shave. She meets my gaze. "They're disgusting and unnecessary. A link to a world that no longer exists."

She's *really* bald—not an ugly bald like an old man, but a smooth bald, like an olive-toned egg. I try not to stare. "Well...all I know is I would've died out here without mine a long time ago."

"You would have adapted. Become nocturnal."

Are we arguing? Barely a complete sentence out of her, and now this inane banter about my suit?

"Maybe." Why don't I just let it go? "But I like to sleep at night when it's cool, you see. I've gotten to like it out under the stars. They remind me that...some things haven't changed. Y'know?"

Trying to wax poetic?

She appears unmoved. "Most things have." She stands and turns toward the dark interior of the cave. "This way."

I rise to follow her but find myself suddenly hesitant. My eyes have adjusted enough to see that this cave extends deep into the mountain. The darkness where she's heading looks impenetrable. Maybe it should be left alone.

"Are we safe now?" My voice echoes after her.

She half-turns to look at me. "What?"

"Before. You said it wasn't safe." I gesture toward the darkness ahead of her. "Is it safe in there?"

"If I said no, would you turn back?"

She has me there—and she knows it. I have nowhere else to go. "Lead on."

I follow her into the darkness and stay close enough to keep her in sight (somewhat), my hand out to the side to brush the cave wall. For some reason, my thoughts drift back to Julia.

She's never far from my mind.

I was just a kid—fourteen or so—and it was right after the first missiles launched around the world. The sector governors had the bunkers ready to go as if they'd been expecting the global chaos to ensue. The Cold War was finally over, and they had to make up for lost time, I guess. The earth rumbled as we were escorted in a rickety elevator down toward its core—a hundred of us taken from our homes that night. Julia and I stood next to each other, pressed in tight like cattle as we made the long descent into the bunker below. We were strangers, but it didn't matter. Our eyes met in the amber light. Our hands clasped and squeezed. We were in this together.

I miss her so much, I ache inside. I wish she'd made it.

More than anything, I hope she can forgive me.

"We go down from here," my companion says.

"What?"

She stops me with a hand on my chest. "Can't you see?"

Is that a rhetorical question? "It's pitch black in here." I frown. "Can you?"

Instead of answering, she sighs. "I'm afraid this will be difficult for you."

What about *her*? She doesn't sound condescending, more like she knows something I don't. And that's already starting to get old.

"You'll need to feel your way." She takes my hand and pulls me down toward what feels like a plastic pipe. "Take this ladder."

"Okay." Blind as a bat, I feel along the pipe until I find the top rung of the ladder she's talking about. "How far down?"

"Twenty meters. I'll go first."

Her garments shift as she begins her descent.

"All right then." I take a deep breath and blow it out, contemplating my odds of surviving a twenty-meter fall to whatever lies below. My boot makes contact, and I rest my full weight on the plastic rung. "There you are." It gives under me, bowing slightly. I bring over my other leg and start down, one rung at a time. The way the ladder bends and creaks as I make each step—it's like I'm the only one on it.

"You still there?"

"Of course." Her voice echoes from far below. She's already at the bottom.

"Didn't even use the ladder, did you?" I recall the way she launched herself down at me when we met.

"No."

Her matter-of-fact tone almost makes me smile. "There's something different about you. Can't quite put my finger on it." My boot slips off a rung, but I catch myself, clutching onto the sides of the ladder and knocking into the rock wall with my shoulder.

"Focus," she says.

"Right." Maybe I shouldn't try to multitask. But then again, I've never been good at following directions. "How close am I?"

"Fifteen meters to go."

"You can see me, huh? I mean—you can see in the dark?"

"Yes."

Maybe she's some kind of mutant. They warned us it could happen if we left the bunker too soon. Sector 43 was auto-locked, programmed to release the blast doors after twenty years passed. By then, supposedly, the nuclear winter would be over, and the atmosphere would have re-adjusted, naturally replenishing itself. But I'm sure there were some bunkers with manual locks, built in basements by folks who were pretty sure they wouldn't make the governors' lottery. The scientists and the soldiers did their best to root them out and eradicate them—for our welfare, of course—but some may have remained on D-Day. People left to their own devices could have come out five or ten years too soon, and the fallout in the atmosphere might have done something to them. Changed them somehow.

"You have any other superpowers I should know about? X-ray vision, maybe?" Silence answers me, so I try again. "You can't see me naked, can you?"

"No. Your urine-suit is in the way."

Humor? Can it be? "You really don't like this thing, do you? Have you ever worn one?"

"Five meters more."

I'm almost there. But then what?

Strange to think I'm actually *inside* my sleeping giants. Deep in these mountains, with no idea where I am exactly or where I'm headed, I'm blindly following a total stranger—just because she happens to be the only other representative of humankind in town. What would the giants have to say about that?

Maybe I'm giving them indigestion.

My boot scuffs across the cave floor as I drop from the ladder. I reach out my hand, and she takes it in her firm grasp. She turns me around, leading me quickly onward. Thoughts of the all-female enclave return, but now I wonder what kind of mutations they might exhibit, or if they're all gnarly and deformed. I guess it really wouldn't matter, since I can't see a thing down here—not even my own glove in front of my face.

"Watch your step," she cautions as we come to a ledge and have to step up. She takes my arm.

"Thanks. How close are we now?"

"Almost there."

"And *there* would be...?" I hope she fills in the blank, but my patience is wearing thin.

"You'll see."

"I hope so. Because right now: nothing."

"Are you afraid of the dark?" She takes my arm again as we mount another earthen step.

"No."

It took a while to get used to the total dark after lights-out in the bunker. When those white, humming fluorescents were on, it was possible at times to forget how deep underground we were. Bright as day. But at night, things could get a little suffocating. My breath would quicken. Sweat would prickle down the back of my neck. Irrational fear would squeeze my insides. Sometimes Julia slept beside me, and with her body snug against mine, I could forget about the darkness. Hell, I could forget about anything but her warm curves.

"Should I be afraid?" I ask. Her responses are so elusive, I have to do what I can to probe the matter. I'll break her down eventually. "Is there something lurking in here I should be aware of?" I keep my tone confident, but I can't help but wonder if I'm going to be fed to some hideous mutant beast. A sacrifice for the good of the many?

"Not that I can see."

"Well, that's a relief." I almost chuckle, but my heart isn't in it. "So I have nothing to fear."

"I didn't say that."

Is she toying with me? She's definitely warming up; that much is obvious. This interchange might even qualify as a borderline conversation.

"You like keeping me in the dark." I hope my clever choice of words isn't lost on her.

"Soon we'll be able to risk some light."

"Is something following us?"

"It was following you."

The rocks and gravel? I was hoping to create a mental block against that. "So...what was it exactly? Mother Earth out for revenge? I'd say we deserve it, after what we did to her." I wait for a response. Anything.

Silence.

I'm done waiting. I want some answers. I need them.

I feel her hand on my arm, guiding me forward, and I clamp down on her wrist, jerking her back as I plant my feet.

"What are you doing?" she demands.

Finally, some emotion out of her.

"I'm not going another step without some answers." She tries to pull free, but I twist my hold on her and draw her close. She struggles. Nothing doing. I'm stronger than she is, after all. "Tell me where we're going—what we're running from. Tell me *now*!"

"We're here."

"What?"

She tugs me forward and breaks free of my grasp, at the same time giving me a shove that sends me flailing blindly into the cave wall. The impact sends a sharp pain from my head down my right side, and I struggle to stay on my feet. But it's difficult to tell which end is up, and I land hard on all fours, cursing.

"You'll be sorry!"

Jackson spits out the blood and wipes his beard on the sleeve of his blue jumpsuit.

"You knew it could be either one of us, Milton."

My jaw works to speak, but the pain is too great—it might be broken.

"Why her?" my slurred words finally come out.

"It's random. Always is. You know that."

"Why Julia?" I scream.

I rise slowly, holding out my hands to show I'm not here to fight. I'm at an obvious disadvantage with her night-vision, anyway.

"I'm sorry." My voice echoes, then fades into silence. I can't sense her anywhere nearby. I can't even hear her breathe. "I just wanted some answers, that's all. Please."

My stomach tightens at the thought of being abandoned in here. My breath quickens. Needles prickle down the back of my neck.

"Don't leave me..."

2. LUTHER
SEVEN DAYS AFTER ALL-CLEAR

We're not alone. We feel it in the wind. Even in this desolation, there is life. A *Presence*.

The earth is wounded. One has only to look out across this barren land to see we have hurt her deeply. Her fields are deserts. Her waters are poison. Her children are missing. Does she weep for them?

We're not her children—we never were. Hers were the innocents we destroyed, the lives we caged and sold and devoured and, in the end, neglected to defend. Now they're gone forever.

Will we be judged? Will the Creator punish us for our great sin? Or have we already been punished enough?

Our destruction is our own. We can't blame it on anyone else. There is no one left. We must shoulder our burden of guilt as we struggle to survive this world we've inherited. As we coexist with an invisible Life Form we cannot begin to comprehend.

The sun disappears behind a range of mountains in the west. I can't help but marvel at the deep red and gold hues consuming the sky. Beauty remains in this world. Rare, but it can yet be found.

"Now?" Plato calls up to me.

I unfasten my face shield and pull off my jumpsuit. As the

dusk light wanes, I turn and look down the hill behind me. Plato stands beside a steel doorway built into the hillside.

"Let's get to work," I tell him.

Plato shoves hard on the manual release, and the bunker door groans, then slides the rest of the way open, stopping with a steel clunk. He whistles, and the men behind him emerge like slow-moving inmates trudging out of the block into a prison yard. They take deep breaths of the outside air as they carry plastic pipes, fittings, canvas tarps, sheets of plexiglass, rope, and hand tools. They know their assigned tasks. I catch the hammer Plato tosses to me.

"Tonight's the night," he says with an eager look in his eyes. "We finally leave the past behind."

I pull down the upper portion of my jumpsuit and tie the dangling sleeves around my waist. A cool breeze whispers across my bare chest. "We should have the shelters finished by morning."

"Some will want to go back. They don't look like it now, but they will. When it gets hard out here."

The energy level of the men is high, as are their spirits, as they work together. A hundred meters beyond the bunker, our attempts at a makeshift village rise up from the dusty earth. The huts are composed of plastic and canvas and steel—anything we could strip from the underground warren where we spent the past decades. Not fancy, but these structures will do the job, serving as our base camp once we begin searching for other survivors.

"I don't think they will." We descend the hill to join our brothers. "There's nothing for them to return to. The bunker is an empty tomb now. We have everything we need right here."

"I'm just saying..." Plato shrugs. "The time will come when they'll crave the familiar." He looks back. "We should seal it shut."

I follow his gaze. The bunker's dark entrance looks like the gaping maw of a half-interred beast. "Not tonight. We have other priorities, my friend. We must be certain our shelters are strong enough to withstand whatever elements come our way."

He nods. "I'm sure it'll become a moot point eventually. Most of the life support systems have shut down. It's only a matter of time before the door mechanisms refuse to cooperate entirely." He casts me a sideways glance. "I'd hate to be the poor fool trapped inside when that happens."

He makes a good point—in a roundabout way, as always. The bunker is a danger. But the men have been told it will be off-limits after tonight. For months now, Plato and I have stressed the importance of looking forward, not back. Our future depends on our ability to work together as one. At this point, after all we have accomplished—surviving below ground, maintaining our sanity, developing a brotherhood of unity, and achieving what will be, tonight, life outside the bunker for the first time in twenty years—only a fool would desire to go back to nothing.

"Do you have anyone in mind?" I pick up one end of a steel support beam and wait for Plato to take the other.

He shakes his head. "It could be any one of us—or more, if they panic. We have no idea what life will entail out here. We could not have possibly prepared for every eventuality."

He shoulders the beam, and we carry it down the middle of our *street*—a wide path through the center of the village—toward one of the last structures yet to be completed.

"We're in this together, my friend," I remind him. "If we remain united, we have nothing to fear."

"Of course," Plato replies. But he doesn't sound convinced.

He's the youngest of us and, in many ways, also the wisest. The philosophical discussions he'd instigate following our evening meals earned him his name from the start. Over the years, I've learned the value of heeding his concerns; but I have to remember to balance them with a certain level of optimism. He tends to believe the proverbial glass is half-empty, and I always have to work diligently to convince him otherwise.

"You're making more work for us, Samson," Plato grunts as we hand off the beam.

Samson—so named for obvious reasons—takes our offering and shoulders it alone. "Standard-issue hut won't cut it. Man my size needs room to breathe." He devoted more time than any of us to building his physique in the bunker gym, at times spending more than three hours a day with the weights. His muscle mass is now double what it was on D-Day, and he was already a large young man back then. "Besides," he grins, baring white teeth. "When we find those women you promised us, I plan on taking two!"

Everyone laughs as he punches me lightly in the shoulder. I plant my feet to keep from showing the force of the impact.

"Yeah, Luther, when are our wives gonna show up?" one of the others calls out, struggling to tie down a roof tarp. He's the oldest of us by far, named Rip (Van Winkle never stuck). "I'm not gettin' any younger, y'know!"

Amid the laughter, the men turn their eyes to me, tools held at their sides as they await my answer. For most of us, it's been the thought of repopulating the planet that has kept us looking forward to the future, whatever it holds. The government scientists selected us for this purpose. Samson, in particular, has mentioned his anticipation daily; it's become his mantra. Over the years, he's often told us how he envisions a future full of his children, filling the earth.

Segregation by sex was easy for no one, but we developed our own coping methods. I earned the name *Luther* for believing that we could—for the time being—live without female companionship just as religious monks in monasteries had done for centuries. (Perhaps *Augustine* or *Lawrence* would have been a more appropriate name, but I kept the one I was given, as was our custom.) Quite a few of the men followed my example, using meditation and physical exercise to free their minds of our God-given urges. Avoiding madness was always the goal.

"All in good time, my friends," I offer with what sounds like certainty. "We've lasted this long. We can hold out a while longer. If the women of today are anything like those we remember, then I doubt that they'll want anything to do with us until we get these shelters finished." I raise an eyebrow at Samson. "And perhaps take a shower or two."

Hearty laughter erupts, and with renewed vigor, the men return to their work, doubling their efforts.

"Well said," Plato remarks once we're alone. "So...when do we start the search?"

My gaze returns to the mountains in the distance, their peaks frosty in the light of the waxing moon. "Sector 50's bunker was near that ridge. But the maps are useless now—the earth has changed. Those may not even be the same mountains, for all we know."

Plato keeps his voice low as we work together, tying down one of the tarps on Samson's shelter. "Do you really think they planned everything out?"

They—the government scientists and sociologists—had known for years the Cold War would eventually thaw, and when it did, another continent could be lost. Or worse: the entire globe. The North American Sectors had grown ripe with underground terrorists—*Patriots*, they called themselves. Rumors circulated about vials of weaponized chemical agents missing from secure government labs. If such dangerous bioweapons ended up in the wrong hands, the only way to neutralize a potential threat would be nuclear strikes hot enough to eradicate a toxic outbreak along with every other living organism for kilometers around.

The scientists worked together unilaterally across the sectors to construct our bunkers—state-of-the-art subterranean prisons designed to safeguard their most valued commodities, as defined by rigorous tests of intelligence and physical stamina. The warmongering factions turned a blind eye to these efforts; their goal was to take lives, not save them, and they did not interfere. Before the time eventually came for a chain reaction of falling bombs, the government officials collected us and took us below ground to safety. For the next twenty years, we stayed alive thanks to their careful planning and preparation. But how far into the future did their foresight extend? Could they have accounted for every eventuality?

"For our sake, and for the future of our species...I hope so."

"You've done well, Luther. You've kept us together, united. The men remain in high spirits." Plato glances around quickly before returning to his work. "But if they were to lose hope—"

"We won't let them."

He looks up at me, and in his eyes is a hint of fear.

"Done!" Rip calls out, slapping the roof with an air of finality as he tosses down his hammer. It hits the hard-packed sand with an earthy thud.

"Done!" echoes throughout our village as the shelters are completed, one by one, and the men move on to the next.

We join forces to finish Samson's, and by morning, as the sun's rays break across the eastern horizon, we find refuge for the first time not beneath the earth, but above it, in shelters of our own design. The men sleep, each under his own roof, exhausted bodies sprawled out across mattresses we exhumed from the bunker below. Snores and deep sighs punctuate the stillness of a new day.

I lie on my back and stare at the plexiglass ceiling, coated with a dark UV protective polymer. I study the edges where thick canvas tarps are tied down. If we made any mistakes in our construction, if something comes loose in a sudden gust of wind, the sun will scorch us in our sleep. Perhaps I should have told the men to wear their jumpsuits, but I wanted them to feel free.

I need to relax. We *are* free now. Finally on our own.

But we're not truly alone. I feel it—that Presence in the air I breathe. I don't know how to describe it. I sense the men around me in their shelters, even when their breathing is quiet. But this is different. It's not simply the presence of another human being. What I sense is much greater. And it is watching us.

When Samuel from the Hebrew Scriptures was a boy, he

thought he heard his elder, Eli, calling to him. But it wasn't old Eli. It was God.

"Here I am, Lord..." My voice hangs in the stillness. The silence that follows is thick, mocking me. I'm no prophet. I shouldn't presume to hear the Creator speak to me.

Something hits the side of my shelter with a loud crack. I catch my breath and sit up.

"Yes?"

No sound answers. I pull on my jumpsuit and fasten the face shield. Pushing through the heavy tarp that serves as my door, I step outside into the white-hot sunlight.

Even with the tinted Mylar on my face shield, my eyes take a few moments to adjust. When they do, I find a large stone lying beside the canvas wall of my shelter. I bend down and pick it up, hefting it in the palm of my gloved hand. We swept this area clean a few nights ago, sending rocks to the bottom of a dry gully south of our village. This stone shouldn't be here. It wasn't here minutes ago when we all turned in for our first day's sleep inside our new homes.

I glance up and down the vacant path between our twin rows of shelters. If one of the men is up to some sort of shenanigan, he's doing a good job of hiding. I stand and face the bunker, a hundred meters away with its mouth dark and inviting. In this moment, I know what Plato meant. It's natural for us to crave the familiar. We were so secure in our underground prison.

I grip the stone in my hand and take a few steps away from my shelter, the gravel crunching beneath my boots. Other than the sighs and snores of the men deep in slumber, everything remains still and silent. I hear my own breath against my face shield and marvel, yet again, at the complete desolation around us, as ashen as a crumbling corpse. We have sinned, and great is our iniquity.

"Forgive us..."

I don't expect a response. I gave up on that long ago. But I continue to pray daily. I know the Creator exists, and He hears me. There is no way we could have destroyed Him.

I bring the stone into my shelter and set it beside the mattress. I keep my eyes on it as I remove my face shield and pull off my suit. I have no idea how the stone came to be where I found it, but I'm too weary to wonder anymore. My eyelids sink heavily and I exhale, falling back onto my bed. My arms stretch out to my sides as sleep draws me into its abysmal depths. I couldn't resist even if I wanted to...

In my dream, I run toward the mountains as fast as I can, but I move so slowly it seems I'm not moving at all. In the distance, so far away yet so vivid, I see the women of Sector 50, their waving locks of hair taken by the breeze that whisks across their lithe, naked bodies. I try to warn them. I try to scream, but my voice emerges in hoarse gasps. I can't get to them in time. Horror overwhelms me as the sun scorches and blisters their perfect skin. They reach out in desperation, shrieking silently. The breeze becomes a wild torrent of wind that blasts through them, scattering ash into a thick cloud that engulfs me, suffocating me. I reach for my throat as I cough. My fingernails become an eagle's talons that sink into my flesh.

I scream.

"Luther?" Plato kneels at my side, his face red, glistening with sweat.

Where am I?

His strong hands grip me by the shoulders.

"Nightmare?"

I look him in the eye as reality reclaims my senses. I nod and wipe beads of perspiration from my brow.

"No wonder. Hot as hell in here." He runs a forearm across his own brow and sniffs as he looks around my shelter. "We didn't plan for this."

I take a deep breath to steady myself. Did I scream loud enough to wake the men? Or was that only in my dream?

"We couldn't have known." The suits have kept us cool during the heat of the day. This is our first without them. Mine lies folded beside my mattress. "We may need to wear them while we sleep."

Plato nods. "I'll tell the men." He reaches for my suit, and as he turns, I see the skin on his back is sun-burned.

"Where's yours?"

"Here—put this on. You'll sleep better."

I pull it on. "You're burned, my friend." I look him squarely in the eye.

"You were screaming." He shrugs to explain his recklessness. "Do you remember anything from your nightmare?"

Of course I do. It was terrifying.

"No." I stand and zip up the front of my jumpsuit. "I'll get yours. You've been burned enough for one day." I stop before I lift the tarp. "It was foolish of you to risk your skin like that. Don't do it again." I snap my face shield shut.

"I hope I won't have to," he says.

The images from my nightmare remain clear in my mind's eye as I step outside and move toward Plato's shelter. I glance at the mountains. According to the maps we printed off the bunker database before our computers lost power, the Sector 50 bunker was built in the foothills. It was there that our female counterparts were held during the nuclear winter. We were told that after All-Clear, we would be united with them.

Unlike other sectors whose members were sterilized prior to D-Day, we and the women had one over-riding purpose: repopulation. It was why we were selected, the only reason we're here now while everyone else in our sectors died that fateful day, twenty years ago. The government scientists knew we would be needed when the time came to recover from their world's mistakes.

But without the women, my brothers and I are only half the solution.

I can't shake the feeling that the women—wherever they are— may be in danger. Thanks to that nightmare, of course. I should deride myself for being so easily influenced by subconscious fears. But it was so real. I saw their faces, every detail. Vulnerable and exposed, standing on that ridge—a hundred or more of them.

We were never told how many had been assigned to the Sector 50 bunker. Samson has his theories. A man with only one thing on his mind, he says it was common knowledge that the population of each female enclave was triple that of its male counterpart. For the purpose of our species' continuation, there would be a greater probability of successful births that way. The government scientists had it all figured out, he says.

But I have my doubts. The Creator was not consulted by the United World government as they carefully planned our future, even as they destroyed our past. It would serve them right—and us—if we were unable to conceive a single child in this post-apocalyptic nightmare of a world.

Something catches my eye as I reach Plato's shelter. A dust spiral rises from the earth just beyond our village, perhaps thirty meters out. Odd—there's no wind blowing against me. The dust devil whirls and builds upward, sucking ash into its center and expanding ever outward like a miniature tornado. I can't shake my gaze from it.

Plato has to see this.

I rush into his shelter and grope blindly, stumbling across his jumpsuit beside the mattress as my eyes adjust to the dim light. I roll up the suit and tuck it under my arm, heading back outside to see—

Nothing.

The dust lies still on the baked earth as if it had never moved at all.

I take a deep breath. First the stone, appearing out of nowhere. Now this dust spiral, forming without any wind and disappearing just as quickly. The stone could have been a prank, but not this. There's no way to explain this.

Unless I'm losing my mind.

Lack of sleep in conjunction with the heat and a wild nightmare... Perhaps I simply need to rest. Shaking my head, I return to my shelter and toss Plato his suit, chiding him again for exposing his skin.

"Fine. Next time I hear you screaming bloody murder, I'll leave you to the bogeyman." He stands as he zips up.

I remove my face shield. "Thank you, my friend."

"I thought we swept this area clear." He gestures toward the stone beside my bed.

"We did." Part of me is glad that he can see it too. I exhale loudly as I fall back onto my mattress, arms out to the sides, eyes closed. I keep my suit on this time. "A memento."

"Get some rest, Luther. You'll need it tonight."

Tonight? Of course. Without the scorching rays of the sun, we'll make our first attempt at locating the women. "Be sure the men have enough to eat. They'll need their strength."

"Before or after we find Sector 50?" He grins.

It's good to see him smile. "Goodnight."

"Good *day*," he says quietly as he leaves.

The perspiration that covered me when I awoke has been absorbed by my suit, already recycled by the cooling system within its fibers. I don't mind the heat at all now, and I'm sure I'll sleep peacefully—and dreamlessly, I hope.

We kept these suits stored away in the bunker along with all the other supplies we would need after All-Clear: medkits, tools, construction frames, extra nutrition and hydropacks—all off-limits until the day the bunker door locks released us, and we stepped outside for the first time in decades. The scientists told us the suits would be our first line of defense against the harsh climate we'd find waiting outside, but they were not designed to be a permanent solution; after their shelf-life, they could be expected to function well enough for six to nine months. The more we used them, however, the sooner they would expire.

I close my eyes and count the number of days I've worn my suit. Three? Four? I should be able to spare a good day's sleep. We all should. We've earned it. And later—when our suits reach their expiration dates and can no longer protect us from the elements—

"Plato can worry about that," I sigh, half-mumbling as sleep overtakes me once again. My body sinks into the mattress as if I'm floating in a lake of cool, fresh water.

We had a small lake house before the end. When I was a boy, we'd go there every year. My parents accumulated their paid leave so they could take my brothers and me for a month in July. We always looked forward to it, so much so that by the middle of June, it was tortuous even to attempt to focus on our studies. Our minds were completely occupied with thoughts of diving, swimming, and kayak races. We'd spend hours hiking through the trees in the sector's only natural Preserve. The government had continually offered us a great sum for our cottage, but my father had always said there were some things in life money could not buy. The property had been passed down from father to eldest son for over a century, and someday it was going to be mine. I never would have sold it...

I float on my back, my arms drifting out to the sides, my legs gently kicking to maintain my position. Eyes closed, I smile under the sun's warmth. The cool, fresh water fills my ears, but—if I pay attention—I can hear the distant shouts of my two younger brothers as they wrestle on shore, no doubt fighting over who will get to use the telescope next to spy on our sunbathing neighbors. This is heaven, floating far away from my studies and all those tests. Here I'm free to *live*.

My brother Alex calls my name—my real name. At first I don't respond; I've been *Luther* for so long now. Then he calls again, and I realize it's me that he wants. I let my legs sink, and I pull myself forward, treading water.

"What? Is Dad back?"

He stands on the pebble-strewn shore in his swimming trunks, his bare skin rosy from too much sun. He shakes his head and points to the house.

"Somebody's here for you!"

I remember this moment. My stomach tightens.

They're here to take me away, back for more tests.

I didn't want to go, but my parents made me. They said it was for the good of us all that I comply. They said it was for our future, and they were proud of me.

I like it fine right here. I lie back and let my arms and legs go limp. Instantly, I'm floating again. Free again, calm, cool and relaxed. The water laps into my ears. I can barely make out Alex shouting anymore.

"They're coming!"

Let them come. I won't go back.

I didn't know then what all the tests were for, but they were sorting out the best and brightest from our sector, the ones there would be room for—made for—in the bunkers, while our loved ones died on the surface. Of course, they never let us or our families know about any of this, only that we'd been chosen by the UW to provide *a better tomorrow*.

When the bombs started falling on D-Day, then everyone knew.

The truth.

The lake turns to sand all of a sudden, and I gag on it. I jerk forward to find myself covered, buried from the chest down. I blink, my eyes stinging. My heart races as I look around me. Our house is gone, as are the trees and blue skies. In their place is an endless sea of ashen sand beneath a blazing sun.

"What have you done?" I rasp, spitting to clear my mouth.

Two scientists in baggy, reflective environmental suits walk across the desert toward me, their mirrored face shields showing my reflection. My arms push out to the sides as I try to pull myself free. But it's no use. I'm stuck.

"What have you done with it all?"

They don't respond. They approach and stand over me, their heads tilted forward as they stare.

"What do you want?" I thrash wildly, swinging my arms at them with clenched fists. "Leave me alone!"

They bend down to reach for me, their gloved fingers curled to grab hold of my arms. I see my eyes—bloodshot with rage—in the face shield of one of them, and my scream is both guttural and unintelligible as I thrust my hand at his throat. My fingernails, suddenly extended long and sharp like eagle talons, rip through his suit and tear into his flesh. I feel the warmth of his blood as it pours over me. He convulses and falls backward.

My hand moves slowly as I pull back and stare at it.

What have I done?

My blood-red claws start to retract into my fingers. I flex them, and out come the talons again. Sharp. Lethal.

What the hell is this? What's happening to me?

The other scientist has let go of my arm. His face shield is trained on my hand. In the reflection, I look like a monster.

"Get away from me!"

I raise my other hand with menace, and a matching set of claws flex outward from my fingers. Before I'm aware of what's happening, my body launches up out of the sand, and I descend upon the scientists with a vengeance that's not my own. My claws rip into them both, blood splashing upward and outward, staining the ground. They writhe under my wrath as I watch, horrified, unable to stop. I shred their suits and their bodies. I squeeze my eyes shut as an all-consuming rage takes control—it's in control, and it's not mine.

I'm not the one doing this to these men. I can't be.

I pray for it to stop.

I sit up from my mattress and cough, choking on the ash covering me. My heart races, pounding like a fist against my chest. I blink, and my eyes sting. Wiping at them only smears the dust from my hands. The interior of my shelter is caked in a layer of ash a centimeter deep. I cough again, feeling the grit coat my throat. How did all this get inside?

I break open a hydropack and rinse my eyes, nose, and mouth. I reach for my face shield and gloves. Fits of coughing erupt from the other shelters.

The men are in danger.

"Luther!" Plato rushes toward me as I emerge from beneath the tarp, fastening my face shield into place. He too is covered in the stuff. "Are you all right?"

"What's happened? A sandstorm?"

"If there was, we slept through it."

I look down the rows of shelters. "Get the men together. We need to assess the situation."

We shout out the names of our brothers as we go from one shelter to the next and help them overcome their disorientation, wash their faces, get their face shields on, and join the group forming in the center of our village. The invisible Presence I've felt before is stronger now, hovering over us as I look upon the men. They stand dazed and perplexed in a half circle, their jumpsuits filthy.

It's as though we've been marked.

A strange thought.

I train my gaze on our surroundings—silent and still beneath the scorching sun—for any sign of movement. I don't know exactly what I'm looking for; anything that can take the blame would be helpful. The men are on edge, and the last thing they need to hear from me are musings on an invisible *Presence* watching us.

"What do we tell them?" Plato stands beside me, his back to the men.

"All accounted for?" I fight to keep my nerves steady.

"We're all here." He curses quietly, shaking his head. "What the hell happened?"

I can't allow the men to panic.

"Hey Luther, did we sleep through some kinda dust storm or something?" Rip pipes up over the murmuring of the others, and some of them chuckle.

I can always count on him to lighten the mood. "Yes—" I begin.

"How did it get inside? I've got ash a couple centimeters deep in my shelter, wall to wall," cuts in one of the men from the back of our assembly. The other men echo his description of the situation, their voices building as tension rises, reaching a crescendo. "No way it could've gotten in on its own!"

I hold up my gloved hands to quiet them. My mind flashes back to the dream where *claws* came out of my fingers. I fight to clear my thoughts, even as I remain unsettled by both of the bizarre nightmares I've had today.

"My friends, you're not alone. We're all in this together. Remember that," I say in a strong, surprisingly confident voice. They begin to quiet down. Their tinted face shields stare at me without expression. "We must remain calm and confront whatever comes our way unified, as one. We're strong together, my friends, strong enough to survive any freak sandstorm that gets us a little dirty." I turn to Plato, hoping I've bought him enough time to develop the sort of rational explanation he's known for. I pat him on the back with a puff of dust and quietly wish him luck as I step aside.

"Luther's right. Only with peace of mind can there be reason." He clears his throat as he steps forward. "While we were sleeping, there was some kind of...wind disturbance that swept through our village, stirring up the dust inside and out—"

"Load of crap! Look—the tarps are clean on the outside, just like we left 'em. There's no sign of any sandstorm." The vocal dissenter elbows his way to the front of the crowd. He's called Holmes, always one for a good argument. "You don't have a clue what's happened. Admit it, Plato. You're dumbfounded, just like the rest of us." He gestures to the others who murmur in agreement. "The truth is, we don't know what kinds of things are living out here on the surface!"

"What are you suggesting?" Samson moves to loom over him with brawny arms crossed, straining the seams of his extra-large sleeves. "You think something attacked us? By sprinkling a little ash in our shelters?" He scoffs, and some of the men chuckle.

"They could go either way," Plato mutters to me. "If they panic, they'll want to return to the bunker."

"Not an option." I clench my jaw.

"We should seal it shut." He grabs hold of my arm as the attention of the men divides between Holmes and Samson, shouts flying from both supporting factions. "There's still time. I can set off the charges."

Will the bunker be the death of us? Already I see the line drawn between the men. Will they split up—some remaining on the surface to face what comes while others go below, back to the familiar security of concrete and steel where we spent the past two decades?

I can't allow them to do so. We must move forward. We must overcome this fear of the unknown rearing its ugly head and press on. There's no viable alternative.

"Do it." Resignation weighs heavy in my tone.

Plato squeezes my arm and moves quickly down the hill.

I watch the men as they argue, turned in on themselves, oblivious to anything else. They've overcome so much, only to fall apart at the first sign of the unexpected. Where is our unity? Where is our strength? Was it only a brave facade?

If we're being watched, we undoubtedly appear weak. If this is a test, then we've failed. If this was merely a preliminary strike of some sort, we may not be strong enough to survive what comes next.

"Are you watching us?" I whisper. I feel the Presence now close around me, encompassing our village. My heart quickens as my senses tingle. "What do you want?"

"We should've never left the bunker—not so soon after All-Clear." Holmes has a good number of the men on his side, gathered around him and nodding, murmuring their assent. "We should've made sure it was safe first before we started setting up camp."

"We did." Samson's posture hasn't changed, and the men siding with him—including Rip—have also adopted it, arms crossed as they nod their approval. "Everything checked out: O2 levels, toxicity, radiation, all of it. We're fine out here."

"You're sure about that? You've made certain there aren't any fallout freaks anywhere in the vicinity?"

Is that what he's worried about? I feel myself relax. At least he doesn't share my concerns. It may be better for the men to think they're up against some band of mutant pranksters instead of an indescribable force of nature—if the *nature* that remains has any force left in it.

"So that's what's got you scared, Holmes?" Samson laughs heartily, throwing back his head. "You think a bunch of mutants came through here while we were sleeping and—"

"Have you got a better explanation?" Holmes demands. "Well? What does the mighty Samson have to say?"

Samson shakes his head slowly, no doubt scowling behind his face shield. "It was just some crazy dust storm, man. You act like we've been attacked or something."

"Maybe we have!" Holmes shouts. "No one knows exactly what's happened, but it happened while we were sleeping. All of us. And if they come again—I don't want to be killed in my sleep!"

The men on his side echo "That's right!"

"*They* who?" Rip retorts, dwarfed at Samson's side. "Did you see any footprints in your shelter? Cuz I sure as hell didn't. You've got no evidence for these worries of yours, son. And that's not like you at all. Get a grip on yourself!"

Holmes backs away, pointing at the older man. "You can stay out here and die if you want, but I'm taking my stuff back into the bunker. At least in there I can sleep in peace!" He reels to face the men behind him and shouts, "Who's with me?"

A roar of approval answers him, and they disband to retrieve their belongings from their shelters. I've seen enough.

"Wait!" Hands raised again, I approach them, pleading with them. "My friends—my *brothers*—please, hear me!"

They stop and turn, but they don't join Samson and the

others. They remain scattered, each headed toward his own shelter. Holmes turns away.

"My friends...Holmes—" His face shield turns back toward me. "You have a valid concern, and you're right: We don't know what's happened. But we can't allow it to divide us. We must stay together, for it's in our *unity* that we've always found our strength." I gesture with my arms outstretched as if to embrace them all. "We're brothers, and if there is an adversary who wishes us harm, then it's only together as one that we can—"

"Preach it to your choir, Luther." Holmes shakes his head. "We don't want to die out here."

They go to their shelters and disappear inside. My arms drop to my sides as I stare after them. I won't attempt to persuade them anymore. Is it because part of me agrees with Holmes? Do we even belong out here on the surface?

This world is no longer our own.

Regardless, the bunker will be sealed shut, and we'll have to move forward with a breach among us the likes of which we've never dealt with before. I'll have to do my best to convince them there is nothing to fear...while convincing myself of the same thing.

Am I the only one who feels this Presence pressing in? I can't be.

"What are you?" I whisper. "Spirit of the wounded earth? Souls of the departed?"

Was there no room in the Afterlife for the billions of lives suddenly extinguished all at once on D-Day? That couldn't be. The Creator exists outside of time and space and would have been able to foresee all the horrific acts His creation were doomed to commit. He would have made room in Heaven for the victims. Hell would have been reserved for those responsible.

What about the other forms of life that once thrived on our planet? Mammals and birds, fish and reptiles, amphibians and insects. They lived and breathed, just as we did, on the surface of our shared world. Before the end, were any of them sent below?

Or had the government scientists believed we could live without them?

The earth is so empty in their absence.

"Are you...?" I whisper, unable to articulate my thoughts.

Could it be that the *Presence* I feel is in actuality the collective spirit of all the creatures who once lived in this world, those for whom the planet was first created? Could it be that they've never left us? That the bioweapons and bombs were never able to completely destroy them? Do they continue to live on...as this brooding life force?

An explosive blast thunders from the bunker, and the ground trembles. I catch my breath, my heart lurching, even though I knew it was coming. Plato has done it.

My fingers tingle strangely, and I look down at them. Sharp claws slowly retract through holes torn in each of my gloved fingertips.

Time stops.

In the silence, I stare at my gloves. I turn them over in between heartbeats and swallow. I wiggle my fingers and see each one through its hole—both hands, both gloves. I exhale in a short burst and grit my teeth.

The dream...

What's happening to me?

Men are shouting and running, all of them moving en masse across the plateau, down the hill.

"Luther—the bunker!" One of them grabs at my shoulder as he rushes by.

I turn slowly, moving as I do in dreams. But as I look down the hill, I know this is no dream. Smoke, dark and thick, billows upward from the bunker's blackened blast door. The rock face around it has caved inward, large chunks of earth lying on top of one another against the sealed door. There is no way it can be opened again, either from within or without. The mechanisms have been destroyed, and even if Holmes wants to dig through the rock face around the door, he'll be unable to penetrate the reinforced steel to enter the shaft below.

The deed is done. There is no going back now, not for any of us.

I look at my gloves again, my feet rooted. A cacophony of shouts echoes below me, and there may be fighting. I can barely hear it though, as all my senses are overwhelmed by one question.

I flex my fingers, and the claws, long and sharp like an eagle's talons, extend outward, gleaming under the sun.

What am I?

3. DAIYNA
FOUR WEEKS AFTER ALL-CLEAR

We've been changed.

I don't know when or how it happened—maybe during that first dust storm that came upon us in the night as we traveled—but something has turned us into more than we were. I try to accept it as Mother has advised us, that this is our new reality.

It's in the evenings like this when I'm alone that these thoughts return. I have to do something to pass the time and keep my mind alert; otherwise I'll surrender to the sleep that lurks in the shadows, and my sisters will be left in danger. Only a couple hours more, then my watch will be over. One of the others will pace across the width of this cave with a makeshift spear, holding the hungry daemons at bay.

The only way we've managed to stay alive is by outwitting them with our *gifts*, as Mother Lairen calls our new abilities. The daemons don't seem very intelligent, even though they're the ones with the vehicles and real firepower. We have only what we were able to piece together after we stripped the bunker bare and headed up to these caves in the mountains. My weapon is an ingenious combination of a two-meter long PVC pipe, some duct tape, and a serrated scrap of steel. I've yet to use it in battle. None of our weapons have been put to the test. Our *gifts* alone have kept us alive.

Mother Lairen—the oldest and wisest among us—believes the Creator in her infinite wisdom bestowed these abilities upon us as an act of divine mercy, knowing we would need them to survive in a strange new world.

She might be right. But I have my own ideas.

We're mutants.

Something in the air we're breathing—or in the contaminated dust at our feet that has a bizarre tendency to move at will—has gotten inside our lungs and changed us. I don't know how, but the results are clear to see. Some of the women can hear sounds from great distances. Others can see farther than humanly possible. A few now have the strength to move large boulders. Most of us can see in the dark, which is obviously helpful during these night watches. Everything I see, from the barren land below to the ridge of the mountainside, is cast in a bright blue monochrome by my gifted eyes.

I'm sure there are sisters in our midst who have yet to become aware of their abilities. That's the funny thing about these *gifts*—they tend to emerge without warning, right when we need them most. Perhaps they do come from the Creator as part of her provision.

But from the start, it's felt like something else.

I sensed it the moment we stepped out of the bunker a month ago and looked out across this lifeless world. Yes, it was empty, missing every living creature that used to thrive on its surface. But even in the desolation, I instantly felt a Presence, one I couldn't name or describe.

We weren't alone—that much I knew for certain.

Maybe it was some sort of intuition, but I had a feeling it wouldn't be long until this Presence—or life force, or energy, as I struggled to give it an identity—manifested itself, either benignly or malevolently. Many of the others, including Mother Lairen, dismissed the idea as medieval superstition. They believed in the Creator as the one and only supernatural force to be reckoned with.

But some of us have come to believe this nearly tangible Presence we feel is more than just a figment of our collective imagination. It's directly related to our *gifts*.

They appeared among us following the sandstorms.

A few days after All-Clear, when the blast door to our bunker finally gave us the green light, we carried everything outside that might later prove useful. The life support systems had shut down as soon as we opened the door, so there was no going back. Some of us wanted to build shelters nearby in case we needed the bunker for safety. There was talk of dangerous rain and other remnants of the fallout we had yet to endure. But Mother Lairen insisted that we let go of the past and move forward to create a new life for ourselves. So we made a mass exodus, all one hundred fifty of us, toward the caves up in the mountains less than a kilometer away. Very slow going at first—until that first sandstorm.

The weird thing about it was that there was no storm, really; there was no wind. The dust and ash started moving at first, seemingly of their own volition, swirling across the tops of rocks and along the ground at our feet, increasing in both volume and intensity. We found shelter in crevices, covered our face shields with our arms as the dust devils whirled the sand and gravel upward, expanding outward. We hid between boulders, beneath the tarps and sheets and mattresses we carried. After the storm, we all were covered in a thick layer of ash.

I remember the taste of it in my mouth, the stale grit on my tongue. My face shield had been shut, fastened to the collar of my jumpsuit, but somehow the stuff had penetrated the polymer. The same happened to each of us. And as we shook ourselves off to resume our climb toward the caves above, we immediately became aware of the strength and agility we now possessed. We were able to leap from rock to ledge, swinging from one handhold to the next with ease, as we scaled sheer rock faces with our supplies in tow. It came as instinct, and we marveled at our newfound abilities. We quickly came to enjoy our gifts as we put them to use.

Mother Lairen later said we'd been born again, christened by our Creator with the dust of a new earth. Yet at the time, she seemed unnerved by it. I'd never seen her so disturbed by anything. She grew very quiet and would not eat with us during our mealtimes. She said she was fasting and praying. It wasn't long afterward that we reached the caves, so we had something else to turn our attention to: making a new home for ourselves. For a while we tried to forget about the sandstorm and our miraculous climb.

Then one moonless night, Sheylia—a frail girl—said she saw something in the distance. A few of us joined her, and though we craned our necks and squinted our eyes, looking left and right from atop our perch on the rock ledge, it was in vain.

"Don't you see them?" Sheylia's small voice carried a dreamy quality. I wondered if she was sleepwalking. "Can't you hear them?"

"Who, Sheylia?" I glanced back into the cave behind us to see if anyone else was there. We stood alone with her. "Who do you see?"

She inhaled deeply, and a slight smile played on her lips. "Visitors." She took another deep breath of the night air, her arms floating out from her sides. "They're coming, Daiyna. Our husbands are coming. We get to be mommies!"

One of the others cursed and turned away. "Can't see a damn thing. Go back to bed." The rest straggled after her, murmuring among themselves.

"Don't they want to meet their husbands, Daiyna?" Sheylia asked me.

I didn't know what to say. Many of our sisters were not keen on the idea of becoming *breeders* in order to repopulate the earth. They'd been able to live without men for years, and they'd gotten used to it.

"Just look around," they'd say. "Would you really want to bring a child into this world?"

Maybe they were right. Mother Lairen chided them gently, as was her way, reminding them it was both our duty and blessing to be mothers of the next generation. It was our *destiny*, she told them. But they would have nothing of it. As a sign of their resistant solidarity, they shaved their heads to the scalp.

"Don't you want to see your husband, Daiyna? Don't you want to know what he's like?"

"We'll probably get the same one, Sheylia." I cast her a sideways glance, and she smiled broadly.

"Then I hope he is both handsome and strong, and that he is kind to both of us." She turned to me with a slight frown. "You really can't see them?"

I shook my head. There was nothing to see.

If only I'd been right.

"They're just over there…" She pointed and brought my hand up with hers, our fingers intertwined, directed westward. "Maybe ten kilometers away now. They can see us too, I think."

I strained to see, but it was too dark and too far. "Sheylia… Have you always been able to see like this?"

"No." She sighed happily and grinned at me. "Pretty neat, huh?"

My mind flashed back to the sandstorm and our climb. I tried to fight the idea that something had changed us, telling myself that Sheylia was only seeing things, hearing things. But then I heard it too: the low hum of a vehicle, maybe more than one. Faint, but distinct and growing louder, carried to us on the cool breeze blowing up the face of a sheer cliff below.

"Is it—?" I listened again. "What you hear, is it the sound of an engine?"

She brightened and clapped her hands. "Yes! Isn't it wonderful, Daiyna? We have to tell the others!" She turned away, overjoyed.

"Sheylia—"

They shot her.

She seemed to float for a moment, hanging in mid-air as a patch of blood blossomed across her gown. Then came the report of a rifle in the distance, and I flinched, crouching instinctively, looking toward its source.

I could see. The night was no longer black as pitch but instead it glowed with a hazy blue light. My focus sharpened as I blinked my eyes and stared. I could see them. Two or three kilometers out from the base of the foothills below, they came at us in two jeeps, the tires sending up plumes of dust in their wake.

"Why, Daiyna?" Confusion froze Sheylia's soft features as she stumbled backward and dropped headfirst over the ledge.

"No!" I grabbed her legs, my fingers digging into her cool flesh. The rock face beside me shattered with a bullet's impact, and the rifle reported again, echoing in the night. I didn't let go of her. "Mother Lairen!" I shouted. "Help!"

Chaos had ensued. A dozen of my sisters came running out of the cave, and two were shot before they heard my warning. With short cries, they fell from the ledge and were silenced by the jagged rocks far below. No one knew what was happening—only that we were under attack. At first, I was the only one besides Sheylia who could see in the dark, but then others became instantly gifted in the same way. Their eyes widened as they pointed and screamed wildly.

The bodies of our fallen sisters were being eaten where they lay, broken and bloody. The attackers—a dozen in all—had left their weapons behind and their jeeps idling as they lunged, one over another like rabid dogs, up onto the rocks to tear into their prey.

Even now my stomach turns at the memory. I have never felt so powerless in all my life.

There was nothing we could do. We had to get Sheylia inside to care for her, but I couldn't pull my eyes away from the feeding frenzy below us. It was my fault; I shouldn't have called for help. That was my punishment: forcing myself to watch. Bile rose in my throat, and my stomach churned. Vomit shot over the ledge and fell onto the filthy savages far below, but they didn't notice.

I wished it would burn them like acid.

"Daiyna, you mustn't." Mother Lairen and another—Rehana, the first of us to shave her head—dragged me, struggling, into the cave.

Sheylia was already on a mattress inside, cared for by two sisters with medkits. I crawled into a corner and watched as others scurried with rocks and boulders in tow to seal up the opening—only one of many in our honeycomb of caves.

"We must go deeper in," Mother Lairen said with tear-stained cheeks. "Those..." she faltered.

"*Men*," Rehana spat.

A murmur ran through the women who quickly gathered around us in a tight circle.

"They must not be allowed to follow us inside." Mother Lairen swallowed and raised her chin. "We must defend ourselves—"

"How?" a frightened voice cried. Others echoed her.

"We make weapons." Rehana stood confidently. It was as if she had expected this moment to come. "Right, Mother?"

I sat curled up in shadows not penetrated by the green light of glowsticks mounted at intervals along the earthen walls. Mother Lairen looked stunned, not one given to quick decision-making. No doubt she would have rather been fasting and praying instead of discussing the sudden need for weapons.

"Yes, Rehana. We must protect ourselves." She held out her arms as if to shelter us all. "We are the fertile womb of the future. Not one of us can be allowed to perish. We must go deep into the mountain and hope that if these...men...find a way inside, they will not be able to see in the dark as many of us now can, praise the Creator."

My mouth tasted bad. I wasn't praising the Creator. I didn't echo Mother Lairen's refrain as the others did. Thanks to this new *gift* of night-vision, I had seen my sisters torn limb from limb and devoured like raw meat. I brought my knees up to my chest and hugged them, squeezing my eyes shut. I couldn't get the horrifying image out of my mind.

In quiet moments like this, it still comes back to haunt me.

I set down my spear and stretch, then take a seat on an outcropping of rock. Every night, I volunteer for the first watch. After Sheylia died, I was determined not to let another one of us perish. I helped Rehana and some of the others make weapons—spears, crossbows, swords, daggers—all out of the supplies the government had provided for our shelters. I don't think those UW scientists ever could have foreseen our need for weapons. It wasn't part of their plan for our future.

But we were on our own now. We had to survive.

The gravel shifts behind me and I reel, spear in hand.

"Nice reflexes." Rehana smiles, her even teeth white against her olive skin.

"Your watch?" I relax, lowering my weapon.

"Soon. Keep it up, you're doing great." She steps out of the cave and takes a deep breath of the night air. A cool breeze rustles her loose cotton garments. "How's the new look?" She rubs her clean-shaven head and points at mine.

"Itches a little." I adjust the scarf tied around my bare scalp.

She half-smiles. "You should take that off. Breeze feels great." She closes her eyes and sighs. "No reason to hide."

I'm not hiding anything. Everyone knows I've done it, along with sixty of my sisters. Mother Lairen has been in seclusion for days, fasting and praying. The fact that we don't want to be the future's *fertile womb* worries her. But I think part of her must understand. After two decades underground, none of us could have expected the first men we met to be cannibals.

"See anything?" Hands on her hips, Rehana scans the ground below. She too is able to see in the dark, but neither of us has the range Sheylia did.

"Nothing. You'd think they would have found us by now."

"They're men," she scoffs. "Out of sight, out of mind."

Are they men? From the distance that night, nearly a month

ago, they looked like it. Since then, we've caught sight of them on more than one occasion, but we have been able to stay hidden. In the dark, we hold the advantage. Only once have they come close to finding an opening in our network of caves. Mother Lairen commanded us to seal it, to be safe.

We have not engaged them. For the past week, it's been so quiet on the plain below that we've wondered if they decided to move on in search of other meat.

"Think they'll be back?"

Rehana shrugs. "If they ran out of nourishment packs already, that makes us the only meal in town."

"Couldn't they have just...asked us for more packs? Why did they have to—?" My voice falters.

"They're not like us, Daiyna. You know what Mother Lairen calls them."

"*Daemons.*"

She chuckles. "Well, don't try to figure them out. They're not human anymore." She punches me playfully in the arm. "So we can't carry their spawn. Right? Human and daemon DNA aren't compatible." Her eyes become dead serious as she gazes out into the night. "We won't be their *cows*. And we won't be their dinner. We should kill every one of them."

"Then you'll need this." I toss her my spear and turn to enter the cave. My shift is over. I need sleep, not talk.

"You know I'm right, Daiyna."

I don't want to hear this again from her. More of us will die if we confront the *daemons*. Mother Lairen has advised defense only —keeping hidden. In any kind of offensive action, we wouldn't stand a chance against their weapons and vehicles.

"Three of us have died already. You really think we should risk more?"

"What did you study?" Rehana raises an eyebrow. "When we were below."

"Biology and genetics—the sciences." Since most of us were sent to the bunker before we finished our secondary education, we were given multi-terabyte databanks and thirty consoles to help us complete our studies. They functioned well enough until All-Clear, providing us with a wealth of knowledge about a world that no longer existed. But what did that have to do with killing the daemons? "Why?"

"Science. Natural selection, right?"

I nod, already guessing where this is going.

"The whole animal kingdom's gone. All that *survival of the fittest* stuff—we're it. We're all that's left. Kill or be killed. We can't keep hiding and hope they'll go away. That's not how it works." She grips the spear with both hands and jerks it toward the darkness below us. "We've got to wipe out those bastards!"

She may be right. If they're still prowling around these mountains, it'll be only a matter of time before they find a way into the caves through some unguarded cleft in the rock. Then more of us will die.

Perhaps even more than if we'd taken the offensive in the first place.

"You should tell Mother Lairen your concerns."

A small rock hits my shoulder from above. My muscles tense. I reach for the dagger at my belt and scan the night for movement.

"What was that?" Rehana is at my side, spear ready as she watches the area above the cave's yawning mouth.

I kneel to pick up the stone.

"Just a rock?" Rehana hisses. "If a daemon's up there, he's going to hell tonight!"

"If it's a daemon, he would've shot us already." I squeeze the rock, smooth and cool in my palm. It's a survivor, like us; but it survived on the surface while we hid below. What horrors did it witness? "It's nothing." I let it fall to the ground. "I'm going to bed. Don't get yourself killed out here."

She gives me the finger before a stone hits her square between the eyes. She curses, doubled over. The rock lands beside the one I dropped. They look identical.

"What the—!" She touches the bridge of her nose gingerly and groans. "Show yourself!" She brandishes the spear. "You cowards!"

"Keep it down."

"Somebody threw that at me!"

"No one's up there. It must have slid down on its own, like the other one." There's no movement above us. "You all right?"

"I'll live." She holds her spear in a defensive posture, facing the cave. "I'm smacking the next one to the moon."

"Have fun." Determined to get to bed, I break into a jog—

"Daiyna. Take a look at this."

Something about the tone of her voice makes me stop and turn back. She's no longer looking above the cave. Now the ground at her feet holds her undivided attention. She stares, frozen, at where the two rocks lie.

One deliberate step at a time, I return. I don't join her side. From where I stand, I can already see what she's looking at: the rocks are scraping across the ground, turning slowly, revolving around a central point in the dust.

"Daiyna?" She licks her lips and takes a hesitant step away, her gaze transfixed. "What's your scientific explanation for *this*?"

I don't have one. The muscles in my stomach tighten, and the back of my neck tingles. Is this fear—or dread? The stones spin faster, whirling like the hands of a clock gone awry. The ledge trembles beneath our feet.

"Rehana..." I hold out my hand, beckoning to her as I back into the cave.

"Yeah, maybe I should—"

The gravel and dust launch upward, hiding her behind a screen of rushing sand. She screams, and the head of her spear swings outward only to be broken off by the power of surging earth. I call out her name, my voice drowned by an avalanche of rocks descending from the slope above, falling in a haphazard pile just outside the cave entrance.

Gritting my teeth, I lunge forward and thrust my hand through the rushing wall of sand. The friction burns, shredding my flesh, and I cry out. But I clutch onto Rehana's forearm, and she clasps mine. I pull with all my strength, and she releases a guttural scream as she passes through the screen. Dodging a shower of rock that plummets straight for us, I yank her to the side, then shove her ahead of me. We clamber up over the growing pile of rocks and crawl deep into the cave beyond. There we collapse, gasping as we catch our breath, deafened by the rumble all around us.

"It's sealing us in..." I can't hear my own voice.

The avalanche covers the mouth of the cave meters at a time. A spasm of pain distracts me. Blue-white in my gifted vision, my outer garment is torn ragged from the elbow down, and the skin on my forearm is nearly gone, dark and wet with blood.

"How?" Rehana squirms beside me and curses. Her clothing has been reduced to rags, and most of her bare body looks as raw as my arm. She needs a medkit ASAP.

"Don't move. I'll be right back."

Clenching my jaw against the pain and cradling my arm carefully, I stumble to my feet and head deeper inside. The rumble of the falling rocks reverberates all around me, and in the caverns on all sides, the others stir and wake, sitting up in confusion. Their eyes stare after me as I pass them.

"Are you injured, Daiyna?" Mother Lairen stands before me.

I stop abruptly and catch my breath. "Rehana...she needs a medkit."

Our Mother beckons two of the girls nearby from their beds. "Tend to our sister. Where is she, Daiyna?"

"At the mouth of the cave." My heart thuds unevenly.

"Go," Mother Lairen dismisses them and faces me. "You need tending as well, my child. Come with me."

I hesitate. Her calm demeanor is oddly out of place considering what's happening.

"Mother, an avalanche has sealed the cave. We need to move into another section, or we can wait and dig our way out once it's over. Some of us gifted with strength could—"

"There is no need, child. We are in good hands. The Creator is protecting us." She turns away. "Come. Let me heal you."

My arm throbs as I follow her through the main cavern. Her bare feet seem to glide across the smooth rock. She is not dressed in her nightgown like the others but in the loose cotton garments we wove in the bunker. They hang on the sharp edges of her frame.

No one has seen her for more than a week as she's fasted and prayed. I hope she has finally found herself. For her sake, as well as ours.

"Sit down, Daiyna." She gestures to a cushion on the ground as we reach her corner of the cavern. An alcove set apart, it's more private than the communal sleeping quarters the rest of us share. "Please."

I hesitate. Maybe because I've never been alone with our Mother before. Or maybe because I know she doesn't approve of my shaved head. But I also know she's not one to hold grudges, so I cross my legs and sit on the cushion, careful not to bump my arm into anything. She retrieves a small plastic medkit from the storage chest beside her bed and pops it open as she kneels before me. She keeps her languid gaze on my ravaged arm as she tends to it, dabbing at the oozing blood with a sterile pad.

"Do you believe in the Creator, Daiyna?"

That catches me off guard, and I stammer, "Uh-yes. Of course I do."

A smile plays on her thin lips. "What exactly do you believe?" She doesn't look up, but I can tell she's waiting for an answer.

I swallow, knowing what she wants to hear. Should I tell her what I truly believe instead? A Creator who allows her entire creation to destroy itself isn't a deity worthy of anyone's belief, but is instead no better than a sadistic daemon.

"I believe—" I cringe as she gently cleanses my arm with fluid from a hydropack. "The Creator has given us a second chance. It's up to us to do what we can with it." I pause, weighing my words. "But I wish she would do more to help us out."

Mother Lairen stops and holds my gaze. In her eyes is the peace and assurance I crave. "Oh She is, my child. Have no doubt. She is helping us more than you know. She has sent Her Spirit, and it moves among us now, bestowing upon us these miraculous *gifts* that are our blessing. Can you not see? Because of Her infinite mercy, we are so much more than any mere mortals have ever been before. This is an amazing time in the history of humankind, don't you agree? And we have been chosen to *live* it."

I wish she would finish healing my arm so I can check on Rehana.

"What about the daemons? How do they fit in with the Creator's infinite mercy?" My tone is not as respectful as it probably should be. "And what about that rockslide and—" My mind flashes back to the sand rushing up from the ground. "This?" I hold out my arm. "How does *this*...?" I trail off, unable to explain what happened to Rehana and me.

But if it was caused by the Creator, then it would seem we're definitely on her bad side.

Mother Lairen wraps my arm in a cool bandage. "Do not confuse the work of our Creator with the work of evil, my child," she says softly. "In Her infinite wisdom, She is protecting us from the dangers without. Even now as we speak, each of the entrances to our caves is being covered by Her hand. We will be safe from the daemons, secure inside this holy mountain. Our Creator has consecrated it for us. We will not come to harm."

How will we breathe? My lips part, but I say nothing.

"Fear not, Daiyna. We are safe again, as we were in the bunker. But now we have the strength of the Almighty on our side—not the technology of a sinful human government. We have nothing to fear. We have Her word."

Her *word*? "You mean, you've..."

She ties off the bandage and smiles. "Yes, Daiyna. She has spoken to me. We have Her word: we will not come to harm as long as we remain in this mountain. She will provide for all our needs, and She will bring our husbands to us. Even now, She is speaking to them through dreams and visions." A hint of sadness creeps into her eyes as she reaches to touch the scarf on my head. "We are Her fertile womb..."

I stand. "Thank you, Mother. I need to check on Rehana, she was in worse shape—"

"Rehana is a danger to us all." Mother Lairen rises to her feet opposite me, and the sadness has been replaced by a cold severity. "She has no thought of the Creator's will, and she leads others astray. She hearkens to the voice of evil!"

I take a step back. "What do you mean?"

"Do not be misled by her, my child," she adds in a gentler tone. "Only harm comes to those who do not follow the will of our Creator."

Nodding slowly, I thank her again for tending to me. Then I excuse myself.

I make my way to the other side of the cavern, all the while feeling Mother Lairen's eyes fixed on my head. A shiver snakes its way down my back. Maybe all that time in seclusion praying and fasting has gotten to her. Or maybe she really did hear from the Creator. Either way, she seems...different somehow.

I ask a couple of my sisters where Rehana is being healed, and they point me toward a bed against the far wall of the main cavern. Most of the other women have returned to their slumber; the quaking outside has stopped.

I glance toward the mouth of the cave as I pass. It's sealed up tight, as silent and still as if it's always been like this. Does every opening to our cave network look the same? That would indeed take an act of God. I'll have to check it out for myself in the morning.

Rehana lies on her back. Her shredded garments have been removed, her flesh covered in a layer of clear healing salve that glistens blue and white in my night-vision. Her chest rises and falls evenly due to the sedative she's been given. Sleep would have been impossible, otherwise.

I look at the earthen ceiling above me. How long can we last in here? If rockslides have covered all the exits, how will we breathe in a day or few? Mother Lairen would say I lack faith. But I don't believe it was the Creator who sealed us inside.

It was that *Presence*, the one I've felt all along. It wants us to die. Somehow, it appeared to Mother Lairen and made her think it was the Creator so she'd let us suffocate without a fight.

I shake my head and release a heavy sigh. My thoughts are out of control, far from logical, and not even close to scientific. I need rest.

I glance back at the effects of the avalanche. There's no longer any need for the night watch. We're safe inside for now. I can sleep.

If I can.

I curl up next to Rehana's bed and pull my knees to my chest. My eyelids sink, and the muscles in my body begin to unclench like an impotent fist...

Darkness slowly dissipates, and in its place I see grass, green and lush, passing swiftly below. Yellow flowers sprout between soft emerald blades and spread out their petals under the sun's warmth. I fly over them, my arms outstretched, my long chestnut hair whisking across my back. I blink into the wind and look up. The sky is clear and blue, its hue rich enough to take my breath away.

The grassy hillside drops away, and I sail out over the sea. The ocean swells reflect the sky, moving with a life all their own. I gasp as a pod of dolphins emerges, jumping out of the water with salty splashes, one after another, only to plunge back nose-first. I want to wait for them to reemerge, but I can't stop. I fly across the entire ocean in a matter of seconds, then I pass over the desert. The ground below me lies bare, cracked, and desolate. As I gaze across it, a sick feeling lurks in the pit of my stomach. There should be life in the desert: reptiles, barrel cactus, sage brush, even flowers. But there's no life here. It's been obliterated.

What looks like a long stretch of mangled highway runs below me now. Mounds of rubble and the twisted remains of buildings stand half-submerged in ashen sand. A great expanse, a level plain covered in dust and gravel, leads to the base of the mountains, thirty kilometers away. My flight gradually slows as I drop closer to the highway. The sun beats hot on my back. A dry breeze catches my hair. Silence reigns as I catch sight of a single figure on the move. Clad in a hooded standard-issue jumpsuit and face shield, he heads toward the eastern mountains at a steady, unhurried pace.

How can anyone survive such loneliness? What does it do to one's soul?

The ground comes alive all of a sudden, gravel and sand flying upward, spraying the figure who breaks into a run—faster than anything I've ever seen. Super-human. Rocks dislodge themselves from the earth and follow, mercilessly striking the figure in the back as if some invisible force is throwing them.

I must do what I can to help this poor soul... Or they'll kill him.

Banking in mid-air fifty meters ahead of the running figure, I hover upright. An enormous cloud of dust rises in his wake, and the gravel at his feet relentlessly launches itself upward, tearing at his jumpsuit, bouncing off his face shield.

I stare at the dust cloud and open my arms wide.

Spirits of the earth, I whisper. *I see you.*

The rocks and gravel hit the ground and lie still. The cloud of dust hovers, then seems to drift away reluctantly. The figure stops running. He's not doubled-over from the exertion, even though he's run thirty kilometers in a matter of seconds.

I'm not flying anymore. I stand on a mountain ledge high above him. But before he catches sight of me, I turn back to the cave—

"You can see them? The *spirits?*" Mother Lairen blocks my path. Her hair is as red as fresh blood, her pupils completely dilated. She grabs me by the throat. "You are unworthy, child." Claws extend from her other hand, and she rakes them across my chest. She grips my throat tighter as I scream. She chokes me silent and lifts me off my feet. "Join him!"

Screaming, I'm hurled headlong toward the figure below. Why can't I fly? The ground rushes to meet me before everything goes black.

"Bad dream?"

Gasping, my heart thumping, I look over and see Rehana's face, her head turned toward me with a faint smile on her lips.

"Hey." I rise onto my knees and take a deep breath. Just a crazy nightmare. That's all it was. "How do you feel?"

"Like hell. What do you think?" She manages a weak chuckle. "They put this goop on me that's supposed to regenerate my skin." She closes her eyes. "Creeps me the hell out. And it stinks."

I sniff at the air. It's stale, the circulation already beginning to deteriorate. We won't survive long like this—not a hundred and fifty women cooped up without fresh air. Mother Lairen is wrong. Even if there is a Creator, she didn't have anything to do with this.

"Spirits of the earth," I mutter.

The Presence? It makes sense—metaphysically, anyway. The life force of the earth, asserting itself against us. After all the destruction we wreaked upon her, it's no wonder Mother Earth would seek to return the favor.

But why were we given our *gifts*? Could it be that these spirits are disparate entities, some wanting to help us while others wish us harm?

"Spirits what?" Rehana frowns.

"Nothing."

I rise and look around. Our sisters are beginning to stir, readying themselves for a new day. How will they react to being shut in? What will Mother Lairen tell them?

Nausea sloshes around my stomach as I remember my nightmare.

"What happened out there, Daiyna?" Rehana sounds almost

like a child. I've never seen her this vulnerable. "What happened to us?"

"I don't know."

"But you've got to have some kind of idea. You're smart, I'm sure you've got a scientific theory or something."

"Everything is different now." I shake my head, avoiding the pleading look in her eyes. "I'm not sure if anything we studied applies anymore. The world has changed. There could be...forces at work that we don't understand."

"Ghosts or something? Those kinds of forces?" She waits for me to respond, but I don't say anything. "Good and evil spirits, something like that?"

"How many pain meds did you take?" I force a smile, even as what she says—despite the implications—makes sense in a weird way.

"I know, I probably sound crazy. It's just...it felt like we were being *attacked*, you know? Like the earth itself was out to get us."

I reach to squeeze her shoulder, but I pull back my hand. I don't want to interfere with the coat of healing salve. "Get some more beauty sleep."

"God knows I need it." Her scarred face relaxes, and she lets out a sigh. "Wake me up if those forces come after us again, all right?"

I half smile as I turn away. Then my brow furrows. *Forces? Spirits?* Is that really what we're up against? My nightmare returns to haunt me, but I can't think about it right now. There's a more pressing matter.

Fresh air.

I make my way up to the sealed cave entrance. It sits just as we left it. Hands on my hips, I survey the rocks piled haphazardly but effectively. It'll take those of us gifted with strength to move the biggest of these boulders, and even then it won't be an easy undertaking. Where should we put them? If we drop them off the ledge outside, the descending racket will be like an invitation to any daemons lurking about. And even if we manage to clear this opening, what if there's another rockslide as we move on to the next cave entrance? Some of us could be stranded outside in the process.

All I need to do for now is clear enough rocks to let in some air. If I can do that at each of the rockslides, we'll have enough fresh air circulating to get us by. Then, maybe, Mother Lairen will be right. We'll be able to survive.

I climb the rock pile and find a large stone surrounded by sand, lodged between two others halfway up. I give it a push, and it doesn't budge, but some of the sand trickles down. I try pulling instead, and it shifts in place. With enough effort, this should work. I pull again, changing the position of my fingers. The stone slips out and falls with a loud clatter before I can catch it. Instinctively, I glance over my shoulder.

"What are you doing, Daiyna?"

Mother Lairen stands watching. Behind her a group has gathered, their eyes fixed on me. How long have they been there?

"I'm—" My stomach tightens. "We need air. I'm just—"

"We have air, my child. What do you think it is that you're breathing?" She smiles, and the others laugh. They look almost identical in their cotton frocks and long hair pulled up tightly, pinned behind their heads.

"Yes, but—"

"Do you doubt the Creator's will for us, Daiyna?"

A hush falls on the other women. They watch me intensely. More join them, a silent throng. I don't see any shaved heads among their ranks.

"Do you doubt Her almighty provision?" Mother Lairen's voice is as calm and gentle as ever, but there's a strange edge to it. Her eyes stare, unblinking.

"No, of course not."

"Then why do you interfere with Her handiwork?" She gestures to the missing stone in the rock wall behind me. "Why do you invite danger upon us all? The Creator has protected us, yet you seek to destroy what She has done?"

A murmur sweeps through the others. There are so many of them now.

"We—we need fresh air, Mother. Can't you feel it?"

She inhales deeply and smiles, turning to the others. They follow her example, filling their lungs.

"We don't seem to notice any difference, my child. Do we?" The throng murmurs in agreement. "Perhaps we have been blessed with a new gift by the Creator, as a result of our protection. We can breathe perfectly fine here. Whereas you..." A sad look crosses her face as she steps toward me. She glances at my scalp. "You apparently cannot."

I draw back as she touches my cheek. "I don't think the Creator did this to us, Mother," I say quietly, hoping only she will hear me. "You weren't there. It was like Rehana and I were...*attacked*."

Mother Lairen's brow creases slightly, and a look of uncertainty flickers through her eyes. "Daemons?"

"No. I don't think so. I don't see how. It was beyond what any human—or whatever they are—could do."

"The *Creator*, child," she says with feeling, as if I'm blind and desperately in need of someone to lead me to the truth.

I shake my head and lower my voice to a whisper. "It's something else. Something that wants us to die. Something...in the earth."

"You speak foolishness, Daiyna. Worse: *blasphemy*. The Creator forgives you, and so do I, but—"

"You said you heard her, that she spoke to you."

"What of it?"

"Has that happened before? Ever? Because if it did, you never told us." That uncertain look passes through her eyes again as I go on, "What if it wasn't the Creator who spoke to you? What if it was something else—and it wants to harm us?"

"Harm comes to those who do not follow the will of our Creator!" Her voice is loud and authoritative. She steps back from me to join the others. They nod and murmur their assent.

"Daiyna, you will bring danger upon us all! Have you no concern for the safety of your sisters? We are the fertile womb of the New Earth, and we must be protected!" Eyes wide, pupils dilated, she points at the rock I removed. "Replace that stone this very instant!"

My heart skips a beat. I can feel adrenaline kicking in, that *fight or flight* choice staring me in the face. I look down at the stone, then over at the space where it was lodged. Behind it, there are slight cracks of light around another stone. If I punch it through to the other side, we should have a boot-sized hole in this *wall of protection*. We'll have fresh air.

Then what? Will Mother Lairen's cows attack me? I'm curious what that might look like.

Without another moment's pause, I turn and reach into the space, shoving the stone on the other side. It falls, clattering as a beam of morning light streaks inside with a burst of cool, fresh air. I close my eyes and inhale deeply, my face warmed by the light.

Sharp fingernails dig into my shoulder, whipping me around to face the wide, furious eyes and red hair of Mother Lairen. She screams unintelligibly and slaps me hard.

"What have you done?" she seethes. "You want air? Here!" She turns me around and shoves my face into the hole, pushing the back of my head with a shocking, brutal strength. "You have defied the will of the Creator, and you are a danger to us all. Harm will come to you. Harm *must* come to you!" She shoves with all her might. "You will replace the stone with your *skull!*"

Should I laugh? It's so absurd, but the pain keeps me frightfully in the moment. I choke, my throat crushed against rock, my arms and legs flailing without purpose. My face stings—from the slap or the sunlight? I can't cry out. I can't fight back.

She jerks my head to the side for a better fit, flattening my ears as she pushes. I can't breathe at all now; my windpipe is cut off. My limbs drop weakly.

Random thoughts spiral through my mind like flurries of ash.

Such a bizarre way to die. I never could have seen this coming. I guess I should have put the stone back. Too late now. Mother Lairen is killing me. What will the others think of this? How long will they last in here? Will I meet the Creator? Or will I simply cease to exist?

Dark. Everything is so dark all of a sudden...

"Let her go."

Rehana's voice comes from kilometers away. Gasps and short cries erupt from the other women. Mother's hold on me releases slightly, but I still can't breathe. My eyelids flutter to sparks of light.

"Rehana, you shouldn't be up. You need to—" Mother Lairen's voice is serene, soothing at first. But then she grates with menace, "Don't you point that thing at me!"

"I said let her go. *Now*."

The hand on the back of my head releases me, and I slip down just enough for my trachea to expand. I inhale in a loud gasp.

"She has defied the will of the Creator," our mother shouts. "Blasphemy is a sin!"

"What do you call *murder*?" Rehana counters.

"What?"

The scream from Mother Lairen is wild and guttural as she falls away from me and hits the ground sobbing.

"Stay back," Rehana warns, her voice approaching me. "Or the next one goes through her heart."

"Damn you," our mother wails. "Vile pagan bitch!"

Able to breathe at regular intervals again, I push with my arms and stumble back from the rock wall. Blood trickles warm out of both my ears.

"You all right?" Garbed only in her bed sheet, Rehana points a loaded crossbow at the other women and swings it side to side, keeping them at bay.

I nod, holding my throat. It'll be a while before I can speak.

"May the daemons devour your flesh!" Mother Lairen writhes

on the ground, unable to stand with the short arrow through her thigh. Blood spreads from both the entry and exit wounds.

"Stay back!" Rehana warns the others again as they press forward. This time she points the crossbow at our mother's head. "Tell them."

Mother Lairen scoffs, clenching her teeth. "You won't kill me, child. They know that." She turns to the others. "Come, my children!"

They surge forward in a stampede. An arrow downs one of them before the crossbow is wrestled free from Rehana's grasp. They come at me, but I spring upward, clinging to the rock wall above their heads. Others gifted in climbing and agility pursue me, and I launch myself through the air, over the throng, landing on all fours in the center of the cavern below.

"Run!" Rehana screams. The others are upon her now, tearing away her sheet and clawing at her ravaged flesh. "Run, Daiyna!"

Where are our other sisters with shaved heads? We have to help her—

You cannot save her, says a voice from deep inside me. *You must escape. His life will depend on it.*

I stand rooted, staring without really seeing. Listening, but not hearing the screams as Rehana dies.

"Who...are you?" I manage.

You already know.

PART II
CONNECTIONS

4. MILTON
NINE MONTHS AFTER ALL-CLEAR

I'm totally in the dark.

I blink my blind eyes and see only impenetrable black, oppressive and smothering. I've given up calling out. It got a little eerie (and pathetic) to hear my voice echo throughout these caverns.

We're here, she said. Then she left me. That was what—two hours ago?

I shouldn't have gotten rough with her. But I'd had it, and she seemed perfectly able to fend for herself. The throbbing pain in my temple is proof enough. I apologized of course, and I'm sure she heard me calling after her, wherever she was going. I just needed some answers.

Now all I want is to get out of here. I've already tried feeling around on my hands and knees, but I almost fell off a ledge. I caught myself in time, heart pounding, adrenaline pumping as my arm plunged through empty space, unable to tell how far the drop was. That got me to stop and think.

I haven't moved since.

But I can't sit here forever. There have to be other survivors around somewhere...besides crazy bald girl. I have to find them.

Why would she abandon me like this? It seemed like she was helping me, leading me through the cave, guiding me through the dark. Somehow, she could see. How was that even possible?

If only I'd thought to pack some glowsticks when I left the bunker. Guess I didn't plan on doing any impromptu spelunking.

I blow out a frustrated sigh, and it echoes like a beast in slumber. I need to focus, figure out some kind of strategy here.

Big hands clamp my shoulders, squeezing as they lift me off my feet. I struggle, carried through the darkness, kicking as viciously as I can, but my boots don't make contact with anything.

"Who are you?" I scream.

The hands swing me sideways and release their grip. I sprawl tumbling against the cave wall. Groaning on impact with the unyielding rock, I curse and struggle to my feet. Terrified but furious, I reel unsteadily, hurling my fists at my invisible opponent. Something cracks.

A bright light burns my eyes, and I shield them with both arms.

"Take his suit," a man's voice says with quiet authority.

"What?" I squint against the light. Two shadowy forms approach, their hands reaching for me. "No!"

They grab at my jumpsuit and dodge my punches, my kicks. One knocks me down and I fall flailing, landing a few good blows. One of them groans, and my adrenaline surges at that small victory. I release something like a wild war cry.

My windpipe closes thanks to a sudden headlock from behind. I choke as my suit is ripped from my body. Its liquid reserves splash across my bare legs, filling the cave with the strong reek of urine.

"Boots, too?" a bass voice rumbles.

A man grunts in the affirmative.

I keep thrashing until I'm thrown to the ground and someone sits on me, nearly crushing my ribs until my boots are tugged off. Then I'm left alone. I cough on hands and knees, naked in the harsh glare of green light.

"Hope you enjoyed that as much as I did," I croak, rubbing my neck.

A hydropack flies at me, slapping against my shoulder.

"Wash yourself," says the authoritative voice.

"You gonna watch?"

No response. I smirk and shake my head, hoping to regain as much of my composure as possible, considering the circumstances. Who are they? What do they want with me—besides my clothes? Are they in league with that bald girl?

It's been months since I had a bath—not since I've been out of the bunker, that's for sure. I probably smell like piss mixed with the foulest of body odors. Good thing I'm immune to my own natural scent by this point.

I tear open the pack and splash the water-like fluid down my chest and back, along my arms and legs and between them, saving some at the end for my face. Refreshing. These folks must have hydropacks to spare if they can waste one like this.

A wad of cotton clothes much like Bald Girl wore comes flying at me, and I catch it. I squint into the light.

"You want me to wear these?" Bet I'm coming across as very astute.

"Yes," the voice of authority says.

"Please," adds the bass voice with a short rumbling chuckle.

I dry my face on the long tunic before I pull it on, then tug the baggy pants on underneath. I stand facing the light, my muscles tensed, arms down at my sides. I can't see anything beyond the light. They've got me cornered, that much I can tell.

"Now what?" my voice echoes, sounding more confident than I feel.

"Now we talk." A shadow steps toward me, and with another crack, the glowstick in his hand flares green, illuminating the sharp features of a well-built man a decade or so older than I am. He comes within a meter of me and stands at ease, his eyes piercing. "I'm Luther. Tell me what you're called."

Introductions after I'm roughed up? What is this?

"Milton," I mutter.

He nods slowly. "*Paradise Lost,* indeed."

"What?"

"The name you were given in your bunker—"

"My parents." I swallow. I haven't thought about them for a long time. I can't believe how much I suddenly miss them. I clear my throat as hazy images of a former life fill my mind. "My parents...they named me. When I was born."

"I see."

"Where's the girl?" I force myself to focus on the moment. "She found me outside, brought me in here." Before abandoning me to these cave dwellers.

"She'll return. Please." He gestures toward large rocks on my left that have been arranged around a flat-topped boulder. Like seats around a table, if I used my imagination. "Join me."

He sits down and sets the glowstick in the middle of the table. He moves with confidence, like a leader. Like Jackson.

Maybe he was the boss man of his bunker, and they all moved up into these caves after All-Clear to avoid the sun. But what sector would they be from? Sector 43 was the only one on the west side of these mountains, the only one for kilometers around. I should know. I walked most of them. Then I ran...

Like I've never run in my life.

"Where are you from?" I take my seat across from him and glance toward the other light, the first one that blinded me in the dark. A massive shadow of a man stands with it mounted on the end of a spear. "What sector?"

"51. You?"

"43. So you were on the other side of these mountains. East of here." Again, I probably appear quite astute. But I don't know what else to say.

"Fifty kilometers due east. So much of this terrain has changed since D-Day."

True enough. An image of the mangled InterSector, my companion for so much of my journey, passes through my mind. "How did you wind up in here?" I gesture toward the earthen ceiling.

He parts his lips to speak, but pauses before saying, "I'd like to hear your story first, Milton. Will you indulge me?"

I contemplate telling him to screw off. But I'm outnumbered, and they did give me this nice new set of duds, so I figure what the heck. It's not like I have anywhere else to be, and he did say the bald girl would be back. I'd like to see her again.

What's her part in all of this? From what I remember, Sector 51 was one of the all-male bunkers full of virile young studs waiting to sow their seed. How did she fall in with them?

"Sure." I shrug. "Where do you want me to start?"

A slight smile plays on the sharp features of his unshaven face. "Start at the beginning, Milton. At your beginning."

My beginning. There isn't a whole lot to tell, but I give it a shot.

"Well, I was born to two members of Sector 43, their only allotted child, before they were both sterilized. I grew up with my mother working the twelve-hour day shift and my father working the night. Trade school started for me when I was four years old, and I progressed well enough through all the requisite levels."

I learned all about the cold wars and other times of peace and conflict in between. It was after the second cold war that half the continent was nuked, leaving it uninhabitable. When the third cold war started to thaw, everybody knew it wouldn't bode well. I was fourteen by then. We heard rumors of bioweapons and other forms of impending doom, but I thought it was just talk. Nobody would intentionally screw over the entire planet. By then, I was on the day shift, and I had more than enough to keep me busy.

"So one day the work bus takes a slight detour, and I end up in a cattle car headed on a one-way trip, straight down." Julia's face fills my mind: her soft blonde hair and green eyes, her warm smile. The way our fingers interlaced, our hands together a perfect fit. "And twenty years later, the bunker door opens. Outside..." I look down with a heavy feeling in my gut. "I found this mess of a world they saved us for."

"It was a long time for all of us." Luther watches me. "How did you cope?"

"Underground?" I feel my face sag. I don't even want to think about that. "Hated every minute."

"How many of you were there?"

I look at the glowstick. How long can it burn? "Fifty, I think."

"Mixed. Male and female?"

I remember Julia's scent as she slept beside me. She smelled sweet, like fresh cut flowers. She tasted even better.

"You were sterilized, then."

Why does he have to bring that up? "We all were."

"Of course. To avoid..." He chooses his words carefully now. "Overpopulation in the bunker, nourishment shortages—"

That was the idea. "Not you, huh? Bursting at the seams with seed, right?" I smirk. "Didn't waste any of it on your bunker buddies?"

He looks a little taken aback. "I didn't mean to offend you."

A little late for that. I glance at the giant with the spear. "Got any food? I was told there would be." Unless that was just part of Bald Girl's ploy to get me to come along.

"Of course." He holds his hand out to the giant. "Samson?"

A protein pack sails through the air, landing in Luther's hand. He offers it to me. With a grunt of appreciation, I take the pack and tear open the plastic seal. Bite off a big tasteless chunk.

"Milton," Luther says, "where are the other survivors from Sector 43?"

"Dead."

"All of them?"

I look him in the eye and nod. Now he'll want the sordid details. But I don't feel like talking about it. None of his business, really.

"How about you?" I say around another mouthful. "How many of you survived?"

"All fifty at All-Clear." He sighs, watching me closely. "But in the weeks that followed..." He leans forward. "How did they die—your companions? Was it on the surface?"

I shake my head, staring into the light on the table. I chew slowly. All I can see is blood, gruesome scenes flashing behind my eyes like an old horror interactive.

"In the bunker, then?"

I nod once, my chin sinking and staying there. I drop the rest of the pack, no longer hungry.

"But how?" He sounds stunned. "Was there a malfunction in the environmental systems? A revolt?" He waits for a response, his eyes boring into me. "Please, Milton... If you were attacked, we may have a common enemy—"

"I don't think so." My voice sounds strange. Lifeless. Why am I telling him this? "His name was Jackson."

"Jackson." Luther sits back slowly, waiting for me to continue. He looks genuinely interested, maybe even concerned. Why should he care?

"Jackson was our leader. He said there was a food shortage." I clench my fists. Why didn't I stop him? "He lied." I was weak, and he was the strongest. But I could have stopped him. "And they all died," I grate out, my eyes stinging all of a sudden. *Tears?* "He killed them, one at a time...until it was just him and me left."

That was my reward. My punishment. He let me live. He kept my name out of the lottery until the very end.

There was no food shortage, no need for the lottery every four months, no reason why one of us had to be selected at random to die every time. Jackson said he had it all figured out, that there would be enough nourishment packs if we did it this way. All fifty of us wouldn't survive until All-Clear as things were, he said. But *he* had to make it, of course, since he was the only virile male among us. The future would depend on men like him. The rest of us were expendable.

"The new earth won't need a sterile labor force," he told me in private. *"More than anything, we'll need to repopulate. And we'll need food."* He *cursed, shaking his head. "I don't know what those government jerk-offs*

were thinking! There's no way we'll survive out there with the limited supply we've got. Cutting back now is our only option, and that means less food down here so there'll be enough up there." He pointed to the surface far above us. "You understand, Milton? We've got to think of the future!"

After he explained the situation to everyone, he instituted the lottery. Every time, one of our group was selected to die. Jackson made a big deal out of it, and we always celebrated our bunker mates for an entire day before their time was up. Then I would take them back into one of the storerooms and shut the door. We didn't have anything painless they could take in their sleep. I don't think the government geniuses had planned for us to kill ourselves while we were underground.

But we did have rope.

"Then what happened?"

"What?" I swallow.

"When only you and Jackson were left—"

"I killed him." I cut him open, again and again, and his blood covered the floor in a thick layer of crimson liquid mercury. "It was either him or me. I wasn't going to let him kill me."

Luther nods slowly, watching me. "I can't imagine what it must have been like for you. To lose everyone—and then face this new world alone." He pauses. "You've been out there for nearly ten months."

"Yeah." I relax my hands and rub between my eyes. I can't think about it anymore.

It will drive you crazy.

"She was the first person you've seen in all that time?"

She was my first love: *Julia.* I managed to keep her name out of the lottery for years—until Jackson found out. When her name was selected, my heart nearly stopped. The others celebrated her all that day, but I couldn't. I met Jackson in the back storeroom, and I hit him as hard as I could. He beat me down hard because of it, and I couldn't walk straight for a week after.

He knew I loved her. He knew she loved me. He couldn't stand to see us happy together.

"Yes," I manage. "She was the first."

Slipping the noose down around the nape of her neck... I couldn't look her in the eye.

"Don't hate yourself, Milton." She gazed at me, her green eyes glistening. *"Be strong. We have to think about the future."*

"There is no future," I grated out through clenched teeth. *"Not without you."*

"Milton." She touched my cheek, swollen from my fight with Jackson. *"The future is a whole lot bigger than you and me. I'm helping others to live by doing this, so the future will be secure for our species."*

Jackson's rhetoric leaking from her lips.

"There was no other—not in all that time?" Luther sounds uncertain, like he's having trouble believing me. "You haven't met any other survivors?"

Well, there was Adam and other skeletons like him, and there was Rocky my erstwhile pet... I should probably keep that to myself. "Just remains in the rubble. Bones. That's all I've found."

I was a scavenger from the moment I stepped out of the bunker. I took all the nourishment packs I could carry, wrapped them in my bedroll, and headed east for no other reason than to see what lay on the other side of these mountains off in the distance. I left Jackson to decay in an empty storeroom. Julia deserved a proper burial. They all did, every one that I'd killed. But I heaved the bunker door shut and left it.

A dark, festering tomb.

"You were running when she found you."

I ran away and left them all behind. But now Luther knows where I came from. If he finds the bunker—

"She says you were...under attack."

"Yeah." I look him in the eye. "Like the earth itself was out to get me. What the hell?"

The giant rumbles with a low chuckle.

"Wasn't funny." It was the weirdest, most frightening thing ever. "What was that all about? She wouldn't tell me anything."

Luther hesitates, again choosing his words carefully. "There are a few opinions circulating among us at present. But suffice it to say, you're not the only one to have experienced something like this. Had you not been wearing that jumpsuit, your skin would have been completely ravaged."

"So why'd you take it from me?"

A sheepish expression crosses his face. "Some of the women don't like the suits."

"And we aim to please," the giant adds, chuckling again.

"This is Samson," Luther introduces him. "He was with me in Sector 51."

Samson brings the light down to illuminate his massive, bearded face. His eyes gleam with good-natured humor as he says, "Howdy." The light rises, leaving him in shadow again.

"Howdy," I mutter. His name suits him. I face Luther. "*Women*, you say. From what sector?"

"Fifty." He smiles ironically. "Our wives, supposedly—the other half of the equation necessary for our planet's repopulation. The government scientists had everything planned out, but they failed to factor in something very important: *free will*. They never considered the possibility that the women would want nothing to do with us as far as procreation is concerned."

"Bunch of lesbians?" Figures. Underground for twenty years, they had to find a way to satisfy themselves. I'm sure Samson and Luther shared a few intimate moments of their own.

"Not exactly." There's a grave look in his eyes now. "We're facing certain dangers...with which you're not yet familiar, it would seem. When we found the women—numbering less than thirty, out of an original complement of one hundred fifty—they made it clear to us that survival was their priority for the time being, not *baby-making*. We agreed, for we'd lost many of our own as well."

Dangers? Worse than killer sand and rocks that decide to pound weary travelers to death?

"So, Mother Earth is after you guys too?"

"If only that were all."

"Hey, it's enough. Believe me, if it hadn't stopped all of a sudden when it did, that dust storm or whatever it was out there would've killed me."

"She saved your life."

"Huh?" I manage to articulate.

"She sees the spirits. They communicate with her."

I'm staring, and my mouth is hanging open a little, but I can't seem to do anything about it. Luther looks serious, but the words coming out of him are complete gibberish. What the heck is he talking about?

"Spirits?" I force a chuckle. "Like ghosts or...?"

"What are your spiritual beliefs, Milton?"

"I don't believe in ghosts." Jackson's face—twisted with surprise and covered in blood—flashes through my mind. I sure hope ghosts don't exist, because if they do... "Is that what was chasing me?"

Ghosts of the departed? All the ones I led to the noose, back now for vengeance?

"What I mean," Luther rephrases his question, "is what are your beliefs about spiritual matters?" He watches me for a moment. "Do you believe in the Creator?"

"God? Hell no!"

Samson chuckles.

Luther appears unaffected. "You feel strongly about it."

"Well, yeah. I mean, how could anybody believe in God after D-Day? How could any all-powerful *god* let something like that happen to the planet?"

Luther raises an eyebrow. "It could be argued that we're the ones who let it happen, and that even so, we've been given a second chance. But I digress. The reason I ask you is because we have seen things—similar to your experience with the rocks and sand—that defy logical explanation. I ask about your beliefs because it will take an open mind to begin to comprehend what's happening here."

I'm staring again. This is definitely the strangest conversation

I've had in a while. Not that I've had many lately, but this one really takes the cake.

"For example..." I hope he fills in the blank.

"Take my hand." He holds it out to me over the light.

Weird, but I reach for it anyway. Samson shuffles his feet as Luther takes my hand in a strong grip, and I return it. Then his fingernails extend outward like long claws, pinching into my skin without breaking the surface.

"What the—!" I jump to my feet, my heart lurching. He doesn't release his hold. "Let go of me, you *freak*!"

"We've been changed, Milton. All of us, in one way or another. You yourself can run faster than any human in the history of the world."

"Changed?" I stare at his claws. A memory of the bald girl sweeps back into my mind: how she launched herself through the air and landed at my feet. And how she could also see in the dark. "Changed how? Why?"

His claws slowly retract, and he releases his grip on my hand. It hangs limply in mid-air. "We've been given certain *gifts*, Milton. I don't know how else to describe them. Some are shared among a few of us, while others are unique to the individual. Many of us have more than one ability."

"Well, aren't you special," I sneer, backing away from the rock table. I have to get out of here somehow, leave these freaks behind and be back on my own, outside where I belong. "So you're all mutants?"

He shakes his head. "Not mutations, as far as we can determine. Seldom is a random physiological mutation beneficial to the organism, and never can it be activated at will. Our changes are unlike anything that's ever arisen in nature." He pauses. "They've helped us stay alive in spite of a well-armed adversary that outnumbers us five to one, according to the most reasonable estimates."

"Right. The ghosts." He's out of his mind, and he's a freak of nature, to boot. I've got to grab that glowstick and make a run for it. The ladder can't be too far away.

"Not ghosts, Milton. These creatures are flesh and blood. Men like us once, but something went horribly wrong and changed them as well."

"They'd be the *mutants*," Samson mutters.

Fresh air, that's what I need. Clear my head. These guys and their bald beauty must have gone stir-crazy a long time ago, probably after their mutations started kicking in. I don't blame them. Probably wasn't their fault. I'm sure they're great folk and all, but they're not my type. I prefer your average variety of human.

I'll keep looking.

"Let me guess: those mutants happen to be cannibals?"

Before Luther can respond, I snatch up the glowstick and make a run for it without any idea where I'm going. The light extends a meter ahead of me, and I hold it out in front as I make my mad dash. I glance over my shoulder, and by the light of Samson's spear I see them move to pursue me. But their movements are so sluggish...like they're in slow motion...

Or is it because I'm moving so much *faster*?

The cavern wall slams into me full-force, and I groan out loud. That's what I get for not looking where I'm going. I almost lose the glowstick as I sprawl sideways, but I manage to right myself, and I tighten my grip on it. My feet barely skim the surface of the cavern floor as I run, and I feel that strange awareness again, the sense that this speed is not my own. A powerful energy courses through me, wild but contained, harnessed like a fuel source.

Have I been changed? Obviously. But I'll figure it out on my own. I'm not staying here with this bunch. I've got to get out.

A sudden blow to the face stuns me. I curse at the blinding pain and fall backward. The glowstick clatters beyond my grasp as I land flat on my back. Then a chorus of cracks fills the air, and the cavern is illuminated by twenty more glowsticks, each held by a bald woman garbed in loose, sand-colored garments. They stand on a wide ledge a couple meters above the cavern floor, the green light reflecting in their eyes as they watch me impassively. Creepy, to say the least.

One of them stands over me with a spear made from PVC pipe and scrap metal.

"You?" I wipe at the blood issuing from my nose.

It's her: the bald beauty, the first living person I'd seen in months. Only now I wish I never laid eyes on her.

"I have him," she calls to the men behind me, the point of her spear held at my throat. She looks me in the eye.

I meet her gaze, not even trying to rise. "Where have you been?"

"Miss me?"

Samson and Luther's footfalls pound toward us.

"Not really." I grab the spear below its head and jump to my feet in a single move, whipping the weapon free from her grasp as I step behind her and shove the sharp point flat against her throat. She's too slow to resist. "Stay back!"

Samson and Luther stand rooted, as do the twenty-odd men behind them who've come out of the dark corners, their eyes glowing in the sickly light.

"Did you see that, Luther? How quick he can move?" one of them stage-whispers loudly.

Luther nods, watching me. "He's embracing his gift."

What are they talking about? Can't they see what I'm doing?

"You too! Keep back," I shout at the women above me. Murmuring among themselves, they hold their position and keep their eyes focused on me. "Everybody stay back! I'm getting out of here, okay? No one's going to stop me." I press my lips against the bald beauty's ear. "Which way?"

"I can't help you escape," she says without fear. "I won't."

"You will, or this spear starts impaling." I tighten my grip on her. "*Which way?*"

"We need you, Milton," Luther says quietly. "Our survival may very well depend on what you can do."

More crazy talk. I look around at them all, and I don't know if it's the eerie light or the bald women or the eager looks in their eyes, but they're really giving me a bad case of the heebie-jeebies.

"Listen, I really don't want to be part of your cave cult, okay? I just want out of here."

A younger man behind Luther steps forward.

"Plato," Luther cautions him.

Plato holds up his hands in response and faces me. "How will you survive out there, Milton? It's midday. The sun is out in full strength. You'll roast."

He's right. "Give me my suit."

Plato shakes his head.

"I'll kill her!" I swivel the spear tip, and it punctures her skin, drawing a narrow bead of blood. She stiffens.

"Please." Plato takes another step forward, his hands hovering. "You're a reasonable man, Milton. You're not a killer."

That's kind of funny. *Ironic* would be a better word for it.

"You don't know anything about me, man. So stay back!"

He lunges forward and spits at me, right in the face. Thick mucus slaps against my eyes, but my disgust lasts only a moment. The next thing I know, I'm doubled over and screaming, scrubbing at my burning eye sockets as they're devoured by acid.

Voices converge on me all at once:

"Daiyna, are you all right?"

"I'm fine."

"We should tie him up."

"I'm sure that would really earn his confidence."

"Nice shot, Plato."

"Nasty, but effective."

"He spit at me? What the hell?" I scream.

"Milton, hold still."

"Stop rubbing. You'll make it worse."

"Flush it out."

Strong hands clamp my head and jerk it back. My arms are held down against their will. Cool liquid from a hydropack pours across my eyelids. They continue to burn, and I continue to scream. I've never felt anything so intense. It's like a raging fire behind my pupils. I can't see a thing. Incapacitated, I'm completely at their mercy.

"Relax, Milton. You'll be fine. Plato's gift doesn't incur any permanent damage," Luther says at my side. His hand squeezes my shoulder.

"As far as we know," says an unfamiliar voice.

I struggle to form words, and when I manage to do so, they erupt in a string of curses.

"Yeah, he'll be all right." Samson chuckles behind me, holding my head back.

"Open your eyes. We need to flush them out." It's Plato. Why is he helping? He's the freak who spat at me! "Pinch his eyelids open."

I struggle, but they overpower me yet again. I scream as they open my eyes and pour the fluid in. After the initial shock, the burning starts to subside; the hydropack seems to have a neutralizing effect. I blink and sputter as they help me sit down on one of the rocks nearby.

"We should tie him up," someone says.

"No." Luther remains by my side. "Can you see, my friend?"

Friend? What's this guy smoking? Didn't I have one of his cult members at spear-point? But I nod, blinking away the fluid as my vision returns, blurry at first but gradually sharpening up. Luther, Samson, and Plato the Spitter appear first in my field of vision. Behind them are the others, men and women dressed alike in the same loose-fitting cotton I'm wearing now. They strain past heads and shoulders to see me.

The bald beauty is not among them.

A pang of remorse strikes me for no reason. She's nobody to me, yet I wish I hadn't hurt her. And I don't know why, but my urge to flee has subsided considerably. Go figure.

"Let's give him some room to breathe, my friends," Luther says.

The others back away, but a scrawny old man mutters, "We should tie 'im up."

"Try it, Grandpa, and I'll hang you with the rope." The words come out before I know what I'm saying.

My stomach drops. I don't want to see another coil of rope ever again.

"I'm sure you could, son," he replies, locking his grey eyes on me and standing confidently, albeit stoop-shouldered. How'd he ever make the cut for Sector 51? "You're fast enough, that's surely a fact."

"Rip, please," Luther says.

"I'm sure you could kill us all if you wanted to, and we'd be too slow to stop you. But is that what you want, son? Do you want to be a killer?"

I stare back at him.

"Use your gift for good," old Rip says. "That's why it's been given to you."

He lets those words sink in, then turns to join the others, their lights fading into the dark recesses of the cavern beyond. I'm left alone with Luther, Samson, Mr. Spit, and some pretty strange thoughts.

I have a *gift*, apparently: superspeed. I've used it three times now. These people have gifts, too: claws, night-vision, super-spit, probably others. But the word *gift* implies it was given by someone.

So...who exactly handed out these bizarre abilities?

"Where do they come from?" My voice is low and sounds a little defeated. I sniff and wipe at my oozing eyes, my bloody nose.

"The others?" Luther frowns, gesturing to the men and women who've left.

"No. The *gifts*." I mime claws with my fingers.

He almost smiles. "We believe... We have come to believe—"

"With Daiyna's help, of course," Plato adds. He looks so young with his bright eyes and hairless face. How old was he on D-Day? A newborn?

"Without Daiyna, we had only vague conjectures and fears. At first, we thought the same as you, that we were somehow *mutating*. Perhaps we left the bunker too soon and were suffering bizarre, unpredictable side effects. I was the first from our sector to be changed. I experienced it first in a dream, then in reality." Luther flexes his fingers, and the claws shoot out.

Samson chuckles. "Gets me every time."

Yeah. Real entertaining.

Luther turns his hand over, marveling at it, apparently still awed even after the time that's passed. "I've yet to grow accustomed to this." He shakes his head and allows the claws to retract. "Daiyna—the woman who found you—and her sisters also experienced newfound abilities emerging among them, all beneficial in some way to their survival. They could climb great heights with ease and see without any light. Some of them, like our Samson here, were gifted with super-human strength."

Samson grins, revealing a mouthful of big teeth. "I don't even have to work out anymore." He shrugs. "But I do anyhow. Gotta look like I'm making an effort. For the ladies."

"Any luck with that?" Plato asks.

The giant's expression darkens. "They'll come around eventually."

Luther clears his throat, and they both return their attention to me.

"But where do they come from? These weird abilities?" He better not say *ghosts*, or I'm out of here for good this time.

"At the same time that my brothers and I were struggling to comprehend what was happening to us, Daiyna and her sisters were doing the same, only they were blessed with a revelation that didn't come to us." He pauses. "Milton, when you were on your journey all those months, did you at times feel...as if you weren't alone?"

Is he kidding? All I felt was utterly and completely alone. I hoped there were other survivors out there somewhere, but the nagging fear always remained that I was the last man on the planet. Not sure yet whether I wish I was right.

"No." I think again. "Well, not until the whole attack of the killer sand thing."

"You felt a Presence?"

"Then? Yeah, definitely. One that wanted to kill me."

Luther presses his fingertips together. "It did."

It? He better not mean a ghost.

"When we found Daiyna and what remained of her group—after we proved we weren't their enemy, which took some doing—we learned a lot from them. None the least of which was that this life force, something we all felt at one time or another yet none could identify, is indeed real. And it can communicate."

"Okay." I nod to show I'm listening and hope he'll go on. "And?"

"Brace yourself," Samson rumbles.

"This Presence, from what we can tell, takes two forms: one that wishes us harm, and another, which has somehow granted us these super-human abilities. We don't know why this dichotomy exists, but we have reason to believe there are forces at work on this planet that desire vengeance upon humankind, while others seek to aid us in our survival. It may be that these are two facets of the same entity, or that there are two very distinct entities. From what Daiyna has been told, it appears to be the latter. There's so much we don't know, and even less that we understand." He leans toward me. "What we know for certain is that months ago, Daiyna saw you in a dream. And in this dream, she knew how to save your life. She was told to save you."

I swallow. "Told?"

"By the spirits of the earth."

That's it. I'm out of here. I'll thank them for their fine hospitality and be on my way. The tough guy approach didn't work, so I'll try being the nice guy.

"Well, good luck to you all." I start to my feet.

Samson steps forward, the joviality absent from his eyes. Is he trying to intimidate me?

"You know I'm too fast for you," I caution him.

"Yeah." He nods. "That's why we need you."

"Milton, please hear us out. If you still want to leave, we won't try to stop you. Right, Luther?" Plato faces him.

"Of course," Luther says quietly.

So they need me. Well, I need them too, because there's no chance I'll find my way out of here in the dark. And I'll need my suit, once I'm outside.

"How about this. You tell me whatever you want while you lead me out of here. You'll have until we get outside to convince me to join your crew." I smirk at their hesitation. "Hey, if you really don't plan on keeping me here against my will, then you shouldn't have a problem with this."

Plato takes the glowstick from Samson. "I'll lead you out."

"I want my suit."

He nods. "Samson will bring it. He'll meet us at the mouth of the cave."

Smart move. Probably thinks I'll take his light and run, otherwise.

He'd be right about that.

"All right. Let's go." I keep an eye on him. He better not try spitting at me again.

"This way."

I follow as he steps past me and to the left. I don't know why, but I glance back at Luther and Samson. They don't say anything or make any gesture of farewell, not that I expected them to. They just watch me go. I can't help but feel a little sorry for them. But I can't help them. I'd only disappoint everybody if I stuck around.

Strangely enough, I wish I could see her one more time. *Daiyna.* Even though she gave me this bloody nose.

I follow Plato's dark silhouette as we make our way through the silent cavern, the green light bobbing in front of him. For a good ten minutes or so, he doesn't say anything, and I wonder if he's given up trying to convince me to stay. Fine by me. As soon as I've got my suit, my nourishment packs, and my bedroll, I'll be back on my way to see what's on the other side of these mountains. I'll put all this craziness behind me and continue my climb. It'll take some work, but maybe I can put my new superspeed to good use.

"Luther is a spiritual man," Plato breaks the silence. "I don't fault him for it."

"Some people are, I guess." Small talk? Give me a break.

"His faith kept us unified for years. Many of the men have adopted his belief in the Creator. They found peace in his religion. It helped them survive."

"But not you?" Why am I encouraging this?

"Careful here," he warns. "The drop is twelve meters, straight down."

I do my best to follow in his footsteps.

"You're right, Milton. It wasn't for me. There may be a spiritual world that coexists alongside our own, a world of *ideal forms* and such, but I tend to find more comfort in reason than the supernatural. And when survival is on the line, I lean toward a more pragmatic line of thought."

"So you don't agree with Luther about the ghosts?"

"He believes the spirits are those of all the animals wiped out on D-Day."

I can't help but laugh. My voice echoes like a madman's.

Plato's silhouette shrugs in front of me as we duck under a low outcropping of rock. "As I said, Luther is a spiritual man. He believes every form of life has a God-given essence, and that the animal spirits were left behind, since there was no afterlife for their kind. Unable to reincarnate as was their way, they remain as some kind of metaphysical residue that over the years, in our absence, coalesced into a dichotomized—"

"He mentioned that." I don't want to hear any more about this. It's insane.

"Right. Well, Daiyna's experiences helped confirm his beliefs, and he's managed to convince most of the others. I agree with him in theory, that it's a possibility, and that it explains some things." He makes a spitting noise, followed by a self-deriding chuckle. "But I think we have more pressing matters."

I smirk. "The mutant problem?"

"You already know about that?"

"He mentioned it. But he was more into talking about *spirits* than anything else."

"Well, that's Luther. I, on the other hand, would have told you about the hostiles. It's where you and your *gift* would come in—how you'd be an invaluable help to us all." He turns, and his light shines on the base of a ladder made of plastic pipes. "Straight up from here."

A wave of relief pours over me. Looks like I'll be getting out of here after all. I couldn't be sure that he was leading me in the right direction, but now I know my doubts were unfounded. He starts up the ladder, and I'm right behind him.

"So how's that, exactly? You need my speed?"

"We need you to disarm the daemons the next time they attack."

"Uh—*demons*?" Are they bad ghosts?

Plato chuckles without humor. "That's what Daiyna and the women called them when we met. The name suited these monsters, so it stuck. We don't know who they are or where they came from, but they have weapons and vehicles, oddly enough. And they're savage flesh-eaters. They devour both the living and the dead."

Cannibals. I knew it.

Plato falls quiet. The only sounds are our hands and feet making contact with each rung of the ladder as it creaks beneath our weight.

"They attacked us twice before we reached these caves," he says at length. "We lost half our men to them. The women suffered losses as well. For now we hide in relative safety, but we can't live this way forever. In fear." He clears his throat. "If you were to help us, we could disarm them and start fighting back. We could protect ourselves—our future. Don't you see how important you are to us, Milton? How much *good* you could do?"

He reaches the top of the ladder and pulls himself onto the ledge above, moving to the right. I follow, hand over hand, and he takes hold of my forearm as I come within reach, helping me up. He looks me in the eye as if he's waiting for my answer.

"That way?" I gesture to the left.

He drops his gaze and releases his grip on me. "No. Follow me." His shadow leads off to the right along the cave wall. "Careful. A deep crevice runs beside this path for the next hundred meters." He falls silent again.

Is he finished trying to convince me to join them in their mighty battle against the demon hordes of hell? So a bunch of his bunker buddies were killed—sorry to hear it, but that doesn't mean I should go toe to toe against the degenerates who did it. I know what it's like to have death take your friends, but this isn't my fight. I don't have to get involved.

Who am I kidding? I'm already involved. I have a *gift* like the rest of them. I can't doubt that. And there's something to be said for us humans sticking together. Hell, I might not even be alive if it wasn't for that bald woman.

"Wait a minute." I stop in my tracks, and he turns to face me. "Before, when Luther said she saved my life. How exactly did she do that?"

"Do you really want to know? It involves the spirits."

"Just tell me."

"She saw you in a dream, months ago. Saw the spirits of the earth attacking you. She told them she could see them, and they vanished. The rocks and dust stopped chasing you. Just like that."

"And then...she did it for real?"

"You tell me." He shrugs. "You were there."

She saved my life, and I threatened to take hers. What kind of gratitude is that? I have to make it right. For all their sakes, for all the lives that have been lost.

For Julia.

I have to help. I'll do whatever I can, and then I'll be on my way. I owe them that much.

No. I owe *her*.

"Her name's Daiyna, right?"

He smiles and frowns slightly. "What is it, Milton? Having a change of heart?"

Maybe.

"So...she told the bad spirits she could see them." I ponder that for a moment. "Doesn't that seem kind of dangerous? For her, I mean." I don't know what I'm talking about. Just a few seconds ago, I was looking forward to being on my own again, leaving all this freakishness behind. But now I'm actually leaning toward helping these people.

"She did it for you, Milton. I think she knew the risks involved."

"What'll happen to her?" I don't want to ask any more. It'll mean I've taken a turn in a direction I can't come back from. But I have to know. "What will they...*do* to her?"

He raises an eyebrow in the green light. "Honestly, Milton? She thinks you're in greater danger than she is. That's why she led you inside these caves. She's never seen anyone pursued as you were. That must mean something." He points at me. "You've been given a very special gift that can be used for good. But there are forces at work on this planet that don't want you to succeed." He lets that sink in. "It's your choice, Milton. We won't force you to join us, not that we even could. But know this: if you leave on your own, you'll be completely alone. Daiyna won't be there to see what only she can, and if you're attacked again, you won't be able to outrun their fury."

He turns away, and we resume our careful navigation through the darkness.

I'm having trouble thinking straight. Maybe I should stop trying. The faces from Sector 43... Will they haunt me forever? I was doing a good job keeping my head clear for a while there. As

I wandered through all that desolation, my one desire besides finding other survivors was to leave these memories behind. And I did, sort of.

But now they're back. Why?

Alone for so long, it seemed at first like I was in some kind of purgatory. I deserved it. But I hoped there would be others like me. In the deafening silence, I clung to the hope that I would hear another voice at some point.

And I was right. There are other survivors, just like me—only different. They've been changed. But so have I. Doesn't that make us all the same?

Why would I want to be alone again? The loneliness was bad enough, but now I have to factor in mutant cannibals and evil spirits. What a nightmare. But then again, wasn't I out there for nine months without any supernatural attacks?

I have to switch over to autopilot until we reach the cave entrance. Clear my head, focus on the bobbing green light and Plato's silhouette in front of me. I won't allow any of these thoughts to resurface. When we get there, if Plato takes me all the way to the end, and if Samson catches up with us and has my suit, then I'll know I can trust them. They won't be liars like Jackson.

No more thinking.

Minutes pass, maybe an hour. Seems longer than last time, with her. Maybe I appreciated the company more then, and the time flew by. Our footfalls, slapping against the bare rock, echo around us. Plato's glowstick shines as bright as ever, lighting our path. We seem to have started up a gradual incline, and the air tastes different. Drier. The darkness fades by a shade or two. I see movement now when I pass my hand in front of my face. It shouldn't be much longer until we reach the mouth of the cave.

Light up ahead—faint, not green. It comes from the sun. Seems like forever since I've seen sunlight. Funny how relative time can be. The same amount will disappear when you're enjoying yourself but drag on for an eternity when you're lost in a dark network of caves. Or when you're blindly following someone who's supposedly leading you out.

"Here we are." Plato pockets the glowstick, no longer needed in the ambient light. He points at the bright patch of white that enlarges as we approach.

Squinting into the glare, I see the dark silhouette of a large man.

"Took you long enough." Samson chuckles and holds up my folded jumpsuit.

"How'd he get here before us?"

Before Plato can answer, Samson replies, "He took you the long way."

"We had a few things to discuss." Plato glances back at me.

"Did he come around?" Samson sounds hopeful.

No more thinking about it. They were both true to their word. "I think I might," I admit.

Plato mounts a few rocky steps to join Samson, and I follow. But soon I become acutely aware of something, and my stomach drops.

This is not the same way I came in.

"Where are we?" I frown and step away from them, out toward the sunlight. "Where have you taken me?"

Plato watches me, a confused look on his face. "Milton, what's wrong?"

"This is wrong! Answer me," I demand. "Where are we?"

He is a liar.

Why ask him anything? He won't tell me the truth.

"We're at the mouth of the cave."

I step out just long enough to check the sun's location in the sky. Not overhead. Not leaning toward the horizon where it should be if this is late afternoon.

I step farther out onto the ledge, shielded from sunlight by an outcropping of rock above the upper lip of the cave. I can't see the sun. It's on its way down to dusk, on the other side of the mountains.

Where I should be. Where I would have been, if Plato had taken me the right way.

"You took me through to the other side."

"You were headed in this direction when Daiyna found you. It only seemed logical—"

"You didn't ask me."

Plato looks at Samson, who shrugs.

They cannot be trusted. They are up to something.

I take another step away. "You didn't tell me."

Samson holds my suit out to me. "Don't you want this?"

Do not go near him. He will take you back into the caves.

"Milton, be careful. You're standing close to the edge."

"Stay back!"

I glance behind me. My heels are centimeters from a fifty-meter drop. The dust stirs between my feet. But there is no wind.

The jagged rocks below look so inviting.

"You just want to use me. My *gift*." My voice sounds distant, like it's coming from someone else. "I'd be a big help to you."

So they say.

I can leave all of this behind. There will be no more faces to haunt me, no more awful loneliness, no more freaks of nature. I can be completely free of it all. I can fly away forever.

I've always wanted to *fly*...

Is someone shouting my name? Calling to me?

The world revolves slowly as I turn to face the open sky, my arms outstretched like wings, my toes curled over the ledge, sand between my toes and swirling all around me now, enveloping my legs and spiraling upward, rushing against me.

Jump.

Fly.

Voices shout, but they don't matter. They don't come from the rocks below, the sharp edges that offer me all the freedom I could ever want. Why are they shouting? Who are they?

"Milton!"

Hands grope, tugging at my sleeves. But they're too late.

A sharp pain pierces my chest, and with it comes a blow like someone kicking me full-force. I'm thrown backward. What sounds like a rifle reports in the distance, cracking from far below. I fall for one long moment, wondering why I'm moving so slowly, until my head meets the unyielding surface of the ledge.

The sunlight turns black.

5. LUTHER

TEN MONTHS AFTER ALL-CLEAR

A bullet from the darkness shatters the rock face above me. I cringe as a shower of gravel rains down. Shielded from the full moon's light by a large boulder, I crouch against it, crossbow gripped in both hands. A rifle reports in the distance, echoing across the desolation.

We counted three of them. A small hunting party, armed with high-powered firearms, bold in their attack. One of Daiyna's sisters gifted with far-sight saw them approach in their jeep, and it was agreed that tonight we would make our stand. We wouldn't hide from the hostiles this time.

We've hidden too long.

Milton can't help us. Yet in a way, he already has. His injury weeks ago at the hands of these daemons galvanized our determination to strike back. His superhuman speed would have indeed been a great asset to us right now, but he must recover from his wound.

I pray he does soon. I pray the evil spirit within him will depart, and that Milton will emerge from his coma healed both in body and mind. I pray for a miracle.

Risking a quick glance over the boulder, I check the location of my comrades. Down the grade, crouched low as I am, Samson lurks armed with a spear and knife. He looks like a warrior of old, every muscle in his frame tensed and ready for action. Ten meters to his left is Plato, biting his lip and darting his eyes furtively, clutching his own crossbow. He never studied battles as Samson did all those years in the bunker. It was a curiosity for him among other topics of interest on the database. None of us could ever have imagined that the tactics he filed away would ever prove useful.

We didn't expect to find a garden paradise when we opened the bunker door after All-Clear. We knew there would be plenty of work involved in making a life for ourselves on this new earth. But we never imagined having to fight for our lives.

Flashes of memory return of the daemons' first attack.

They came six days after Plato sealed our bunker door shut with explosive charges. Tensions were running hot among the men. Holmes had succeeded in dividing them, and despite my best efforts at maintaining unity, he and those who sided with him would have nothing of it. Perhaps by agreeing to seal the bunker, I'd earned their distrust. Regardless, we were split down the middle, and as the saying goes, no community divided against itself can stand.

The time came for us to seek out our female counterparts, to find the survivors from Sector 50. Samson, Plato, Rip, and twenty others joined me, and we set a time to start our trek toward the mountains. We packed the maps (many of them useless) and nourishment packs, and we checked our jumpsuits to make certain the waste recycling functioned properly. Samson was the most eager for us to get on the move. He mentioned more than once a certain illustrated text from ancient India he'd found on the database, and he couldn't wait to meet his wives and tell them all about it. I suppose each of us was excited in his own way.

But Holmes and his men refused to join us. Perhaps he wished only to spite me. He said they were fine in the village we had built and that we should send word if we found the Sector 50 women. He emphasized the word *if*. I wondered if he planned to take the men with him farther east to find shelter in the wasted ruins of a city instead of the barren wilderness.

The mountains were closer. They were our logical destination.

Holmes was motivated by fear, which can cause one to toss logic to the wind. On the database, the government scientists left us information about certain dangers we'd likely face after All-Clear. Areas to avoid included city ruins due to the potential for airborne toxins to still be viable in enclosed spaces, despite the years that had passed. It was all speculation, of course.

Perhaps Holmes assumed the scientists were wrong. They didn't know everything. They couldn't have.

But Holmes never had a chance to find out.

We were less than five kilometers out when we heard the distant hum of engines and the short reports of firearms. We reeled and looked back, stunned to see an all-out assault on our village, on our brothers.

We took off running as fast as we could, back to a scene that became more horrific the closer we approached. We could do nothing but watch. It was immediately clear we weren't outnumbered, but that was little consolation.

Three solar-powered jeeps stirred up the dust and ash as they circled our shelters. In each vehicle, men with guns fired at our brothers, shooting them in the legs, the abdomen, the back, downing them as they scattered, desperate for cover.

We had no weapons. We never thought we'd need them.

Who were these men? Where did they hail from? Our brothers cried out in fear and pain, but by the time we reached them, they were screaming in agony.

The shots had ceased. The jeeps sat idling and empty. Our brothers lay sprawled out across the ground, face up or face down, wounded and bleeding, immobile...or being eaten.

Their attackers—strange-looking men with exposed, sun-charred leather skin and wild, unkempt hair, wearing only rags—roved quickly from one fallen victim to the next in a starved frenzy, gleaming blades drawn as they cut into our brothers and ate their flesh, pulling out wet organs and fighting among themselves over every piece.

Our shock at the sight lasted only a moment. In its place erupted white hot fury. Screaming, the muscles in his neck straining against the jumpsuit's collar, Samson led the charge. We rushed the cannibals just as they became aware of us. Their attention had been completely consumed by their gruesome feast, but no longer. They turned with eyes bulging from deformed faces, fresh blood dripping from twisted mouths. Sharpened fangs flashed gruesomely.

Two figures rose up from a ravaged body as Samson came upon them. Both his large gloved hands shot out and grabbed their heads, smashing them together with a burst of blood and brains. Their ragged bodies fell limply in his wake. I'd never seen such a brutal display of strength.

I followed close behind, leaping over one of my fallen brothers as I flexed the sharp claws from my fingers. They extended through holes in my gloves as I descended upon one of the monsters. He raised his knife and cried in a garbled voice, but I raked my talons across his face and chest, and he staggered back. Then I plunged my hand into his throat and ripped out his trachea. He fell writhing, incapacitated, and I moved on, fueled by a wild ferocity I'd never known before. I lashed out without thinking, as if driven by animal instinct, and even though I'd never killed anything before in my life, I knew how to destroy these creatures.

I'd seen it happen in a dream.

Something crashed to my left. One of the hostiles had broken the face shield of my brother with a knife, then forced the blade out the back of his skull. The attacker moved on, but my brother swayed unsteadily on his feet, his head twitching strangely before he collapsed and lay still.

Rage boiled within me. I charged after the monster as he ran to one of the waiting jeeps. Out of the corner of my eye, I saw three other savages fleeing toward their vehicles. I looked ahead.

The stock of a rifle sat next to the driver's seat. Were they running in retreat? Or merely to fetch more weapons?

Indecision gripped me as I weighed my chances of dodging a bullet. But I didn't alter my course, and as the creature reached the jeep and lunged into the seat, I took a flying leap. I hit the ground hard, nearly knocking the wind out of me. The jeep tore off at full speed, spewing sand and dust against my face shield. The other two vehicles followed, headed in the same direction: east.

Samson found me as I got to my feet, staring after them.

"We got eight of 'em. The other four escaped." His broad chest heaved as he caught his breath. His jumpsuit and face shield were splattered with blood. "One of them left this...in Reagan's face." He wiped the knife across his sleeve and handed it to me. "Military. Government issue."

I took the hilt of the dagger and noted the UW insignia laser-engraved into the steel blade. "How many of ours?" My voice sounded hollow.

"All of Holmes' bunch. And Reagan." He cursed. "Maybe fifteen were..." He couldn't bring himself to say it.

"I know." Carved up, butchered. *Eaten.* "We'll bury them." I handed him the knife.

"What if those freaks come back?" He faced the cloud of dust retreating into the distance.

"We'll dig quickly."

We buried all of our fallen brothers. For some of them, it was only what remained of their bodies. Plato kept watch, armed with our only weapon—the military dagger. We left the mangled bodies of the cannibals to rot in the sun.

It was strange to see their exposed skin, hard and blistered. Their mouths gaped open, revealing teeth sharpened to points, obviously for tearing into human flesh. Their eyes, yellow and bulbous, oozed a foul-smelling mucus, as did their ears and noses. Their faces were severely deformed, their shoulders and backs hunched over and thickly muscled. It was obvious they had suffered some sort of genetic mutation, but we could offer only conjecture as to what could have caused it.

Had they left their bunker too soon, before All-Clear, and fallen victim to whatever radioactive toxins remained outside? How fast had their DNA been damaged to manifest such bizarre physiological changes? And why had they turned to cannibalism? Had their nourishment packs run out?

Something horrendous and incomprehensible had happened to these men. But we spared no sympathy for them. They were the enemy, predators intent on hunting us down to the last meal.

Another bullet blasts the rock above me and I cringe, tightening my grip on the crossbow. They know where I am. They must have seen me take cover here. My claws flex outward involuntarily, then retract as I weigh my chances at changing location. As if to punctuate the futility of such an attempt, another bullet ricochets, followed by another.

Then everything is quiet. I hear only my own breathing—rapid and too loud. Below me, footsteps crunch the gravel at the base of the slope where it levels out. A rifle bolt cracks, shattering the silence.

The daemon is reloading.

I jump to my feet and aim the crossbow at him. He stands twenty meters away, staring back at me with lidless eyes as his misshapen hands deftly load the rifle. The full moonlight casts a surreal backdrop to our silent face-off. Time slows. I can't tell what lies behind his bulbous yellow gaze. Instinct? Conscious thought? Is he even human anymore?

I don't call out. I don't want to alert the other two daemons on the opposite side of the ridge. Daiyna and her group have attempted to flank them, and I hope they've been successful.

Silence holds the moment.

The daemon's rifle is loaded. My finger tightens on the trigger of the crossbow. He snorts, involuntarily it seems, as thick mucus oozes from his gaping nasal cavity. Then he raises the rifle with practiced ease and takes quick aim.

Samson appears on the daemon's right and plunges in his spear. Taken by surprise, the daemon lurches against the blade in his ribs and throws back his head to cry out. But Samson is too quick. In an instant, he's behind the daemon with knife in hand, slashing his throat in one swift movement and dropping him gurgling in his own blood. Samson pulls the spear free, then plunges it in again to be sure the daemon is dead. Satisfied, he looks up at me and grins, holding up one finger.

I nod. One down. Two to go.

My boots crunch across the gravel as I join my brothers. I try to quiet my footsteps, stepping heel to toe. There's no sign of the other daemons.

Plato retrieves the fallen rifle and examines it closely, his hands unfamiliar with such a weapon. Nevertheless, he holds it up and shakes it triumphantly. I can't hide my smile. It's a victory, our first in months. We now have one of their firearms. A step in the right direction, but balancing the scales in our favor will take more than a single rifle.

Plato points at the insignia on the stock. There it is again, the same that's on the dagger Samson carries: United World. Another military-grade weapon?

Shots ring out from the other side of the ridge. Samson grabs the rifle from Plato and gestures for us to follow. Warily, we begin the climb. More shots. Bullets ricochet off boulders, blasting dust into the air. We charge up the slope, keeping our weight forward as sand shifts at our feet. Samson falls prostrate with rifle in hand, tucked against his shoulder. Plato and I hit the ground at his side.

Below us, Daiyna and five of her sisters have scattered across the hillside, finding cover behind lopsided boulders jutting out of the ground. At the bottom of the grade, two daemons stand brazenly in the open, firing their rifles at will. Between volleys, they wait patiently for any movement, their eyes twitching side to side, their mouths sagging open. They tilt their heads one way and then the other like a pair of deranged hunters, toying with their prey.

"Go to hell," Samson grates out quietly, taking careful aim through the rifle scope.

"You know what you're doing?" Plato whispers

Samson shrugs. "We'll see."

He pulls the trigger, and the rifle kicks back hard against his shoulder, startling him. He curses as he quickly regains control of the weapon. The shot was wide, causing the daemons to cower and shriek. They glance at each other, then turn and charge toward the ridge.

Straight toward us.

"Brilliant," Plato mutters, pressing himself against the ground. "Now what?"

Samson takes aim. But he hesitates.

"You've got this," I encourage him.

One of the daemons calls out, his voice guttural and the words garbled, echoing against the hillside. Both creatures look up in our general direction and fire their weapons before Samson can get off another shot. The gravel and dust fly upward on impact, less than a meter from our faces. The same daemon calls out again. Is it taunting us?

We should fall back.

"I've got him." Samson squeezes the trigger, and this time he manages to hold the rifle steady despite the impact against his shoulder.

The bullet hits one of the daemons in the midsection, and he doubles over, screaming wildly as he's thrown backward to tumble down the hillside. Samson fires again and hits him in motion, taking off half his head with a burst of blood.

Samson holds up two fingers and grins.

The remaining daemon glances at his fallen comrade. Then he lunges straight for us, rifle held low as he drills us with a barrage of fire.

"Fall back!" I tug at my two brothers, and we slide down from the ridge.

"How is it firing so many rounds?" Plato shouts over the din as the raining bullets slam into the ground above us, sending up plumes of dust.

Samson turns his rifle over, studying it. "Must have an automatic mode."

We dive behind an outcropping of rock just as the daemon mounts the top of the ridge and stops, scanning the hillside below, undoubtedly spotting our scuffled tracks. He snorts and reloads his weapon as Samson takes aim.

"Wait." I start to my feet. "Cover me."

"What are you doing? Are you *insane?*" Plato hisses.

I raise a hand to him and rise above our shelter. The daemon locks his eyes on me, but his fingers don't move any faster as he reloads his weapon. I'm no threat to him. I'm his next meal.

He's the hunter. I am merely prey.

What am I doing?

"You there!" I call up to him, my voice echoing confidently even as I fight to keep my knees from trembling. "Can you understand me?"

He snorts, mucous drooling from where a nose should be. Instead there are only two holes, like the face of a skull. The rifle is loaded now, and he raises it, aiming at me. Any second, Samson will take him out with a head shot. But first I have to know.

"Why are you doing this?" Can he speak?

The daemon grunts, shaking his head oddly as if there's a fly buzzing in his ear.

"Get down, Luther!" Samson roars, jumping to his feet. "Go to hell, daemon!"

He squeezes the trigger. Nothing. He ducks down quickly, and I fall beside him as the daemon descends the ridge. With him comes another barrage of fire, blasting against the rock sheltering us.

"What happened?" Plato yells, covering his ears and cowering.

Samson curses and scowls at his rifle, pounding the weapon with his fist. "Jammed!"

The daemon's automatic fire rains down, growing in intensity as the creature fast approaches.

Then it stops. Our ears ring in the sudden silence.

We glance at each other. Samson hesitates before attempting to return fire. He points away from us and pulls the trigger. A round explodes from the muzzle and burrows into the earth. Satisfied, he peers over the outcropping of rock.

"Hold!" Daiyna's voice calls out. "It's down."

"Hello, Ladies," Samson says, cocking an eyebrow as he rises to his fullest height. "Decided to join the fight?"

A daemon lies at Daiyna's feet with two arrows through his neck. The bloated chest heaves with gasps rasping through jagged teeth. His rifle has been kicked aside.

"We've been here all along," she retorts, gesturing for the woman behind her to finish off the daemon with a spear.

"Really? I could've sworn you just arrived." Samson winks at her.

"Through the heart, Shechara. If a daemon has one." Daiyna points, turning her back on Samson.

"Wait." I step forward. She frowns at me. "Please."

Daiyna halts her sister, but the frown doesn't leave her brow. She watches me, they all do, as I kneel beside the fallen daemon and look at him closely.

"Careful, Luther," Plato warns. "It still looks hungry."

The oozing yellow eyes twitch as they focus on me. The stench of rotten meat is almost unbearable, but I don't draw back. Is that human hide he wears as a second skin?

"Who are you?" I whisper.

He stares back at me, but it's impossible to tell if there is any conscious thought behind his eyes. They have the look of a wild animal's, fueled by instinct, driven by hunger. Thick saliva drips out of his gaping mouth, and his stomach churns at my proximity.

"Where do you come from?" When we were first attacked, the daemons came from the east, and it was there they fled when we drove them out of our village. "Was your bunker compromised?" Did biotoxins somehow manage to get inside? "Did you leave your bunker before All-Clear?"

Nothing registers in his gaze.

"Can you understand me?"

A gurgle erupts from his throat where the arrows pierce him. His gnarled hand jerks up and clamps my jaw, sharp fingernails digging into the sides of my face as he pulls me toward his mouth with unyielding brute strength.

"Luther!" Daiyna cries.

"I've got him!" Samson bellows, firing three rounds into the daemon's legs.

The grip on my face tightens. The gurgling grows louder, strained, as if he's trying to speak. The fangs reek of carrion.

"Shoot him again!" Plato yells.

"No," I manage. "He's—saying—"

"He's trying to eat your face!"

Samson may be right. But if this creature is attempting to communicate, we might not be afforded another opportunity to learn about their kind. We have to know our enemy so we'll know better how to fight them. What are their strengths? Their weaknesses? Motivation?

The daemon's teeth clamp down on my ear, piercing through the flesh.

Ignoring the cries of alarm around me, the hands that fight to free me, the additional rounds Samson fires into the creature's legs, I flex my talons and plunge them into the daemon's chest, tearing into his ribs. A guttural scream erupts from the deformed mouth, and the fangs lose their grip on my ear lobe. I fall back, refusing the aid offered to me.

"Satisfied?" Daiyna takes the spear from Shechara and drives it through the daemon into the ground. The creature exhales a long, wheezing gasp and lies still, bulbous eyes staring vacantly.

"What were you thinking?" Plato frowns at my ear.

I feel for missing flesh and find only a set of fresh piercings that bleed down my neck. "I had to know."

"Know what exactly? That these things want to eat us? I thought that was already well-established." Plato shakes his head. "You need that wound cleaned out. Come with me." He takes me by the shoulder and turns me toward the cave high above us.

I look back at Samson, and he grins, holding up three fingers. "Three rifles, too. And a jeep," he booms. "Not bad for one night, eh Luther?"

"Not bad at all, my friend." I should share his joy at our first victory in battle. We accomplished what we set out to do, and the Creator has blessed us. Not one of ours was lost.

"Shechara." Daiyna turns to her sister. "Go with Luther and Plato. Make sure no other daemons are out tonight. Take this." She hands her the daemon's fallen rifle.

Shechara nods, keeping her gaze downcast as she takes the large weapon and slings it over her shoulder by the strap. Then she moves to my side. She's been blessed with far-sight, and it was due to her gift that we knew this band of daemons was headed our way.

"Thank you for your help tonight, Shechara." I look at her, but she doesn't return my gaze. Her dark eyes remain fixed on the ground before her, waiting for us to begin our climb toward the caves. "You have a great gift. May the Creator bless you for your courage."

She stiffens, drawing back slightly.

She's attractive, as are all the women from Sector 50. Their lack of hair doesn't interfere with their beauty. Shechara tends to be quieter than most, but when I've been graced by her eyes, I've found a world of feeling behind them.

Plato leads the way up the steep grade, and I follow with

Shechara close behind. I glance down at my hand, extended claws wet with the daemon's blood. I avert my gaze.

Three rifles and a solar-powered vehicle will be a great help to us. When day breaks, we'll set out in search of the creatures' place of origin. We must know how many there are, whether they have other machines, tools, or technology we could put to use.

Why do their weapons carry the UW insignia? Did they happen upon a military bunker after they emerged from their own? Or were they supplied with weapons and vehicles from the start? If so, why would the government scientists have equipped these creatures with such things and left us entirely without? We now represent three sectors—43, 50, and 51. Three separate bunkers. Not one of them was supplied with a weapon or vehicle of any sort.

Most of our supplies are nourishment packs—hydro, protein, vitamineral. We should have enough to last a year if we ration them well. In that time, with the Creator's help, we hope to make it to the northern sectors. According to the bunker database, the Preserve is an untouched wilderness sheltered from the ravages of war by some sort of energy field. I have to believe it remains, that it's still there waiting for us. To think otherwise would lead to despair.

Ironic that we have plenty of nourishment, but no weapons or vehicles that would help us in our journey north, while the daemons possess what we lack. Yet they have no food. Why else would they resort to eating the flesh of their own kind?

Perhaps they no longer think of themselves as human, if they are even capable of rational thought.

The changes in their physiology could not have happened since All-Clear. Their deformities would have taken years of exposure to the biotoxins and radioactive waste to develop. The daemons could have been on the surface longer than any of us, perhaps years. Long enough for their skin to change, for their noses, ears, and eyelids to drop off, for mucous membranes to overdevelop and coat their facial orifices against the relentless heat of this dry, barren land. The fangs and fingernails didn't grow that way; they were sharpened intentionally, proving these creatures have embraced their new identity, leaving their humanity behind. They have become something new.

We all have been changed.

"What did you have to know, Luther?" Plato casts over his shoulder as we reach the last portion of our climb. "When you insisted on speaking to that thing."

I pull myself up the rock face behind him, my hands gripping the crevice below his foot. "I had to know...they're not like us. There's no humanity left in them." He waits for me to continue. "It was because of war, brothers and sisters killing one other...that we were sent deep into the earth. Part of me wondered if we're heading down that same path." Shouldn't every life that survived D-Day be given a second chance to live? "But they're not human anymore. And if we don't destroy them, they will keep coming after us...until none of us is left."

"We must kill them all," Shechara says quietly with conviction.

The rifles and jeep are only the beginning. From this night forward, we fight back against the daemons. We will go to war.

Plato pulls himself onto the ledge and reaches down for my arm. Once I'm up beside him, we offer our hands to Shechara. She smiles slightly and swings up beside us on her own. Adjusting the rifle strap on her shoulder, she gazes out into the distance. The ashen, cratered landscape looks much like the moon's under its own light.

"Anything?" Plato turns east.

Shechara shakes her head. "Perhaps they've had enough for one night."

I hope they didn't hear their comrades die and decide to return in stronger numbers. "We should bury them."

"The daemons?" Plato faces me. "They don't deserve that. Let them rot."

"We can't allow the next hunting party to find them. They may retaliate, and we'll have lost what ground we gained tonight."

With a reluctant nod, he turns to our brother who's kept watch from the northernmost cave. "Shechara will relieve you," Plato tells him.

"You put on a good show down there," says the tall, strong man we named Ali. He grins.

Plato points toward Samson, Daiyna, and the others on the east side of the ridge below. "Tell them Luther wants the daemons buried. Go."

Ali's grin fades. Nodding grimly, he takes a running leap from the ledge and glides through the air using the strong fabric of his cloak as makeshift wings. He floats, landing within meters of the group below. Hitting the ground in a forward roll, he springs to his feet, instantly the center of attention.

A smile spreads across Shechara's full lips as she watches. Was Ali's impressive display for her benefit?

"Luther." Plato beckons.

I follow him into the cave and blink my eyes as they adjust to the lack of moonlight. He takes a glowstick from his belt and cracks it. Instantly our path through the earthen passage is splashed in green light.

"Take me to Milton."

"Your ear—"

"Tend to it there. Please."

He nods mutely. I have yet to memorize all the twists and turns of these passages and caverns, but navigating them has come to Plato as second nature. Perhaps it's one of his gifts. He's promised to make a map for me, but he knows we'll eventually leave the caves. There's no reason to think of them as our home. We're here for protection only—from the sun and the daemons.

We turn down to the right, pass through two smaller caverns, then duck our heads through a low opening into a much larger cavern lit with glowsticks around the perimeter. The men and women lie asleep, divided by sex with the main floor between them. Milton's mattress is propped against the far wall. Old Rip watches over him.

"How is he?" I whisper, clasping my brother by his bony shoulder.

"Besides being comatose and possessed, you mean? Healing up, I guess." Rip chuckles quietly. "Hey, what happened to you, Boss?" He taps his own sagging ear lobe.

"Curiosity," Plato mutters.

"It's nothing." I kneel beside Milton's bed. "Get some rest, my friend."

"Don't have to tell me twice." Rip turns away. "How long until daybreak?"

"A few more hours."

"How'd we do out there?"

I nod, meeting his gaze. He nods in return.

"So we're on the warpath, then." He sighs heavily and leaves me with, "You know what you're doing. It has to be done."

I watch him go, hoping he's right.

Milton jerks involuntarily, lying on his back dead to this world, yet very much alive as a battle rages within him. Daiyna tended to his bullet wound, and it's healing well. No infection. But there was nothing she could do about the evil spirit inside him.

She says it's the same sort that entered the leader of her bunker and nearly a hundred of her sisters, driving them to mass suicide. They allowed themselves to be shut inside a cave southeast of our current location, and they died for lack of oxygen. Daiyna tried to save them, but they would have killed her if she hadn't managed to escape with Shechara and the others.

"Hold still, Luther. This'll sting a little." Plato opens a medkit at my side.

I wince as he cleans my wound with the bedside manner of a laborer. "What do you think? Where do the daemons come from?"

"The east." Plato shrugs.

"Yes, but...how did they come to be as they are?" My gaze rests on Milton's face, twisted, scowling as though he's having a nightmare. "Was it the radiation or biotoxins that changed them, or something altogether different?"

"The *spirits of the earth?*" Plato scoffs.

"Is that so difficult to believe? They changed us. Doesn't it seem logical that others could have been changed as well—in detrimental ways?"

"Very few things seem *logical* anymore, Luther."

"Do you deny your own gift?" Granted, it's a strange one, his ability to spit a blinding substance. He's always seemed ashamed of it.

"No." He wipes the blood off my neck with a swab. "What are you getting at?"

"I'm not sure." I blow out a sigh. "But I can't help wondering if other forces at work, malevolent ones, may have turned the survivors from an eastern sector into these...*hostiles* we've encountered."

"An intriguing hypothesis." Plato applies a healing salve to my pierced ear. "But I hope you're wrong." He gestures at Milton and snaps the medkit shut. Without another word, he heads over to his mattress for a few hours' sleep.

For Milton's sake—and ours—I do hope I'm wrong. But if the evil spirit intends to change him into a hideous daemon, then there is nothing we can do about it.

I envy Daiyna's ability to communicate with the spirits, to *see* them. Yet even she's been at a loss with regard to Milton. She can see the spirit fighting against his mind, striving to overcome him, but she can do nothing about it. Once it's entered a host, she says, only the host can rid himself of it. This she was told by the spirits who've helped us to survive this strange new world by giving us our gifts.

I place my hands on Milton's forearm and pray to the Creator of the universe for his healing. I see no spirits. I hear no voices. But I pray, knowing that my voice is heard. I pray it is enough.

It has to be.

The men around me are fast asleep, oblivious to the battle

we've won tonight. Plato lies among them now, his eyes closed, his breath even and unlabored. I gaze across the cavern to where the women lie. We won't always be separated like this, divided down the middle. There will be coupling, and there will be children, firstborns on a new earth. Perhaps Ali and Shechara will be the first of us joined in marriage.

But not yet. We must strike back at an enemy that has terrorized us for far too long. Now is not the time for human mating rituals. For now, we must do our best to survive each day. The time will come for sexual relations, and I long for it as much as anyone else. One or two of the women have already caught my eye—

We must wait a while longer.

I pull the bundle of maps from my belt and quietly unfold them beside Milton's mattress. My thoughts have turned to the future as they so often do, to a time beyond our present hardships. My finger traces a nameless mountain range, a series of jagged lines crossing the paper from north to south. On the west side is a large circle and SECTOR 43—LABOR FORCE in bold print. The scale, mm to km, has them approximately one thousand kilometers west of these mountains. Milton came a long way indeed if these maps are still accurate.

But we have our doubts. The scientists who downloaded them to our bunker database lived in a different world, after all.

My eyes drift to the SECTOR 50 circle—FEMALE PROGENITORS. Daiyna said their bunker was located in the foothills on the east side of the mountains. I slide my finger east slowly, tracking the distance, 70km, to the circle marked SECTOR 51—MALE PROGENITORS. Years ago, people would have spent their entire lives in search of their purpose, their reason for being. And here we have ours, spelled out clearly in black and white.

If only it were that simple. If only everything had gone according to plan.

The scientists could never have predicted the shifting sands or the spirits of the earth or the daemons. What sector do they hail from, these mutant men from the east? I slide my finger in search of a Sector 52 or 53, but the map ends fifty kilometers east of our bunker. I was able to print out the sectors north of ours before the database went offline, and I arrange them now, lining them up. Like a child with a favorite puzzle, I've done this many times before. The mountain range extends to the north another two hundred kilometers. On the west side, northwest of our current location, nothing is labeled. But one hundred fifty kilometers due north of the Sector 51 bunker is SECTOR 31—TRADE WORKERS. Fifty kilometers beyond that is SECTOR 30—ENGINEERS. These two bunkers would have held all the supplies and skilled tradesmen necessary to start rebuilding. Undoubtedly, the engineers would have chuckled at the sight of those shelters my brothers and I constructed. I'm certain we would have done far better with the proper tools and materials.

Why were we divided this way? Did the United World government actually believe the world of the future would function in the same way as their own? The North American Sectors had been governed by the nations of the UW for decades, ever since the collapse of the United States of America following the second cold war. Each of our sectors had its own specialization, whether that be the arts, sciences, labor, engineering, trade, human reproduction, peace-keeping, or anything else the UW deemed important. We supplied them with everything they needed. In turn, they kept us divided, yet thoroughly efficient. They didn't want to see us unite as a nation again, but they wanted us to continue contributing to the world as our ancestors had for centuries. Most citizens were content with the arrangement. But there were, of course, dissenters who called themselves *Patriots*. No one took these rebels seriously.

Until they released their toxic bioweapons, and the UW governments unleashed hell on earth, retaliating with nuclear strikes intended to annihilate every trace of the toxins as well as those who were infected, both human and animal. The scientists, sociologists, and psychologists in charge of the North American

Sectors Survival Program rounded us up and sent us below to the bunkers they'd prepared for us. Everything was carefully planned and executed. No glitches.

For twenty years underground, I looked forward to the new life we'd build together upon leaving the bunker. I never questioned our purpose. But now? All I have are questions. Perhaps I'm no longer the man I was.

I tap Sector 31 with my index finger. How many of the trade workers have survived? Are their supplies and materials still intact? How far north do the daemon raids extend?

Plato, Daiyna, and I have discussed various options for the next few months, and we've agreed on few. But one thing we know: we're stronger now together than we ever were apart. When we eventually decide it's the right time to make our journey northward, we'll go together, all of us. Or we won't go at all.

I line up the remaining two portions of the map and smooth out the wrinkles of the uppermost page: SECTOR 1—PRESERVE. A lush, heavily forested wilderness interrupted by flower-speckled meadows, gurgling streams, and windswept lakes of fresh water. On D-Day, no bombs were dropped in the Preserve—off-limits in times of war. The rebels' bioweapons decimated all animal life, but everything else would have remained.

So we were told by the bunker database.

Plato has his doubts. Even if world leaders had managed to protect the Preserve, the nuclear winters that ravaged the earth after D-Day would not have halted at the threshold of Sector 1 and proceeded no farther, regardless of any energy field in place. The atmosphere would have carried fallout for years as ash and poison drifted down into the soil and groundwater below.

I have to believe the Preserve still exists, in one form or another. How else would we be able to breathe? Nothing grows in these southwest sectors. The oxygen must come from somewhere.

Once we're able to subdue the daemons, we'll leave the caves en masse in the solar-powered vehicles we obtain, invite the engineers and trade workers from Sectors 30 and 31 to join our ranks, and then make the trek northward to begin living off the land as did the pioneers of old: building homes, planting and harvesting crops of real food, raising families. A good life, one unlike anything we've ever known. There in the Preserve, we won't be divided; our sectors will no longer have any meaning.

My eyelids sag, and I catch myself before I nod off. As soon as day breaks, we'll send a group east in our newly acquired vehicle to scout out the daemons' nest. Dawn will arrive before I know it. I should try to get some sleep.

I gather the maps and fold them back into my belt. My gaze falls on Milton before I turn away and head to my mattress. He's sleeping easier now, no longer tossing restlessly. Perhaps my prayers were heard.

Or perhaps the evil spirit has won the battle inside him.

I shake my head. Of course the Creator heard my prayers. He hears and sees all, as He has for all time. I can't allow myself to doubt. To do so only leads to despair.

A shadowy form moves toward me from beneath the low cavern arch. I can tell by her gait and slim, muscular figure that it's Daiyna.

"No change?" Her voice is quiet as she gathers her flowing cloak to keep from brushing the bare feet of our sleeping brothers.

"He's at peace." I watch her as she looks at Milton. "What do you see?"

In the faint green light, her dark eyes focus on Milton's sleeping form and remain there for a few moments before turning back to me. "The battle is over for now."

She has my full attention. I envy her gift, and she knows I believe her, unlike some of the others in our midst. "Is the spirit gone from him?"

"No." She shakes her head and bites her lip. "But it's not fighting against his will. It's like they've agreed on a ceasefire."

"He's been fighting all day. Yet it hasn't overcome him."

"I don't know what's really happening, Luther. Only what I see. And I don't know why I can see and hear these things." She wipes her brow and sighs, exhausted. "The daemons are buried, as you asked. We could've torched them just as easily."

"Others would have been drawn to the smoke."

"Let them come. We'll kill them too. How's the ear?" She looks at it with more interest than concern.

I touch it gingerly. The healing salve is still wet. "Fine."

"You're not going to turn into one of those things, are you?" The makings of a smile curve the corners of her lips. Before I can fully appreciate the sight, the curves vanish. "Seriously".

I restrain a chuckle. "I certainly hope not. But if I do, you have my permission to put me down."

"I wouldn't need your permission." The glint in her eye softens her words. "Ali is armed and watching over the vehicle until daybreak. We didn't know how to start the engine, so it's right where the daemons left it, fifty meters out. Shechara has night watch on the ledge until dawn. Everyone else will be coming in for a few hours of sleep. We all need to rest."

The meaning in the look she gives me is clear, and I nod. I plan to get an hour or two of sleep if I can. "Ali and Shechara left alone? Do you think that's wise?"

The curve returns to her lips. "You've noticed it too?"

"I don't know what you're referring to." I fail to maintain a straight face.

She almost laughs. "I think you do!" she whispers, glancing around at our sleeping brothers and sisters to be certain they haven't been woken. "What do you think?" She steps closer to me. "Should we discourage it?"

"Did you leave them together on purpose?"

"What are you suggesting?"

"It's a simple question." I feign an impassive shrug.

She shakes her head, eyeing me as she backs away. "Go to bed." With a hint of the smile left intact, she moves across the cavern to her mattress in the midst of our sleeping sisters. Her feet barely seem to make contact as they glide across the cold rock.

I catch myself watching her go and dip my chin, turning my attention to the waiting mattress closest to the arched cavern entrance. Exhaustion weighs my steps until I sink heavily onto the firm cushion and roll onto my back. My senses swim dizzily and I close my eyes, more than willing to surrender completely and be carried away by the darkness.

"Luther!" Samson's whisper, much like the rest of him, is bigger than most. He grips my shoulder as he collapses onto the vacant mattress beside mine. "You awake?"

"No, of course not, my friend." I rub my eyes and face him. "Don't tell me you're going to sleep with that."

Beside him on the mattress where a lover might be, cradled under his brawny arm, is the rifle he confiscated tonight. He strokes it tenderly and grins.

"This is but the start of a beautiful relationship, Luther. I'm not letting her out of my sight. We've got plenty more daemons to dispatch."

He needs his wives. And soon.

"Just be careful not to shoot your head off in your sleep. Or mine, either."

He chuckles quietly, but not quietly enough. Bodies stir around us. He notices and cringes, still grinning. His eyes wander to the other side of the cavern, enshrouded in shadows, where Daiyna has undoubtedly already fallen asleep.

"I might have a chance with her, you know. Daiyna. She's warming up to me, I'm sure of it." He sighs a long gust of air. "We'll have strong children. Ten boys and girls. Ten of each. We'll have to talk about that." He closes his eyes, still stroking the rifle, his loud whisper becoming a low murmur. "I will bed her soon...Luther..."

As he drifts off to sleep, I have to wonder if Daiyna is aware of his intentions. If not, I'm certain she soon will be.

She made it perfectly clear from the start, when the men and women from our bunkers merged to share sleeping quarters, that there would be no recreational sexual activities among us. She's been responsible for keeping her side of the cavern on the straight and narrow path to celibacy, and I've done the same with my brothers. The stipulation has been that if any coupling takes place, we men would no longer be welcome here. We would have to find our own shelter elsewhere. With the daemons outside, that's been a strong enough motivator.

No contraceptives were included in any of the medkits. Obviously, the scientists expected us to be fruitful and multiply. But with the constant threat of the daemons and the spirits who may wish us harm, we've agreed it would be wise to postpone our government-mandated purpose for the time being. There will be plenty of time later for procreation.

So far to my knowledge, none of us has yet attempted to alter our arrangement, but it's only a matter of time before someone's sex drive overpowers his or her willpower. Then nature will take its course.

Samson is my brother, my dear friend. He's a mighty warrior, and I trust him more than any other to lead us into battle against the daemons. But he's always had only one thing on his mind at all times, and I hope he can keep it in his pants long enough not to jeopardize our current situation. Our strength is in our unity, and we can't allow anything to divide us.

Daiyna's smile passes through my mind as I close my eyes. She didn't seem irritated by the obvious attraction between Ali and Shechara. On the contrary, she seemed amused by it, perhaps intrigued. Strangely enough, I reacted in the same way. I should have expressed fear at the danger their pairing could bring. Instead I beheld her smile as a starving man would gaze upon a feast set for him alone. I couldn't bear to see it fade.

During the rare moments I've caught her smiling, she's always been with her sisters. Never with me or our brothers. Our discussions have been more serious, more strategic and matter-of-fact. Tonight was the first time she—

An explosive snort erupts from Samson as he begins his nightly sonata.

"Roll over, my friend," I urge him quietly, as is our ritual.

Mumbling, he turns onto his side, cuddling the high-powered rifle as a child would a teddy bear. His massive back expands and settles with each gust of breath.

I close my eyes and feel myself instantly drift away again...finally, to sleep.

Daiyna smiles at me again, but now she stands on a grassy meadow in the Preserve, her sheer white garments billowing in the breeze that catches her glossy raven-black hair and plays with it, casting it side to side. She looks directly at me, her eyes inviting me closer. Her radiance consumes my vision. All I can see are her eyes, her smile, her gently waving locks. Her lips move, and she whispers to me, but I can't hear her words. I move closer, and as I do...

A single thought enters my mind: I don't want Samson to bed her.

6. DAIYNA
TEN MONTHS AFTER ALL-CLEAR

They merge as one, like many waters coming together as a rushing river, like the murmur of an enormous crowd, yet every word spoken is clear and distinct. The emotions conveyed range from playful and mischievous to anxious, sometimes angry, combining to form a multi-faceted voice that's rich and powerful yet quiet, unlike anything I've ever heard in my life.

It startles me every time they speak.

I don't know if anyone could truly understand what it's like. Luther seems open to the unseen world with his continual talk of the Creator, but that always sets me on edge. Mother Lairen believed in the *Creator* as well, and she ended up suffocating with most of my sisters. *Cows*, Rehana called them. But Mother Lairen and the others were possessed by evil spirits, like Milton is. This truth was revealed to me by the spirits who've changed us, gifting us with these incredible abilities.

Possessed. According to Plato, a suicidal urge came over Milton weeks ago. Entirely at peace with the idea, he'd been ready to throw himself off a cliff before he was shot by the daemons—which, ironically, ended up saving his life. He collapsed onto the ledge, and Samson hauled him back into the caves.

This morning, he lies comatose in our central cavern as we ride east at full-speed in the solar-powered jeep we took from the daemons. Our shoulders knock into each other, jostling over every bump along the rocky terrain. Samson drives, hunched low over the steering wheel to see through a clear patch in the dust-caked windshield. Apparently, when he wasn't building his muscles and practicing his award-winning charm down in the bunker, he studied weapons, warfare, and war machines. After a few false starts, he figured out how to get this vehicle running. Beside him sits Luther, holding Samson's rifle with one hand and gripping onto the dashboard for dear life with the other.

They're both dressed as we all are now in the loose, sand-colored garments the women in our bunker wove while we were below. Our heads are wrapped in the same material while black goggles shield our eyes, and standard-issue gloves and boots protect our hands and feet. It didn't take long to convert the men to our style of dress. We made it clear they wouldn't be allowed within a kilometer of us smelling like urine. They received their new attire when they moved into the caves with us, and the jumpsuits were placed in storage. We may need them again someday, but I hope that day never arrives.

In the back of the jeep stands Shechara, hanging onto the roll bar as she gazes ahead of us for any sight of the enemy. Gifted with the same far-sight as Sheylia, she's been a great help to us. I sit beside her and hold the other rifle ready, gripping the rail. Samson is a wild driver, and the way he chuckles every time we hit a bump makes me think he enjoys giving us a scare. I'm not afraid of being thrown from the jeep. I'm only concerned that if he damages this vehicle, we'll be stranded out here at the mercy of the daemons.

And there will be no mercy.

"Anything?" My muffled voice is loud enough for Shechara to hear.

Her goggles turn to me briefly, then return to the east. She shakes her head. No sign of any hostiles yet, despite all the dust we're churning up.

It's really insane, when I think about it: the four of us driving full-speed toward wherever the daemons come from, our only defense being two rifles, a knife, and the superhuman gifts we possess. We have no idea how many of them there are or what other weapons they might possess. Odds are we'll be killed and eaten—hopefully in that order.

But we're not alone.

"You don't know what we're up against, Luther. It's too soon to take our only vehicle and weapons to face these creatures. If they overtake you, we'll be right back where we started." Plato shook his head, seated cross-legged beside me. *"It's rash."*

Luther regarded him with a steady gaze across the circle. He'd called this meeting early in the morning after I'd woken him.

"I understand your concern, my friend. We'll be careful, believe me. But we won't be alone." He looked at me, his eyes bright with hope. *"Daiyna has heard from the spirits."*

Plato dropped his gaze. I knew he wouldn't like what I had to say. Of them all, he was the least supportive of the belief that spirits of the earth existed. He had even more difficulty believing that they could communicate, and that they chose to do so with me alone.

I cleared my throat, glancing at Shechara beside me. She nodded, encouraging me to speak. *"They'll go with us. We have nothing to fear."* I faltered. *"That's what they told me, anyway."*

"Nothing to fear?" Plato pointed across the cavern toward where Milton lay. *"Didn't one of your spirits do that to him? How can we trust anything they say?"*

I looked him in the eye. *"I don't know if we can."*

"We can." Luther sounded confident. *"Daiyna is their vessel, and they've chosen to join us in our journey east. I say that bodes well."*

Plato cursed under his breath. *"Where's the logic in that, Luther? Are you listening to yourself? None of this makes any sense, yet you're so willing to believe it!"* He faced me. *"They told you to rescue Milton, right? When that sandstorm was attacking him? Why would they do that, then make him try to kill himself later?"*

I had no answer. I could have argued semantics, that it might have been the good spirits who told me to rescue Milton and it was now an evil one *inside him. But I wondered if there was really any distinction between the voice that spoke to me and the force that attacked Rehana, or the entity that chased Milton when I first came upon him. None of it made any sense.*

"You must believe, my friend." Luther's voice was calm and quiet, in contrast to Plato's angst. "We're living in a different world now, and there's much about it we don't fully understand. We must have faith—"

"In what exactly, Luther? These spirits? This Creator you're always talking about? Where would you have us direct our faith?" Plato rose, leaving us without another word.

There's no sign that the spirits are with us now. Tens of kilometers away from the safety of our caves, this sun-scorched earth reminds us how alone we are.

Maybe we should have waited. We could have ambushed a few more of the daemons' hunting parties, taken more vehicles and weapons. Hunted the hunters in stronger numbers. But if we come upon a hundred of the daemons, armed, hungry, and waiting, it won't matter either way. Likewise if spirits of the earth decide to attack us with rocks and sand, it won't matter how prepared we are.

I can only hope there are good spirits with us now, and that they'll protect us on this journey as they said they would.

Maybe I shouldn't have woken Luther and told him. But he's made it clear he wants to know every time I hear the spirits' voice. He seems obsessed, always asking if I've *heard anything*. Maybe he wishes the spirits would speak to him as well. I'd gladly let him or anyone else take this ability from me. I don't know why I was chosen. Of us all, Luther is the most spiritual. He should be the spirits' *vessel*. I've never been one to care about the supernatural, and since D-Day, the idea of anything remotely spiritual has been the furthest thing from my mind.

Samson takes us over the lip of a large crater, and we plunge headlong toward its bottom. He laughs out loud while the rest of us hold on with all our strength. I grit my teeth to keep from biting off my tongue. We're thrown back against our seats as he accelerates up the opposite side of the crater, and we sail through the air for a moment, clearing the rim and landing hard, skidding sideways on the chunky tires. Samson pounds the dashboard with his fist, obviously delighted with himself.

Luther needs to reel him in. He's going to get us killed.

"Let's avoid the craters as much as possible, shall we?" Luther's voice emerges clearly through his head covering. His claws have extended through the holes in his gloves, digging into the dashboard.

"My bad." Samson's chuckle is as deep as thunder. "Just wanted to see how much power this thing's got!"

"I believe we've tested its limits sufficiently."

They make an odd pair: the well-built intellectual and the hairy Neanderthal. But they seem as close as blood brothers. Samson, despite being bigger and stronger, always defers to Luther.

"Up there." Luther points ahead to a bluff on the left, his claws retracting. "That should provide a good vantage point."

Samson nods, steering the jeep in that direction. He guns the engine as we top the rise, then slams on the brake once we reach the plateau, jerking us forward. We collect ourselves as the dust clears.

"First stop, folks." Samson hauls himself out of the driver's seat as we exit the vehicle. "A whole lot of nothing!"

Always in high spirits. So obnoxious.

But he's right. There's nothing ahead of us that we haven't already left behind: more ashen sand, gravel and craters in the desolate earth. The same moonscape under the same unforgiving sun we've seen for kilometers, and no sign of our quarry.

"You think they know we're coming?" I ask Luther.

His goggles stare straight ahead as we move to the edge of the plateau, our boots shifting through dust on the cracked hardpan. "They would have no reason to make themselves scarce."

"Unless word's spreading around mutant-ville that we're not your average variety of human. If so, we could finally be off the menu." Samson stands with arms folded across his broad chest, feet spread. "Or they could be planning an ambush. And that wouldn't be pretty."

I shake my head. "It's open space out there. I don't think we need to be afraid of—"

"Who said I was *afraid*?" Samson looms over me. His tone is as confident as ever, and I'm sure he's cocking an eyebrow under his head covering.

"Do you see anything, Shechara?" Luther places his hand on her shoulder briefly, but she backs away from his touch.

She scans the distance for a few moments, south to north. Then she shakes her head. "I don't see them."

"Well, maybe these spirits of yours are helping us out, after all." Samson pats the middle of my back with his paw. "Scaring off the hunting parties so we can find Camp Daemon!"

I turn away from him, doing my best to ignore his touch. If he tries it again, I'll have to hurt him. I'm not one of his brothers. He shouldn't be so comfortable with me.

"Do we go on, then?" I ask Luther.

"We have more than enough daylight." He catches himself. "For Samson and me."

Shechara and I can see as well in complete darkness as we can in the light.

"I don't want him driving in the dark. The ride is wild enough as it is."

"Hey, I don't see anybody else volunteering," Samson rumbles. "But be my guest." He holds his hand out toward the driver's seat as we climb back into the vehicle. "No takers?"

He chuckles and squeezes himself behind the wheel, starting up the engine. We veer backward, then jolt forward, down the same way we came up. I half-thought he would take us sailing off the plateau's edge.

Shechara leans toward me as we resume our eastbound journey, the dust and gravel flying upward in our wake. "Where are they, Daiyna? Why can't I see them?"

I slide my arm around her shoulders and pull her close. "You will. When they show themselves, you'll be the first to spot them."

It's her gift. And her curse.

She rises to her feet and grips the roll bar, her goggles fixed forward. When the spirits gave her the gifts of far-sight and night-vision, they gave her something else she never had before: self-confidence. She's so different from the quiet, invisible girl I knew in the bunker.

You must save them.

The spirits' voice surges within me, and I catch my breath.

She will not see it coming.

My head whips side to side. What's coming?

"Stop the jeep!" I hit Samson's shoulder with my fist.

"What?" He doesn't slow down.

"What is it, Daiyna?" Shechara faces me.

"Keep looking!" I point her forward. I punch Samson's shoulder again, the muscle rock-hard. "Stop the jeep!"

"All right, all right," he grumbles, braking abruptly and throwing us forward in our seats. Shechara clings to the roll bar as the vehicle skids to a stop.

"Daiyna..." Luther faces me. The dust we've stirred passes over us in a thick cloud, obscuring our view of anything else.

An explosive concussion slams into the ground in front of the jeep, sending it upward and us right along with it. Deafened by the blast, I fall sprawling to the sand and cower in the rain of gravel and clumps of ash.

Then the world is silent, save for an incessant ringing in my ears. Dust and smoke billow around me, and I taste them both through my head covering.

A large hand grips my arm and pulls me to my feet, jerking me away from the jeep as another blast rocks the earth. The vehicle erupts in a fiery mass of twisted metal, jagged pieces flying in all directions. The hand on my arm throws me to the ground, and a massive body falls on top of me, crushing me into the sand. I scream, but I can't hear myself. The earth beneath me trembles as pieces of the jeep rain down like plummeting birds of prey.

The body climbs off and pulls me into a run. I gasp for breath, recognizing Samson. He has my rifle in one hand and my arm in the other. Shards of metal from the jeep pierce his back and shoulders with blood spreading from each wound. He runs straight for a boulder ten meters away, one large enough to shield us both. I struggle to keep up. He drags me every time I falter, his grip forcing me to stay on my feet.

Another explosion hits the ground behind us, and Samson pulls me close, taking us into a dive behind the boulder. I land hard, my arm nearly wrenched from its socket. No one hears my silent scream as dust from the blast passes over us. Samson aims the rifle toward the remains of the jeep, waiting for the dust to clear.

Shechara? Luther? Where are they?

You must save them.

The dust isn't clearing. How would I find them? Are they even alive?

We will shield you from their sight.

Whose sight? Who attacked us? Daemons?

They will not see you. But you must hurry. They are coming.

If they reach Shechara and Luther before I do—

I shout something to Samson, but I can't hear it, and neither can he. I move to rise, but his arm shoots out and knocks me back to the ground without interfering with his aim. I land on my backside, seething with fury. There's no time for this.

I roll away from him and lunge upward, clearing the boulder with a single leap and touching down in a full sprint toward the jeep. The dust swirls past me, obscuring my vision. Apparently, my gifted eyes can't see through particulate matter.

Ahead, the dust darkens to black, the smoking rubble of our vehicle. A body lies face down, covered in soot.

Shechara! I fall to my knees beside her and roll her over. There's no blood. Her neck—her jugular—there's a pulse. She must have been thrown clear of the jeep, the blast knocking her out. Or the fall knocked the wind out of her.

I jostle her with both hands. She has to wake up. They're coming, and the dust is beginning to dissipate.

You must save her.

What about Luther? Where is he?

Shechara stirs, coughing. The head covering around her mouth pulses outward. I help her up, and she touches her ears instinctively, dismayed by the deafness and ringing. I pull her to her feet, draping her arm over my shoulder.

Straight ahead is the boulder and Samson. But what about Luther? Will I have time to come back?

Run.

Shots ring out behind me, sharp popping sounds. They send a jolt of adrenaline through my system, and I take off as fast as I can, half-carrying, half-dragging Shechara as she stumbles along. I risk a glance back in time to see Luther emerge through the clearing dust, staggering backward with a rifle held low, firing blindly across the jeep's remains. He sees me, slings the rifle over his shoulder and breaks into a run. Catching up with us, he takes Shechara's other arm, and we carry her ten paces, then ten more.

We should be at the boulder by now. Only there is no boulder. No Samson. In the dust cloud, I've lost my way.

"Keep moving!" Luther's voice sounds garbled, like he's under water.

Where are we? Where's Samson?

"Daiyna—they're *coming*!" Luther pulls Shechara forward and me along with her.

More shots punctuate the distance, but this time they come from the opposite direction. The daemons have us surrounded. Luther pulls us to the ground and holds his rifle ready on one knee, swinging side to side, aiming for the first daemon to show itself.

The spirits said they would go with us, that we would have nothing to fear. Where are they now?

Get down.

"Luther—get down!" I grab hold of his arm and tug him to the ground just as a massive figure charges out of the dust with a rifle in each hand.

Samson.

Three hideous shapes emerge behind us. Grunting, the daemons rub at their bulbous eyes, irritated by the dust.

"Stay down!" Samson roars at us, leveling his weapons over our heads and squeezing the triggers, holding them tight. A twin burst of automatic fire explodes from the muzzles, and the three daemons convulse as the rounds hit their marks. The mutants flail their arms and scream, weapons hitting the ground moments before they do as well, torn and bloody and lying still.

Then everything is quiet. Samson discards empty magazines as he steps over us and scavenges what he needs from the fallen weapons. He looks at me.

"That was suicide. You going back." He glances at Shechara and Luther. "But good work, Daiyna."

I don't need his praise. I get to my feet and take up two of the daemons' rifles—one for me, one for Shechara.

"You're hurt." I gesture at Samson's back.

"Flesh wounds." He shrugs.

"The dust... It's providing cover." Luther gazes around us.

"They're doing it." I offer Shechara the butt of her rifle, and she pulls herself to her feet. "But it won't last."

"The spirits." He nods. "They fight with us."

"How many, do you think?" I give one of the daemons a kick to make sure it's dead.

"Three fewer now." Samson clears his throat. "They hit us with some kind of grenade launcher. A Stinger, I think."

"I didn't see it," Shechara says quietly. "I'm so sorry, Daiyna."

"No way you could have." Samson faces her. "They took us by surprise."

Shots pop in the distance, farther away than before. They'll leave us stranded out here, then come back and take us out one at a time. What were we thinking? Why'd we travel so far from the caves? We should have waited for Milton, for his speed. He could have run them down, disarmed them, and shot them before they even had a chance to see him.

But that doesn't matter now.

"We need another jeep," Samson states the obvious. He stands rooted, looking toward where the shots originated.

Luther nods. "What do you have in mind, my friend?"

"We take one."

Luther turns to me. "Would the spirits be willing to help us?"

I don't know. "How?"

"A full-on sandstorm would be nice—one that targets only the daemons. Think they could swing that?" Samson shifts his weight. He looks like he's ready to take off running. "I mean, from what you said, they did a good job attacking Milton."

"Those were evil spirits," I mutter.

How do I explain something I don't understand? Are the same spirits who speak to me the ones that stirred up the sand and attacked us in the past? Is the voice I hear from the same entity that ravaged Rehana's skin? What voice did Mother Lairen hear? What did Milton hear before he tried to kill himself?

"Can the spirits go on the offensive, or do they only defend us?" Luther asks. He seems to believe without questioning. What kind of faith is that?

"I don't know, I really don't." I shake my head. "They haven't told me."

Samson shrugs again. "How about you ask them?"

I wish I could. "It doesn't work that way. They speak to me only when they want to."

"Convenient," Samson mutters.

"It's almost gone," Shechara says.

She's right. It's happening quickly now, like a vacuum is sucking away all the dust. In moments, we'll be completely exposed.

"Can you see any daemons?" I ask her.

Her goggles face north, beyond the charred ruin of our vehicle.

"They're moving off." She stands tall now. "Four of them. One carries a long pipe on his shoulder."

"That'd be the Stinger," Samson says.

"You don't see a vehicle?" Luther steps beside her.

She shakes her head. The last of the dust cloud has settled, and the dark figures moving in the distance are too small for my eyes to distinguish any details.

"We must be close to their camp, if they attacked us on foot." He sounds eager to pursue them.

"We've just managed to escape with our lives," I caution him.

He points after the retreating shapes. "This is why we've come, Daiyna. Now we'll know what we're up against, what other weapons or technology they possess. There may be communication devices, ways to contact other survivors—"

"Condoms?" Samson chuckles. No one joins him. "What? Don't tell me it didn't cross your mind."

"Honestly? No." I face Luther. "We're stranded out here. We need to find a way back to the caves."

"Agreed. We'll take one of their vehicles after we've surveyed their camp. We have to know how many there are before we can mount a full assault."

We can't journey north to the Preserve until the daemon threat is neutralized. And we can't risk a full-scale attack on them without knowing their numbers. We need to find their base camp or whatever hell-hole they live in before we do anything else. But the thought of being on foot, unable to flee from potentially dozens of these creatures when they come back for us...

It's enough to turn my legs to ash.

"I sure hope you can still see 'em, Small Fry, because they're just about off my radar." Samson shields his goggles against the sun's glare with one hand.

"I can see them," she replies evenly.

Luther steps forward and turns, walking backward. "Shall we, my friends?"

"Count me in." Samson follows.

Shechara turns to me. "Daiyna?"

I sigh, watching Luther with his hands out to the sides, seeming to invite an embrace as he backs away.

"I think they need us, Daiyna." Shechara pats my arm. "We should go with them."

Maybe she's right. It's what we came out here for, anyway. We've lost our means of transportation and escape, but we've gained two more rifles, so now each of us is armed. That's something. And so far, the spirits have helped us. I can't deny that.

I have to hope they'll continue to do so. If they do...then we'll have nothing to fear, just like they said in my dream.

But in my dream, we still had the jeep at this point.

"All right, if you say so." I shoulder the rifle by its strap. The UW insignia on the stock catches the sunlight. I hope we find an explanation for that among everything else that lies ahead of us. "We're in," I call to Luther as Shechara and I catch up. "On one condition."

He turns mid-stride as I come alongside him. "And that would be?"

"We make finding a vehicle our top priority. Before we do anything else."

"Always have an exit strategy. One of the primary rules of engagement." Samson chuckles. "Just what I was thinking. Great minds think alike, eh Daiyna?"

If I didn't know he was from Sector 51, I'd seriously doubt he has a mind at all in that huge head. Maybe that's unfair. He does know how to drive, after all.

"Reasonable enough." Luther nods.

"They're dropping into a crater, out of sight now." Shechara picks up her pace. "We should hurry."

We break into an easy jog, passing what's left of the jeep as we continue northward. Hills and craters lie ahead, lifeless, crumbling into ash. Do the daemons know we're following them? What if only a few of them broke away from the pack, and the rest lie in wait to ambush us again?

"Keep your eyes open, folks," Samson says, seeming to hear my thoughts. He holds his rifle low, at the ready. "We don't want them doubling back to surprise us."

Eyes darting, I wipe at the dust caked on my goggle lenses. Now they're smeared, but I can't waste a hydropack to clean them. The sun beats relentlessly against my head, my shoulders, my back. Sweat trickles across my skin, beneath my garments. I wish I could take them off. I wish the sun wouldn't scorch me if I did.

"They climbed out of the crater, but they dropped down an embankment on the other side." Shechara points. "I can't see them anymore."

"Think they caught sight of us?" Samson scratches his chin through his head covering.

"They haven't looked back." Shechara breaks into a run, beckoning. "Let's go!"

We follow close behind. It seems too easy—tracking these creatures straight to their home. They must know we survived their attack and killed three of their own in the process. Could it be they simply don't care?

I can't shake the feeling we're not alone. Maybe because we're not. The Presence I feel could be the spirits, moving with us, keeping the evil ones at bay who would rise against us in the rocks and sand. They told me we had nothing to fear. Do I doubt them?

I hope they'll warn me again if trouble heads our way.

"Great spot for an ambush," Samson remarks, clearing his throat. He surveys the low hill formation up ahead and an outcropping of rock across from it. We'll have to pass in between to remain on course. "If they've got any brains left in those mutant skulls, they would've thought to leave a couple sharpshooters there and there. Pick us off as we pass by."

I drop the rifle from my shoulder and hold it ready as our pace slows.

"Anything, Daiyna?" Luther asks.

I shake my head.

"Then we must assume it's safe. If they haven't warned you..." He looks at me for a moment. Then he runs ahead, beckoning us to follow.

Samson charges after him, then Shechara. As they pass by the rocks, my abdomen tightens. I half-expect to see a well-armed band of daemons rise up for the slaughter.

But Luther and the others make it through without incident, and I quickly join them.

"Didn't think we'd make it, huh?" Samson mutters to me.

Of course he noticed my hesitation. "I was covering you." I raise my rifle.

"Sure you were." He chuckles.

Shechara points out a massive crater in the earth ahead of us, one that would take just as long to circumvent as it would to cross. "That's where they dropped out of sight before."

Samson curses. "They sure did bomb the hell out of this place."

"Indeed they did," Luther muses. Not referring to the daemons but rather the United World government that unleashed nuclear hellfire on D-Day.

"All because of those stupid rebels."

"Misguided, perhaps," Luther corrects him. "But far from stupid. They thought they were patriots, but their homeland was a figment of their collective imagination."

"Exactly. Stupid idiots. What were they thinking?" Samson curses again and moves ahead.

"I heard they wanted to drive out the UW and unite the sectors." I frown, trying to remember history that wasn't included in the bunker database. "The *United Sectors of America*, they wanted to call it. Their posters and graffiti were all over the place when I was a kid."

Luther nods. "No one took them seriously. Until the end."

"How many sectors did they infect?"

"At first? Merely a handful. There were no symptoms for weeks. They targeted sectors with a large UW presence. Then they started shifting to global targets, and they made their demands known once the symptoms emerged. It didn't take long for the plagues to spread worldwide."

He remembers more details than I do. I guess he would have been a little older at the time.

"That's why the bombs fell."

"A teacher in one of my secondary courses taught us ancient world history." He pauses. "He told us that the original nations of the UW, back in the twenty-first century, held in their possession enough nuclear weapons to destroy the earth a hundred times over. And he found that peculiar, since destroying the planet once would probably be bad enough."

"And here we are." I sum up the devastation of the world in a trite statement.

"Yes. Here we are."

We stop at the rim of the crater, the toes of our dust-covered boots sending small cascades of gravel down the side. The drop is fifty meters down from here, and it's a kilometer or more before another fifty-meter climb up the opposite side. I could make the leap downward with ease, but the climb will take some doing with the shifting sand and ash.

"What do you think?" A hot breeze ripples Samson's garments as he stands with arms crossed and the rifle slung over his shoulder. "Across or around?"

Luther tilts his head to one side. "Which would be faster?"

"The drop's easy enough. We can slide down. But I don't know about the other side." Samson shuffles his large boot and sends another ashen trickle off the rim.

Luther moves toward the left. "Then around it is."

I turn to Shechara. "Where did they drop out of sight?"

She points straight ahead at the opposite rim. We're close. Is she afraid?

"If they're hiding in a depression over the other side, we'll be too exposed if we go around." I point down. "We should go across."

Samson shakes his head. "That will give them the higher ground while we're climbing out."

"Only if they're expecting us."

"You don't think they are?"

"They never looked back," Shechara says.

Luther watches her. "We split up. I'll look out for you as you cross the crater. Shechara can come with me. If you reach the opposite rim before we do, you can let us know how to proceed."

I'd rather go with Shechara, but it makes sense for her to go around with her far-sight unobstructed and for me to go across with my agility at climbing. There's no time to argue, anyway. It won't be long before the daemons meet up with others of their kind and come back for us.

"Let's go." I leap from the rim and fall quickly, the side of the crater rushing behind me as the bottom rises up to meet my boots. I land in a crouched position, then spring to my feet.

Luther pats Samson on the back and jogs around the side with Shechara. The big oaf is left alone, looking like a small child standing at the deep end during his first swimming lesson. Will he decide to follow Luther instead? I can hope.

Before I know it, he's on his backside, sliding feet-first with a plume of dust flying upward in his wake, gravel flinging from his boots as he makes his way down to the bottom of the crater. He holds the rifle out in front like a kayak paddle and shifts his weight awkwardly as he hits larger rocks. I can only imagine what his rear end will feel like once he touches down. Will there be any material left to cover it? A scary thought. An image of a hairy gorilla passes through my mind as he lands on both feet and stumbles toward me, righting himself after almost pitching forward face-first.

"Impressive," I offer, then turn and break into a run.

Surprisingly, he's able to keep up. "Thought you'd like that."

"Sore?"

"Like you wouldn't believe," he mutters.

As we cross the level ground, I glance over my shoulder to check on Shechara and Luther's progress. They're making good time, but we'll reach the opposite side long before they do.

"Can you climb?" I face Samson mid-stride as we pass the center of the crater. "Gravity won't be working in your favor."

His goggles glance my way. "Are you asking if I can get up?" He waits for his lame double entendre to sink in. Then he chuckles. "Not a problem."

If he can't make it, I won't be able to help him. He's too heavy. And I won't wait for him. Get a vehicle and get out—that's our priority. If he ends up stuck in this crater, we'll tow him out later. Might take his arrogance down a few pegs. Not a bad idea at all.

Within minutes, we reach the steep, sloping wall of sand and gravel at the other side, and without a word to him, I take a running leap, launching myself upward and clearing the first ten meters. My boots sink instantly into the shifting, cascading mix. I hurl myself forward and upward, pausing long enough between lunges only to take a breath until I reach the rim and crouch down quickly.

A desolate valley opens below. The descent from here is a short drop, then a gradual slope downward. Four small, distinct shapes move at a leisurely pace across the hardpan in the distance, the ash-colored earth rising up around them at an even grade. Less than five kilometers ahead of them, spread out across the valley floor like a child's sand castle smashed by bullies, lie the broken remains of a large city.

The devastation is incredible. Mangled frames of what were once skyscrapers lean sideways at awkward angles. Rubble in mounds nearly as high cover what would have been urban neighborhoods. Everything lies caked in a thick layer of ashen dust, making it look like it's been forced up out of the earth and rejected.

There you must go.

My nerves stand at attention. "Why? What will we find?" All we need is a vehicle to get out of here. If we come back, we do so in greater numbers—and with Milton, who can outrun anything.

What do you fear?

Honestly? "That place down there." An image passes through my mind of frenzied ants covering a disturbed hill. "It's probably crawling with daemons."

The spirits' voice is silent.

Heavy breathing and grunting breaks the silence behind me. I whirl around, rifle ready.

"Stand down, soldier." Samson hangs a few meters below me, his brawny arms elbow-deep in the side of the crater. Behind him is a track of holes he's punched along the way up. He chuckles, pulling one arm free from the shifting gravel and slamming it in half a meter above his head. Then he heaves himself upward by it. The spirits have indeed gifted him with strength.

"Anything?" he manages.

I nod. I can't find any words to say.

"Keeping low?" He punches in his other arm and hauls himself up to the rim, throwing over his forearm to brace himself. "They haven't spotted you."

"No." I swallow. On one knee, I turn back toward the valley. "Not yet."

He pulls himself forward onto his hands and knees, head down as he catches his breath a moment. Then he looks up.

He curses. "So that's where they live? Nice digs." He takes his rifle from his shoulder and slides forward onto his belly, the scope flat against his goggle lens. "There they are." His finger curls around the trigger.

Is he going to shoot them? "Wait—"

"For them to catch sight of us?" He curses again, taking careful aim. "Not a chance."

"You won't be able to hit all four of them. They'll run ahead and warn the others." What is he thinking? We're all alone out here. We can't afford to take risks like this.

"Have a little faith." He squeezes the trigger.

I jerk my rifle scope up to my goggles in time to see the daemon on the far left crumple to the ground and lie still. The other three stop to look at him. One of them nudges the fallen daemon's back with his rifle. They seem strangely unaffected by the loss of their comrade.

Then they turn and look our way.

My stomach drops. Through the scope, it's like they're looking right at us. The one with the large pipe on his shoulder drops to one knee and fires without a moment's hesitation. Why didn't Samson shoot him first?

"Get down!" Samson roars, clamping onto my arm as he dives headfirst down the side of the crater.

A short cry escapes me, and the sky between my boots is all I see until a blast rocks the earth and a hail of sand and gravel fills my vision, pelting me from head to foot. I raise my free arm to shield my face and cry out again, this time in pain. Samson shouts something, but I can barely hear him. We slide to an abrupt halt, and I swing outward then fall back, my arm still in his grip, nearly wrenched from its socket. I look up. Samson has planted his arm into the side of the crater, and we're anchored by it for the time being. I glance down between my dangling boots and see another thirty meters to the crater's bottom.

The staccato popping of gunfire reaches my ears. Two shadowy figures stand at what remains of the crater's rim above us. The shadows jerk at the sound of each shot.

Samson shouts again. I wish he would let go of me. I don't need his help.

The gunfire subsides, and the shadows move, becoming larger as they approach. The sun glints in their goggles. It's Shechara and Luther, closer to our position than I would have thought. The blast took out a large piece of the crater's rim. They hold out their gloved hands, Luther with the holes torn in the fingertips. Relief swells within me.

Did they take down the remaining three daemons? If so, we're no longer in danger of being discovered. Or have we announced our arrival?

Samson lifts me up over his head, and I clasp Luther's forearm as he pulls me up. Ears still ringing from the blast, I find my footing and turn to Shechara.

"Did you get them?" I shout.

She nods, turning me with a hand on my shoulder as she points. The bodies of the daemons lie where they've fallen, dark forms on the dusty valley floor. I look beyond them, and there's no movement in the dilapidated city sprawl, no indication we've been spotted. Either they didn't hear the rocket blast and rifle fire, or they're waiting patiently for us—wherever they're camped.

Samson heaves himself upward without much help from Luther and bellows, "So what do you think? City of the living dead?"

Luther turns toward the valley and nods. "It would seem to warrant a closer inspection."

"We get a jeep, and we go back." I'm more adamant than ever.

Luther nods slowly. "Of course."

Samson starts down the grade toward the valley. "Let's roll. Looks like we've got some more firepower waiting for us."

The fallen daemons' weapons—the rocket launcher, in particular—lure him onward. As we follow him down, I can't help but notice that we look a little worse for wear. Our garments are dirty, soot-stained, torn and ragged. Bloody in spots, threadbare in others. For the most part, they still shield us from the sun's rays, but we'll need to exchange them for fresh clothing when we return to the caves.

"Milton said he passed through city ruins like this. Wreckage from D-Day. He was able to scavenge supplies and find relief from the sun. But this is the first I've seen for myself." Luther faces me as we walk. "You?"

I shake my head. My ears are starting to work right again. "We went straight to the caves as soon as we were out of the bunker. Sightseeing was never much on our minds."

"For us either. Everything was very clear-cut then: build shelters, find our wives—"

"Wives? Is that what you called them?"

"You." He pauses to clear his throat. "Your sector, that is."

"We had another name for them."

"Oh?"

"Cows."

"Not *mating partners?*" His tone is playful.

"*Reproductive companions,*" I recall from the bunker database.

"That's right," he laughs. "I remember the film."

"They made you watch it, too?" What am I thinking? Or course they would have.

"I'm sure ours was more tailored to the male psyche. Regardless, we thought *wives* was a better term to use, considering the connotations."

"And those would be?" When he says *we*, he usually means himself, with Plato's input. Why would they use such an archaic word as *wife*?

The only sound is that of our boots across the gravel. Samson has pulled ahead, but Shechara remains beside me.

"*Wife* connotes a bond more meaningful than a mere *procreation partner*. Of course, rebuilding our species is the greatest purpose we must shoulder in the years to come, but we're sure to have other challenges along the way. And to meet them effectively, I knew the men would need wives. Companions for life." He holds up his empty hands. "It's how the Creator first intended us to live. He said it wasn't good for us to be alone." He pauses. "A better word than *cows*, at any rate."

My lips curve into a smile beneath my head covering. But it fades as I remember Rehana. "The daemons were the first men we met outside the bunker. The thought of being reproductive companions lost its appeal rather quickly. But one of us was calling our other sisters *cows* long before that. She didn't like the idea that bearing children was our only purpose in life. She rebelled against our leader, and many of us followed her example." My voice falters.

"What became of her?"

My eyes sting, and I swallow. "The *cows* killed her. But they didn't really know what they were doing."

They were possessed. Like Milton.

Ahead of us, Samson stoops to retrieve the rocket launcher from one of the dead daemons. Shechara jogs to join him.

Luther lowers his voice. "Have you heard anything?"

My mind is cluttered with images of Rehana and Mother Lairen, and I feel hollow inside as these memories resurface, thoughts and feelings I've fought so hard to bury. Isn't it obvious to him I'm not thinking about the spirits right now? I thought he was more intuitive.

But what did I expect? When he lowered his voice, did I hope for him to offer me some kind of consolation? Did I want him to touch me? That was my mistake.

"No." My tone is flat. "Nothing."

I move ahead to join Shechara. Deftly, she removes the ammunition from the three daemons' rifles while Samson turns the launcher end to end, acquainting himself with it. Luther's goggles are fixed on the city before us.

"What's this?" Shechara holds a miniature version of one of the rifles—a handgun.

Samson glances up. "Smith and Wesson nine millimeter semi-automatic." He returns his attention to the rocket launcher and chuckles with delight, rising to his feet as he hefts his new war toy to his shoulder. "This'll be a fun one. Can't wait to try it out."

"Let's hope you won't need to." Luther shakes his head. "Strange to see a city like this. An entire sprawl, laid to waste."

"Home to our friendly neighborhood cannibals?" Samson turns to Shechara. "See any more of them, Small Fry?"

Her goggles slowly pan the ruins from left to right. She wants to be absolutely sure before she says anything.

There you must go, the spirits said. Why? What will we find? *You have nothing to fear.* Does that mean we won't come across any daemons in there? Or will the spirits fight for us?

We've had some close calls so far, but we're alive and relatively uninjured. Maybe I was wrong to doubt them. But it frustrates me when they're silent like this, when I want them to speak to me, offer assurances, and they don't. I want them to lead us, but at the same time, I want them to leave me the hell alone.

Part of me is glad when their voice isn't surging through me. I can feel like myself again. Yet I also feel utterly alone.

"There's no movement, none that I can see." Shechara gives Samson the handgun. "You can have this one. It's too small for me." She steps past him, the rifle slung over her shoulder.

Samson takes the gun but hesitates before jamming it into his belt. He doesn't seem to know how to take her remark. "Okay?"

Leaving the corpses behind, we follow Shechara across the valley floor. Somewhere beneath all the sand and ash under our feet there must be concrete and asphalt, multiple InterSector lanes that once brought people by the thousands in and out of this great city. The green signs with white letters posted on strong steel supports must lie buried as well. If I let my mind wander, I can almost hear the rushing vehicles traveling at speeds near two hundred kilometers per hour. The rush hours when traffic ground nearly to a halt and drivers insisted on changing lanes, always thinking the one they were in was the slowest. The daily accidents when drivers racing home would suddenly slow down and look for carnage, causing more traffic congestion behind them, then speeding up if the accident wasn't serious. So morbid.

If they could only see their city now, I'm sure they would stop and stare—with good reason.

The wreckage looms larger with every step we take toward it. In the silence, interrupted only by the rhythmic pattern of our footsteps, I sense an eerie calm, one that reminds me of the bunker when we first entered. As if this city has known we would be coming, and it's expecting us.

There you must go, the spirits told me. *You have nothing to fear.* I wish I could find courage in those words.

"Does-uh...anybody remember what this place was called?" Samson has his rifle in one hand and the launcher balanced on his shoulder with the other. His gaze swings side to side, watching the two burnt-out buildings that will flank us as we enter the city.

Luther seems distracted. "What sector would this be?"

We traveled east by jeep, then north on foot. "Thirty, maybe?" I take my rifle down from my shoulder.

Luther nods. His claws extend through his gloves. "Yes, perhaps... But the maps had it farther north." His goggles are fixed on the building to our right as though he's seen something stirring. He holds his rifle ready. Then he turns back and joins our triangular formation behind Shechara. "It could be thirty-one. A trade sector would still have many useful things for us."

Samson scoffs, but it sounds half-hearted. "If the daemons haven't taken it all. You know, that might explain their UW gear. Wasn't this where all of it was manufactured?" He curses softly. "Now entering hell. Visitors welcome."

Our boots cross into the shadow cast by the tilting remains of a skyscraper.

"They always come from the east," Luther says.

"What?" I glance at him, then return my gaze to the buildings on either side, tangled steel supports with charred clumps of concrete clinging to them.

"The daemons," he says absently. "When they attack, they come from the east...every time."

"So what're you saying, Luther?" Samson half-turns as if he saw something move. He shakes his head and keeps walking. "You don't think they're camped out here after all?"

"They never come from this direction."

The big man chuckles. "I hope you're right. That would mean

we have nothing—"

"Nothing to fear." Luther faces me. "As the spirits told you, Daiyna."

I don't say anything.

Shechara stops beside the concrete sublevel of a blown-out structure. She peers down inside, then turns and beckons us to follow. Shelter from the sun. We could use a few minutes' rest. To drink some hydro, grab a bite or two from our protein packs. One of us will have to keep watch, but we can alternate.

Shechara drops in first, followed by Samson. Luther gestures for me to go next, but I shake my head and let him go before me. Samson sighs loudly and smack his lips, already drawing from his hydropack in the shadows below. I hesitate before joining them.

I turn and look back, out of the ruins, past the four daemon bodies baking in the sun. Beyond the crumpled rim of the crater where the rocket blast blackened the sand, beyond the charred remains of our disabled jeep, a cloud of dust rises up from the earth, a single plume headed this way.

He is coming.

The spirits' voice catches me off guard and I stumble forward, nearly dropping my rifle.

"Who?" I strain to see. "Shechara..." I whisper, unable to find my voice.

"Daiyna?" Luther steps behind me. "What is it?"

My boots shuffle away from the sublevel, one step, then two, toward the approaching dust cloud. Faster than any vehicle could possibly move.

He is coming.

Dust and ash streak upward across the valley floor in his wake, and before I know it, he stands in front of me in his filthy urine suit, his face shield dull and cracked.

"Milton?" I fall back from him, my heart skipping a beat as the dust passes over us and settles.

"They're dead." Milton's voice emerges unlabored. He stands at ease, arms hanging limply at his sides. "They're all dead."

PART III

POSSESSION

7. **MILTON**
TEN MONTHS AFTER ALL-CLEAR

Wake up.

My eyes open as a jolt of energy courses through my body. I jerk upright to find myself sitting on a mattress inside a dark cavern. Voices shouting, people running like there's some kind of emergency. Gunshots and echoing screams punctuate my confusion.

"Milton, you're awake!" An older man with stooped shoulders grabs my arm. "Get up, quick!"

Rip is his name. He wanted to tie me up earlier, when that weird spitter blinded me.

"What's happening?" My voice is husky, like I haven't spoken in a while. I move to rise, but pain shoots through my chest, and I look down to see I'm bandaged. My head swims, and the rock floor shifts beneath my feet. I land back on the mattress with a groan.

"You've got to pull yourself together, man. We've gotta get you out of here!" He throws one of my arms over his bony shoulders and steadies me on my feet. "The daemons are—"

An explosion cuts him short. The entire cave trembles as dirt showers us.

"They're armed to the teeth!" He pulls me forward.

I struggle to put one foot in front of the other at first, but then

I start getting the hang of it. We head out under an earthen arch into another cave, this one filled with natural light pouring in from the mouth at the other end. Silhouettes move side to side there, jerking awkwardly, fighting against one another. Gunshots explode. Shadowy figures fall and writhe. Screams echo from all directions, some shrill, others guttural like they're from wild animals. But that can't be. There aren't any animals anymore. I should know. I was out there long enough—

Rip pulls me into the fray.

"Is this the only way out?" Why's he taking me this way if we're under attack?

"We need you outside," he grunts under my weight.

I pull back. "What do you mean?"

A strong hand grabs my shoulder. "Milton." It's that weird spitter: Plato. "You're awake!"

How long was I asleep? "What's going on?"

Plato leads me toward the mouth of the cave, and I try to resist, but it just looks like my feet aren't cooperating.

"They came without warning, dozens of them. We're outnumbered and outgunned. We need you." He turns and the light falls on his face, splattered in blood. Some of it looks like his own. "We need your help. Your speed, Milton. Disarm as many of them as you can, and bring us their weapons."

A scream, wild and hoarse, tears through the din. Plato barely seems to notice.

"They've scaled the cliff. We can't hold them back much longer. If they get inside, it'll be a massacre."

Why can't we escape farther into the mountains, back to the west side where they found me? "What about the passages that lead—?"

"Caved in," Rip cuts me off. "All at once, like it was planned. Right when the daemons showed up. Some of the ladies are sayin' it happened to them before, that evil spirits caused it."

Spirits? Right. Those. Like I believe in spooks. Regardless, we're trapped here.

No. *They* are. *They*'re not going to make it without the weapons *they* need to even the score. *They*'re all going to die.

Not me.

"Will you do it?" Plato takes me by the shoulders, his eyes fierce with intensity. "We don't have much time."

Get out.

I catch my breath at the sudden voice inside my head. The back of my neck prickles.

They are already dead. There is nothing you can do.

The sensation is so bizarre, like someone else is thinking through me. Surreal, yet strangely familiar. Without a word, I move toward the mouth of the cave.

"You will, then," Plato's voice echoes behind me. He sounds hopeful. He thinks I'm going to save them.

Let them kill each other. We will see who survives.

No. I shake my head and squeeze my eyes shut. It's obvious who will survive if I do nothing. I'll be the only one the cannibals don't kill. I'm too fast for them. Everyone else here will die.

Who are they to you? The only one who matters is not here. These can perish.

I open my eyes and move ahead, quicker now, one foot in front of the other. As I do, something weird happens: everything around me slows down.

I can't help but stare. They're all running in slow motion now, their voices moaning, garbled. I step closer to the light and see each of the rounds fired by the mutants below. The casings glint under the sun as they float by. I dodge them easily.

My forearm tingles and starts to burn. Even at this speed, my skin isn't safe from the sun. I retreat out of the light, ducking back into the caves to retrieve my jumpsuit. Quickly pulling it on, I make sure the gloves are zipped to my sleeves—a compulsive little habit.

Leave. Now.

I pull up the hood and attach the cracked face shield. Instantly, my view of the mayhem is tinted. I become detached. A couple of glowsticks and nourishment packs sit in my pockets. Maybe I should bring more.

There is plenty of food where you are going.

"If you say so." Whoever *you* are. Guess I shouldn't worry. Everything appears to be in order.

I step aside as a half dozen of the ugly mutants appear, climbing over the ledge with gleaming military-issue daggers in hand. They're really hideous creatures. Eyes bulging wide, jagged teeth drooling, they charge into the cave to wreak havoc. My boot just happens to catch one of them in the shin as it passes, causing it to pitch forward and fall headlong. Plato plunges a spear into its back as it hits the dusty floor of the cave. Score one for the good guys.

Then Rip lets out a shriek. Two of the cannibals have converged on him, tearing him apart in a slo-mo feeding frenzy.

I can't save him now. It's too late. But I could avenge him.

What good would that do? These people are outnumbered. Survival of the fittest.

Leave. Now.

I hesitate for one last indecisive moment. Then I take flight, moving with a speed and strength that's not my own. A wild energy floods through me. Without glancing back, I plunge down the cliff, my boots barely making contact as I cross over rock and crevice, leaving a cloud of dust in my wake.

The mutants turn, distracted momentarily as I pass. There are so many of them, more than Plato estimated. Could this be all of them? Some kind of final assault on their prey? I count at least twenty solar-powered jeeps and easily more than a hundred of the rifle and rocket launcher toting freaks. They seem to be moving in ranks, yet there's no form of communication that I can see—only grunting and drooling. They're running on instinct, like animals.

They are not animals.

The voice inside me is sharp, like a slap in the face. I slow reflexively, but I don't stop.

"Who are you?" My own voice sounds weak and hollow in comparison. What's happening? Have I finally lost my mind?

Go northeast. She is there. She is all that matters.

"She?" The climber—Daiyna, they called her—is the first person who comes to mind. "Is that who you mean?" Why is she so important?

An explosion rocks the earth behind me, and I reel around to see large chunks of the cliff face shoot outward in all directions. Three of the mutants kneel, rocket launchers on their shoulders, aimed up at the cave. They're reloading.

I have to do something.

Leave. Now!

I will. But first...

Before the next barrage of rockets can be fired, I run to intercept. With a push here and a well-placed nudge there, I turn the slow-moving mutants on their own ranks. Then I run as fast as I can to avoid the blasts to follow. The makings of a grin tug at my face as the rockets find their new targets. Solar-powered jeeps fly into the air above fiery billows of smoke, and mutants by the dozen are scorched out of existence.

That should even things out some. I wish I could do more. I wish I could stay. But I can't. I don't belong here.

More explosions echo behind me as this superhuman speed carries me on its own energy, driving me into the unknown. The sandy, ash-colored moonscape is a blur on all sides.

"Where am I going?" I venture to ask. I feel only curiosity, not fear.

I'm invincible. Nothing can hurt me. I'm too fast.

The voice doesn't answer.

Kilometers of desolation pass beneath my feet in a matter of minutes. I glance down and marvel at how fast my legs are pumping, yet I feel no effort or strain, no fatigue. It's almost like I'm flying. Nobody else has ever experienced this, that's for sure. I've been given this *gift*. I've been *chosen*.

Me, of all people? I'm not complaining, but there had to be better candidates.

Craters, deep and yawning, suddenly whip by on both sides, and before I know it, I'm headed straight for the broken remains of a city. Is that my destination? After being out in open spaces for so long, it'll be strange to feel the confines of concrete and steel again. What will I find there?

A lone figure garbed in dirty, sand-colored cloth stands next to the sublevels of a ruined building and watches me approach. He or she looks vaguely familiar, even with the head covering and goggles masking any facial features. I feel my pace slow.

Then abruptly I'm no longer moving at superspeed. I'm standing before the lone figure.

"Milton?" It's her voice that comes through the head covering —Daiyna's voice. She takes a step back from me as if I've startled her. Must be the smell of my suit. She never liked it.

The dust I've stirred settles around us. I'm covered in the stuff, my face shield hardly transparent anymore.

"They're dead," I manage. The image of Rip being mutilated and eaten by the gruesome cannibals returns to my mind. "They're all dead."

Her black goggles stare back at me without expression. She stands rooted. There's something familiar about her, a connection we both share. Energy surges within me like a wild dog lurching against its chain, so strong it takes my breath.

"Luther—" she gasps, doubling over with a hand to her midsection as she backs away. Repelled by my presence?

Another figure, dressed as she is, climbs up out of the dark sublevel. "Daiyna." He catches her as she falls against him. "What is it?" Then he sees me. "Milton?"

"Hey, Luther."

"What are you doing here? How?" He's at a loss. I don't blame him.

Two others climb up from the shadows. One of them is bigger than Jackson—Samson, probably. The other one is smaller than Daiyna. Both are armed with what look like high-powered rifles.

"You're...well?" Luther asks me. It's like I'm the last person he expected to see. "Your wound—"

"They're all dead," Daiyna murmurs, pulling away from him and leaning heavily against the charred concrete wall.

Luther keeps a hand on her shoulder. "Dead?" He faces me. "Who?"

"All of them." I shrug. I don't know how else to say it. "There were more than a hundred of those cannibals you mentioned, with jeeps and rifles and rocket-propelled grenades. After the cave-ins, your people were trapped inside the mountain."

"What the hell are you talking about?" Samson growls, starting toward me.

Luther stops him with an upraised hand.

"He's saying they had help." Daiyna's voice is cool. She keeps her distance from me.

"Help?" the big man demands. "From who?"

"The spirits?" Luther turns to Daiyna.

She nods.

I shrug again. "I don't know about any of that, but it sure looked like those freaks meant business."

"How'd you get away?" Samson grates out through clenched teeth. He doesn't come any closer, but he grips his rifle with menace. "How'd you find us?"

I open my mouth, but no words show up. I'm glad the face shield hides my dumb look. What do I say? I don't even understand it myself.

"He had help, too," Daiyna says. Everyone is quiet as her words sink in.

Does she know about the weird voice in my head? How could she?

"You mean he's still..." Samson's loud whisper trails off, and he backs away a couple steps.

Luther and Daiyna confer quietly. He stands with his back to me, blocking my view of her. Samson shifts his weight awkwardly. The small one remains silent with her rifle slung over her shoulder, but her goggles watch me. I wish I could read their thoughts. Now that would be a real *gift*.

The memory of those screams in the cave is fresh in my mind. Raw. I really should have done more to help Plato and the rest. I could have saved them all.

Daiyna pushes past Luther, ignoring his words of caution. She points straight at me.

"Spirit of the earth, I see you!" she cries.

Luther restrains her. "Daiyna, not like this." His hands grip her shoulders. Then he whispers something I can't make out, and she pulls free from his grasp, turning away and crossing her arms.

She is the only one who matters. Kill the others.

Overcome by a sudden wave of dizziness, I stagger backward, unable to breathe. The ruins around me sway and lurch, then tip over on top of themselves as my head hits the ground. The rest of me crumbles to join it.

"He's bleeding. Quick, get him inside." Luther's voice is followed by a grumble and curse from Samson.

Strong hands and arms lift me up, and I'm carried down into shadows, cool and musty. My face shield is removed, and the fluid of a hydropack pours across my forehead, down into my eyes. Careful fingers open my jumpsuit at the chest. I wince as the bandages are gently ripped away.

"It must have reopened. Apply pressure here." Luther attends to me.

He is dangerous. Kill him.

Fabric tears beside me.

"Not the most sterile solution, but it'll have to suffice. Samson, prop him up." To me, Luther says, "One would think you'd heal faster with your gift of speed."

That makes sense, I guess. Why isn't that the case? And why isn't my stomach growling? Shouldn't my metabolism be faster, too?

"The spirit is interfering with his gift." Daiyna keeps her distance.

Some kind of ghost—is that what's talking in my head? I sure hope not.

Luther pauses as he wraps the strip of fabric around me. He looks me in the eye, and even in the shadows his uncertainty is clear to see. "Are you...aware of it, Milton?"

"I don't know what she's talking about." Partially true.

He resumes his work on my new and improved bandage.

"So-uh...who shot me?" I ask.

Luther pauses again as Samson scoffs.

"Don't you remember?" the big man growls incredulously.

"One of the daemons, Milton," Luther says. "They had you in their sights. But fortunately, Samson was there, and he brought you back to us."

I don't remember any of that. "I was following Plato out through the caves. But then things get kind of fuzzy." They go black, actually, like I've got amnesia or something. Why can't I remember?

So the cannibals shot me. Bastards. I should've killed them all when I had the chance. Maybe there's still time. I can go back to the mountain and wipe them all out, the gun-toting freaks!

Kill him now.

My breath catches as Luther ties off the bandage under my armpit. His eyes remain focused on his work. I'll strangle him before he can lift a finger to resist me.

No. I can't. Why would I?

"Luther." Daiyna wants to talk to him again in private.

He glances up and meets her gaze. "Take it easy, Milton." He squeezes my shoulder and leaves my side with, "I'll be just a minute."

Samson remains crouched behind me, muttering something to himself about wasting time. The smaller one, her head covering and goggles no longer in place, steps toward me. Her bright eyes stand out in contrast to her smooth, dark skin.

"Did you see Ali?" she asks quietly, kneeling at my feet. "Do you know him?"

"Don't get too close, Small Fry," Samson warns her. "This one's not altogether... together."

I smile and give him the finger.

"Did you see Ali fall?" By the way she clenches her jaw, I can tell she's fighting back tears. She's doing a good job of it, though her eyes are glassy.

You can kill her easily.

"No!"

She jumps to her feet at my sudden outburst and steps back, eyes wide. Samson adjusts his hold on the rifle. Luther and Daiyna watch me from across the room.

"No, I'm sorry. It's just the pain, that's all." I gesture lamely at my chest. I close my eyes for a moment, let my nerves settle. "I don't remember anyone named Ali. I wasn't there long. I mean I was, but I wasn't conscious, I don't think."

I look up at her and hope she can tell how sorry I am.

Weapon at the ready, Samson steps between the girl and me. "So why aren't you covered in their blood?" he demands, glowering.

"What?"

"The daemons. Didn't you fight them?"

"I did what I could." I grimace as I try to sit up. "There were too many."

"For you?" He laughs. "I don't think so. I've seen how fast you can move." He glances over his shoulder at Luther and Daiyna, deep in conversation, and drops to one knee, keeping the muzzle of his rifle aimed in my general direction. "You know what I think?"

"Nope. I really don't."

"I think you ran away." He nods. "Yeah, I think you got scared, and you figured you'd just look out for number one. You could've killed every one of those freaks, but instead you ran off. Because deep down, you're nothing but a *coward*."

I could kill him right now. Before he even knows what hit him, I could be on my feet and take his rifle, jam the muzzle up under his chin and blow off his big fat head. His strength would be no match for my speed.

But I'm not a killer.

So says the Sector 43 hangman.

I shut my eyes and grit my teeth. A low moan escapes me. Samson's boots scuffle as he backs away, muttering something about an *exorcism*.

Their faces return to haunt my mind's eye, each with a noose around the neck. They stare at me, condemning me for what I did in the bunker. What I was made to do.

I *am* a killer. I know it as well as they do.

"Milton."

A strong hand squeezes my shoulder again, and I open my eyes to find Luther crouched beside me. Behind him, out of earshot, Daiyna speaks with the other two in low tones.

"Are you in pain?"

Does mental anguish count? But no, he's referring to my chest wound. I try to take a deep breath. It catches, and I wince a little.

"I'll live. Thanks."

"We need to find a vehicle. Can you walk?"

I ran all the way here. I could come up with something witty to say, but instead I just nod. I don't want to be left behind.

"Where are we going?" Bracing myself against the wall, I struggle to my feet.

Luther helps me up. "Through the city. We'll see what can be salvaged."

Samson sounds like he's refusing to go along with Daiyna's plan, whatever it is. She stands her ground, apparently calling the shots. Maybe he doesn't like that. He looks like a chauvinist.

Luther catches me watching them.

"Difference of opinion?" I offer.

I wonder if it has something to do with me. Maybe Luther convinced her that I should come along, and now she has to convince the Neanderthal of the same thing. The other girl stands by, attentive but silent.

"They're both very strong-willed individuals, and my brother is accustomed to winning arguments. He finds it difficult when things don't go his way." The beginnings of a grin tug at the corners of Luther's mouth. "How about you, Milton? Do you fight to win?"

I'm not sure what he means. "Uh..."

"There's a battle raging inside you."

My muscles tense up.

He squeezes my shoulder again. "The only way you're going to make it is by fighting as hard as you can—for your life." He pauses, glancing at my chest. "There's little more that I can do."

He's talking about my wound—not the voice in my head. That's a relief. "Right. Fight to win." I raise a steady fist. "I'm a fighter."

He watches me a moment longer than necessary before releasing my shoulder and turning back to the others. He's a spooky guy, that's for damn sure.

Samson lumbers our way, head covered and goggles in place. He hasn't let go of his rifle since I arrived. Slung across his broad back is a grenade launcher—something you don't see every day. Must've snagged it from one of those mutants.

"Moving out," he rumbles, his tone a bit dejected. Daiyna must have won their argument.

Luther nods, and the others start wrapping up their head coverings and retrieving their weapons. I zip up my suit and pull on my hood, fastening the face shield. I probably should have a gun, too. There's no telling what kind of freaks could be running around loose in these ruins—besides us, that is.

Shoot Luther first.

I squeeze my eyes shut and clench my fists. I don't know how much more of this I can take. They're not my thoughts. If I shoot anybody, it'll be Samson. I have nothing against Luther.

He is dangerous.

Shut up! Leave me alone!

"I'll take the rear." Samson steps past me and stands with his boots spread shoulder-width apart.

Daiyna and the other girl climb out of the sublevel first, followed by Luther, who reaches back to help me up. I stare at his hand without really seeing. It's like I'm not the one inside my own body right now. I'm not in control.

The voice in my head is taking over. I'm possessed or something crazy like that, and it's going to use my body to kill these people.

I've really got to get a grip here.

I take Luther's hand, and he pulls me up. A spasm seizes hold of my chest, but I'll live through it. I take a deep breath once I'm out in the open and look around as the pain subsides.

This place in enormous, not like any of those ghost towns I passed through on my way to the mountains. Along the Inter-Sector—what was left of it, anyway, twisted out of shape—there were blown-out remains of diners and motels and border stations, but nothing like this. I gaze up at the deformed skyscraper skeletons, giants without internal organs. This must have been a big city before D-Day, but which one was it?

The others have already started out, so I hurry to catch up. Glancing over my shoulder, I see Samson following me close enough to make it clear he's keeping an eye on me. I wouldn't mind killing him. He reminds me of Jackson. Maybe they were brothers.

I've seriously got to clear my head.

"Where-uh...Where is it we're headed exactly?" I ask Luther.

His goggles pan the hills of rubble on either side of us as if he expects mutant cannibals to come popping out. He holds his rifle ready, but not with the same ease as Samson.

"We need a vehicle to take us back."

"Back? To the caves, you mean?"

He nods.

"But... There's nobody left." What didn't he understand about *They're all dead?*

He faces me. "That remains to be seen."

He doesn't trust me. None of them do.

Kill him now, before it is too late.

"What do you think we'll find?" I manage.

"I suppose it will be just as you say. But we must be certain. There may be survivors." He glances back to mark Samson's position. "They would need our help."

What if there are survivors...and they saw me run away?

More crazy thoughts. With all those hungry cannibals around, no one could have survived that onslaught. Let this bunch find their vehicle. Hell, I'll even help them. I don't have to be afraid of anything or anyone ever again. They can't do anything to me.

I'm too fast.

"I mean, do you think any vehicle we find is still going to run? It's been twenty years, right? The batteries would be dead."

He acknowledges me with another nod. "Perhaps. But our friend Samson may be able to work a miracle."

I doubt that.

"Do you believe in miracles, Milton?" Luther's goggles are trained on me, their black lenses reflecting my sand-caked face shield.

"I-uh..." What does he mean? "I really doubt anything can be brought back to life."

He watches me for a moment, then returns his wary eye to our surroundings. "Stranger things have happened, my friend."

That's true enough. And he hasn't even heard the voice in my head.

Where the hell did it come from? One minute, I'm following that guy with the super-spit through those cave tunnels. The next minute, I'm waking up in the middle of *Attack of the Killer Mutants*, and I've got a voice in my head—unlike any voice I've ever heard in my life. It's more like a whole crowd of voices blended together, rushing through me as strong as a river in the

Preserve. It could be coming from my own thoughts, yet I know it's not.

Or have I finally lost it? I've snapped. And this is what schizophrenia feels like.

Daiyna gestures to Luther up ahead, and he nods. We've arrived at an underground parking structure, several sublevels below a skyscraper skeleton. The concrete looks stable enough, and the gnarled steel frames of the floors above don't look like they've shifted much in the past decade or so. It's a little eerie, though. Dark and silent like a tomb.

Our pace slows noticeably as we draw near.

"What do you see?" Luther asks the women as they both peer down inside.

How can they see anything in there? Beyond the first fifty meters or so—littered with the molten remains of several abandoned, long-forgotten vehicles—it's pitch black.

Then I remember. She can see in the dark. I guess the other one can too. How special.

"Nothing we can use, not on this level." Daiyna turns toward him. "We'll have to go farther down."

Nobody says it, but I know what they're thinking. Not really—I don't have that ability yet. But I can guess: It's dark and spooky down there, and it's likely we might bump into a clan of inbred mutant cannibals. A reasonable concern. For them.

I don't have to worry. I just have to outrun the rest of this bunch.

She is important.

"Right." I wince. This time the voice brought a little friend: a splitting headache. "I won't leave her behind. Happy now?"

Samson shoves me aside as he passes by. "Talking to yourself?" He joins the others above the concrete ramp that once served as an entrance to this garage.

Resisting the urge to kill him, I follow.

"We can look elsewhere," Luther suggests, offering an alternative in light of everyone's uneasiness.

Daiyna shakes her head. "It won't be any different anywhere else. The only vehicles left intact would be parked in the lower levels. This structure or the next, it doesn't matter."

"Daiyna and I can go ahead," the smaller one adds quietly.

"You're not going without us, Small Fry," Samson rumbles. "I don't care if I'm blind as a bat. I'm not waiting around out here."

"Agreed." Luther nods. "We go together."

Daiyna seems a bit reluctant. She glances at me, then turns to lead the way. The other girl follows her with Samson close behind. Luther beckons me to join him at the rear, and we descend the cracked incline. No one speaks as we enter the garage.

It's more like an auto morgue with all the wreckage in assigned parking spots. These vehicles were people's prized possessions at one point in time. I'm sure they were either sleek and fuel-efficient or solar-powered. Difficult to tell one from the other now. They all look the same: frozen puddles of plastic and steel.

The sunlight quickly dissipates, and we're covered in shadow. Goggles come off and head wrappings drop to their shoulders. I remove my face shield and toss back my hood. It smells bad in here, like tires were cooked in motor oil, then baked into the concrete. Instinctively, I cover my nose. Hope we don't plan on staying long.

Daiyna gestures *this way* and points out a stairwell on the opposite side of the sublevel. It should lead us down into the depths of this place, where I'm sure it'll smell even better.

The tension among the others is palpable as we move forward. Even with their special abilities and weapons, they still fear the unknown—though none of them would admit it. Strangely enough, it doesn't affect me. I don't feel the least bit nervous.

Shouldn't I? Just a little? Yet I'm completely at ease, and it's exhilarating.

The shadows loom darker as we reach the doorway at the foot of the stairs. Our boots scuff across the floor and echo against the concrete walls. The smaller girl shoots furtive glances to and fro. Luther and Daiyna are more guarded in their expressions, but they don't fool me. They're just as nervous as she is. Samson's focus is set straight ahead. His eyes flick from side to side as he holds his weapons at the ready and does his best to cushion his oversized footfalls. I don't see the point. If anybody's down here, they would have heard us already.

Images from a zombie film I saw as a kid pass through my mind. It was made in one of those Eurasian countries, centuries before my time. Four people were riding in a little car, and they ran out of gas under a long overpass. Or it was some kind of tunnel. No, the car had a flat tire, and the people had to change it as fast as they could. The zombies were coming, running full-tilt, not staggering stupidly like in older films. They ran like the devil was chasing them. The *infected*.

Wouldn't it be funny if that's what we find down here? Forget about mutant cannibals armed to the teeth. We've got a new monster in town, folks: your friendly garage-dwelling zombie! Be afraid.

I almost laugh out loud.

What is fear, really? Where does it come from? Is it rooted in our mortality? What if we could live forever—would we fear *anything*?

This sense of total freedom flooding through me is enough to make me giddy. I have nothing to fear. It's amazing.

No, there's still one thing I'm afraid of: That the voice will speak to me again.

"Watch your step," Luther whispers over his shoulder as we enter the stairwell and head down. "Try to feel your way along."

That's about all I can do. Unlike the two women, I can't see my own glove in front of my face right now. Reminds me of when Daiyna first found me and we tried some informal spelunking together. I had to feel my way down a ladder in the dark. She could see fine, but I was completely blind.

She sure is keeping her distance. It's like she doesn't want to be anywhere near me. I'm trying not to take it personally. Probably just the smell of my suit.

You are not alone.

I brace myself against the wall as my knees go weak.

"What do you mean?" Are there really zombies down here?

Kill them. Before you are discovered.

I can't even see them. How am I supposed to kill them? If I start moving around at the speed of sound, what will keep me from planting my face in a wall?

Kill them!

A searing pain knifes through my skull. A wimpy cry escapes me as I collapse, cradling my head. Whispers assault me, jumbled, too loud. Hands grasp at my arms, but I pull back, retreating up the steps one at a time.

What's happening to me? What are they doing to me?

"Milton." Luther's voice comes through clearly, and I stop moving. "Milton, you're not alone."

I know. The voice told me the same thing. But what does it mean?

"Milton. Focus on my voice." Luther crouches down beside me. "I know you're in pain. You feel alone. But we're right here. We won't leave you."

I grunt. It's all I can manage. I cower, cringing against the wall. Make it stop!

Kill them.

Why? Haven't I killed enough people already?

Then a few more should not matter.

Luther is whispering. What's he saying? He's not talking to me or Samson or anyone else here. He's praying. For me. I don't know if I should laugh or cry. Isn't God dead?

The pain subsides instead of increasing in intensity. My eyes open, but all I see is black. I take a deep breath, and my body relaxes. My chest wound stings like multiple bees are having their way with me, but it's nothing compared to that barrage of cranial agony I've just endured.

Luther squeezes my shoulder. "Are you going to be all right?"

Is there something living inside me? If it wants me to kill these people...will it hit me with killer headaches until I do it?

It should take over my body and be done with it. No, this is crazy. I don't want them to die—most of them, anyway. I just want to be left alone. But I don't want to be alone. I want this voice out of my head. That's what I really want. It scares the living hell out of me.

This is what it's like to lose your mind. Weird.

"I'm fine." I get to my feet and keep my hand on the wall for support. "Thanks."

"We need to keep moving," Samson half-whispers.

Does he know what's coming? I bet he does, the bastard. He's probably in league with them. In league? Who talks that way? I'm thinking, not talking. Does he know what I'm thinking? Does he know I want to kill him?

I could kill him. I killed Jackson. Same size.

"We can wait here, if you need to," Luther suggests.

I shake my head. I don't want to be alone with him. He might pray again or do something else equally bizarre. "Let's go."

We follow the sound of the footsteps from our seeing-eye women. I almost laugh at that. Why don't we light a glowstick or two so the rest of us can see where we're going? It's not like we're making a silent approach here. Not now. Our clomping boots echo throughout this level of the parking structure despite our best attempts to quiet them.

The zombies are waiting for us. They're probably watching us right now. They can tell that three of us are blind. What are they waiting for? Jump us already! Get it over with!

The footsteps ahead of us have stopped. Luther and I approach the whispers and Samson's blundering attempts at keeping his voice down. I bump against the smooth steel body of a vehicle. We've found one. So now what?

"Talk us through it," Daiyna says.

Samson grunts negatively. "I've got to see what I'm doing. We need some light."

"Well, unless you brought a glowstick—"

"I've got one." I reach into the leg pocket of my suit and retrieve it. I hesitate before cracking the light. "Shall I?"

Silence holds the moment as indecision weighs heavily on them. Then Luther says, "Do it."

So much for the element of surprise—or what little we have left. I snap the stick across the middle, and instantly we're washed in its green glow. It takes a few moments for my eyes to adjust after the initial blast of light, but when they do, blinking overtime, I can read the bold lettering stenciled on a nearby support pillar. We're on the garage's third sublevel. There are enough parking spaces down here for hundreds of vehicles, but the only one left intact stands alone in front of us. It looks like a utility truck. The others are skeletons, stripped for parts long ago.

"What do you think, my friend?" Luther asks.

Samson doesn't look optimistic. "This one will need fuel just to get it started. And to keep it running." He surveys the remains of the other vehicles. "Solar panels and battery cells are missing on those. Somebody's already been through here. And they knew what they were doing."

"So what are you saying?" Daiyna stands on the other side of the vehicle with a hand on its hood. "We need to find gasoline? Or look for another one?"

He shrugs and tries the handle on the driver's door. Unlocked. He reaches under the steering column, and the hood pops up slightly with a thud that echoes like a gunshot. Daiyna backs away. He steps around the front of the truck and releases a latch behind the grill, then lifts the hood with ease, propping it up with one hand. He looks over the engine with the focused intensity of a medic gauging injuries, touching things here and there.

"A little light." He gestures for me to move closer with the glowstick. I toss it to him instead, and he catches it in one hand with quick reflexes. "Thanks," he mutters. The hood remains steady in his grip as he leans close to the engine. An ancient circus performer sticking his head into a lion's gaping mouth. "Yeah, it'll run if we get some gas," he says at length.

Luther nods. "We should find enough in these other vehicles."

Samson shakes his head. "They're all solar-electric. Or they were, before the vultures got to them."

"Daemons?" the small girl asks in a whisper.

"Doubt it. Like I said, whoever did this had skill. What we need are earlier models—hybrids, anything that ran on fuel. We can siphon it out of their tanks. They would've been air-tight to prevent the gasoline from oxidizing. Most were, back then." He looks at Daiyna. "We should try the next level down."

None of them want to admit their fear at the idea of going deeper into this crypt, but I know they feel it. I can almost see it emanating from them like an aura. But their faces are brave. Impressive how they're able to keep it together.

So I encourage them with: "Anybody else feel like we're not alone?"

Daiyna turns away. The girl next to her stares at me. Samson mutters something under his breath and drops the truck's hood, shutting it as quietly as possible. Luther turns to me with an uncertain look in his eyes.

"Have you heard anything, Daiyna?" he asks calmly.

She doesn't turn around. "No."

"We have nothing to fear," he says half to himself, like he's said it before. His mantra.

"Just trying to lighten things up a bit," I offer with a lame shrug. "Sorry."

Samson tosses the glowstick back at me with a glowering look and I catch it against my chest with both hands. I could run behind him and cram it up his ass before he has a clue what's going on. Now *that* would be funny.

Daiyna meets Luther's gaze, and he nods. How cute. They're telepathically linked.

She checks her rifle and leads the way, the other girl close behind. Samson follows, then Luther. I stand there holding the glowstick, not knowing what to do with myself. There's no way to turn off the light, and I don't know if they want me to bring it along. I have a fresh one in my pocket, so I could leave this one by the truck to burn itself out.

But they're already across the sublevel, approaching the door to the stairwell. So I stuff the glowing stick into my pocket and hurry to catch up. I come alongside Luther with a bright green bulge in my pants.

"So much for a miracle, huh?" I say.

"How's that?" he asks, his face in shadow.

"The truck. Samson couldn't work his magic."

"Don't count him out yet. He'll come through for us. We need fuel, that's all."

"Gasoline. Right. I'm sure there are barrels and barrels of the stuff hidden somewhere below, just waiting for us."

My sarcasm isn't lost on him. "What would you suggest we do instead, Milton?" He sounds genuinely interested.

It's a good question, but unfortunately I don't have much of an answer. "I guess I don't see the point in going back. To the caves, I mean. We've managed to escape from those cannibal freaks, and going back seems like suicide."

He's quiet for a moment. "We left our friends, Milton. If there's even a chance one of them is still living, it's worth the risk. You haven't had the opportunity to get to know us very well, much less our other brothers and sisters, but surely you can understand." He pauses. "You had friends in your bunker before things went badly, yes?"

How does he know about that? I must have told him. How much did I tell him? I can't remember. Does he know about Julia?

I nod mutely. Of course I understand. I'd go back for her. But not for the rest of them. They don't matter to me. She's the only one who matters.

I look down at the bobbing shapes in the dim glow cast through my pocket. I can vaguely make out Daiyna's form, farthest from me. What would she look like with long, flowing hair instead of stubble? Would she look like Julia? Would her bare skin be just as soft?

I need to be alone with her. And I would be, if I killed the others.

Are these my own thoughts? I can't tell anymore. They sound like the same ideas that came from that voice in my head. But the voice has been silent ever since that last killer headache.

Below, the others leave the stairwell and enter the next sublevel. The stench in here is stronger, the air thicker, more stagnant. I cough involuntarily as I follow Luther out into Level Four. There's only one more level beneath this one, so if we don't find what we're looking for here—

"Light." Samson holds out his hand expectantly.

This time, I don't toss it to him. I retrieve it from my pocket and hold it shoulder-high as I move to his side and stand there. He looks irritated. Satisfied, I wink at him.

"All right, what we're looking for will be located toward the rear of the vehicles, above one of the tire wells," he says. "A small hatch. We'll disconnect hoses from under the hoods to siphon out the gas, and we'll need containers to carry it in. If we all split up, it'll go faster."

"Out of the question." Daiyna's stance is resolute. "We stay together."

Again, Samson looks irritated. I can't hide my grin.

"In case you haven't noticed, the air isn't great. We split up, we cover more ground in less time." He gestures around us to where more than thirty vehicles are parked. Many of them have been surgically stripped, but others don't fit that category. They look like small city commuters. "Let's get this done and get the hell out of here."

Daiyna looks at Luther to make the call.

"We'll break into two groups," Luther says. "Samson, go with Daiyna. Shechara, we'll need you to come with us in case the light goes out."

So that's the smaller one's name—Shechara. Besides seeing in the dark, what else can she do? Samson and Daiyna set out across the sublevel without a word spoken between them.

"Meet back at the stairs," Daiyna casts over her shoulder.

Luther nods, turning to Shechara as she joins us. "Do you see what Samson spoke of?"

Her large, dark eyes scan the vehicles around us, seeming to penetrate them with X-ray vision. "There." She points to the far wall, maybe fifty meters away. She sets off in that direction, and we follow.

"You can see really well," I thoughtfully articulate. She doesn't respond. "With your night-vision, I mean. That must come in handy." No response. Is she scared of me?

"Shechara is quite the chatterbox, once she gets to know you. Just wait and see," Luther says. "There will be no stopping her." The girl's lips turn upward slightly as she glances back at Luther, but that's all. More than I got.

We reach two parking spaces where a pair of small vehicles sit side by side. In the green light of the glowstick, I see the hatches over their rear tire wells.

"So these run on gasoline." I look at Luther. "How do we tell if there's any left in the tank?"

He stares at the vehicle in front of him. "I have no idea."

Shechara tries the driver's door and, finding it unlocked, ducks inside like Samson did with the truck. The hood pops, and she comes around to lift it.

"He said there would be hoses," she says, frowning at the engine.

"Right." Luther joins her and points. "Could that be one?"

The blind leading the blind. But I'm no help, either. We all rode public transports back in Sector 43. Nobody had their own auto in a labor sector, except for the governor and his cronies.

"I'll go get Samson," I offer. "Be back in no time."

Luther looks up at me. He almost says something but stops himself, nodding instead. "Very well. Tell him we've found two gas-powered vehicles, but we're...currently at a loss."

I grin. "Will do."

"Milton." In his eyes, the uncertainty has been replaced with concern. "Be careful."

He shouldn't worry about me. That's ridiculous. I have enough light to keep me from slamming into a support pillar or anything, and I'm too fast for any zombie. I'm too fast for Samson.

Julia... I can't wait to be alone with her again.

I take off, the green glow lighting my path between parked vehicles that rush past on both sides. It feels so good to be moving like this again. The freedom is intoxicating.

But all too soon, it's over.

"What are you doing here?" Samson glares at me in the sudden light. It makes him look like some kind of hulking monster. "Why aren't you—?"

"We found a couple gas-powered autos. Over there." I point, but I watch Julia—Daiyna. She winces with a hand to her stomach, backing away. It's like she's allergic to me, or the sight of me makes her sick. "They need your help. Something about hoses." I hand him the glowstick. "You'll probably need this."

He eyes me warily. "Okay." He glances back at Daiyna and frowns. She looks like she's in pain. "You all right?"

She nods curtly, biting her lip. Avoiding eye contact. "Go on. I'll be fine."

Of course she'll be. We'll be together again. After so long... I hope she can find it in her heart to forgive me for what I did. What Jackson made me do.

The big man stares at her stupidly. "Keep looking. We'll need all the fuel we can get." Glowstick in hand, he heads across the sublevel in a primitive trot.

Gradually, the light recedes with him until Julia and I are in shadow, then total darkness. I can't see her at all now, but I know she can see me. It's her *gift*.

"What do you see?" I break the silence.

"Do you really want to know?" Her breath catches slightly.

"Tell me. Why have you been avoiding me?"

"I see the spirit inside you. It wants to destroy us."

"Not us." I shake my head. "Only them."

"It will destroy *you*, Milton. It's already begun," she gasps. "Can't you tell? What it's doing to your mind?"

"You can't see inside my head."

"I don't have to. I know you want to kill Samson."

Jackson, she means. That's no secret.

"He deserves to die!" Tears sting my eyes. "It's all his fault!"

Silence.

"Milton..." Her voice is quiet and gentle, just like Julia's in the middle of the night. "Milton, you can fight this. You're strong. But you have to let go of the past."

What is she talking about?

"Spirit of the earth—"

Something stirs within me. My heart pounds double-time, every nerve in my body instantly set ablaze. I gasp for air and pitch forward blindly.

"Spirit of the earth—"

Take her!

The voice rushes through my mind, and with it comes a flood of memories: Julia's bare skin against my own as we kissed, tumbling over each other in the heat of passion, moaning with pleasure, hot sweat dribbling down our backs, her eyes, her smile, her gasps of delight—

"Spirit of the earth, leave him now!"

"NO!" I lunge forward with both hands and close my fingers around her throat.

"I saved you once," she struggles for her voice, fighting against my grip. "Let me save you again."

I shake my head. Tears streak my cheeks. I squeeze with all my strength.

"You can't."

8. LUTHER
TEN MONTHS AFTER ALL-CLEAR

The spirit inside him is taking root. Daiyna believes she may be able to rid him of it with the help of the spirits who speak to her, but she's told me he must be willing. He must want her to help him. Samson believes Milton is nothing more than a coward, that he saw the daemons attack and ran for his life. He blames Milton for their deaths.

Do I? How will I react to seeing the remains of my brothers scattered across the caves? With his superhuman speed, Milton could have saved them all. He could have put an end to the daemons.

It was our hope that he would. But when given the chance, he didn't. What does that mean? Is he a threat to us?

When I look into his eyes, I see the same high-spirited, strong-willed young man I met when Daiyna first led him into the caves. He carried a secret that haunted him, but there was also an unaffected innocence about him. He had yet to witness the unspeakable horrors of this new earth, and he seemed able to function completely without fear. He was confident, perhaps arrogant—that hasn't changed since his coma. But there's something else now when I meet his gaze.

It's like looking into the eyes of a wild animal.

"Do you think there will be any left?" Shechara asks.

I turn back to her and our project: a small commuter vehicle with a gas tank. I can't see a thing in the darkness that has descended upon us in Milton's absence, but I face her voice.

"Gasoline?"

"When we go back, I mean," she murmurs. "Any survivors."

"I hope so." I pray so. I take a deep breath, recalling how she and Ali were enjoying the early stages of a mutual affection. He's obviously on her mind, and I wish there was more I could say to keep her from losing heart. "We must have faith."

Even as I say these words, I feel hollow inside. Despair lurks close by.

"Here he comes."

I turn around to see the bobbing green light. That didn't take long. Samson will know how to remove the gasoline from the tanks of these two vehicles, and soon we'll be on our way.

"He's alone," Shechara says.

"What?"

She can't be right. Samson would not have left Daiyna with Milton. We already discussed the fact that it would be unwise, considering the effect of the evil spirit's proximity on her.

Unless it was her idea. She may have convinced Samson to return alone. But when had she and Samson ever agreed on anything?

I break into a run as Samson draws near, his grim features illuminated by the glowstick in his hand. "We agreed they wouldn't be left alone together." I reach for the light and move to pass him.

He grips the stick tightly and grabs me by the shoulder, halting me. "Luther, she knows what she's doing."

"How do you know? Do you have any idea what's happening?"

"I don't claim to." He swallows, his broad face a mask of bewilderment. "But she said it had to be this way. Even before Milton came over to us. She said the spirits told her so."

My stomach drops as Daiyna's bold voice echoes across the sublevel: "Spirit of the earth..."

I try to pull free of his grasp. "Let me go, brother."

"She said we can't interfere."

"We don't know what he's capable of!" I struggle against his hold on me and contemplate using my claws on him.

He tosses the glowstick to Shechara and grips both my shoulders, immobilizing me. "I want to tear that little coward a new one, but this is how it's got to be." His eyes implore me. "It's like that faith you always talk about. We have to trust her on this."

Daiyna's voice echoes again, the same words.

"We've got to have faith Daiyna knows what she's doing."

My shoulders sink into his grasp. "We have nothing to fear." The words hold no special meaning for me now. I know she's in danger, but I'm powerless to do anything about it.

"Spirit of the earth—leave him!" she cries.

"NO!" Milton's hoarse scream rips through the darkness.

Adrenaline blasts through my system. Samson releases me, his hands clenched into fists. We glance at each other—long enough to confirm our course of action. We turn to run just as Shechara sprints past us. If Milton dares harm Daiyna in any way—

The sudden roar of an engine fills the garage as a large vehicle revs up the ramp from the level below. Headlights chase away the darkness with a deluge of blinding white. Our boots skid to a halt.

"Quick—find cover!" Samson hits the ground beside an abandoned vehicle and rolls underneath, rifle in hand, dropping the rocket launcher to the concrete next to him.

Shechara quickly follows his example. I crouch behind another vehicle and hold my rifle at the ready. Even with this unexpected intrusion, Daiyna remains my priority. I must get to her.

Another vehicle follows the first, as large and as loud, headlights overwhelming in their intensity. The second vehicle stops with squealing tires at the top of the ramp, engine idling, while the first one rolls forward, veering around a support column and heading in our direction. It looks like an armored assault vehicle, black and gleaming. Well maintained, without a speck of dust on it.

Daemons? No. Survivors? There's no way to tell. The windows are tinted black, and as it rumbles our way, we're washed in the floodlights mounted on its roof.

"Luther—get down!" Samson growls.

"Daiyna..." I stare across the sublevel.

"You can't help her if you're dead!"

Gritting my teeth, I drop to the cold concrete and roll under the nearest automobile, just as the armored vehicle squeals to a halt. For a few moments it sits there, engine thrumming, massive tires filling my view. Was I spotted?

A passenger door swings open, and a pair of military-issue boots drop to the ground. The bolt of an automatic weapon clinks, echoing with menace. Instinctively, I grip my rifle, training the muzzle on the boots with blue camouflage pants tucked into them.

A man clears his throat confidently. "Well, I'd say we have a couple options here. We can either do this the easy way...or the hard way." He waits for the echo of his authoritative voice to fade. "We know you're not mutos. You understand human speech." A pause. "We've been watching you. The security cameras in here are rigged with night vision and infrared thermoptic. We know right where you're hiding." His boots remain rooted. "So I'd like you to come on out and lay down your weapons for the time being, just until we get to know each other. We don't want any trouble. But if it's trouble you're after...rest assured that we've got you outnumbered, and we will not hesitate to put you down." His tone does not change. "The choice is yours, of course."

I look across at Samson. He'd sooner fight than hand over his weapons. He glares back at me, knowing this is my call. I look for Shechara but can't see her anywhere nearby.

Daiyna? Milton? Where are they? Is she all right?

We must have faith in our gifts, that even without the weapons we've obtained, we're still able to defend ourselves. I pray for strength. Then I slide—carefully, with my rifle held up in one hand—out from under the automobile.

"Well, hello there." I'm greeted with a broad smile by a slight man in full camouflage and a black beret. He wears a transparent oxygen mask and holds a pistol at rest, aimed at the ceiling. "That didn't take long at all. I was thinking there'd be more of a stand-off." He chuckles, his noticeable Adam's apple jerking spastically.

"My weapon." Slowly, I set it down at my feet, my eyes fixed on him as I rise. The large assault vehicle beside him—twice the size of the mutants' jeeps—doesn't appear to be solar-powered, and it could easily carry ten men. Are they inside? Or is there only a driver?

"Great, thanks. Just a precaution, you understand. Until we all get ourselves acquainted properly." He frowns then, scratching the back of his ear with the pistol. "How about your friends?"

I hope Samson is of a mind to cooperate. We have no idea what sort of situation we're in here. "Yes, they—"

Samson rolls out and gets to his feet, rifle in one hand and Stinger in the other. Brow furrowed, he steps to my side. He doesn't relinquish either weapon.

"You mind?" The man in the beret gestures mildly toward the rifle at my feet. He doesn't appear to notice my brother's formidable nature. "Set them down, please." He sounds like he's speaking to a child. "Right there."

"I don't think so." Samson shakes his head. "Not until I see some proof that we're *outnumbered*, like you say."

Another broad smile stretches the man's thin lips along with his narrow mustache. "Seeing is believing, eh?" He chuckles. "That can be arranged. But I must say, I'm a little disappointed. Could it be that you'd prefer things...the *hard* way?" He raises his voice with a sudden edge to it, and the vehicle's other doors fly open. Seven armed men in camouflage and O2 masks land on the concrete with a cacophony of hard-soled boots. Across the garage at the top of the ramp, the same scene unfolds at the other armored vehicle, perfectly synchronized.

Samson stands rigidly, eyeing the short-barreled automatic rifles trained on him. I know he must be weighing his chances. That's the kind of man he is. I can only pray that he gives in to reason.

"Take 'em." He drops his gaze, defeated, as two soldiers relieve him of his weapons. One stoops to retrieve mine.

I relax, realizing only then that I've been holding my breath. I must stay calm. Already, I can feel my claws begin to flex outward.

"That wasn't so bad, now was it?" The leader chuckles again. "So that leaves three more of you, right? One male, two females. Should I send my men after them, or do you think they'll follow your fine example?" He eyes me squarely.

I look across the garage. Already, the seven men from the other vehicle have spread out with weapons at the ready. Where's Daiyna? Milton could disarm these men before they even catch sight of him. But what is his state of mind right now?

Shechara rises to her full height half-way across the garage, between two abandoned automobiles. An audible murmur sweeps through the soldiers. She raises her rifle in one hand and keeps her other hand where they can see it. Their murmurs become louder, more suggestive, as she moves to join us.

"You'll have to pardon my men," says the leader. "We've been without the...*benefits* of female companionship for some time now. They're just doing what comes naturally, I'm afraid." His beady eyes rove up and down her body as she approaches. "Why thank you, darling," he says with a wink as she hands over her weapon.

She keeps her gaze set straight ahead, her face an expressionless mask as she steps between Samson and me. From the corner of my eye, I see her tremble briefly before regaining her composure. A shiver of fear? Disgust, more likely.

"So, two more then. A man and woman. Didn't seem like things were going too well for them. He might've had her by the throat when we pulled up." He chuckles at my expression. "Like I said, we've been watching you ever since you arrived. Cameras all over the place. But here's the weird thing: soon as we pull up, those two disappeared. Just like that, they're off the grid. Vanished. Poof!" He takes a step forward, his eyes fixed on me, his pistol cradled against the side of his O2 mask. "You wouldn't happen to know anything about that, now would you?"

Milton could have carried her away, using his speed to avoid detection. But why would he have had her by the throat?

"I don't know about you, but that sure seems like something that should be shared amongst God's children." He tilts his head, squinting an eye up at me. "Some kind of invisibility cloak or some such? Yeah? Wouldn't that be the ticket? Sneak up on those mutos out there and wipe 'em out, once and for all!" He laughs. Then his features abruptly go slack. "But you don't know what the hell I'm talking about."

Before I can respond, Samson says, "He wasn't one of us. We just let him tag along."

"And the woman?"

Samson nods slowly, weighing his words. "She's our...sister."

"*Sister*, you say? Well then. I reckon you'll want to find the magic man who disappeared with her as much as we do. The weirdest thing, the way they just went off-grid like that." He shrugs. "We'll find 'em, eventually. Even if we have to scare 'em with a few rounds shot here and there. So, how about some introductions? I'd be Captain Willard, and these fine young soldiers are my men, the very best of the Eden Guard." He holsters his weapon, his eyes never wavering from Shechara. "Now who would you be?"

We say our names, but that's all.

"Uh-huh." Willard eyes us one at a time. "Where do you hail from?"

I tell him, and briefly I explain why we're looking for a vehicle, how ours was destroyed. There's no point in lying to him. Strange that I'd even consider it.

"Sorry to hear that. Those mutos are a bad lot, all right. We've managed to keep them out of here, but they keep coming back and stealing our stuff. It's like they're drawn to these ruins for some reason. Linked to them somehow. Creepy, really."

He gestures to the men at the other vehicle and calls out, "They couldn't have gotten far." He takes four of the soldiers with him to join in the hunt. The remaining three keep their weapons trained on us, their severe postures in stark contrast to their leader's nonchalant demeanor. "I really don't see the point in you all goin' back to your caves and whatnot. Sounds like suicide, really. Besides, the mutos will likely follow your trail here. And when they do, it sure would be nice if y'all would lend us a hand in Eden's defense."

"Does that mean we get our weapons back?" Samson rumbles.

Willard chuckles. "Now don't get ahead of yourself, big boy. I still don't know if I can trust you. Believe me, I'd like to. You're the only natural children of God we've met since All-Clear! But I can't take that to mean we're on the same side here, no matter how much I want to. We've learned to be careful over the past few months. It's kept us alive."

I watch him closely. He's a talker, and I'm uncertain whether his words are crafted out of honesty or deception. "How might we gain your trust, Captain?"

"All in good time, Luther my man. All in good time. I just want to get to know you a little better, for starters. You seem kinda tight-lipped."

"Perhaps we'd be more at ease without your men aiming their weapons at us."

Willard raises an eyebrow and nods slowly. "Maybe so." He taps his mask all of a sudden. "And maybe where the air's a little better, eh?" He steps away from the vehicle and gestures for us to get inside. "Go on. Hop in."

"I'm not going anywhere." Samson snorts, crossing his arms.

"Where will you take us?" I ask Willard.

He chuckles and shakes his head. "C'mon now, it's not like we're going to eat you! What have you got to be afraid of?" With a petulant sigh, he turns to his men. "Lower your weapons, boys.

You're making our new friends agitated." He glances at me and shrugs. "Don't tell me you like it down here."

I turn to Samson and Shechara. I see in their eyes that they don't like our current situation any better than I do. But I also see their courage. They have faith in me to lead them.

Will I lead them to their deaths? What do these soldiers want with us? Who are they, really? What's worth guarding in the rubble of this city?

Shechara nods. With resignation, Samson does the same. I turn back to Willard.

"Very well. We'll go with you."

"Fantastic." Another broad smile stretches his gaunt face, but his eyes remain steely. He orders one of his men to take the driver's seat and another to ride shotgun. He then gestures for us to climb into the back seats. "After you."

We do as we're told, sliding in side by side across the wide cushioned bench. Willard climbs in behind us, as do two of his men. The driver revs the engine, and the doors slowly swing shut on their own, locking automatically. Samson glances around the interior and mutters something about a *hummer*, whatever that means.

The tires squeal against the concrete and we lurch forward, heading toward the ramp at the end of the garage. But instead of returning to the surface, we veer down to the level below, leaving Willard's other men spread out among the rows of abandoned vehicles. The lights mounted on their rifles sweep to and fro in search of Daiyna and Milton.

I pray they're all right, someplace safe. I pray that Milton didn't hurt her, that she was somehow able to exorcise the spirit from him. I struggle to control the anxiety and adrenaline coursing through me, my hands clenched into fists, my claws piercing into my palms. I have to control myself. We don't know if Willard and his men have been gifted by the spirits. If not, then they may not react kindly to seeing our changes.

Willard's first response at seeing someone *vanish* wasn't that it was a special ability, but that it was some kind of unknown technology—an *invisibility cloak*. And his talk of *natural children of God* has filled me with apprehension.

We must not use our gifts in front of these men until we know for sure. Or unless they leave us no other choice.

Outside the vehicle, there lies only darkness, but the path before us is washed white in the headlights' glare. The driver navigates our course at high speeds, careening through the lowest level of the garage around another gathering of abandoned vehicles. Then he floors the gas pedal as the opening to a large concrete tunnel presents itself in the far wall. I'm thrown back against my seat at the sudden acceleration. I glance at Samson, who appears to be appreciating the ride, his eyes kindled with interest. I'm sure he'd prefer being behind the wheel of this powerful vehicle.

Behind us, Willard leans on the back of our seat, his head between Shechara's and my own. "So, Sectors 50 and 51, huh. Together at last?" He chuckles. "How's that going for you? Any buns in the oven yet?" He winks at Shechara, but she ignores him, her gaze still set straight ahead.

I choose my words carefully. "The mutant threat has been our primary concern. We made our journey this far in hopes of locating their...origin."

"Good luck with that." His smile fades. "We haven't been able to figure out where they hail from. Plenty of them out there, though, and that's a fact. Tracked 'em here, you say? The ones that blew up your jeep?"

I nod. I already explained as much.

"Well, you can forget all about them for the time being. They never venture where we're headed." Another chuckle. "I've got a feeling you're really gonna like Eden, Luther."

"Do we have a choice?" Samson mutters.

Willard grins, unaffected by my brother's grim demeanor. "I don't know what you're insinuating, but once you see where we're going, I truly doubt you'll want to go anywhere else. We've managed to make quite a life for ourselves. At the risk of sounding a bit conceited, I'd have to say it's the closest thing imaginable to the way life used to be." He clears his throat suddenly. "That's not to say cave-dwelling is without its charms..." He winks again, this time at me. "You'll be surprised by how many conveniences we've managed to resurrect."

Should I trust him, believe what he says? As we hurtle through this tunnel with no room to spare on either side, I find that I can no longer sense the life force of the spirits. Where have they gone?

"So, you were out there quite a while," Willard says.

"How's that?"

"Since All-Clear, you've been on the surface. Isn't that right?" His eyes bulge, unblinking, through his mask.

I nod slowly, unable to discern the course of this conversation. "And you?"

"Our bunker opened into these old tunnels. We think they were for diverting groundwater to subterranean reservoirs. We've never been out of the city, never needed to leave. Everything we could possibly want is right here." He catches himself. "Well, *almost* everything." He nods at Shechara.

"Sector 31?" I try to distract him.

Willard shrugs. "Probably. A trade sector would make sense, what with all the leftovers. But really, those old titles don't mean much anymore, do they? Sector 50, Sector 51, Sector 31. Who the hell cares?" He pats his own uniform. "The Eden Guard is starting everything over from scratch, Luther. We've hit the reset button. We're forging a new life for ourselves, a new nation, making things the way they ought to be."

There are no markings on his uniform for any sort of rank. The pale light reflected from the headlights is little help, bounced around the sides of the tunnel. A UW insignia could have been on Willard's shoulder at one point, but it's been ripped off.

"How much longer until—"

"Till we reach paradise?" he interrupts me with a grin.

"Shouldn't be long now. Lieutenant Jamison up there, our trusty navigator, he knows these tunnels better than his own balls, and that's a fact. I'd be lost without him. He's got a mind like a steel trap, that one. Knows every crazy turn down here."

The truth of the matter is easily inferred: It will take some doing for us to leave on our own, when we're eventually allowed to do so.

My stomach sinks.

The caves. If any of our brothers or sisters survived the attack and are still clinging to life, how will we reach them in time? And what about Daiyna? Is she all right? The spirits told her we had nothing to fear on this journey, but now that I cannot feel their presence, does it mean they no longer go with us? Have we been abandoned to our fate?

Regardless, we've achieved our primary objective, as unlikely as that seems at the moment. We have succeeded in finding a vehicle that can take us back to the caves.

We're in it.

"Procreation," Willard muses. "How's that for a life purpose? Be fruitful and multiply. Get busy! Am I right?" He punches me in the arm lightly, but there's no mirth in his eyes. "How's it feel to be alive just because of your genes? Isn't that how you all were selected? The best and brightest?"

I think back to the rigorous tests we underwent, locked in those rooms with computers and no windows. "It wasn't our choice. Many of us were taken against our will."

Willard dismisses the fact with a wave of his hand. "What I'm getting at is how most of us were selected because of our skill sets. Abilities that would be necessary, y'know, in a brave new world. They knew we'd have to rebuild from ashes, pretty much. But you folks, you have nothing to do with any of that. Know what I mean? It didn't matter what skills or education you had. God made you the way you are, and because of that, you were chosen. All because of your *genes*."

Once again, I feel the need to change the subject. "Have you met any other—?"

"You'd be the first!" Another grin pulls his face taut. "Besides the mutos, you're the only other survivors we've met since All-Clear. So you'll be putting our hospitality to its very first test!"

Samson starts to reply, but he thinks better of it and remains silent. I assume he was about to comment on the hospitality shown to us thus far.

"There was no one else here when you entered the city?"

Willard shakes his head, staring out through the windshield now. I wait for him to elaborate, but he doesn't.

"And...how many of you are there?" I watch him. He seems mesmerized by the white-washed concrete whipping by on all sides.

His eyes twitch to meet mine. "You'll see. You're outnumbered, don't forget that." He winks, then drops his gaze. "What happened to your gloves?"

I look down at my hands. I should have kept my fists clenched.

"Been doing some climbing, huh?"

I wiggle my fingers, each tip visible through the holes my claws made months ago. "In the caves—"

He reaches forward and grabs my wrist, pulling it closer. "Are these blood stains?"

"Yes." I nod and hold my breath.

He stares at me, eye to eye. Then he glances back at my gloved hand. "I'll get you a new pair." He shakes his head and chuckles as he releases my wrist. "Luther, you folks are entering the land of plenty!"

As if on cue, the tunnel ends, opening into an enormous subterranean dome lit as bright as day. Willard counts off the dimensions for us: fifty meters high, half a kilometer in diameter, more than five stories below ground. Steel structures elevated on solid supports around the perimeter are living quarters; they look like apartments. I lean forward to gaze up at the high arched ceiling and the lights mounted at intervals, evenly spaced. Everything here is so clean and new. It's as if we've entered another world.

"Jamison, get the windows," Willard tells the driver, who hits a pad on his console. Instantly the dark-tinted windows slide down. Willard removes his mask and takes a deep breath. "Nothing quite like purified air. Better than nature intended, and that's a fact." He sighs. "Oh yeah. Delicious."

I inhale, hesitantly at first, then deeply. He's right. The air is...*pure*. As fresh as it was at the lake house when I was a boy. Perhaps even fresher.

"How?" is all I can manage.

Willard chuckles heartily. "All in good time, buddy. For now, you just enjoy it."

What's in the air we've been breathing outside? I shudder to think. The contrast is tangible.

Samson reaches across Shechara to nudge me. "Look." He points off to our right as we drive past a transport vehicle lifting stacks of provisions on pallets, wrapped in plastic. "Is that food? Real food?"

Willard eyes him with an upraised eyebrow. "What do you mean by *real*? If you're referring to a good meal instead of a flavorless protein pack, then yes indeed, we have real food. We also have running water. And electricity, obviously." He gestures toward the lights and smiles broadly at our expressions. "I told you, folks. It's paradise!"

Unable to respond appropriately, I turn back to stare out the window at my side. There's so much movement in this place; every corner is alive with activity. Willard wasn't exaggerating: we are definitely outnumbered. I count at least fifty men moving about, conferring with one another, driving small electric vehicles carrying pallets of supplies, working with tools on large machines. Everyone wears the same blue camouflage uniforms, and everyone keeps busy. It reminds me of a bee hive made of concrete and steel, filled with soldiers. When we entered the city ruins above, I never could have imagined a place like this existed beneath its surface.

"Right here's good, Jamison." As the driver slows to a stop and exits the vehicle, Willard nudges my shoulder and points above us at one of the apartments. "Home sweet home."

"That's where you live?" I crane my neck to look up. The structure is suspended by steel supports from the side of the dome, seven or eight meters in the air. A ladder leads from the floor beside us to a wide catwalk above.

"Nope. It's where *you* get to live. Eden's guest quarters." He slaps me on the back with a chuckle. "Let's go!"

Samson fixes me with a wary look. Shechara bites her lip briefly as she stares outside. They wait for me to make the first move.

"Very well." I step out of the vehicle as the door automatically swings open. The driver stands with his short-barreled rifle across his chest. He doesn't bear the hardened demeanor of a soldier. He seems ill at ease.

"This way, folks." Willard gestures to the ladder and starts climbing up, leading the way with a quick familiarity.

Samson glances at me and follows, pulling himself up easily. Shechara is next, and I follow. Two soldiers bring up the rear with assault rifles slung across their backs. Despite Willard's congeniality, the inescapable reality is we're their prisoners. They found us in their city. What they do with us next is anyone's guess.

Captain Willard waits for us to reach him on the catwalk before he takes a ring of keys from his pocket and unlocks the solid steel door, sliding it aside.

"Welcome, welcome," he sings, beckoning us to enter. "Hot showers await!"

Samson stares him down at the doorway before taking a look inside. Shechara peers around his formidable frame. Her jaw drops slightly.

"Like what you see?" Willard winks at her. A familiar tic by this point. "Go on in."

"Do we have a choice?" Samson rumbles, his boots rooted to the catwalk.

Willard's smile drops from his face.

"A hot shower sounds fine to me," I attempt to diffuse the situation, squeezing past my brother as I step into the unit. I make it to the middle of the room before I stop, unable to believe that what I'm seeing is real.

There are two large, chocolate-colored couches with plush pillows and thick, rust-toned carpet. There's a fireplace with flames flickering within a stone hearth. Recessed lighting glows from the ceiling, illuminating artwork circa two decades ago hanging framed on earth-toned walls. To the left is a bar and a small kitchen; to the right is a short hallway with doors to other rooms and other wonders. Straight ahead, beyond the hallway, is a bathroom.

A hand grips my shoulder, and I turn to see Willard's gaunt grin. "What do you say?"

I don't know what to say. "It's...wonderful. How—?"

"Q and A time's later. For now, you just get settled in. Take a shower. Take two! No offense, but judging by the smell, you folks decided on going back to nature months ago." He beckons impatiently to Samson and Shechara who remain on the catwalk outside. "C'mon, you two. Look at what you're missing!" He chuckles benignly. "Get in here already!"

Samson turns to glare at the two soldiers behind him. Did they just try to crowd him? Not a wise choice. He looks down at Shechara and raises an eyebrow. She nods reluctantly, and they move to join me.

"Good, good. This way." Willard leads us down the hallway and points out the two adjoining rooms. "Two bedrooms, closets with clean clothes. Make use of anything you find." He turns toward the bathroom. "Just one shower, so try not to fight over it. Though I'm sure you could double up." He winks at Shechara and chuckles again.

Samson clenches his fists. Shechara avoids Willard's gaze.

"Thank you. We look forward to—" I begin.

"Make yourselves at home, and I'll be back in an hour or so to check up on you." Willard clasps his hands behind his back and ducks his chin, heading toward the front door with quick, long strides. "Carry on!" he barks like a military commander.

Before we have time to register what's happening, he steps outside and his men heave the steel door shut with a solid thud. A heavy bolt slides into place, locking us in.

Samson curses.

"This isn't good," Shechara says.

I nod, scanning our surroundings. Are there cameras in here, as there were in the garage above us? "We must be careful."

"What kind of freak show is this?" Samson bellows, unable to contain himself any longer. "A *fireplace*? What the hell?"

It's an interesting point for him to focus on, but I know what he means. After struggling to survive for the past months, the extravagance of this place—these comforts from a past life—are now so alien to us. What's their purpose? I find it difficult to believe every unit in this dome would be so luxurious. But what if this is the case? Is this underground community truly paradise?

Running water...

Without a word, I go to the sink in the bathroom—and I'm immediately startled by the face in the mirror. Clear blue eyes stare back at me, familiar but for their haunted look. My skin's creased, dark with grime. My beard's scraggly and grey along the sides of my jaw, matching the temples where long, unkempt hair is pushed back from my furrowed brow. I lean forward and turn to get a closer look at my ear, the one bitten by that daemon. It's healing well enough, thanks to Plato's quick work with the salve.

The cold water handle creaks as I turn it. A sound from another life. Water rushes out, streaming into the sink, swirling down the drain. Such a beautiful sound.

But I shut it off. I shouldn't waste it.

"What're you doing?" Samson fills the doorframe, ducking his head as he enters. "We've got to get out of here!"

I look at him, but I don't really see him. "They have water." I turn the handle on, then off, catching the cool stream in the palm of my hand, splashing it in the basin. I stare at the shower's frosted glass door.

"They've got it made, I'll give them that. But something isn't right here, Luther. Everything... It's messed up somehow. I can feel it."

"There are no women."

He turns sharply to find Shechara behind him. "What's that, Small Fry?"

"I saw them. All of Willard's people, as we drove in. There are only men." She bites her lip. Then she holds up a woman's floral dress on a hanger. "But I found this in the closet."

Samson curses again. "What did I say? Messed up!" He reaches for his belt beneath the folds of his outer garment and pulls out a handgun, dwarfed in his paw. "When that scrawny captain comes back, we make a run for it."

"Where did you get that?"

"One of those daemons we shot." He holds it up with a shrug. "Captain Freakshow didn't ask for it, so—"

"You've had it all this time?" I marvel at his restraint.

"Just waiting for the opportune moment." He gestures at my hands. "Not like you're completely unarmed."

My eyes flash a warning. These walls may have ears. If so, then Willard will already know about the gun when he returns. Samson wasn't thinking clearly. I point to my ear, then to the walls and ceiling. He scowls at me, then registers what I mean and hastily stuffs the weapon back into his belt.

Shechara returns the dress to the closet, leaving the door open to expose racks of women's clothing. Very odd...assuming there are only men in this dome. Were there women here at one time? Do they work elsewhere, out of sight?

Samson pushes past me and pulls open the shower door. He jerks the handle to the side, and the water thunders into the drain. Glancing at me, he turns on the shower head.

"Don't waste it," I caution him. How have these people managed to create running water? I can't help but marvel at it, almost hypnotized by the sight and sound.

He nods and grabs my shoulder, pulling me close. "Get in."

Before I have a chance to react, he pushes me into the downpour and I sputter, blinking against the spray. He ducks his head inside and sticks his tongue out as the water clings to his beard.

"Tastes like the real stuff." He licks at his mouth.

I part my lips and let the water rush in. He's right. The hydropacks don't do it justice. This is the real thing. Drenched, I look down at my slick boots and the streams of muddy rivulets cascading from my soggy garments, rushing down the drain. I hear laughter, like music. Shechara leans against the doorframe, her hand over her mouth, her eyes sparkling. I've never heard her laugh before.

"Quite the sight?" I call out to her. She giggles, holding her stomach now. "All right, you've had your fun." I move to step out.

Samson shakes his head, dripping wet. "They can't hear us in here."

What's he talking about?

"If you're right, if they've got this place bugged, then the sound of the shower should interfere with whatever gizmos they've got hidden in the walls." He wipes at his eyes. "I'd join you in there, but I don't think there's enough room."

I rinse and spit to clear my mouth. "Allow me to state the obvious, then. They're not soldiers."

"They don't carry themselves or their weapons like UW troops. And they're not trade workers, either. This place is too...advanced."

"Engineers then, from Sector 30. Wouldn't that be a peculiar twist of fate? We planned to meet up with them on our way to the Preserve, and they find us first."

"Fate?" He frowns. "Maybe. But why bother playing soldier?"

I shrug, rubbing at my face beneath the stream of water. I

might as well put it to use. "Perhaps they found the weapons and uniforms when they first entered the city."

"Why set up this underground colony? Engineers should've been able to use what's left on the surface and turn those ruins back into a metropolis. That's what they do, right?"

"Willard mentioned they've had to contend with the daemons as we have. Perhaps that's what drove them below. The daemons have a way of interfering with our best-laid plans, it would seem." He grumbles knowingly, and I weigh my words before asking, "Do you believe them to be...gifted as we are?"

"I don't know. Doesn't seem like it."

If only Daiyna were here, she would know. If only the spirits would speak to me, as they do to her. If only I could sense their presence as I did on the surface.

"Until we know for certain, we continue to keep our abilities hidden. Agreed?"

Samson nods, glancing over his shoulder at Shechara. She nods her agreement. "So what now?" He reaches for his gun.

"I'm going to enjoy a hot shower." I start tugging off my waterlogged garments.

He backs away and shuts the shower door. "That's our cue, Small Fry. We don't want to see this." They leave with a thud of the bathroom door.

I drop my filthy clothing to the shower floor and nudge it aside. I let my boots fall on top of them. My skin's tender at first beneath the pelting streams of hot water, but after a minute or two, the sensation is incredible. I use the soap awkwardly, as if I'm recalling how to perform each step of a ritual from a past life. I move quickly so as not to waste any of this precious water, savoring every moment in its numbing warmth.

I could never have imagined this, not in a million years. How have these people achieved so much in the past months, while we've managed barely to survive?

I shut off the water and open the shower door. The room is filled with fog. Grabbing a thick white towel from the cupboard, I wipe at my face. The towel smells fresh, like it was washed recently. I wipe at the mirror. This time, the face looking back at me is almost familiar. The eyes are still haggard. When was the last time I slept through the night?

In a smaller cupboard beside the mirror, I find a straight razor and a bottle of shaving gel. I nod to my reflection. The beard must go.

I wrap the towel around my waist and begin the arduous task of removing thick bristles from my neck, my jaw line, and beneath my nose. With a minimum of spilled blood, I'm eventually successful, and when I look into the mirror this time—despite the pieces of tissue attached here and there to sop oozing cuts—the face I see looks more or less like the man I remember. He's a good ten years younger than that hermit who greeted me earlier.

As the steam dissipates, I glance at my torso's reflection before I leave the room. All of the muscles are where I left them. They may be necessary, should we have to fight our way out of here.

I open the door and head down the hallway, keeping a firm grasp on the towel around me. Perhaps there's a closet full of men's clothing near the women's dresses. That was odd. I can only hope Willard gives us a straight answer when he returns.

"Try the next one down."

I turn to find Shechara standing behind me, her head tilted to one side as she looks at my face.

"The next one?" I hold my towel with both hands. "Here?"

She nods. "There are two closets full of men's clothing." She starts to smile. "You shaved."

I'm sure she's noticed my battle scars. "I had a fight with a razor. It was a close shave, but I believe I was victorious." I throw open the closet door she referred to and step behind it, out of view. The racks hold men's shirts and pants, just as she said. No fluid-recycling jumpsuits to be found among them.

The bathroom door shuts quietly, and I glance back to find

she's disappeared. Perhaps she too has decided to take advantage of the shower. Samson might want to consider following suit if he plans on ever wooing the wives of his dreams.

I pull down a pair of folded boxers and a pair of coarse blue pants—*jeans*, they were called—as well as a white button-down shirt. I leave the socks on the shelf. I like the way the thick carpet feels between my toes.

"All squeaky clean?" Samson smirks, sprawled out across one of the couches in the front room.

"Highly recommended." Buttoning up the front of the long-sleeved shirt, I take a seat on the couch adjacent to his.

"You find those duds here?"

I raise an eyebrow at his obvious question.

He nods and grunts something, rubbing between his eyes. "Right. You know, I forgot guys used to dress like that. It's been so long." He fails to stifle an enormous yawn. "What time do you think it is?"

"After nightfall, I'd assume." I look around the room.

"No clocks in here. I checked." He sighs, shaking his head. "Weird, huh? It's like we're back in the old days, when we were kids. And this is what house arrest felt like."

I give him a cautionary look. We should refrain from saying anything that could be construed as negative for the time being, in case we're being monitored.

"The running water..." I trail off as the sounds of Shechara's shower fill the moment—splashes, bare feet thumping on the shower floor. "I don't know how they've done it."

Samson listens, but I'm sure his mind is occupied by the usual. There is, after all, a naked woman only a few doors down from him. "They must've found some protected groundwater or something. Started purifying and recycling it, maybe." He glances toward the bathroom. "You think she's all right in there? I'd hate for her to slip and fall. Maybe I should—" He moves to rise.

"Steady." I shake my head. "She's fine. You, on the other hand..."

He scowls and falls back onto the couch. "What's that supposed to mean?"

I maintain a straight face. "Let's just say it might serve you well to take a look in the mirror at some point. If you plan on ever charming that wife of yours."

"*Wives*," he corrects me.

"If you plan on winning their affections anytime soon, you might want to make sure you still recognize the face in the mirror. Take my word for it."

A broad smile creeps across his face. "Scared yourself in there, did you?"

"Perhaps."

He throws back his head and laughs heartily.

Laughter. Running water. Couches and carpet. A fire in the fireplace—gas, no doubt, but amazing to see, just the same. In stark contrast is the steel door, locked from the outside. No windows. It's as Samson said: we've been arrested. But we're in a very comfortable cell block.

Where is Daiyna? Milton? Have they been captured as well? Are they in another one of these luxurious apartments? Or did they manage to escape in time, before Willard's soldiers went on the hunt?

According to Willard, Milton had her by the throat. What was going on there? Was he trying to kill her? It had to be the spirit inside him, acting through him. I can't allow myself to speculate whether he was successful. But with his superhuman speed, no one could stop him.

"They've got books." Samson gestures at the rosewood cupboards along the far wall. "Hardbound, all kinds. Not the digital stuff we had in the bunker. The more *illegal* variety."

"We had everything," I remark absently. I read most of what the database had to offer, but it was far too extensive even for the most avid of readers to exhaust, given twenty years or a lifetime.

I step across the plush carpet toward the row of enclosed shelves mounted on the wall. The small door opens with a short creak. Instantly I'm met with the ancient aroma of print, paper, and glue. Yet there is nothing ancient about these books. Were they printed here, by these people who seem to have no end to their modern conveniences? Or were they printed before, decades ago, by trade workers in blatant defiance of the UW mandate?

"Well?" Samson yawns again. This place is putting him to sleep. "See anything you like?"

All of the bindings are similar, a forest of green leather with titles embossed in gold. One stands out: *A Holy Bible*. My breath catches as I reach for it. How long has it been since I've held the word of God in my hands? My fingers tremble as I slide it out from the books on either side. I cradle it in my palms, letting it fall open. But it does so reluctantly. The binding creaks and the pages remain in clumps. No one has opened this book before.

"They're new." Reverently, I tuck the Bible under my arm and reach for a random title. *Robinson Crusoe*. It's in the same pristine condition. So is *Great Expectations* and *Les Miserables* and *War and Peace*. "They've never been read."

Samson grunts and scratches his belly. "Weird, huh? I don't think anybody's ever lived in this place." He winks at me and raises his voice. "You sure don't get this kind of hospitality everywhere you go!"

Anywhere would be more like it, but his comment was meant for anyone listening in. There is no hospitality on this planet, not anymore. There are no comforts outside this strange place. Unless I am mistaken, and this is merely one of many subterranean returns to normalcy. How long have they lived like this, while we've fought for our lives on the surface?

Was it a mistake to leave the bunker when we did? Perhaps we too would have found some sort of tunnel to this place or another like it if we'd only looked. If I hadn't been so determined for us to make a new life for ourselves outside.

Defeat overwhelms me as I think of the lives lost since All-Clear. Could we have avoided all that suffering?

"They've really rolled out the red carpet, that's for sure."

Samson rubs between his eyes again and blinks. He looks as though he's fighting a losing battle against the weariness overtaking him. "But I hope they can answer the hundred or so questions I've got for them. Because right now, no matter how I look at it, I can't get much of this to add up."

"Our gracious host will return soon." I wish we could speak freely. I have a feeling Captain Willard is far from the gracious type.

"Find a good one?" He leans over to take a look at the Bible in my hands, but his interest fades. "Oh."

"Not one of your favorites?" I turn to the middle, having always found solace in reading the Psalms of King David. Samson, on the other hand, has always found strength in himself —despite the irony of the name we bestowed on him years ago. For the Samson of the Bible, strength came only from Jehovah.

"Not much of a reader," he admits. "Unless I'm into the topic. Sex, weapons, warfare, you know. The usual."

"You might be surprised by what you find in here." I almost smile. "Have you ever heard of King Solomon?"

"Maybe. Why?"

"He had hundreds of wives."

Samson blinks at me, his face expressionless. "How did he manage to...?" He shakes his head. "Wow. What chapter is he in?"

The shower shuts off. We both look up, then glance at each other. In his eyes, I can tell what he's thinking. "Have a sudden urge to visit the bathroom?" I know him too well.

"No." He gestures to the Bible. "Where's this Solomon guy?"

"But you were thinking about it."

"What?" He looks up, catches my gaze, and quickly averts his eyes.

"You were imagining her naked."

"Was not." He points at the Bible again. "Show me."

"Don't try to change the topic."

The lobes of his ears start to flush. "Are you going to show me or not?"

"When you admit it."

The bathroom door opens, and Shechara emerges wearing clothing from the hall closet. Unlike me, she thought ahead, bringing a pair of jeans and a cream turtleneck sweater with her. She too is barefoot as she steps lightly across the carpet to join us.

"All washed up?" Samson manages, jumping to his feet and not seeming to know what to do with his hands. Or his eyes.

Shechara's figure—normally hidden by her loose garments—is shapely in the form-fitting attire. Her scalp shows a day's growth. She must have decided not to shave it. My mind wanders, imagining her with a full head of dark, thick hair.

Daiyna's face flashes through my mind.

"Your turn." Shechara looks up at him, her tone congenial but with enough of an edge to achieve the desired result.

"Right." With a short nod and his eyes focused on nothing in particular, Samson drops his head and stomps toward the bathroom like he's marching to war.

Before he can reach his cold shower, the bolt on the front door slides open. I clench my fists quickly as my talons flex outward, piercing the palms of my hands and drawing blood. I grit my teeth and will them back where they belong. Staring at the steel door as it's shoved aside, I force a pleasant expression.

"Settling in, I trust?" Captain Willard strides toward us with three of his armed soldiers and a familiar grin stretching his face. His eyes wander to Shechara and linger, roving slowly across her curves. "Forgive me for barging in like this, but the situation calls for it. Your friends are here."

Daiyna and Milton? "You've found them?" I step forward, my pulse racing.

Willard chuckles and shakes his head. "Not exactly." He pauses as a loud commotion echoes outside in the dome—tires squealing, orders barked over loudspeakers, boots pounding to and fro. "It's the mutos. They're back. All of 'em." He turns to wink up at Samson. "You'll be needing that gun in your belt."

PART IV
ORIGIN

9. WILLARD

SIX WEEKS AFTER ALL-CLEAR

We have to kill them. Every last one. It's the humane thing to do. Something's in the ash out there, and it's messed with them—altered their genetic makeup somehow. It's so bizarre, I can't really wrap my head around it, but it's happening. That I'm sure of. We've got to do something before it's too late.

And we've got to get the hell out of here.

We've managed to extend life support since All-Clear these past few weeks, but we're engineers, not miracle workers. It won't last. We'll have to go outside eventually...but not here. Dust and ash as far as the eye can see, like a desert wasteland from a Dali painting. There has to be another way out, somewhere, kilometers from here, and we've got to find it.

I blow out a sigh, and it hisses loud against my O2 mask. I'm stressing again, losing my cool. Just one step at a time—that's the mantra. I've got to take it easy, keep a level head here. Can't change a thing by worrying, and that's a fact.

Tucker joins me at the bunker's exterior door. He's got his mask on and the same government-issued jumpsuits we're all wearing now. I hope it's enough to keep out the ash if there's another freak sandstorm on the horizon. Fortunately, the door mechanisms still function, thanks to our tender loving care. Any swirling dust devils amble our way, and we shut it. I don't care who's still out there.

"Any sight of 'em?" He leans against the thick steel door frame and gazes out across the barren plain before us, a sickly grey in the fading light.

I shake my head and curse. "They take much longer, they'll be running on reserve power." I gesture toward the sinking sun. "We'll give 'em half an hour, then lock up for the night."

"I could go after them." They took a jeep, but we still have one down below. "They went south this time." Tucker nods. "I could track 'em easy enough."

"It was her idea to go. She can find her own way back."

"I'm sure she will."

Silence. Everything is so quiet out there, so dead. If we could make it work, I wouldn't mind spending a few more decades in the bunker. It has all we've needed for twenty years now: food, water, entertainment. Plenty to keep us busy. Unlike those poor bastards in Sector 51, we weren't segregated by sex. Sure, they sterilized us for obvious reasons—a limited food supply doesn't allow for babes in arms—but that didn't interfere with our coital recreation. It kept us busy, inspired us like nothing else. Some of my best ideas always came after a good orgy.

But that was before.

It's been twelve days since I first noticed the change in them. I've been counting. And I'm not letting a single one of them near me ever again.

"You think they found anybody?" Tucker sounds hopeful.

Survivors. Would they be ash freaks, too? Or did they have the presence of mind not to come into contact with the stuff? "Going by the maps those government geeks left us, there should be bunkers to the southwest, but who knows? Nothing looks right out there. You'd think there would be ruins, some sign this used to be a major city. But after two decades, the desert has reclaimed everything that used to be ours."

"She said they found an InterSector coming from the east.

Mounds of sand covering what's left of all the vehicles, frozen like statues. Maybe some things are still there. All we need to do is find 'em and make 'em right again."

"Silk purses from sows' ears, eh?" I give him a half-hearted grin.

He laughs and nods. He's right, though. It's what we do. We have all the tools, materials, manpower, and know-how. But I don't have a mind to.

It isn't safe on the surface. We have to stay underground. It's the only way we'll survive.

"We can't assume the other sectors made it. So far, there's no proof we aren't the only ones left."

Tucker sniffs. "I can wait for 'em, if you want to go below."

Will she be wearing her O2 mask? Probably not. The others will follow her example, sucking down all that particulate matter in the air, letting it infest their lungs.

"It's all right." I cross my arms and widen my stance. "I'm as eager as you to hear what they've found. Must be something. She doesn't usually cut it this close."

The sun sinks into the west as a rippling crimson orb. I take a deep breath, feel the brief chill in my lungs. I hate wearing this mask. Give me a room full of filtered air over this any day. But anything is better than the alternative. I can imagine the dust particles from the infected ash and sand out there finding their way into my respiratory system, taking root, changing my DNA, mutating me into something unnatural.

Like she is. Like the others are. Bastardized children of God.

We should shut the bunker door and seal it, once and for all. There has to be another way out. The UW geeks would have planned for every contingency. They had no way of knowing that two decades, on-the-dot, would be enough time for the nuclear winters to end and all that ash to dissipate, for the atmosphere to replenish itself. Our rations and our air weren't intended to last forever. The geeks must have designed an alternate exit somewhere in the bunker below, some kind of underground passageway. We just haven't looked hard enough for it.

We're not rats in a maze with only one route to the cheese. And once we've found our emergency exit, we'll go as far away as it takes us—hundreds, thousands of kilometers away from this alien world and its mutant dust.

"Maybe they got caught in a storm or something," Tucker offers with a shrug. "Like that other time."

I clench my teeth and attempt a smile, acknowledging his remark.

That other time. Two weeks ago. She came back from scouting with three of the other women. The jeep was caked in dust so thick the vehicle didn't even look like one of ours anymore. They were covered in it, too. Every centimeter of their jumpsuits, their O2 masks, their gloves, their boots—the stuff clung to them like paste. She said a sandstorm had come out of nowhere as they were driving back to the bunker. The dust engulfed them, and despite cowering in their seats and covering their heads, the stuff had managed to get into everything, even through the impenetrable polymer of their masks.

That's when I knew something wasn't right. Wasn't natural.

"There they are." Tucker points, moving to step outside.

"Wait."

He halts, glancing back at me with a frown behind his clear face shield. I squint into the weak light. The jeep should be sending up a plume of dust behind it, enough to turn us all into mutants. What did Tucker see?

"There." He points again.

I see them. Four small shadowy figures heading toward us. On foot.

"Where's the jeep?" I curse. If she's left it behind, there will be hell to pay.

"Must've run out of juice."

"The sun just went down." I shake my head. "They would've had reserve power."

He steps outside, the sole of his boot landing with a puff of dust.

"Get back in here, Tucker."

He glances over his shoulder at me. "They might need some help."

Clenched fists tremble at my sides as fury boils in my belly. "Get in here," I grate out.

He hesitates, and for a moment it looks like he's going to try his luck with me. But then he drops his head a little and steps back across the steel threshold. Dust sticks to his boot like fungus.

"You'll need to clean that off." Just the sight of it turns my stomach.

What was he thinking? What's gotten into him lately? Maybe he's gotten into her, and she's turning him into one of *them*.

I'll have to keep an eye on him. Might need to put him down for his own good.

The shadow-figures enlarge, taking shape as they approach, their waving locks of hair caught in the cool breeze. Their O2 masks are off, swung down at their sides with every sauntered step. She knows I'm watching. She's rubbing my nose in their blatant insubordination.

I curse under my breath. How much has she inhaled by now?

"What's that?" Tucker turns toward me as if I said something.

"Get the hose. Take care of your boot first."

He nods, heading down the corridor to the elevator like a good lap dog. He'd better stay that way if he knows what's good for him.

"Well look here, ladies. Willard's come up to welcome us back. How sweet!"

She struts toward me like the leader of a wolf pack. The other three chuckle, their faces cracking with the dust covering their skin.

"Where's the jeep?" My jaw muscle twitches.

"What's that?" She cups her ear. "I can't quite hear you with that stupid mask on. You know there's O2 out here, right?" More cackling from the others.

"The jeep. Where is it?"

They approach within a few meters and stop. Only then do I notice the wet splatters across their jumpsuits.

"Let's see. How do I put this?" She bites her cheek, hand on her hip. "We ran into a little trouble, you might say."

"Not much," adds one of the others. They all laugh.

I don't have time for this crap. "If you've damaged it, you'll pay with your rations."

"You hear that, girls? Willard's gonna put us all on a diet." She turns and pushes out her posterior. "You think I'm *fat*, Willard?"

I grit my teeth and wait. After she's had her fun, she'll tell me. I have to be patient—and not react.

She moves toward me, her hips exaggerated in their movement. "You never used to complain about my *fat*." She gropes herself suggestively. "We always had a lot of fun, you and me. Isn't that right? A *lot* of fun." She winks suggestively.

"Don't come any closer." I swallow. She's covered in dust, and it doesn't seem to bother her one bit. But what's this other stuff splattered all over her? "Tucker's bringing the hose."

I yell over my shoulder to hurry him up.

She snickers. "Paranoid as ever."

"What's that on you?" If only there was more light. It looks like—

"Yeah. About that." She takes a deep breath, sober now. "We're not alone, Willard."

What the hell does that mean?

"Got the hose," Tucker mutters, trudging up the narrow hallway from the elevator.

"Let 'em have it." I gesture toward the women, and they brace themselves.

Tucker grimaces, twisting the valve at the end. The hose bucks in his hands as the air blasts outward, but he's got it under control. With a short warning, he turns it on the women.

Water would be more ideal, obviously, but this is the best we can do for now. They'll need to scrub their skin down with a few hydropacks before we let them inside. And we'll need to wash out the suits. Tucker can't do anything about the stains, so I send him below after he's done with his part.

"You know the drill," I tell her. Now they have to strip down.

"Gonna watch?"

The thought of it repulses me.

"What's come over you lately, Willard?" She frowns as she pulls the zipper down her torso. "Used to be you couldn't keep your hands off me."

"Is that blood?"

She stops and looks at her suit. "We-uh might've run into some...creatures."

"Animals?" I didn't think there were any left.

She shakes her head, shrugging out of the upper portion of her jumpsuit. Her bare skin is flecked with dust.

The suits are a useless defense against it. I will never set foot outside.

"Not animals." She gives me a direct look.

"What then?" My mouth is dry. "Mutants?" I scoff.

Survivors from another sector? Infected by the dust as she is, but changed to a greater extent? *Creatures?*

"I wouldn't know. But they came out of nowhere—a dozen or more. Armed to the teeth." She drops the suit to her ankles and pulls her legs free, one at a time. "Guns, believe it or not, and plenty of them. They wanted the jeep, and they took it."

I toss her a limp hydropack and lob three more at the others. They tear them open and begin to wash themselves, pouring the synthetic water across their bare skin and rubbing the stuff around.

"You let them take it." I can't believe I'm hearing this.

"We were otherwise occupied." She closes her eyes as she cleans her face. "Managed to kill half of them, but the other ones piled into the jeep and took off."

"Kill them? How?" Did she manage to wrestle away their guns?

"Funny thing, Willard. It didn't really matter that we were unarmed. Those creatures were too slow for us. I don't know what it is exactly, but this planet isn't the same Earth we used to know and love. We feel different out here now. Can't really describe it." She chuckles, cracking one eye open. "We killed them with our bare hands."

Wonderful. They've tasted blood. Now it's only a matter of time before they turn on us.

"But I almost forgot. We brought you back some souvenirs, just in case those creatures decide to head this way, and you need to defend the homestead." She turns to the other women. "Ladies."

They reach into the pockets of their crumpled jumpsuits and retrieve a small arsenal of handguns and knives. I can only stare.

"Picked 'em off the ones we put down. Military-issue, by the looks of it." She points out the insignia on the grip of one of the guns. "Genuine United World merchandise. Only the best for our Willard."

She moves to hand me the booty, and the others follow her.

"No." They're not clean yet. "Toss them to me."

"Whatever, Mr. OCD." She lobs the gun at my feet and gestures for the others do the same. The weapons clatter across the concrete on my side of the threshold. "You're really gonna have to get over yourself if you want to go into town with us."

I shoot her a glance as I bend down to retrieve one of the four guns—a semi-automatic. I check the clip. Five rounds left. "Town?"

She grins, obviously pleased with herself. She pours some of the hydropack fluid across her chest and rubs it around. "We hit the jackpot. A trade sector city—what's left of it, anyway. Fifty kilometers southwest. It's got everything we'll ever need to start over, just sitting there. All we've got to do is ride in and take it."

I turn the gun over, weighing it in my hand. Twenty long years since I've held one of these. It feels good. Familiar. I squeeze the grip.

"And the creatures? They won't be a problem for us?" I don't look up.

"Not for us," one of the women remarks, and they all chuckle.

"Of course. You can kill them with your bare hands. How could I forget that?"

My tone isn't lost on her. She stops scrubbing herself. "I thought you'd be happy, Willard. It's what we've been looking for."

"Oh I'm sure it is. You can make a wonderful life for yourselves and your mutant friends out there." I slide a round into the chamber and let the bolt snap back with a clink.

"We can't live in the bunker indefinitely, Willard. The O2 won't last, no matter how much you fiddle around with it. We're just prolonging the inevitable."

She's right. I am. I have been for far too long.

I bring up the gun and pull the trigger in a single movement. The round burrows between her startled eyes with a crimson patch of blood. She goes back like a felled tree.

I've forgotten how loud a gunshot can be. But the smell—absolutely delicious.

The other women don't take long to get over their shock. Their movements are impressively quick and catlike as they spring at me, launching themselves through the air with fingernails extended like claws and teeth like fangs, bared in a wild-eyed rage. Somehow, they've taken the form of savage panther-creatures.

Good thing I've been expecting this—not exactly, but something equally bizarre—or I'd be freezing up right now. I've known all along something hasn't been right with them. This display confirms it.

They're mutant freaks.

I drop one of them with two shots to the chest, and she falls against the other two. That slows them down long enough for me to hit the door release lever and back away. They clamber over her dead body, lunging inside as the steel door slides shut. I stumble backwards, firing the last two rounds as the women cross the threshold. The bullets hit their mark, downing the first one who falls in the path of the bone-crushing door. But the last one leaps over her as the steel door seals itself shut and locks automatically, trapping us inside the hallway together.

She stalks me on all fours, grinning. She knows I'm empty.

I point the gun at her anyway. "Stay back!"

She laughs. "You should've taken one with more ammo, Willard." The other guns and knives lie behind her at the threshold, near the bloody splintered remains of her friend. "You want to come back and pick out another?"

I keep the muzzle aimed at her head. I didn't plan this very well. I didn't plan it at all, really. I can admit that. It just happened. And now I'm stuck.

I back away slowly, down the corridor toward the elevator. She matches me step for step like an alley cat toying with its prey.

"What're you gonna do, Willard?"

My mask is fogging up. I rip it off and throw it aside. "I told you to stay back!"

"Or what? You'll throw that gun at me?"

Time for a new strategy.

"Fine." I drop the gun and raise both hands. "You've got me. Now what? You kill me in cold blood? Like those *creatures* that attacked you? Can you do that?" I'm gasping, panting. I've got to calm down. "I'm not like them. I'm a child of God. Unarmed, defenseless. Can you really kill me like this?"

"We'll see." She snickers, fangs gleaming, slick in the jittery fluorescent lights above the elevator doors.

"Could you live with yourself? You're an engineer, for crying out loud—not a killer! You're a daughter of God. Think about this, just think! Is this really who you are? Look at yourself! You're naked, crawling around like an animal with...claws and fangs! What's *happened* to you?"

She slows half a step, confusion clouding her eyes. "You shot them..." she trails off.

"They weren't right. There was something wrong with them. I could tell. But not you—you're different. Why do you think I didn't shoot you first? You don't want to do this. You don't want to kill me."

She scowls, looking down at the concrete floor. "But you *killed* them."

My rear end bumps into the elevator doors. I hit the DOWN pad, my hand fumbling spastically, my heart racing. I have to keep talking, keep her listening.

"You don't have to be like this. You didn't ask to be this way, did you? Of course not. Those three back there, there was no hope for them. But you'll be fine. We can make you better. You'll be yourself again in no time."

My words are having an effect on her. She's glancing down at the claws protruding from her fingers and toes. I've got to keep adding to her confusion, keep her distracted.

"You want that, don't you? To be yourself again? You weren't created like this, not by God. It's the ash out there that did this to you, that demon-dust. The earth's not the way we left it. They did something to it, something bad, when they nuked the hell out of it, and it's infected you. But we can make you the person you used to be."

Am I getting through to her? Is she faltering?

Her head snaps up, eyes locked on me. "I like myself this way."

With a shriek and a growl, she lunges at me. I cower, shielding myself. Her claws rake across my forearms as she descends on me in a vengeful frenzy. I fall back against the elevator doors, my head colliding with them repeatedly as I fend off her wild blows. Her fangs flash. She's going to sink them into my jugular. It's only a matter of time.

I can't fight her off much longer. She's too strong.

What'll happen to all the others below? Dozens and dozens of them with no idea what's going on up here... Will she kill them too, one by one? Or will she turn them all into mutant freaks, biting them like a vampire?

Will she turn me into one?

The doors slide open without warning, and I fall inside with her on top of me, her jaws snapping at my face.

"Willard? What the—!" Tucker gasps.

"Guns! Get the guns!" I scream.

"Guns? We don't have—"

"The bunker door—GO!"

She jerks her head up to hiss a warning, and he leaps backward, trembling and wide-eyed.

"What the hell!" he yelps.

I throw my elbow into her face, smashing her nose. The blow stuns her for a moment, long enough for me to wave Tucker in the right direction, for him to squeeze past us. He takes off as fast as he can for the bunker door, his boots pounding up the corridor.

All too soon, she regains her composure. She looks down at me with blood oozing from her nostrils and laughs. She's enjoying this—the thrill of the hunt. Will she kill me now or go after Tucker, save me for later?

"You're pathetic." She spits into my face. Then she pulls me up by the throat for a brutal head butt.

I fall to the elevator floor with a dagger of pain slicing through my forehead. Everything goes black for a second, then flashes white. Her shadow whips away and wild laughter echoes after her.

She's going for Tucker. She'll dispatch him quickly, and then she'll be back for me...and the others.

I have to get up. No. I have to get down. The DOWN arrow. But everything's black again, and I'm so exhausted...

I have to warn the others below. The DOWN arrow. Where is it?

The sound of a gunshot explodes, echoing all around me, followed by another and another. Surging adrenaline sends me to my feet. I hit the pad on the wall, and the elevator doors slide shut slowly but securely. My lungs shudder as I struggle for a deep breath. I grip the handrail behind me, falling back against it.

They'll believe me now. They'll have to. We can't go out there. Not ever. We'll have to find another way out. We'll disable the elevator, seal the doors. Find another exit. Somewhere, far from here, where the demon-dust can't find us.

Seconds pass like minutes as I'm carried down the shaft. My forehead throbs, tender to the touch. My forearms ooze thick streaks of blood where her claws lacerated my flesh.

The elevator touches down, and the doors slide open. Sucking in a breath, I step across the threshold and into the security of our bunker. Our fortress. The last bastion of humanity, the way God intended us to be.

His Chosen People.

"Code red! Code red!" My voice comes out stronger than I would've thought possible. "Fall in!"

Heads turn and stare. Folks drop what they're doing and swarm me from all corners of the bunker, murmured voices mingled. I raise my arms high, and gasps echo at the sight of all that blood.

"Willard, what's happened?"

"What's going on, Willard?"

"Quiet down!" I clench my fists in the air. "Listen to me. We have to disable the elevator so what's up *there*—" I point. "Doesn't come down *here*."

"What do you mean?"

"What's up there?"

"Listen!" I keep one foot in the elevator to hold the doors open. "Somebody get me a toolkit—on the double."

Perch and one of the women scurry away to retrieve what I'll need to open the control panel and cut the hard lines. Then let that she-devil just try to come down here.

It would be nice to have those guns and knives. But no, not an option. Can't risk going topside ever again. This is the only way.

Perch is back. "Here you go, Willard." He holds up the toolkit, then tosses it to me over the heads of the throng.

I catch it with both hands. "Keep these doors open."

"Sure thing." Jamison shoves his full weight against the open door.

"What are you doing?" someone cries.

"That's the only way out! You can't!"

They press against Jamison, but he does his best to hold them back.

"Take your time, Boss," he grunts with a grimace.

I turn to the control panel and activate the toolkit. "Just a temporary solution, folks," I explain over my shoulder. "You don't want to go up against what I've seen." The cover plate is off. I drop it to the floor. "It's like nothing you could imagine."

"Some kind of animal up there?" Perch calls out from the back of the mob. They quiet down to hear my answer.

"Not exactly." The rhythmic vibration of the toolkit in my hand is familiar, soothing. I feel my pulse slow down as I activate the cutter and aim for the wiring behind the panel. "She used to be one of us. Before the ash got to her."

"There he goes again," one of the women mutters. Others scoff, mocking me. Some of the men join in, too.

"There were four of them." One of the lines snaps and hangs limp. Two more to go. "They attacked me as soon as they got back from scouting."

The scoffing dies out. Now it's only whispers and low tones.

"Sharon and the girls?" Jamison manages hoarsely. "They did that to you?"

The next line snaps. On to the third. "Don't say that name." I shake my head. "She hasn't been herself since the first time she stepped outside. None of 'em have."

"Where's Tucker?" Someone finally notices his absence.

"He didn't make it." The last line is cut. I shut off the toolkit and pocket it. I turn to face Jamison. "You can let go."

He lifts his hand and backs away a step. The doors don't

move. In this case, that's a good thing. The elevator is no longer an issue.

"So now what?" snaps one of the women. "We all die down here?"

Of course not, idiot. I choose to ignore her. She might have gone out on one of the scouting trips, now that I think of it. There could be demon-dust festering in her lungs. I'll need to keep a close eye on her.

"Let me through." Another woman pushes her way toward the elevator. She left the group earlier when Perch went for the toolkit. Her name's Margo. As far as I know, she hasn't been on the surface yet. But I could be wrong.

"Clear a path, folks." She's carrying a medkit.

She'll want to tend to my arms. Should I let her? Or should I shove my toolkit into her stomach and turn it on high? I've never thought of using it for that sort of thing before. I wonder what would happen. Probably make a nasty mess.

"Show's over, everybody." Perch attempts to disband the masses as he follows Margo. "Nothing here to see."

They don't seem to agree. And they don't seem very happy.

"So what do you expect us to do now, Willard? Go back to our chores?"

"I'm not leaving until Willard explains himself!"

"How long does he think we can survive down here?"

I hold up my arms again, and the uproar dies faster than it began. Unblinking eyes focus on the jagged claw marks and trails of blood.

"Listen up!" I shout so all ninety-odd of them can hear me. Margo waits nearby with the medkit, her dark eyes attentive. They're all watching me, expecting something. I can't say too much here. Some of them might be dormant ash freaks waiting to come into their own. "Folks, we can't go out on the surface."

"Tooting the same old horn, Willard!" shrills a woman's voice in back. Low murmurs of dissension follow.

"I'd say it's a little different now." Perch gestures at my arms.

"So shut up and listen, Catherine. All of you. Let's hear what he's got to say." He stares some of them down, his block jaw set. Then he turns to me. "Go on, Boss."

Has Catherine been outside? I should've taken those guns. Things got out of hand up there too fast. I was outnumbered, and they attacked me. The way it happened was the only way it could have. But what about Tucker?

I take note of the disdain here and there amongst the faces staring back at me. My mustache itches all of a sudden.

"I know we can't make it down here much longer. We've managed the impossible already. The fact that we're still breathing O2 is a miracle, and each one of you is to thank for that. We all play our parts for the greater good." I let those words sink in.

I'm not the bad guy here. I'm their savior—they just don't realize it yet. They're not enlightened, but I'll show them the way. They need to be calmed down, reassured first. Then they'll fall in line.

"Like I said before, things aren't right on the surface. There's no life out there, nothing. It's not the way they told us it would be. Those government scientists had no clue what would be waiting for us after All-Clear. They couldn't have known what would be in the air."

Hushed whispers travel from mouth to mouth.

"Sharon said it was fine," Catherine counters. "She's gone out there multiple times looking for—"

"She was reckless. She lost one of the jeeps, and she lost more than that." I nod my head slowly. They're hanging on my every word now. Even Catherine is listening, her big fish mouth hanging wide open. "Sharon lost her mind." I hold up my arms again as proof. "I did what I could to defend myself. She'd been changed—all four of them. They weren't...*human* anymore. They were savages."

Gasps echo.

Jamison stammers, "But how? What changed them? How'd it happen?"

I have my theories, and I'll tell him later, in private. I'll tell him how we need to isolate everyone who's been topside and monitor them for any behavior out of the ordinary. But for now, I play dumb.

"I don't know what caused it, but this much is clear: they've been out on the surface, scouting things for us since All-Clear. More than once, I've seen them return without their O2 masks on. So it's got to be something out there, in the air. It turned them into dangerous psychotics. And I sure as hell don't want that to happen to anybody else."

Margo clears her throat quietly. "And they're..." She looks upward.

"Who is it?" Catherine demands. "They have names, Willard. Don't talk about them like they're—"

"They're not who they were!" My outburst echoes loudly, and silence follows. "Get that through your head! It wasn't Sharon or Anna or Kelly or anyone you know. They stopped being human and turned into something else. Something unnatural." I swallow as an image of her gleaming, snapping fangs passes through my mind. "An *abomination*."

Catherine stares back at me, biting her lip. Is she afraid? No longer worried about her friends above us, now she's only concerned about herself, what she might become. I see it in her eyes. And I'm glad.

"So what do we do?" Margo asks. "After I clean up those wounds of yours." She steps closer, and my abdomen tightens. Because of her proximity?

The DOWN arrow on the elevator lights up with a sudden ding, followed by gasps all around me. It can mean only one thing.

"Who is it?" someone whispers.

"Somebody up top...wants down," another one states the obvious.

It could be her, the last one. She's finished off Tucker, and she wants more blood. Or it's Tucker. He took her out, and he's wondering where I am, why I left him. That wouldn't be good. He's supposed to be dead.

He didn't make it. That's what I told everybody. It would definitely make things awkward to have him join the land of the living again. I would lose my credibility.

Better for him, better for all of us, if he stays dead.

"Not to worry." I gesture at the disabled control panel. "There's no chance anyone can get down here."

"Or any of us can get topside," counters a fellow in the back named Mathis. "How long did you say we'd keep the elevator out of commission, Willard?"

I didn't say. And I don't like his tone. Has he been out on the surface too?

"Long as we need to. Long as we can." What we need are those guns. I could jury-rig the elevator one last time, take Perch and Jamison up with me. The bunker door was shut, but given time, she'll probably open it. She won't want to stay in that hallway forever. She'll leave the weapons, won't have any use for them. Not with her fangs and claws. "Eventually, she'll get tired of pushing that button." Another ding holds the moment. I clear my throat to quiet the furtive whispers. "She'll get bored and move on. She'll get hungry." No, probably not. With those bodies up there, she'll have plenty to feed on. Assuming that's her diet now. "She'll get cold, and she'll have to move on. We just have to wait her out."

But if it's Tucker...

The same would apply to him.

"I don't think we've got that long, Willard." Mathis points at the vents in the walls. "Without fresh O2 from above, we've got nothing to filter through the system." He shakes his head. "It could go kaput in the middle of the night. What then?"

I step into the middle of them. This is the moment I've been waiting for.

"There's another way out," I say with absolute certainty.

Eyes widen. Murmurs flow. Catherine and Mathis are suddenly without words. But of course they are. They had no idea about this. Neither did I.

I hope to God I'm right.

Time for the big reveal. I let the silence run on long enough for their anticipation to build sufficiently. Then I let them have it —as much as I can *engineer* on short notice.

"There's a system of tunnels behind one of the walls in our bunker. Used to be for groundwater routing, back in the old days. Now it's empty."

I point vaguely in the direction of our southwestern corner. If these fortuitous tunnels exist, they should take us right up under that town the panther-women found.

"They're just waiting to lead us to our new home. Might require a bit of elbow grease to get the job done, but I think we're up to the task." I grin at the looks on their faces. Wonderment now. Glances are exchanged, shoulders drop with relief. I clap my hands once, loudly. "So what do you say we break those sledgehammers out of storage and get to work?"

Voices rise with enthusiasm. Most turn away with newfound optimism, but every party has its pooper.

"How come you haven't told us about these *tunnels* before now, Willard?" Mathis steps forward, his voice raised. The disbanding of the masses slows to a halt as they turn to watch me. "You've never mentioned them. Not even once."

My jaw muscle twitches as I meet his insubordinate stare with as much confidence as I can muster. I know I'm right. I have to be. There's another way out of here, and it's behind the southwest wall. We just have to punch through the concrete, then they'll see. The sledgehammers should do the job nicely.

Almighty God, I pray I'm right.

"Tell me, Mathis. Would you take the emergency exit if the front door was wide open?" I grin at his confused look. "Until now, we haven't needed another way out. But now we do. That's why I've decided to *mention* it. You don't want to stay down here forever, do you?"

My response seems to satisfy everyone else, and they drift away, chuckling among themselves. Perch leads a handful to the storeroom with, "Sledgehammers this way!"

Jamison moves to join them. I grab his arm. "The southwest wall. Start there." Makes sense, that being the direction of the *town* she found. But I feel dizzy all of a sudden... My knees give out.

"Steady there," Jamison grunts under my weight. He helps me to the concrete floor, wet with my own blood. He glares at Margo.

"Don't give me that look. I didn't want to interrupt him." Margo douses my arms with fluid from a hydropack. "He was on a roll."

"You could've tended to him while he was giving his speech," Jamison mutters. "Just look at him."

"He's lost some blood, but he'll be all right. Help me cut away his sleeves—what's left of them." Her hands are soft and gentle on me.

Jamison stands. "Southwest wall!" he directs the others. "Get started!"

So it begins.

Ding. The elevator again. Guess she's still interested in me.

I have to smirk at that.

"Looks like a tiger came after you, Boss. What the hell?" Jamison curses.

Tucker's reaction was the same: *What the hell?* Maybe the demon-dust is from hell. That would explain a lot. The nukes from D-Day opened a portal into the dark side, and now... I'm not thinking clearly.

"It was like nothing I've ever seen." My tongue is sticky. I try to swallow.

"Drink." Margo holds the remainder of the hydropack to my mouth, but I hesitate. "*Drink*," she insists, and I obey.

Much better. I swallow easily. "They morphed somehow, teeth

elongating into fangs, fingernails and toenails into claws. It was...surreal." I shake my head. "Can't explain it."

Jamison bites his lip. "And Tucker? Did they... I mean, how did they—?"

"Morbid," Margo interjects. She's cut away the shreds of my jumpsuit sleeves, and now she applies the healing salve, glistening in the spare light.

"I just want to know what we're up against." He faces me. "You don't have to answer, if it's too hard on you. He was a good friend to us all."

He was that. *For the good of the many, Tucker ol' boy. For the good of the many.* He would have done the same in my place. He never was the selfish type.

"They converged on him. I managed to crush one with the bunker door." I can't mention the guns. That wouldn't make any sense. Why would the women give me weapons to use against them? "He killed one, broke her neck. I took out the other one, but I paid for it." I glance down at my arms as explanation. "He was a bloody mess when I saw him last. What was left of him, that is. They clawed the life out of him."

My fiction inspires another curse from Jamison. "And there's still one of them left up there?"

I nod.

"Maybe Catherine's right. About their names." Margo's dark eyes implore me. "Who is it, Willard? Sharon or Anna, or—?"

"I told you. It wasn't them. Not anymore."

"Right. Abominations, I get it. Claws and fangs. I can't argue with what I'm seeing here." She takes a breath, weighing her words. "But if we know who it is, couldn't we help her? Bring her back to reality?"

I shake my head. "It's better you don't know. As far as we're concerned, we've got a wild animal up there, and it's hungry. No matter what, we can't let it get down here."

"We should kill it," Jamison growls.

"There's been enough killing for one day," Margo says.

I don't know that I agree, but I pretend to look like I do. Muttering something, Jamison rises and heads toward the far wall where Mathis and Catherine have attracted a small group to sow discontent. He claps his hands as he approaches them, gesturing for them to join the demolition crew. Heavy metallic thuds echo from the southwest corner.

"They could be trouble." Margo watches Catherine and Mathis lag behind the others that Jamison has herded in the right direction.

I face her. Ever since the first scouts came back, I've withdrawn from the women. I knew something wasn't right about them. Margo could be infected too, for all I know. Yet I find that I trust her. Can't really explain it.

"Those two?" I grin. They're no trouble. "Constructive criticism never hurt anybody."

I'll put them down the moment they become a real threat. For now, I'll just watch them. And at the first sign of any sort of change, I'll know what to do. I did it once, and I'll do it again.

But I need those guns.

"I'm just saying, if we're going to make this work—meet up with survivors from the other sectors, head up to the Preserve—we'll need to stay strong. United."

When have we ever been *united?* She never listened to me. Not Margo—the other one outside with the bullet in her brain. When she was Sharon, she always cut me down. The sex was good, but she never really respected me. She always belittled me in front of the others.

"They have their doubts, I'm sure. Bet you do, too." I wink at Margo. She doesn't respond with a smile. Not even a hint of one. "But you'll see. When we break through that wall and find the tunnels, Mathis will change his tune. Believe me. Everything is going to change."

Hours later, maybe twelve, maybe twenty-four, after some mis-attempts, grumbling and complaining—even the makings of a half-hearted mutiny—the hammers eventually break through as I said they would.

I have to hide my surprise. Of course I was right. Who am I to doubt myself?

Perch coughs, covering his face. The others do the same, waving away the dust from the broken concrete. "The air's stale in there, but it's just like you said, Boss." He reaches into the tunnel with a glowstick and takes a quick look around. "Wide enough for the jeep."

Excitement mounts among us. This is a big step in the right direction.

"Suit up. We're going for a little drive." I beckon to Jamison, and he nods, heading across the bunker to where the jeep's parked. The batteries better be fully charged, or this will be a short trip. I'm not up to scouting on foot. "Want to tag along?" I turn to Mathis.

He thinks for a moment, leaning on his sledgehammer. He'd be a fool to pass up this opportunity.

"Sure," he shrugs.

Margo approaches me. "Don't you think your doctor should join you?" She holds up a medkit.

Might be a good idea. I'm not at a hundred percent. "Suit up, Doc."

She smiles and takes off in a jog toward the locker room. My gaze lingers on her round backside.

The jeep revs, lurching forward. Jamison honks the horn to clear a path. "Juice is at eighty percent." He leans toward me over the driver's side door. "All reserve power."

"So, forty-kilometer range. Give or take." How far is the town she mentioned? I can't remember much of what she said before I ended her.

"Each way? Yeah, that would be the farthest. Might be able to stretch it a little."

"Then let's not waste what we've got." I slap the hood as I pass around the front. He ignites the headlamps. "Perfect timing." I grin at Margo who jogs back with an extra suit.

"For you." She hands it to me as she tugs on her O2 mask. "You need the sleeves."

I look down at my arms. Strange. With the salve on them, it feels like they're already covered. "Right."

Jamison rolls forward. Suit and mask on, Perch runs up and climbs into the back. Margo assists me in a quick suit change, then we climb in as well. I ride shotgun as she slides in next to Perch. Jamison shifts into gear, and we accelerate toward the gaping hole in our southwestern wall.

All ninety-odd of the others line up on either side to send us off. Their optimism, smiles, and cheers are contagious. Waving and grinning, I feel like a victorious UW general returning from a battle already won.

"Where's Mathis?" Margo leans forward, her voice muffled behind her mask.

I shrug. "You snooze, you lose." Someone slaps my shoulder as we pass, but it's not a friendly gesture. It's Catherine.

"What do you expect us to do while you're gone?" Sour as ever.

I wink at her. "Hold down the fort."

Jamison guns the engine, and we enter the tunnel as the cheers reach a crescendo behind us. The white light from the headlamps extends twenty meters ahead, illuminating space that hasn't been disturbed for decades.

"So what do you think? Some kind of groundwater channels?" Perch leans forward.

"That'd be my guess. I doubt they've seen a drop since D-Day."

"This is awesome." Jamison chuckles as he accelerates. "How the hell did you know this was down here, Boss?"

How did I? "Just a hunch. Thank God I was right!"

Our laughter rises above the engine noise echoing from the tunnel walls.

"Really? You had no idea?" Margo leans forward next to Perch.

What is she implying? Her tone is hard to decipher with the mask's interference.

"Before they attacked me and Tucker, they told us they'd found the remains of a city to the southwest. I put two and two together, figured the government scientists were counting on us and wouldn't have left us with only one escape route. And voila!" I gesture toward the dark recesses beyond the headlamps.

"So that's where we're headed—the city?" Perch glances at Margo.

"The surface is no longer an option. But we'll see what kind of materials and supplies are available in the sublevels below the ruins. We've got to get everybody out of the bunker before the O2 runs out." I nod, half to myself. "I've got a feeling we'll find exactly what we need."

Jamison taps the steering wheel. A nervous gesture. "We'll have to juice up at some point."

True. Solar cells are difficult to charge without sunlight. And the sun prefers to shine on the surface. Can we do without the jeep? It could be a long distance to haul all our tools and supplies on foot.

"We'll cross that bridge when we come to it. For all we know, there'll be parking structures full of gas-powered vehicles where we're headed. Wouldn't that be something?"

Perch lets out a loud sigh and falls back into his seat, fingers interlaced behind his head. "A 2042 Mustang..."

Jamison joins in the reverie. "A turbo-charged Hummer..."

"I'd be happy with a clean water source, gentlemen." Margo shakes her head. "And some real food for a change."

I grin at her. "Dream big. Can't hurt any, right?"

"Since when have you been the optimist, Willard?" She gives my shoulder a playful slap.

She has a point there. Before All-Clear, I was more of a cup half-full kind of guy, but since the scouting teams started coming back covered in demon-dust, I became a prophet of doom and gloom. With good reason, it turned out. But that's all over. We're on a new path now. I'll be their prophet again, this time leading them to a new Promised Land.

"God's on our side. Why wouldn't I be optimistic?" I wink at her again. This time she dips her chin—the appropriate response for a lady. "He's with us, and he'll guide us along the way. I'm sure of it."

Perch and Jamison shout "Amen!" in unison.

"Are you sure God is gender-specific?" she asks quietly, so that only I can hear. "You're certain *she* isn't with us?"

What's this? Conversation to pass the time?

"I'm a traditionalist," I offer with a shrug. "I still have a hard copy of the scriptures in my bedroll. Right next to *Mein Kampf*."

She grins. "Weren't all those burned?"

"Which one?"

"Both." She shakes her head. "Only the government editions on the database were legal."

"I'll show you when we get back." Weeks ago, I might have added something suggestive about sharing my bunk and reading passages from Hitler and Moses during foreplay.

Her lips curve upward as she says, "I'd like that." She falls back into her seat.

Did she just read my mind?

"How far out have we driven?" I turn to Jamison.

"Almost ten kilometers." He doesn't take his eyes from the tunnel ahead of us. There isn't much room for error in here.

"How's the juice?"

He checks the gauges. "Under seventy percent. Going faster than I thought. I should've charged it up this morning."

"We'll make do."

He glances quickly in my direction. "You really believe God's with us, Boss?"

"Yes. I do." What kind of prophet would I be if I didn't respond that promptly and confidently?

He blows out a sigh and nods. "Good. Because it's starting to get to me a little—how alone we are. All that talk about what happened to the scouts, I was just thinking..." He lowers his voice. "What if we're not the only ones down here?" He darts me another glance. "What if there are others infected like Sharon?"

He's letting his fear get to him. "Have faith, soldier. Everything's gonna be all right."

"How do you know?" He sounds like he wants to believe me.

"Because we aren't mutant freaks." I grin at him. "We're all-natural children of God, and we've got his blessing upon us because of it. Chase those fears away with the truth, son. As sure as I've ever been of anything, I'm telling you: he's with us."

The more I think about it, the more it makes sense. God would favor the naturals over the abominations. It's always been his way. The only problem—and it's a big one—is if we're the only natural children of God left on this sorry planet. If the survivors from Sectors 50 and 51 have already become infected by the dust, that would not bode well at all for the human race. They're the only ones still able to procreate. Reproduction is their post-All-Clear mandate.

We'll have to cross that bridge, too, when we come to it.

A few more kilometers pass, each one identical to the last. Concrete everywhere you look—up, down, both sides. Water and lots of it would have passed through here once upon a time. But now it's just us, rumbling along like we own the place. I glance at the compass in the center console. The needle is still jiggling in a southwestern direction. I lean over to check the odometer.

Jamison slams on the brakes, and I lurch forward against my lap belt, just as Margo shouts, "What's that?" and points. The tires squeal, shuddering against the tunnel floor. I follow Margo's finger toward what lies ten meters before us, washed white in the jeep's headlamps.

Looks like there was a big cave-in a while back. No way we'll be taking the jeep any farther.

"Shut it down." I gesture lamely toward the ignition switch, my eyes fixed on the rubble. "Keep the lights on."

Jamison nods, his gloved fingers fumbling. The engine groans and dies.

Silence, punctuated only by my breath, loud against the O2 mask. Nobody moves.

What is this? How dare it stand in our way?

Stand is the wrong word. It protrudes through the roof of the tunnel with large piles of broken concrete on all sides below, engulfing it. The enormous thing is covered in dust, frosty in the light of the headlamps. There might be enough room on either side to squeeze through on foot and take a closer look.

My curiosity overwhelms my anxiety.

"Let's check it out." I climb out over the jeep's side door and drop to the tunnel floor. I beckon for the others to follow as I venture toward the rubble.

"From the surface?" Jamison's voice echoes behind me. He hasn't left the jeep.

I nod, pointing at the large cylindrical shape piercing the crumbled ceiling. "Came in through there." I drop my hand to gesture at the chunks below. "And did a nose dive."

"It's *huge!*" Margo keeps her voice near a whisper. Maybe we all should. I doubt there have been many sound waves traveling through here lately. We wouldn't want to start an avalanche. "What do you think? Leftover equipment from when they built the bunker?"

That wouldn't make sense. We're over twenty kilometers out.

"How far down are we?" Perch joins us.

"Fifty meters." I shrug.

"The bunker's that deep. What if the tunnel..." He angles his forearm upward thirty degrees. "What if it brought us closer to the surface?"

My abdomen tightens. "What if it did?" Where's he going with this?

He strides forward, taking big steps over fallen pieces of broken concrete, heading for the gap on the left side of the cylinder. "Then I might know what this is." He glances back to make sure we're following. Then he reaches into the pocket on his pant leg and retrieves a glowstick. He cracks it, washing himself in the sickly green light. "Awful dark on the other side."

Margo and I draw the sticks from our pockets but wait until we're beyond the range of the jeep's headlamps before cracking them. I follow the path Perch has taken, sidestepping debris, climbing over rubble. Is that dirt mixed in with the broken concrete? Demon-dust from the surface? I check my O2 mask, make sure it's secure.

Perch reaches the left side of the cylinder and steps through the gap easily. As he disappears from sight, he curses vehemently. I pick up the pace, clambering over concrete to reach the gap. Perch stands with his head cocked back, gazing upward in the green light. He turns to me and points a couple meters above his head. The large grey lettering on the cylinder is obscured by dust but still legible: UW GUARDIAN MISSILE. Right next to a radiation hazard symbol.

"It's a nuke," he says flatly.

That much is obvious. I stare, unable to string any words together.

"Still in the missile chamber." He curses again. "Undetonated."

"Undetonated..." I echo. "A live warhead."

Margo appears around the corner, adding her light to ours. It doesn't take her more than a moment to assess the situation. "We need to get out of here. Now. It could be leaking radiation, and these suits won't protect us." She starts back toward the gap. "*Now*," she beckons. "We can come back with the right gear and check it out later. It's not going anywhere."

She's right about that. It's wedged in there pretty tight. We follow her back to the jeep with the threat of leaking radiation hard on our heels.

"So what is it?" Jamison is right where we left him, behind the wheel.

"Start her up." I climb into my seat as Perch and Margo quickly follow suit.

"I don't think we can fit through, Boss," he shakes his head as he restarts the engine.

"We're going back." I glance at the missile.

"To the bunker?"

I nod. "ASAP."

He doesn't ask any questions, not until he's managed to rock the jeep up and down the walls of the tunnel to turn us around. He takes us back faster than he would have dared on the way out. Now the path is familiar to him.

"So..." He glances at me.

"It's a nuke."

"Whoa."

If the warhead is still viable, would we be able to harness its power for, say, a nuclear reactor that could provide us with enough energy to rebuild? It's not my area of expertise, but I know someone who's qualified. She's sitting in the back seat. But if the warhead was damaged during its collision with the tunnel, it's now a radioactive hazard blocking our only exit route out of the bunker.

Radiation sickness is a horrible way to go out. Hair loss and nausea and such.

I can't let myself think that way. God's on our side. He works in mysterious ways, and we're blessed to be a part of that work. He'll use everything for good, even this unexpected nuclear missile. It'll be part of our salvation. It'll have to be.

We ride in silence. Only the noise of the jeep's engine echoes all around us. We'll have to do without our vehicle on the next trip out. It'll be kaput after this run. Our boots will carry us in hazard suits. Glowsticks will be our guides. Just like those educational films they made us watch before D-Day: *Worst Case Scenario*. We'll troop through the tunnel, past the nuke, and find the sublevels of that southwestern city. Then we'll start a new life there.

Within minutes, we reach the hole we smashed through our

bunker wall, and Jamison eases us inside. Everything's quiet. Too quiet. Where the hell is everybody?

A gunshot explodes, fired over our heads. We duck, crying out in alarm and indignation.

They swarm the jeep then, all ninety-odd of them. They don't look happy to see us. They glare at me, most looking like confused sheep without a shepherd. Mathis and Catherine and a couple other women hold handguns trained on me. Where did they get those?

The fools. They must have repaired the elevator in our absence.

"You've got a lot to explain, Willard," Catherine grates out, both hands gripping the gun, trembling with rage.

She's probably right. I do have a few things to explain.

And I'll do fine. Like always.

PART V
CAPTIVES

10. DAIYNA

TEN MONTHS AFTER ALL-CLEAR

My eyelids flutter open to faint moonlight and a black sky with scattered pinpoints of light.

I jerk upward and inhale with a loud gasp. My heart rushes, pumping wildly. Where am I? How long have I been here? The ground beneath me is cold and uneven, scattered with rock and debris.

I'm too exposed sitting here in the open. It isn't safe, I need to hide. The mangled ruins of the city, smothered in dust and ash, tower over me in every direction. How did I get out here, lying in the middle of the street? Wasn't I underground before?

The muscles in my back ache to the bone as I stagger to my feet. I was armed. I remember carrying a rifle we took off a dead daemon. Swaying unsteadily, I close my eyes for a moment. I've got to get a grip on things, sort everything out. But my foggy memories are no help at all.

Stiffly, I shuffle toward what looks like the remains of an EV station. The chargers, once a meter high, are now frozen puddles of steel half that height. They've probably looked like this for the past twenty years. The exchange office sits farther back, a twisted heap of steel supports, but it should provide sufficient cover while I get my head straight.

The others—where are they? Shechara, Luther, Samson?

Milton... He was losing his mind. He thought I was someone else. I tried to help him, but I couldn't. He wouldn't let me. The spirit inside him was taking over.

I crouch behind a pile of rubble and touch my neck. I swallow painfully. Did he try to strangle me? Why can't I remember? We were below the surface, two or three levels down in a parking structure.

How the hell did I get out here?

My stomach growls, and I glance at the moon. It must be well after midnight. If the sun had come up, and I was still lying there in the street, unprotected...

I find my head covering, loose around my chest, and quickly wrap it back into place. My muscles tighten at the thought of what could have happened—my face, charred by the morning sun. My head doesn't need the protection right now, but it makes me feel better having it ready. It'll keep me warm, at any rate. It's freezing tonight.

My stomach churns again, and I reach for a protein pack, tucked beneath my outer garment. I rip it open with my teeth, and the noise is too loud. I pause before taking a bite.

It's so quiet here. Am I being watched? Maybe it's just the spirits. Do they know what happened to me?

A protein pack never tasted so good, despite the total lack of any flavor. I devour it in three bites. Eventually my stomach relaxes, and I take a deep breath.

I have to find the others. Where's that parking garage? It could be in any direction. I'm nowhere near where we entered this city from the south. By all indications, I'm in the middle of the city ruins.

I feel naked without a weapon of any kind, rifle or spear. I'd settle for even a knife. I look around at my deformed surroundings. Sector 31, Luther said. A trade sector. There should be plenty of...just about everything. In storage, below ground—if the daemons haven't already gotten to it.

The daemons. Right. I definitely need a weapon.

Keeping low, I set a course along the edge of the street and look for any blown-out buildings with open sublevels. As I move, I can't shake the feeling that someone's watching me.

"Is it you?" I whisper, knowing better than to think the spirits will answer. They speak only when they want to. I'm not surprised or disappointed by the silence that answers me.

Milton had me by the throat. The memory returns, more vivid this time. I remember his eyes, wild yet defeated as he tightened his grip. As if he knew he was losing the battle raging inside him. But then something happened—the sound of an engine approached from the level below us. I can't remember what happened after that. The next thing I knew, I was waking up in the middle of the street.

My boots skid to a halt as I look over my shoulder. What was that sound? Is someone or some*thing* following me?

I step sideways into the rubble of what could have been a restaurant at one time. It's difficult to tell. Were those tables?

When I was a little girl, I'd lie back and look up at the clouds with my sister, and we'd find all sorts of shapes and creatures. It's the same with these ruins. This could have been an auto parts store specializing in solar panels and electric cells, as far as I know. But right now, it's a fine Italian restaurant, and I can almost hear the music...

Silence. I wait a few moments longer to be sure no one's following. I thank the spirits for my gift of night-vision. The shadows provide no cover for anyone foolish enough to try and hide from me.

The ground crunches, closer this time. A footfall? Or something I disturbed as I passed by, something that hasn't been passed over in years?

I need a weapon. If only the spirits had given me claws like Luther.

I kneel and grab a jagged chunk of concrete twice the size of my hand. I hold my breath at the sound of another crunch—gravel and debris under a boot sole. Someone is tracing my steps, closing in on me. Human or daemon? Do others lie in wait down the street? I tighten my grip on the only weapon I have and weigh my chances. Should I force a confrontation or flee? I can't hide indefinitely. My tracks through the ash end here.

It's only a matter of seconds before I'm found.

"Who's there?" my voice hangs in the silence as I stand. I'm aware of my breathing, too loud, all I can hear. That and my heartbeat, throbbing in my ears. "Milton?"

The stillness of the night mocks my foolishness. Why would Milton be following me? Come to finish me off? The spirit inside him wanted to kill us all. What about the others? Did he already get to them? I can't make any sense of it. Why did the spirits want me to save him in the first place if this is how it ends?

"Are you alone?"

My heart lurches at the deep voice suddenly behind me.

"Who are you?" I whirl around, eyes darting. But no one's there.

"Don't run off. I won't hurt you."

"Prove it. Show yourself." I brandish the concrete and face the voice in the shadows.

"The dark suits me fine right now." A metallic clink echoes. "Put down your rock. Then we'll talk."

"Where are you?" Is something wrong with my eyes?

"I said drop it. I'm not fooling around here."

"Neither am I! Step out into the moonlight."

A gunshot blasts my eardrums. The rubble behind me explodes, pieces scattering in all directions. I drop the chunk of concrete.

"That's better." Another clink. He's armed and invisible. A dangerous combination. "Now answer me. Are you alone or not?"

"Yes." My voice sounds flat, not frightened. I grit my teeth to keep it that way.

"What's your name?"

"Daiyna."

"Where are you from, Daiyna?"

"Sector 50."

"A *breeder*? What're you doing here?"

"We were—"

"You said you were alone!" he shouts, stepping closer.

"I am." I raise my empty hands slowly. I'm no threat to him—not yet. "I am alone now. I don't know where the others are."

"How many? How many of them?"

"Three." And Milton. "Four."

"Which is it? Three or four?"

"Four." I try not to imagine an invisible gun barrel aimed between my eyes. "We were separated. I don't know where they are now."

"Why'd you come out here?" he demands.

The short version? "We needed a vehicle. Ours broke down. We were attacked, south—"

"Mutos?"

Mutants—the daemons? Who else? "Yes."

"Yeah, they can be troublesome." He curses. The ground crunches as though he's shifting his feet. "So you're all alone, and you don't know where your friends are."

If he plans to rape me, he'll get more than he bargained for, invisible or not. "That's right."

"What about that guy who left you in the middle of the street? Who's he?"

"What do you mean?" My voice catches.

"You tell me. Why would one of your friends dump you in the street back there and take off—like the *wind*. Never seen anybody move that fast."

Milton. He brought me to the surface and left me? Why?

"I don't know." I frown, pressing my throbbing temple. "I can't remember what happened. I woke up and saw the stars, no idea how I got there." I feel him watching me. "Which way did he go?"

"Couldn't really tell. Too fast."

I nod, trying to grasp the situation. "Are you still pointing that gun at me?"

His feet shuffle again. "Not since you dropped your rock."

My shoulders relax. Good to know. "So who are you?"

"I'm a ghost."

That would explain my inability to see him.

"Your friends," he says, clearing his throat. "Where'd you see 'em last?"

"We came in from the south, looking for a vehicle. Ended up in the sublevels of a parking structure, figured it might have what we needed. That's the last I saw of them." I must have blacked out.

"And you...didn't run into anybody else down there?"

The sound of an engine, bright lights... That's all I remember. "No. Why?" Do daemons live beneath the surface? Is that who came out of the darkness?

He sniffs. "No reason. Only if you did, I'd say your friends are in more danger than if they ran into the mutos."

What does he mean by that?

"I need to find them." If I can locate that parking structure, I should be able to track them from there. But I'm all turned around now, and the stars are no help to guide me. What North Star? The constellations look all wrong.

He mutters something to himself, but I can't make it out. His boots shift as though he's turning away.

"Can you point me in the right direction?" I hope I don't sound desperate.

If he wants to leave, fine. I can wait for the sun to come up and find my own way.

"You don't want to go down there."

I wait for him to elaborate. The silence runs on. At this rate, it'll be morning before I find the others.

"Why not?"

"If they were taken below, then only I can find them." His footsteps move out toward the street.

Should I follow? I have no idea who or what he is. Why the hell can't I see him? "Will you help me or not?"

The crunches stop. The impressions in the ashen dust are clear to see, but there's no one to go with them. Is he really a ghost? Of course not, that's ridiculous.

So what is he then?

"Follow me." The footprints proceed onward. "And stay close."

What choice do I have? Hide out until the sun comes up so I can get my bearings, or follow this invisible man. He didn't kill me when he had the chance. He seems to know his way around; at least that's the impression he gives. But can I trust him?

The fact that I can't see him confuses me as much as it intrigues me. Another incredible gift from the spirits? He's no daemon, that much is obvious.

"So, do you have a name?" I follow his tracks—footprints. His feet are bare. I hope he's not naked. "Or should I call you the *invisible man*?"

"I had a name. But nobody's used it for a while." He stops. His voice faces me. "Tucker."

I don't know where my eyes should focus in the empty space before me. "And where are you from, Tucker?"

The footprints start away, and I follow.

"Here," he says.

Sector 31. "You were a trade worker?"

He mutters to himself again. "No."

Maybe I wasn't clear. "What was your sector? Before D-Day?"

"Thirty."

So he's an engineer, one of the survivors we planned to meet up with on the way to the Preserve. But their sector was farther north. What's he doing here? Are they all hiding from the daemons? Or is he the only one left...like Milton was?

"If I tell you to take cover, you do it. No questions." He keeps moving. "Dawn's coming, and the mutos will be waking up soon."

Do daemons sleep in the sublevels beneath these blown-out buildings? I imagine them pouring out like ants as soon as the sun comes up. Not a welcome thought.

The spirits said there was nothing to fear. I'm not sure if I believe them anymore.

"How many?" From what Milton said about the attack on the caves, it sounded like all the daemons had amassed there. Have we totally underestimated their numbers?

He sniffs, mutters, "Hard to tell. They keep gettin' scared off. A whole bunch of 'em left yesterday, drove west in their jeeps. A lot of 'em are still around, though. But they can't see me."

Neither can I. All of our abilities are somehow related to the animal kingdom that thrived on this planet before D-Day: Shechara's sight, my agility, Luther's claws, Samson's strength, Milton's speed, even Plato's...spit. But where would this ability to disappear come from? What sort of creature could make itself invisible?

I try to focus on what he said. The daemons drove west, toward the caves. Milton already told us what happened, but I hoped he was wrong, untrustworthy with that evil spirit inside him. Now my hope dies within me. There won't be any survivors left.

"I walk right up to 'em and poke out their eyes sometimes. Easy targets, big as yellow ping pong balls. Took some doing to get over the smell, but they're harmless really. Long as they can't catch you."

Harmless? Obviously, Tucker has never seen anyone dear to him devoured by the hellish creatures. But I don't argue the point. He's talking, and I need to learn as much from him as I can.

"You're too fast," I offer, hoping to bait him into telling me more about his gift.

He chuckles. "I've got to be. I don't aim to be their next meal."

"Is that what happened to the other engineers?"

His tracks stop. We've reached a hill of rubble that was once part of the surrounding buildings, now a massive, dusty heap. He sniffs.

Did he hear something? I look around. Nothing moves.

"There's food in there," he says. "Down below."

Is he pointing? "Protein packs?"

"Food." His voice faces me. "The real thing. I've been eating it for months now." His invisible feet shuffle forward. "I have to remember this spot, remember, remember," he mutters.

What sort of *real* food would be in these sublevels? Canned goods, maybe. Has he been scavenging in the ruins of this city since All-Clear? Surviving alone. If the daemons got to everyone else from his bunker, then his gift was the only thing that saved him.

Survivor's guilt is a heavy burden to bear.

"So where are the others...from your sector?"

We venture through what was probably a busy intersection in the distant past. Now the asphalt lies rippled as if a giant chef was mixing in some ingredients and gave up on the recipe halfway through. We have to climb over large chunks of the street in order to cross. Easy for me with my gift of agility, and I don't hear any labored breathing from him. Staying one step ahead of the daemons has kept him in shape.

"They're around," he says. "You know what I think? It's all a big government experiment. We're not the last survivors on earth, nothing like that. This is a controlled environment, and they're watching us. I'm telling you, if we took a vehicle far enough east, we'd find everything just the way it used to be, the way it's been all those years we were underground." His feet shuffle, and he starts muttering to himself again.

His conspiracy theory is a bit extreme, but I wonder if there's a grain of truth to it. Why haven't I questioned the way things are? Why have I so blindly believed everything we were told on the bunker database?

"The mutos, and this weird invisibility thing I've got, and whatever night-vision thing you've got... Don't deny it. I was watching you back there, and you move around through the dark like it's daylight. All part of their experiment. They've done stuff to us, unnatural stuff, and now they're monitoring how we react. We're just glorified lab rats, that's what we are."

We reach the other side of the mangled intersection, and his footprints through the dust take us along a broken side street between what may have been two tenement buildings. I keep an eye out for any early-rising daemons and wish I still had my rifle.

I can't help mulling over what Tucker's said. For the first time, I find myself wondering if the voice in my head never came from supernatural entities. Instead, could it be from the same government scientists who sent us below long ago? They could be watching us through cameras hidden throughout the rubble, studying our every move.

My cheek rubs against the inside of my head covering as I smile. If I'm not careful, Tucker might draw me headfirst into his delusions. From what I can tell, he lost his grip on reality a while back and instead chose to create one he could understand. I don't blame him. It probably makes things easier to believe we're test subjects and at any moment, the ones running the show will appear and give us our results.

"I mean, think about it. They took us below after the first nukes were launched, right? But we never saw them fall. Did you?" He doesn't wait for me to answer. He plows through his theories while his tracks forge through the rubble. "Just video on the web, right? Fake, all of it. I'm telling you, there were no bombs, no insurgents with toxic bioweapons. It was all made up!"

"Why?" He sounds like he's trying to convince himself of the truth, like he's gone through this monologue many times before.

"Haven't you ever wondered why they had all those bunkers ready to go, waiting for us at the drop of a hat? A quick elevator ride underground, and we're safe from harm."

"They'd been preparing for years." I shrug. "That's how things were done during the cold wars."

"Nope. No cold war. That was all made up too." His tracks stop. "UW—*United World*, yeah? The nations of the earth were at peace, for crying out loud! There wasn't any *war*."

It's not easy to remember the way things were. Everything I know about the Old Earth comes from the bunker database. Most of us were sent below at a young age, during our second stage of education. We learned some things about current events at the time: the rebels and their frequent attempts to make their voice heard. They wanted to unite the sectors, drive out the UW. I remember talking to Luther about it... Only yesterday? Seems like a lifetime ago.

"The whole world is still at peace, and they're watching us," Tucker continues. "We're on a post-apocalyptic reality show! I'm sure the ratings are great. And now a word from our sponsors..."

Boots crunch across the ground behind me, and I turn in time to see a daemon stagger out of a sublevel's open doorframe a few meters away. I freeze. We're in the shadows, hidden from the moonlight by a structure on our left. Tucker's footprints haven't moved. He must see it, too.

The vile creature snorts, grunting to itself. Then a stream of urine issues forth from its crotch, splashing aimlessly across the broken pavement. The daemon stretches, arms over its head. Half asleep? Unarmed. Would I stand a chance against it hand to hand? I glance around at the rubble I could jump onto and climb out of reach, if need be. My muscles are tense, ready to spring into action. I watch, I wait. Maybe it will go back inside when it's done relieving itself.

"Die, you freak!" Tucker shouts.

The daemon turns on us with a snarl, just as an invisible gun fires beside me. The shot explodes through the creature's bulging, lidless eye and out the back of its head with a burst of blood. It grunts, staring at us stupidly, head wobbling like it's on loose. Then the legs give out, and the daemon drops to the ground.

A strong hand grabs hold of my arm, and instantly my invisible companion materializes into flesh and blood before my eyes. Startled, I draw back from him, but he holds me tight, raising the handgun in front of his lips. "Shh," he whispers. "They don't like it when I wake 'em up early."

As if on cue, snorting and grunting sounds come from both sides of the street, and footsteps scurry toward us through the dark. My stomach drops. It's just as I feared. These ruins are like an ant hill. And we've disturbed them.

"What were you thinking?" I hiss, turning my fear into anger and directing it at the man beside me. The one I can see now. "You knew this would happen."

"Usually does." He shrugs and grins, the blond stubble on his tanned cheeks folding back in creases. "They're nothing if not predictable."

I stare at him, too furious to say more. His grip on me is firm as he guides us behind a mound of broken concrete from which we'll hold a vantage point in the shadows. I could pull free of his grasp, but I don't.

Can I see him now because he's touching me? Is he visible now, or am I invisible like he is?

The scurrying feet of the daemon horde become pronounced footfalls as the creatures emerge from all sides, stumbling blindly in the dark. Quickly they come upon the one Tucker shot, and they crowd around it, grunting loudly, shoving against one another. Dozens of them...and more on the way. They pass by us without any sign of noticing our presence. But all it will take is one to alert the others.

I glance at Tucker's face. Grim, jaw set, staring hard at the creatures. Did he know there were so many? Does he have a death wish?

The grunting and shoving among the daemons subsides as they turn their attention to their surroundings, arching their backs and craning their necks at odd angles, their arms dangling limply at their sides. Looking, listening.

For us.

One of them snorts loudly. Then another one does the same, sniffing the air. Smelling us out.

We can't stay here. I pull against Tucker's grip, but he locks his icy blue eyes on me and shakes his head. His meaning is clear: we stay put.

Please help us, I pray to the spirits. Where are they now?

The daemons—fifty of them, maybe more—snort with their heads tilted back, their oozing nasal cavities directed skyward. They stumble away from the fallen member of their clan and spread outward. Six of them come within a few meters of us. Two face us. I hold my breath as they stagger closer.

Every nerve in me is ready to spring upward and make a run for it. I've seen them move. I would have the advantage.

Tucker raises his gun, keeping it level with the skull of the daemon closest to us. As the creature steps ever closer, snorting intermittently, Tucker tightens his grip, finger curled around the trigger.

Now it's my turn to shake my head. Unless he has enough rounds to take them all out, this would be suicide.

I tug against his hold on me, trying to get his attention. But he ignores me, his eyes fixed on the daemon now close enough to touch us if it swings one of those misshapen arms our way. The stench of rotten flesh is strong, the fluid dripping from every facial orifice defying description, it's so foul. I fight the gag reflex forcing its way up my throat.

The daemon is close enough to lose its head if Tucker pulls the trigger. The mutant stands oblivious, twitching its eyes as it halts its approach. The others have done the same. They sway slightly on their feet, holding their position. Silently.

Then one of them farthest from us grunts and turns away. The others do the same, one after another, staggering into the darkness. Within a minute, they've all disappeared, back into the sublevels they came from. All except the one near us. It hasn't moved.

It stands rooted, swaying strangely, head cocked to the side onto its large, deformed shoulder. The yellow eyes stare straight at us, unblinking.

What's it waiting for? If it knows we're here, why doesn't it do something? I look at Tucker. If he shoots it, we'll be right back where we started, with all its friends climbing out of the woodwork.

Why's Tucker grinning?

He lowers his weapon, tucking it into the belt of his jumpsuit. He stifles a chuckle at my reaction and gestures to the daemon, then pretends to nod off. I turn back to the daemon in disbelief. It's *asleep*?

"They gotta have their beauty winks," he whispers, letting go of me and vanishing in an instant.

The daemon disappears as well, blinking out of existence. But after the sharp crack of a bone breaking and the thump a body collapsing, it reappears, lying on the ground like a rag doll with its head twisted violently to one side.

"Probably should've done the first one that way." Tucker becomes visible again as he grasps my arm.

"I'm invisible when you touch me."

He nods.

Fear and anger squirm within me. When he let go of me to break that daemon's neck, I was exposed. For that brief instant, he allowed me to become visible while he committed that brutal act.

No. Killing any daemon, awake or asleep, armed or unarmed, is never a brutal act. It's necessary.

"We should keep moving," I mutter.

"You mind?" He squeezes my arm slightly.

"As long as they can't see me, hold on."

He grins. "Those scientists are geniuses, I'm telling you. I don't know how they pulled it off, but I ain't complaining. Everything I touch—poof! Like a magical cloak."

He guides me around the heap of rubble, and we resume our trek through the city. I move with more caution now, avoiding anything that will crunch under foot. Even if we are invisible to the daemons, I don't want to go up against that many of them again anytime soon—not without enough fire power to put them all down.

I glance at Tucker's hand on my arm, just above my elbow. No man has touched me like this before, as though he's escorting me to some fancy party. Samson has touched me, or tried to. He jerked me around a few times yesterday when we were attacked, and he might have saved my life in the process. The big oaf. I hate to admit it, but I miss him.

Only yesterday? It seems like so long ago.

We walk in silence for a kilometer or two. My gaze roams from one blown-out structure to the next, keeping an eye out for any other daemons startled from their slumber. The sky is a deep indigo now. The stars are fading, the moon a faint disc. Morning is coming, maybe an hour or so away.

"How does this invisibility of yours work in daylight?"

He turns sharply on me, as if he forgot I was there. "Oh. You know. Comes and goes. Works best at night, for some reason. Not so good after sun up." He shrugs. "Hell if I know why. But that'll be the first thing I ask 'em."

The government scientists. Did any of them survive?

"So what did they do with all the animals? Birds, reptiles, you name it. Where'd they go?" I might as well probe his theories.

He frowns at me like I'm speaking nonsense. "None of those around."

"Right...not anymore. But there used to—"

"Not here," he scoffs. He shakes his head. "It's not like Earth."

I try to follow his reasoning. "Not like it was."

"You think we're still on Earth?" He casts me a sideways glance. "Seriously, does this look anything like Earth to you?"

Of course not. The nukes from D-Day changed everything. But it's still the same planet. I'm sure it is.

"They took us off-world." He nods to himself. "The bunkers were really in the bellies of space ships, and it took them twenty years to reach this planet. Haven't you wondered where everybody else is?"

Now I'm lost. Wasn't he just saying earlier that the rest of the world is watching us?

"They...didn't make it." I remember what Luther told me about what happened in Milton's bunker, Sector 43. "Or the mutants ate them." Or the evil spirits killed them, as they did to Mother Lairen and the others from my sector.

He shrugs. "Or their ships never made it, got lost in space or something. The sun'll be coming up soon." With one hand, he pulls up his hood and reaches into his pant leg pocket to retrieve his face shield. "No suit, huh? Where'd you get your duds?"

I glance down. The material is filthy now. "We made them." Rehana's face returns to my mind, never far away, then Shechara's. I miss them so much.

He grunts and raises his eyebrows, impressed. With the face shield in one hand and my arm in the other, he takes us along the remains of a street that stretches on for more than a kilometer ahead of us. On either side stand the skeletal remains of skyscrapers leaning awkwardly against each other. Ashen dust clings to every twisted red iron steel beam, caked in a layer built over decades. Below them, most of their concrete sublevels are still intact. How many daemons sleep in there?

I still can't tell which direction we're heading. "How much farther?"

He mutters to himself yet again, his eyes darting side to side. I can't make out what he's saying. He seemed the most at ease when he was sharing his outlandish conspiracy theories. Now he's agitated. His grip on my arm tightens and relaxes spastically.

"The parking structure at the south end. How close are we now?" I turn toward him and make an attempt at eye contact.

He avoids my gaze. "Not going there."

I resist the urge to hit him. I keep my voice low so it won't echo. "Then where are you taking me?"

"To your friends."

"So you know where they are." What else hasn't he told me? "You've known all this time?"

He shrugs, shaking his head. "Not for sure. Where they might be, yeah."

"And that's where we're going."

He nods, avoiding eye contact.

"So how close are we...to where they *might* be?"

He mutters to himself until I tug against him and repeat my question.

"We'll be there before sun-up," he says. "I forgot my boots."

I look down at his bare feet. If the sun comes up before he finds some kind of footwear, he'll never be able to walk again. My fleeting sympathy is overridden by the fact that he won't be able to follow me with sun-scorched feet. Because as soon as this invisibility cloak goes on the fritz after dawn, I'm leaving him behind. And I'm taking his gun.

"How do you know that where we're headed...is where my friends could be?"

"It's where they'd be taken. If they were found."

Taken—by the daemons? Wouldn't they just feast and call it a day?

"Who else is here?" My voice carries the foreboding I feel.

He turns to face me then. There's a haunted look in his eyes, and his features sag. For once he seems completely lucid. "They're not like us. They're...like the way we were before all this. Before the ash." He swallows. "They're *natural*."

A glow emerges on the horizon. We're heading east.

"The ash," I echo. I thought he believed we were changed by government scientists on another planet as part of some elaborate experiment.

"There's something in it," he says, near a whisper. "Willard always said there was, but nobody believed 'im. And then it was too late. He started killing them, any of 'em that had gone out on the surface, one by one. Didn't matter who they were." He sniffs with a vacant look in his eyes. "He killed 'em all."

Sector 30 had a lot in common with Milton's 43, by the sound of things. But as much as I'd like to stay and hear the sordid tale in its entirety, I have people to find.

In a single movement, I grab hold of the gun in his belt and pull my arm free from his grasp. He vanishes for only an instant.

Then his strong hand clamps my wrist, just as I tug the gun free. His eyes bore into me.

"If Willard has 'em, they're gonna die," he says hoarsely.

"Let go of me."

"Let go of my gun."

"I'll shoot you in the leg." My finger curls around the trigger.

"And call those mutos back? I don't think so."

Fury boils within me. I'm trapped. Of course I won't pull the trigger. But he has to let me go.

I chop the blade of my open hand into his throat and he chokes, startled by the sudden blow. He releases my wrist and blinks out of sight. I take off running, veering south, climbing, leaping over every obstacle in my path. I glance back for any sign of pursuit, any tracks made by bare feet through the dust.

Tossing caution to the wind, I sprint down the middle of a mangled street. Too much time has been wasted already. I can't allow fear to slow me down. If the daemons show themselves, I'll take out as many as I can with this gun and out-maneuver the rest. Mid-stride, I check the chamber, the magazine. Six rounds left. Better than a chunk of concrete.

The sky glows brighter, anticipating dawn's arrival. A new day is coming.

So much has happened in the last twenty-four hours. Yesterday at this time, I awoke with a message from the spirits. We had *nothing to fear*. We were to travel east and, in so doing, leave our brothers and sisters to be slaughtered in the caves. *They're all dead*, Milton told us. How can I make any sense of that? Do the spirits want to destroy us? Why won't they speak to me now?

Their silence is as unsettling as the first time they spoke to me. No, this is worse. It makes me wonder if it was all in my head to begin with. Hearing voices—not the sort of thing usually associated with a healthy psyche. Maybe I'm like Tucker. Over the edge, unable to deal with my own survivor's guilt.

They say when you've lost your mind, you're the last one to

know about it. Who are *they*? I must have read it in the bunker database.

So if I'm completely out of my mind, and if there are no spirits of the earth who've been guiding me all this time, then everything is my fault. The attack on the caves, our getting stranded, the disappearance of Shechara, Luther, Samson. The only reason they came here in the first place was because of that voice I heard. A voice that no longer exists.

My eyes start to sting, and I curse. Tears trickle down my cheeks and cling to the inside of my head covering. My lungs shudder, but I don't slow down. I can't. A short sob escapes me before I can stifle it. When was the last time I wept like this? What the hell is wrong with me?

Rays of morning sunlight illuminate the thick layer of dust and ash that covers the ruins around me, making them shine like the broken remains of a celestial city. The blue haze of my night-vision fades, and now everything is tinted by the goggles I wear. I can only imagine how golden the sun must look to the naked eye. I can almost remember it. I focus on that memory until the tears stop trickling. I take a deep breath as my boots beat a steady rhythm across the ground.

Less than a kilometer ahead, the street dissolves into an expanse of desert sand. The south end of the city. I'm getting close. I look east, then west. Where's that parking structure we found?

There they are—the charred remains of those skyscrapers, maybe two kilometers west of my current course. The farthest one, angled awkwardly, held the parking garage in its sublevels. Hope stirs within me. I'm close now, so close. I will find them.

"With or without your help," I mutter—either to the spirits or to my own psychosis.

A bullet skids across the crumpled pavement a meter in front of me as a firearm reports from the right. Adrenaline floods my system with a jolt. I leap sideways and back, finding cover behind a frozen puddle of plastic and steel that might have been a large commuter vehicle at one time. I grip Tucker's gun with both hands, ready to take out the first daemon to rear its lumpy head.

Grunts echo as boots crunch toward me from the other side of the street. At least three of the creatures, from the sound of things. Strange they didn't hit me; they're usually better shots. Maybe they're not as good with moving targets. Or they're not completely awake yet. Regardless, they know where I am now. I'll have to make each bullet count.

A loud grunt becomes a garbled cry cut short. Something clatters to the ground. Shots are fired, but not at me. Then everything is still, silent.

I risk a quick glance over the mound providing my cover. Three daemons lie in the street, two shot dead. The third's head is on backwards, its weapon missing. I frown as one of its boots disappears into thin air, then the other. Its legs jostle as the footwear is tugged free.

"You followed me." I stand, the gun down at my side. I don't know if I should be glad or annoyed. My gaze drifts across the daemons' bodies.

Boots scuffle, sounding like he's putting them on, buckling them up. He doesn't say anything. He doesn't even mutter to himself.

"Thanks." I gesture lamely at the fresh corpses.

"I can't take you into that parking garage," Tucker's voice comes from the empty space beside the barefoot daemon. "They've got infrared and thermoptic scanners set up in there. They'll see me."

"They?"

"The *naturals*. I told you about 'em. But I know another way in, east of here. I can take you there, and we can look for your friends."

What more does he have to do to earn my trust? Why am I so reluctant? I can't shake the feeling that something isn't right—with him, with me... I don't know.

"All right." I pause. "But tell me more about these *naturals*."

The boots shuffle, making tracks toward me, before they stop beside the other two daemons. Their fallen weapons—short-barreled rifles with large clips—vanish. "Ain't safe up here now." His boot prints approach me. Cold steel bumps against my arm. He appears briefly, like a flickering image in a failing holo-emitter. "Take it. Looks like an Uzi—submachine gun, automatic. Plenty of ammo."

I fumble with the weapon as it appears in my gloved hands, then I shoulder it by the thick strap. I tuck the nine millimeter into my belt, beneath my outer garment. He sniffs and tells me to follow, his tracks heading off to the left, down a side street. As we come around the corner of a dilapidated structure, we leave the cover of its shade and step out into the brilliant morning light. The sun hangs in the sky just above the horizon now, at the end of the street. We head straight for it.

Behind Tucker's tracks in the dust, a dark form hovers across the ground: long and awkward, exaggerating each of his otherwise invisible movements.

"Your-uh..." My voice breaks the rhythm of our boots. "Your shadow's showing."

He chuckles. "Yeah. Weird, huh? Can't really figure that out. I try to stick to what shade I can find during the day. Keeps the mutos from getting interested."

"Should we ?"

"We're here."

His tracks stop in the middle of the street, a section that seems to have avoided whatever catastrophe tore up the rest. The shadow of his hand wipes at a layer of ash on the ground, clearing what looks like a circular hatch. Raised lettering set deep in the steel reads: SECTOR 31—15TH STREET.

"They thought of everything," I mutter, making an attempt at levity. If he's right, that we're on some other planet and all of this is a re-creation of our world, then the attention to detail here is incredible.

"They?" His shadow turns toward me. His hand stops wiping.

"The scientists." I falter. "The ones experimenting on us."

His shadow turns away as he resumes clearing the hatch cover. He mutters "mind reader" to himself, agitated again, cursing under his breath. "Give me a hand here."

His shadowy fingers grapple with the hatch, but it's no use. Even with my help, it won't budge. He curses and lets go, muttering some more. His shadow turns away, disappearing into the sublevel of a ruin behind us. After some clattering around in there, he returns with a long, slender shadow in his hand.

"Been a while," he explains, whatever that means. There's a heavy metallic thud as he drops whatever tool he found onto the hatch. Then his shadow uses it to pry upward. It creaks, metal on metal. A gap forms between the cover and the rim around it. "A little help," he grunts.

We manage to lift the heavy cover and slide it aside, letting it drop with a puff of dust. Just inside the hole, steel rungs of a ladder lead down into the dark—which my eyes transform into a hazy blue.

"After you." The shadow of his arm sweeps toward the ladder. "Unless you've got a glowstick I can borrow."

"What's down there?"

His shadow shrugs. "You'll see better than me. I have to feel my way along, usually." He sniffs. "Some kind of tunnel—probably for water or sewage back in the day."

If I go first, what's to keep him from dropping the cover into place and sealing me inside? "How close are those *naturals* you mentioned?"

"This shaft goes for a ways before it connects to the network they use. We won't see them for a while. But we'd better get a move on." His shadow glances back. Did he hear something?

"What'll keep the daemons from following us?"

"They won't. Too scared." He sniffs. "The naturals...do stuff to 'em."

"You're going to tell me everything you know about these *naturals*."

"Yes ma'am," he says gravely.

I hold the rifle against my side and step into the ring. The rungs of the ladder whip past me as I fall, the drop at least ten meters. The concrete of the tunnel floor below is dry as I land on all fours. Slowly, I stand. The curved concrete above is less than a meter from my head as I step away from the ladder and take off my goggles, leaving them to dangle around my neck.

The tunnel goes on in both directions as far as I can see. Silent. The smell... I can't quite place it. Not entirely pleasant, but tolerable. The air is stale. It hasn't been disturbed recently.

"You've got some skills, I'll grant you that." Tucker's voice echoes as he steps down a rung at a time, completely invisible again. "Wouldn't mind being able to do that myself."

After seeing so much dust and sand on the surface, this smooth, clean concrete seems out of place, sitting down here all this time, abandoned. Forgetting Tucker's half-witted theories, I think back to what Sector 31 must have been like in its prime. As a trade sector, it would have been the center of all design and manufacturing. From food to clothing to vehicles, even the weapons we carry, everything was manufactured here. I turn the Uzi over and glance at the stock. The UW insignia is right where I expected it.

I guess it makes sense, if this is where the daemons strike out from and where they return to sleep and gather supplies. Home sweet home. But why the cannibalism? Didn't Tucker say there's food here—*real* food? If so, I've yet to see it. Could be another one of his delusions.

Tucker's boots land on the tunnel floor behind me.

"Which way?" I don't bother looking back at him. I won't see anything.

"Straight ahead. We've got maybe a kilometer or more until we reach the junction shaft down."

"Plenty of time for you to talk."

I wait for him to mutter, "Yeah, right," and begin his tale before I take another step forward. I probably won't believe half of it, and only half of what's left will be true, but it's better than nothing. I have to know what we're up against. "You mind?" He puts his hand on my shoulder. "I'm blinder than a bat down here."

I don't resist his touch. He begins his story.

The way he tells it, these *naturals* have never been out on the surface. By somehow managing to stay underground since All-Clear, they've avoided contact with the ash—which their leader believes to be infectious, causing anyone who breathes it to become contaminated and turn into a mutant freak with bizarre abilities. Maybe not so far from the truth. Anyone they suspect of being infected is tested, then summarily executed.

For the first month or so after All-Clear, their numbers dwindled drastically as every day some among them—usually women—were found to manifest some type of mutation. Eventually, everyone who'd set foot on the surface was eliminated. Those who remained, close to fifty men, set about creating a subterranean paradise in one of the old groundwater storage domes, deep beneath the city. They call it *Eden*.

But that's where Tucker's story breaks down. He says they have purified air, running water, *real* food, even apartments where they enjoy all the conveniences we had prior to D-Day. They have everything they could ever want, he says—except women. And they're more than willing to share their bounty with any *all-natural children of God* who come their way.

"What will they do to my friends?"

"Are they like you and me?"

"They have...special abilities." *Gifts*, Mother Lairen called them. I never thought they'd be cause for a death sentence.

"He'll try to cure 'em first," Tucker says. "That's what he calls it. Always ends up killing 'em, though. He's an engineer, not a healer. He can build things, take 'em apart, then fix 'em and make 'em better than ever. That's his *gift*. A structural engineer. But it's not the same with folks. And besides," he adds with a sniff. "I think he wants 'em all dead."

I clench my jaw and try to keep my voice even. "Don't they

fight back?" Luther's claws, Samson's strength—they would not be subdued easily.

"I'm sure they try. I know I would. But he's got all his men working together like some kind of military organization. They even call 'im *captain* now, like it's official."

"What's his name?" I grate out. I close my hand on the rifle.

"Arthur Willard. A real bastard, that one. Left me to die, once." He chuckles. An odd moment to find humor. "But I've been able to get back at 'im plenty. He thinks I'm haunting him for what he did to me. I show up when he least expects it and whisper things into his ear. Scares the crap out of him, let me tell you!"

"He has no idea you're alive?"

"Nope. Oddly enough, the lights down there don't make my shadow stand out like the sun does. I'm pretty sure he thinks it's my ghost coming after 'im. Payback's a bitch!"

"Ever thought of killing him?"

"I'm no killer," he answers sharply.

Our boots echo against the concrete all around us.

"What does he do to—" The daemons. "—those creatures outside?"

His hand on my shoulder tightens and relaxes. Agitated again. "The mutos? He runs tests on 'em, tries to figure out why they don't show any other mutations—besides the obvious deformities. No special abilities or anything like that. He doesn't understand it. But he doesn't have to, not in order to use 'em like he does."

I wait, but he doesn't go on. "Use them how?"

He mutters to himself and curses, sniffing. "Like slaves, wired to fetch. Remote-controlled to get what he wants from the surface. So he never has to leave Eden."

I hope I'm hearing only the paranoid ravings of an invisible madman, that just a fraction of what he's saying is true. But even that much would be disturbing.

It's entirely possible we'll find the engineers from Sector 30 down here. With their varied skills, I'm sure they could have survived well enough for months beneath the surface of a trade sector with plenty to scavenge. But the rest—all this talk of executions and tests and programmed daemons. It's insane. It can't be true.

A dozen meters ahead, the tunnel dead-ends with another ladder leading down. My pace slows.

"What do you see?" His breath gusts past my ear as he strains to peer ahead.

"Another ladder—"

"Take off your boots. Quick." He releases my shoulder and scuffles across the concrete, unbuckling his pair. "We're getting close. Leave 'em here," he whispers. "So they don't hear us."

How close are we for it to matter? But I do as he says. He grasps my shoulder, and we proceed to the ladder. It stretches for what could be a hundred meters, straight down. At the bottom, the concrete is illuminated in a small patch of light.

"Might not want to jump this time," he mutters.

"What's down there?"

"Old access tunnel, big enough to drive a truck through. They use it for storage on this side." He chuckles. "I get some of my best stuff down there. Usually a couple guards posted. Armed."

"You go first." They won't see him, and by the time I reach him, he can lend me a hand and share his invisibility. He mutters to himself at first, sounding like he'll protest. But then he squeezes past me and starts down the ladder as quietly as possible. I follow, one rung at a time. Slow going. I can't remember the last time I used a ladder instead of leaping. Back in the caves, Mother Lairen had us construct ramparts and catwalks with ladders for the sisters not gifted with agility. I helped in the construction, using pipework and other materials we'd gleaned from the bunker. But I never climbed them. There was no need.

I glance down between my stocking feet, straight through Tucker. Have I jumped this far before? I doubt it, but I'm sure I could do it. I'd use the ladder to slow my descent if it turned out to be too long a drop for my knees to cushion the fall.

Not an option now. He's in the way.

Rung by tedious rung, we approach the bottom where the patch of light gradually enlarges. We don't speak. If our boots on this ladder would be heard, so would our voices.

Soon I'll find out how much of Tucker's stories are true and how much are the result of his solitude in the ruins above. I can't imagine what that must have been like for him. Scavenging, avoiding the daemons, avoiding his own kind—if what he said about these *naturals* is true. Completely alone.

I haven't felt that way for months now. The voice of the spirits —startling me every time it's emerged in my mind—has kept me from ever feeling alone. Something else was always there, always with me.

Was I possessed? Just as Milton was possessed by an evil one, could I have been possessed by one of the others?

My muscles shudder. Is that what keeps gnawing at the back of my mind—that something isn't right with me? Is the spirit gone? Why would the spirits possess me and then abandon me? It makes no sense.

I blink my eyes and focus on the ladder. Maybe Tucker isn't the only one who's gone off the deep end.

The spirits said there was nothing to fear. If they haven't spoken to me lately, so what? They haven't spoken to Luther, and yet he believes without question. I need to dig down deep and find that kind of faith. Seriously, if I believe only when I hear, that isn't faith at all.

I believe in you. My voice echoes in my head as if I'm alone in an empty room. *I know you're there, watching over us.*

It sounds like a prayer. To the spirits? The Creator? I don't know. But I hope it brings me closer to wherever Luther and the others are.

Tucker's hand grips my ankle and I stop, glancing down to find his silhouette backlit by the light below. The ladder vibrates with the hum of large machinery filling the air. The air... It's so *fresh*. I inhale deeply. What have we been breathing on the surface all this time?

Tucker gives my ankle a tug and lets go, resuming his descent and his invisibility. Close behind, I reach the last rung hidden within this shaft. The remaining rungs lie exposed for at least five meters before they reach the floor below.

I wait and listen. Has Tucker already touched down on the concrete floor? Is he taking out the guards? I can't hear anything. No scuffle, no bodies slumping to the ground. Maybe there's no one here. If so, then he should come back and lend me a hand, make me invisible so we can look for Shechara and the others.

What's taking him so long? I clench my jaw and grip the short rifle in one hand, bracing myself. Time to jump out into the open.

Before I can let go and drop, loud voices echo and boots pound across the concrete. I see their shadows before I see them. They encircle the ladder below with weapons drawn. Without warning, they fire.

What feels like a thousand volts of electricity shoots through me, igniting every nerve in my body. A guttural scream explodes from my lungs as I fall through the air to land hard on my back, convulsing uncontrollably, my arms and legs flailing, my head jerking spastically. I'm out of control.

My body's in agony, unable to function—yet my mind's strangely detached. I can't see anything beyond blinding flashes of white, but I hear everything: the laughter from men with guns, the monotonous drone of machinery nearby, the measured approach of another set of boots.

Tucker's voice:

"Well, I did like you asked, Captain. I got one of 'em. And this one, she can see in the dark." Muttering, half to himself. Agitated again. "So what do you say? Can I?" Sniffs. "Can I come back now?"

11. LUTHER

TEN MONTHS AFTER ALL-CLEAR

The daemons have returned. They must have followed our tracks. They slaughtered and feasted upon our brothers and sisters in the caves, and now they are here to finish us off.

"It's the mutos. They're back," Willard said. What else could it mean?

Our footfalls pound, ringing across the steel catwalk as we leave the apartment and jog after Willard. His men close in tightly from the rear. One glance at Samson tells me all I need to know: he plans to use this sudden diversion to aid in our escape. I glance at Shechara and see fear in her eyes. I'm sure they mirror my own.

Willard barks an order as he takes the ladder down quickly, demanding a situation report.

Amid the commotion below, one of his men turns and looks up. "They've breached the east tunnel, Captain!"

A jeep blows past us with three armed soldiers checking their rifles.

Willard's boots hit the concrete floor, and he beckons us to follow. "Pick up the pace, folks. You won't wanna miss this!"

I start down the ladder and try to keep my breath steady. I focus on each rung in my grip. My claws have retracted, but I don't know how long they'll remain that way with so much tension in the air. I glance up as Shechara follows me, her bare feet less than a meter from my hands. Her blue jeans hug the curves of her hips and thighs. Another jeep squeals past us. The concrete is cold and slick as the soles of my feet make contact.

"Perch!" Willard shouts to one of his men on the catwalk—the one foolishly attempting to stare down Samson as he climbs onto the ladder. "Get these people some proper uniforms ASAP." He claps me on the back once I'm within reach. "You ready to fight for humankind, Luther?" He grins broadly and winks. "Hey, did you shave? You're lookin' good." He turns away to confer with his troops.

Everyone is in motion around us, but it's far from chaotic. They all seem to know exactly where to go, what to do, and how to go about it. The voice on the loudspeaker must have something to do with the well-ordered chaos. The scene has every aspect to it of a military drill, one that's been practiced repeatedly. Regardless of whether these men were truly soldiers prior to D-Day, they now play the part well. How many times have they needed to scramble to arms? How often have the daemons attempted to invade this underground sanctuary?

Shechara steps beside me, followed by Samson. Willard's men slide down the ladder by its vertical supports. The one named Perch, a stocky man with a protruding jaw, takes off running to follow his captain's orders.

"Get our guns while you're at it!" Samson shouts after him. "They expect us to fight with them, they'd better give us back what's ours," he mutters to me, folding his brawny arms and glaring straight ahead.

He has no intention to join this fight. I would ask what he has in mind instead, but the remaining two soldiers stand close by. They no longer train their weapons on us, but it still seems we're their prisoners.

"What do you see?" I ask Shechara quietly.

"Everything," she whispers.

"Is that where we came in?" I gesture briefly and scratch behind my ear.

She glances toward the south tunnel where three armed soldiers stand guard, talking among themselves. They watch others race past in jeeps, headed for the east tunnel, close to a hundred meters off to the right. They make no motion to leave their post. Shechara nods.

Samson watches the guards. He would be able to subdue them easily. Shechara would be our eyes through the darkness beyond, and eventually we would reach the parking structure where we were separated from Daiyna and Milton hours ago.

Only hours? It seems like days have passed since we left the caves and ventured into the city ruins above.

Willard returns and dismisses the two soldiers by us. They break into a trot and join the three at the south tunnel. I glance at Samson. Our odds have changed.

"What about our friends? Have you found them?" I turn to Willard.

"Your *sister*, you mean?" He grins, and I remember that's how Samson referred to Daiyna. "And the tagalong? Nope. Can't say that we have. But don't you fret. They'll turn up. We'll pick up the search soon as we give these mutos some serious hell."

Perch returns, boots pounding as he jogs back with three camouflage uniforms. He tosses them at us, one at a time.

"Put 'em on," Willard says.

"Not without our weapons." Samson glares at him.

Gunshots echo in the distance. "Enemy engaged," reports the voice over the loudspeaker.

Perch curses. "We don't have time for this."

Willard nods, his features tight. "If they get in here, we're done for. We could use your help. But if you'd rather wait upstairs..." He gestures toward the apartment above us. Our comfortable prison cell.

I pull off the jeans and quickly tug on the crisp UW uniform, one leg at a time. Samson and Shechara reluctantly follow my lead. If we plan to escape anytime soon, we must stay out of that locked apartment.

"You forgot their boots." Willard glances at Shechara's bare feet and shakes his head at Perch, who curses and trots away on his second errand in as many minutes. "Doesn't always think straight, that one." Willard's eyes linger on Shechara as she struggles to fit into her uniform. "You make a mighty fine soldier, darlin'. Really fill everything out in all the right places." He winks at her.

Samson's fist blindsides him, whipping his head to the side. With a groan, Willard crumples to the ground and lies still.

"That's about all I could take." Samson pulls the gun out of his belt and holds it ready.

"You're a patient man." I stoop to grab Willard's pistol from its holster.

"Timing is everything," Shechara says, smiling up at my brother.

But time is in short supply. Already we've drawn the attention of those five men at the south tunnel—our only escape route. Two of them hold their post while three fan out with rifles at the ready, trained on us. They shout commands to lay down arms and remain where we are. Erupting with foul obscenities, Perch charges toward us, his face livid.

"Now what?" Shechara steps beside Samson, dwarfed by his frame.

"We get the hell out of here, Small Fry," he growls. He fires a warning shot over Perch's head, who throws himself prostrate to the ground.

"Stand down!" shouts one of the approaching soldiers.

Willard stirs. We have to make a run for it before he comes to and summons more of his men. Samson fires another warning shot, and the closest soldier ducks low, staring at us in disbelief. The other two flank us and close in. But they don't return fire. Have they been given orders to keep us alive?

Shooting a daemon is one thing, but these are men, like us. Do I have it in me to kill them?

Shechara snatches the gun from my grip and squeezes the trigger twice before handing it back to me, the shots exploding, echoing like bombs. The soldiers flanking us cry out, clutching their legs as they topple over. Their rifles clatter to the concrete, and Shechara scoops them up mid-stride, leveling them on the two men at the entrance to the south tunnel. Wide-eyed, they drop their weapons and step aside as she draws near.

"Let's move." Grinning with admiration, Samson chases after her, pausing only to send a couple more rounds back at anyone foolish enough to follow. I stay abreast of him. "Good work!" he shouts to Shechara.

She tosses him one of the rifles as he approaches.

"You boys might want to high-tail it." Samson swings the muzzle toward their kneecaps, and the two remaining soldiers break into a run in different directions. "Posers," he mutters. Then to Shechara, he says with a big smile, "Lead the way."

She nods, glancing at the two men she shot. Their moans and curses echo across the floor. Regret flashes through her eyes. Then she runs into the tunnel and we follow, immersing ourselves in the darkness.

I race after the sounds of Samson's heavy boots and Shechara's small feet as naked as my own. We're making a prison break—from a prison that would have provided everything we need. Regardless, we were held against our will, and now we're free to find Daiyna and Milton, to take one of the vehicles from the parking structure and return to the caves.

But we don't get far before Willard's voice echoes all around us.

"That ape's got a solid right hook." A loudspeaker crackles in the tunnel. "But you're too smart for this, Luther. I would've thought you had it all figured out. Maybe I gave you too much credit. You are just a *breeder*, after all. The only brains you've got dangle between your thighs."

Lights glare white hot all around us, and we squint in their sudden brilliance, stumbling to a halt. A heavy creak rumbles behind us. We turn in time to see a solid steel blast door drop from the roof of the tunnel and slide into place, groaning as the locking mechanism holds it securely, shutting us out of the dome. We stand rooted, glancing at the door, at the lights above us, at the darkness beyond their range. What's Willard doing? Why would he want to keep us from going back? Returning to *Eden* is the furthest thing from our minds.

Then Shechara gasps, staring into the pitch black beyond the lights.

Willard chuckles on the speaker mounted over the blast door. "I really wish this was a two-way radio. I'm sure you've got all manner of choice words for me right about now. But maybe you should just listen instead."

He pauses, and from the darkness I begin to hear the shuffle of approaching footsteps. Too many to count.

"What the...?" Samson scowls into the black and grips his rifle.

"They're coming." Shechara's voice is hoarse as she backs toward the blast door, her eyes unblinking.

Another chuckle from the speaker. "You'll probably hate me for this, but... It wasn't really the *east* tunnel the mutos breached."

Samson stares at me, his features slack as a multitude of guttural sounds emerge from the darkness. The footsteps increase their pace. They'll be upon us in moments. I shove the pistol into my belt and flex my fingers, breathing a quick prayer as my claws extend.

"Well, good luck to you all. I'd say *God be with you*, but I don't think he much favors your kind. Anyhow, these are the same bunch that ate up all your friends, so feel free to show 'em no mercy. For as long as you can, that is." The speaker clicks off, cutting his chuckle short.

"There are so many..." Shechara cringes against the steel door, unable to bear what only her eyes can see.

"Let them come," Samson rumbles, clenching his jaw.

"God be with us," I manage as a sickening chill snakes down my back.

The daemons emerge from the shadows and jerk strangely in the light, unable to blink their lidless eyes. They shield them with deformed hands and stagger toward us, grunting and shrieking in a wild rage, jaws snapping hungrily. Samson fires his rifle and the first line of creatures falls flailing to the tunnel floor. Their limbs look skeletal, rags hanging loosely on narrow shoulders, ribcages protruding through charred flesh. The stains of fresh blood are absent, as are any weapons.

Samson wastes no time and fires again, dropping another line. Shechara fires her weapon and takes down a few more. But they keep coming, and we won't be able to shoot them all. There are too many. And from the sound of it, more are on the way.

I step forward as one of them launches itself into the air to avoid the barrage of weapons fire. It stares at me like a starving animal as it descends, fangs chomping in anticipation of its first course. I thrust my hand into its throat, and my claws pierce straight through. The yellow eyes remain fixed on me as its warm blood gurgles, flowing over my hand. The daemon convulses before its head drops limply to the side. I let it fall and watch it lie still, my eyes immediately drawn to the blinking light at the base of its neck. I lean forward, sure I must be seeing things. But there it is: a pulsing pinpoint of red light, almost hidden by the flap of human hide the daemon wears. The miniscule bulb blinks once more before it fades out.

Samson drops the rifle and grabs his handgun, able to dispatch two more daemons before the weapon is emptied and cast aside. Then he tightens his fists, cracking his knuckles, prepared to use all that he has left: the strength he's been given by the spirits. He will exact as much damage as he can with his bare hands.

Where are the spirits now? Will they fight with us? Or have we been abandoned here?

I toss Willard's pistol to Shechara. "Save a round."

She nods, stuffing it into her belt and quickly aiming her rifle to take down the last daemons she can before the magazine clicks empty. Then she grips the weapon like a club with both hands. I step beside her and plant my feet. We don't plan to make it easy for these creatures to feed on us.

Recognizing we're now unarmed, the daemons surge forward en masse, their bulging eyes finally accustomed to the light. Sharp fangs gnash out a syncopated rhythm as they advance. The ones foolish enough to attack Samson outright are no match for his strength. He crushes their skulls against each other and uses their limp bodies to beat back the ones following close behind. Those that manage to avoid his radius of mayhem quickly find themselves slashed and gutted by the sharp talons I've been gifted with. I show no mercy.

Blood sprays in all directions, all I can taste and smell. The thick, coppery stench sickens me, but I don't stop. I can't. We have to survive. We'll paint this tunnel in a fresh coat of crimson if we must. But my muscles begin to ache in the face of such overwhelming odds. We won't be able to hold them off indefinitely. There are far too many.

"Luther!" Samson shouts, and I notice he's stacking the bodies of the daemon corpses as they fall around him. "Send 'em this way!"

I tear through two more throats and shove the dead daemons toward his bloody pile. Undoubtedly putting into practice a lesson learned from his studies of warfare, he's creating a barrier to impede the progress of the hordes still on the way. If we can slow them down enough in their advance, we should be able to dispatch the ones who climb over without being overwhelmed by their numbers. In theory, anyway.

"How many?" I cast over my shoulder as three more daemons lunge my way.

Shechara swings her empty rifle like a baseball bat, crushing daemon skulls with a vengeance. We work together, sending the slain creatures toward Samson's macabre pile.

"I can't count them. They keep coming." She seems resigned to the fact that we're going to die in here.

"We will survive this." I make eye contact with her, but her gaze is vacant, her face spattered with blood. I wish I hadn't told her to save a round. A bullet to the brain would be better than dying at the hands of these monsters, but only as a last resort. "We will survive!"

She screams as a blow lands between my shoulder blades, driving me to the concrete. The daemon wields Samson's fallen rifle, swinging it downward like an axe, aiming to crack open my skull. I roll to the side, and the stock crashes against the floor centimeters away from its target. Two others fall upon me, biting at the air in front of my face as I hold them off. Their eyes bulge fiercely, excitedly. They know they have me. The one with the rifle uses it to pin my left forearm to the ground. I swing my right, punching and slashing at their hideous faces. One manages to grab hold of my wrist with both hands, and I'm unable to wrest it free. They grunt loudly in victory. Then they close in on my exposed torso with fangs bared for feasting.

I grit my teeth and pull my legs up, thrusting with my right heel. It makes contact, striking the pouch-like chin of the one holding my wrist. The impact stuns it for a moment, and I jerk my right hand free, using my claws to slice through its hamstring. With a garbled wail, it falls to one knee. The other one dives at my throat, but a shot rings out. The bullet punctures the back of its head with a burst of blood, sending it to the floor in a heap. The one with the rifle turns on Shechara, and she pulls the trigger again. But there is no round in the chamber this time, and it clicks empty. The daemon grunts something like a laugh and brandishes the rifle overhead, prepared to strike.

I heave myself upward and lash out with both hands, tearing open the thick flesh on the daemon's back. It drops the rifle instantly and collapses, screaming, into my open arms. I grasp its deformed head and prepare to break its neck quickly—

A light pulses near its collarbone, red, the same as before. The daemon struggles against me, but I hold it still, incapacitated, its arms dangling uselessly.

"Shechara, look." She stares at me, but I'm not certain she sees anything. She may be in shock. "Look here. What do you see?"

She doesn't approach. She doesn't need to. "A red light."

What could it be?

"While I'm honored—" Samson grunts as he beats a daemon senseless with its own severed limbs. "—that you apparently think I can take on all these freaks by myself—" He plants his fist through the gaping face of another. "It'd be awful nice if you could lend a hand or two!"

I break the daemon's neck and watch the light dim to black. Then I join my brother. The stack of bodies now extends the full width of the tunnel, over a meter high. The daemons continue to clamber over it as if driven by some unseen force, unhindered by the havoc they meet on our side.

"You'd think they would get the idea—" He rips the head off one of them and winces in the sudden spray. "—that coming this way is a really bad idea."

I slash through the next two that descend upon us. "I don't believe they're acting on their own volition." I shove the bodies away.

He scowls at me, then tears apart the next three daemons in quick succession. "What do you mean?"

"They're being controlled." Shechara stands beside us with a thin strip of metal in her hand, blood covering her fingers. "Somehow." She points at what looks like a micro-transmitter of some kind. The blinking light.

"They're all wearing those things?"

She nods. "Around their necks." She reaches toward one of the bodies stacked before us and pries away the fold of rotten hide at the base of its neck. The steel collar is clear to see.

Samson curses, staring at the device. Absently, he breaks the neck of a daemon that drops in on us. "So... Who's pulling the strings?"

"One guess," I manage, tugging my claws free of a fresh corpse.

"Captain Freakshow." He nods. "What kind of jerk-off does...*this*?" He gestures at the collar with both hands. "I mean, if he wanted to kill us, he had plenty of opportunity while we were in that weird-ass apartment."

"I don't believe that to be his intention here. I don't know what he wants, but his men made no attempt to shoot us down when we escaped. It was as if they *wanted* us to head down this tunnel." I keep my voice low. Willard said he couldn't hear us through his radio-speaker, but to say I don't trust him at this point would be a serious understatement.

"Why would he keep us alive only to trap us in here?" Shechara stares at the collar in her hand.

"He's testing us," I say aloud before I have a chance to weigh my words.

Samson takes out the next pair of daemons with a single right hook that shatters their jaws like a train crashing through glass. "Testing? For what?"

I don't know. But I have a feeling Willard somehow knows about our gifts, even though he and his men don't seem to exhibit any themselves. His talk of *natural children of God* could have been in contrast to the daemons, but now I wonder if he thinks of us as *mutos* as well. Does he plan to collar us and use our gifts for his own purposes? Is this why the spirits led us here? To become slaves at the hands of a madman? If Daiyna were here, she would know our purpose, what the spirits would have us do. But what if Willard has her already? Would he be able to use her to hear from the spirits himself?

I'm not thinking clearly. I must have faith. The Creator hears my prayers, and if it's His will, there will be answers soon enough for the questions that plague my mind.

"So what do you think he'll do after we pass this test?" Samson mutters, keeping his wary gaze roving along the mound of deformed corpses. For the past thirty seconds, no daemons have attempted to climb over. "Assuming we do, of course."

"I can't hear them." I listen closely. All's quiet on the other side.

"Think we got 'em all?" He grins. "Must be near a hundred piled here."

I never would have thought there were so many. When they attacked us in their jeeps, they always came in small bands of three or four—a dozen at most. Yet stacked before us lie the lifeless bodies of dozens upon dozens.

They look as though they were starving. As they fought us, they didn't exhibit the same strength as others we've met in battle before. Even so, they were a formidable adversary, and without our gifts we would have been no match. But what effect do these collars have on them? Have they been controlled from the start?

"We should take a look." Samson glances at Shechara. "See what's going on, if we can make a run for it. I don't want to be here when Freakshow and company reopen that blast door."

Shechara hesitates, unable to see over the heap of bodies. She moves to the side, straining on tip-toe, and gazes into the darkness of the tunnel beyond, her eyes steady, focused. Eventually, she looks back at me.

"They're gone," she says.

"All of 'em?" Samson raises his eyebrows.

She nods.

"Not bad at all." He grins, wiping blood from his large hands onto his soaked pant legs. A futile effort. "Score one for the good guys." He gestures toward the darkness. "Shall we then?"

We need to return to the surface and put as much distance as possible between us and Willard's Eden. We'll start up one of those vehicles we found in the parking structure and head back to the caves. There may yet be survivors, and they'll need us. But first we have to find Daiyna—and Milton. We won't leave the city without them.

Why do I hesitate? Part of me feels that we should linger here.

Is it fear? The daunting prospect of escaping through a pitch-black maze of tunnels with lurking daemons? I don't feel dread. It's more a sense of leaving behind unfinished business. The spirits, through Daiyna, led us here for a reason. If we leave now, will we have failed in our purpose?

They said we had nothing to fear. Does that mean we won't come to harm, whether we stay or leave? Or have we been misled from the start? I would not fault them for seeking to destroy us, after the way our kind mistreated this planet. And if this is the case, then we are decidedly on our own.

I nod to Samson and Shechara. "Let's go."

The speaker crackles. Willard's dry chuckle echoes against the blood-soaked concrete around us. "Well, I must say, you folks put on quite a good show. You're a tribute to your kind. Only three of you up against all those hungry mutos—and you without even a scratch! Wish I could say I'm surprised, but that wouldn't be the honest truth. I knew you had it in you. Impressed, though? Definitely. I didn't think you'd get through them so fast. If I'd known, I would've let more of 'em loose!" He laughs out loud. "So yeah, you've probably figured it out already—"

"What do you want with us?" I demand, but he goes on uninterrupted.

"—a couple cameras in there. Yep, we saw the whole damn thing. Didn't even need those weapons you kept whining about, did you? You did just fine with your bare hands! And boy oh boy, are you *vicious*. I sure wouldn't want to cross you." A short pause. "So here's the thing. I know that you want to escape and all, and I don't really blame you. It's not like you belong here. You're not like us, obviously. And you want to go back to your own kind."

The locking mechanism groans, releasing the blast door behind us. We turn as it slowly recedes upward. Boots clatter as Willard's men duck inside with weapons trained on us.

"But here's the problem, folks," Willard's voice confides through the speaker. "I just can't find it in my heart to let you go."

The men fire their weapons. A shock of electricity tears

through me, exploding like a shivering fire. They hit me again and again, and I fall, unable to control my limbs or the wild sounds escaping me. Shechara screams, and Samson curses, groaning. Then everything goes black as a heavy-soled boot collides with my skull.

Damp from the light rain, I pass through cool sheets of mist that cling to the branches and broad green leaves of trees overhead. My heart keeps a steady rhythm as my rubber-soled shoes strike the forest path beneath me. I run not out of necessity but by choice, inhaling deeply, feeling free here, completely at peace. There's a slight chill in the morning air, but I barely notice it. A woodpecker knocks on an oak's hollow trunk in the distance, and I look for it between the trees. The knock sounds again, breaking the silence, striking in quick succession only to pause at untimed intervals. I can't see it anywhere on the left side of the trail, the side where, if I were to venture far enough through the tall overgrowth below the leafy canopy, I'd eventually find myself standing at the lakeshore.

Perhaps I'll go for a swim after my morning jog. Last year, I swam across the lake in the rain, and the water I stroked through carried the texture of a million raindrops. I smile at the memory.

"We're all going to die here, Luther."

Milton stands rooted in the middle of the path before me. I skid to a halt. His jumpsuit is filthy with dust and blood stains. He holds his cracked face shield down at his side. His eyes are hollow as he stares at me.

"They don't want us to live," he says.

I open my mouth to speak, but no words come. I clear my throat as the rain falls heavier now.

"They want me to help them." He shakes his head, his sodden hair swinging in clumps against his face, drawn and unshaven. "I can't fight them. They're too strong."

Who? Willard and his men?

I look up, and the rain pelts my eyelids, forcing me to close them. I extend my arms out to the sides and breathe. Milton isn't here, he can't be. I'm seeing things, hearing things. I listen to the rain rushing through the trees, building in intensity. I'm sure there are white caps out on the lake.

"You have to stop them, Luther. Before it's too late. If they succeed, there won't be any of us left." Milton shudders as if suddenly chilled to the bone. "They've taken her."

Wake up!

A jolt of electricity pierces my midsection and I cry out. My eyelids blink against hot white light. I pull my arms and legs against steel shackles clamped onto my wrists and ankles. I twist with my torso and swing slightly. I'm suspended from the ceiling by chains. My head jerks forward, and I look down.

I'm naked, covered in gooseflesh.

"Have a nice nap?" the block-jawed Perch grins at me. He grips a shock prod down at his side. It sparks eagerly. "Hope you enjoyed yourself. You won't be gettin' any more winks for a while, I'm afraid."

We're alone in a small room with cold steel walls. A solid, windowless door stands a few meters beyond my chained feet. I can't see anything on either side. Perch moves behind me and rattles something on a metal tray. I drop my head back to find a cart, upside-down from my perspective. Perch holds a pair of large pliers and winks.

"The boss is gonna fix you up good. But first, I gotta make sure you won't be any trouble." He chuckles and nods down at me knowingly. "Been a while since you had a manicure, huh?"

He jams the prod into my side, just above my groin, and I grit my teeth to keep from screaming. My claws flex outward against my will, and he's ready with the pliers. He clamps on and rips the talon out of my index finger with brutal strength. It feels as though my finger's been torn from its socket. A hoarse scream escapes me as he lets the bloody claw drop to the floor. I pull against my restraints with all my might and arch my back. Then I fall on the chains and swing against him. He steadies me with one hand.

"Easy now. One down. Nine to go." He chuckles. "Hurts like hell, I bet."

He's a sadist. My head swims, dangling below my shoulders as the room spins. Pain blooms, and I look at my finger, wet with blood.

Will the claw grow back? Will the spirits bless me anew?

Where are they now?

Perch pulls out the next one from my middle finger, stripping me of my gift one claw at a time. I scream again, unable to control myself. The lights blink out, and everything goes black. Have I lost consciousness? The glaring white returns as the pliers rip the claw from my third finger. I scream, enraged. With all of the determination I can muster, I focus on willing the remaining talons to retract. I can't tell whether they obey me. I'm beginning to lose feeling in my limbs. Perhaps that's for the best.

"Hey now, don't you try anything cute." Perch jams the prod into me again, but the pain is nothing compared to the pliers. He hits me with it again on a higher setting. The jolt of electricity courses through me, shaking every nerve in my body. "Good boy." The pliers tug out another claw and send it to the floor.

The lights go out again. This time, they don't return.

I stand at the edge of the lake. A grassy slope descends toward dark silt beneath the lapping water. Rain falls heavily, and a wind has picked up from the north, driving short white crests onto shore. Raindrops plummet into the choppy surface, and I long to dive into the tumult. But my feet are planted to the ankles in the soil. No matter how hard I pull, I stand rooted here like a tree.

I turn my face to the sky and keep my eyes closed in the downpour. I feel the presence of the Creator. He's not in the rain or the wind, but they both are from Him. They are His creation.

"What are mortals, that You should think of us?" The words emerge from deep in my mind. They escape me in a whisper, a prayer. The fresh water rushes between my parted lips, and I swallow. "You put us in charge of everything you made." We were unworthy of such responsibility, yet He already knew the end at its beginning. He gave us free dominion of His creation, knowing what we would do with it. And even so, He's given us a second chance. For He was, and is, and forever shall be the God of second chances. "Behold, all things are made new..."

Before my eyes, the lake and everything around it is instantly transformed. The clouds, overloaded with precipitation, disappear, and in their place expands an empty grey sky with a scorching sun. My feet are planted in sand now, not damp earth. The trees have been replaced with an arid, ash-colored moonscape that's all too familiar to me. A sinking feeling hits the pit of my stomach as I gaze across an empty crater and blink against the dry wind that flattens my sodden clothing. It won't be damp for long.

"A new earth," I hear the words rasp from my chapped lips. "A new heavens, and a new earth."

The exposed skin on my face begins to burn, but I can't raise my arms to shield myself from the sun. My hands are restrained by an unseen force at the wrists, my fingers cut off and bleeding. I stare at what remains, overwhelmed by loss. A tear skids down my cheek, dropping to dampen the sand an instant before it's swallowed by the thirsty ground.

"Why have You forsaken me?" I gasp.

Wake up!

High voltage rattles my rib cage and I cry out, my eyes jerking wide open with a start. I focus on my limp, bloody fingers, dangling from the steel shackles. They're still intact, but severely maimed.

"Perch says you took it like a man for the most part. Not too much blubbering." Willard grins at me, his head upside down, his thin face stretched too tightly across the skull underneath. "I told him that you would, but he had his doubts. Anyhow, what's done is done. And now you're on the road to recovery, Luther my man. Say, you don't want these, do you?" He extends an open palm. In it, he holds all ten of my talons, sharp at the tips and oozing fresh blood at the roots. "Mementos from a former life? What do you say?"

I cough against a surge of bile and jerk my head forward, my body swaying violently from the chains.

"Perhaps not. Okay, toss 'em." He hands them to Perch, who takes the claws without a word and heads for the door beyond my suspended feet. Willard wipes the blood from his palm onto a towel and casts it aside. "Bring some water. Luther's been through quite the ordeal today."

With a noncommittal grunt, Perch heaves open the steel door and leaves it to slam shut behind him. The walls reverberate from the impact.

"So." Willard scrapes a metal stool across the floor and seats himself beside my head. "How're you doing, buddy?"

I turn slowly to look up at him, but I say nothing. I clench my jaw, for the first time appreciating the chains that restrain me. Otherwise, I'm afraid I might kill this man.

"You're angry. Sure, I get it. Believe me, you're not the first person to hate my guts, and you won't be the last. Not everybody understands the Eden Guard. They don't realize what we're protecting. But they all see the light, eventually." He winks down at me and pats my bare chest with his clammy hand. "So will you, Luther. You're a reasonable man, after all." He catches himself. "You will be, that is—once we've got you back to normal. Once you're *fixed*."

I cough again, clearing my throat. "Where are my friends?" I manage, my voice little more than a croak. Dizziness washes over me in waves, and I struggle to remain conscious. I don't know how many more jolts from that prod my heart will be able to take without shutting down.

"They're no longer your concern. Think of them as dead, if that helps any. Right now, you've got just yourself to worry about. And that's more than enough, believe you me." He reaches for my right hand and surveys the work of his henchman. He clucks his tongue at the damage. "I'm sure it was tough to see them go.

They've probably come in real handy out there on the surface with all the mutos and what-not to contend with. But now you're one step closer to—"

"How do you control them?"

His beady eyes rotate to meet my gaze. "Hmm?"

"The collars. How do they work?" I strain my neck muscles to keep my head raised.

"You wouldn't understand. It's fairly complicated." He releases my hand.

"How many of them have you fitted with those collars?"

He regards me for a moment, his eyes cold. "Why don't you ask what's really on your mind, Luther? The burning question that demands an answer." He pauses. "Did we send the bunch that went after your cave buddies?"

My jaw muscle twitches. "Did you?"

"We didn't even know you were out there. And besides, it's not like we've got *all* of the mutos collared. For every one we capture, there are easily five more topside running around loose." He curses. "We can't seem to get 'em to turn on each other, no matter how high we increase the settings. It's an extermination problem, really. We've just got to figure out a way to wipe out the rest."

"Sounds like you could really use a nuke." As soon as the words leave my mouth I'm filled with disgust, but the irony isn't lost on him. He laughs out loud, echoing against the walls.

"Yeah, wouldn't that be the ticket! Too bad they're in such short supply these days." His laughter subsides. "So here's the deal, Luther. One of my colleagues will be in here shortly to run a few tests on you, just to make sure you're on your way back to being the way God intended. We'll need to take some tissue samples and maybe a little blood—nothing major." He pats my chest again as he stands. "You just hang tight." He strides toward the door.

I clear my throat, drawing his attention before he leaves. "You're not soldiers, any of you. We know who you really are."

He raises an eyebrow. "Oh?" He waits.

"You're engineers. From Sector 30."

"We were." He bites his lip. Then he shrugs. "Structural, chemical, molecular, genetic, nuclear—you name it. But that was a lifetime ago." He heaves the door open. "No longer relevant."

"We—" I grit my teeth against a sudden wave of nausea. "We were going to find you...on our way to the Preserve. That was the plan, to start a new life together."

"It's all gone, Luther. The Preserve—" He makes an explosive sound that puffs out his hollow cheeks, and he gestures with both hands. "Kaput. We're in a forbidden zone here—the whole continent. Or what's left of it. The rest of the world doesn't want to have anything to do with us." He chuckles dryly. "Sounds like you really need to be brought up to speed on a few things."

My head swims. I can no longer hold it up. The muscles in my neck give way, and my skull snaps backward, dangling. Willard says something before he leaves, but his words are slow and garbled. The door slams shut, and the walls reverberate again. So does my brain.

I can't lose consciousness. I don't want to be shocked awake again. But I don't want to be awake anymore. My eyelids close, falling like a black curtain, and the last thing I see is the metal cart behind me.

I can't sleep long. I need to wake up before Perch returns with his prod. Water? Is he bringing water? I'm so thirsty.

I should dive into the lake and swim past the buoy, something I always did with my brothers during those hot summers at our lake house in the Preserve. Gone forever? Was the Preserve obliterated on D-Day? What does that mean for us? How can we survive in this barren wasteland? Perhaps it's a moot point. My eyelids crack open to glaring white lights and bloody fingers dangling without feeling from the shackles. I may not survive this room, let alone anything beyond it.

What did he mean about a *forbidden zone* and the *rest of the world*? Has he been in contact with survivors on other continents?

How many of them are there? How could he possibly communicate with them?

My eyelids collapse against my will. This time, I have no strength left to deny them, and I surrender to whatever comes next.

When I see light again, I find myself lying on a narrow bed with clean white sheets. Medical machines sit on each side; tubes and hoses of all sizes protrude from my arms and groin, connecting me to these machines. The walls are not steel as they were in that torture chamber. I'm now in a hospital room without any windows, and the only light emanates from above the headboard of my bed, fluorescent and jittery.

Just beyond the foot of my bed, a lone figure stands in the shadows with its back to me. Garbed in a white medical coat that hangs limply from its thin frame. Dark, matted locks of shoulder-length hair. Who is this person?

My wrists, raw from the shackles, are no longer restrained. Yet I can't move a muscle. Am I paralyzed? What have they done to me now?

I take a breath to steady my nerves and look over the equipment around me. Then I try to ask *Where am I?* only to find a weak, unintelligible moan come out of me instead of a voice.

The lone figure doesn't stir. "You may not be able to articulate speech for a while," a woman's voice emerges from behind that curtain of unkempt hair. She sounds as lifeless as she looks. "We have you pumped full of muscle relaxants, sedatives. Probably feels like you're paralyzed, but that's temporary. Just while we run some tests."

Willard said there would be tests. I survey the hoses attached to my body. What are they taking from me? Or injecting me with?

I close my eyes and struggle to take in another deep breath, but it comes shallow. How long have I been here? Why didn't I wake up when they removed my chains? The one named Perch didn't seem able to keep his prod to himself. But if I blacked out completely, they may have had to bring me here to revive me.

That would mean these tubes are for my benefit, feeding me nutrients, keeping me hydrated. But what about my groin? What could that possibly be for?

"So far, you've checked out. The best case we've seen so far. For most of the others, there's no going back, not once the physiological transformations have become permanent." She drops what sounds like a file folder onto the cart at the foot of the bed. Then she turns, and the light illuminates her skeletal features, bruised and swollen. At the base of her neck is a thin strip of metal with a blinking red light. "It looks like you're actually going to make it." Her heavy-lidded eyes stare at me bleakly from their hollow sockets. "Good for you, Luther."

Who are you? I want to ask, but another moan shudders out of me instead. I frown, mouthing the words. No recognition sparks in her vacant eyes. I try again, working my mouth sluggishly around the silent words. Despite my best efforts, I'm not rewarded with a response of any kind from the woman. She looks directly at me, but she doesn't seem to see me.

"My name is Margo. That's who I am." Her voice takes on a haunted quality. "That's who I was...before."

I blink, a poor substitute for a nod. *What do you do here?* I mouth the question once, twice, three times before she responds.

"I'm the closest thing they have to a doctor." Her bony shoulders twitch up and down. "I was a nuclear engineer, but I also studied genetics, and I had some medical training. It's the only reason I'm still alive. All of the rest are—"

Her head jerks suddenly as the light on her collar flares brightly. She falls back a step but steadies herself with a hand on the footboard of the bed, her eyes wide in their deep-set sockets. She whimpers involuntarily and hangs her head as the light on her collar fades, returning to a steady pulse.

The room must be *bugged*, as Samson calls it. Willard or his men are listening in, perhaps through the collar itself. Why have they fitted her with one? She's no daemon, no threat at all by the looks of her.

She shuffles away, into shadows beyond the reach of the fluorescent light above me. I attempt to clear my throat, to release a word or two into the silence. Another moan is the best I'm able to manage. It sounds pitiful. I close my eyes and try to move my arms, my legs. Nothing, not even a tingle of energy through the muscles. My body's useless. How long will these drugs maintain their hold on me?

My gaze wanders past the shackle scars on my wrist to my ravaged fingers. Am I returning to the way I was before, a normal human again—a *natural child of God*? I didn't ask to be gifted by the spirits of the earth, and at first my claws filled me with a certain degree of horror. It took some time to come to accept them, but I did. They became a part of me as I embraced my gift.

A flash of recent memory tears through my mind: Perch with pliers in hand, removing pieces of me against my will, ripping them away and sending them to the floor. They were supernatural, beyond comprehension, a sign of intervention by a higher power on our behalf. Cast aside like so much garbage.

Seething with anger, I stare at the ceiling and take a breath to steady myself, to shut out any thoughts of vengeance. The Creator would not be pleased. *Vengeance is Mine...* As difficult as it is to believe right now, He has extended the same second chance at life to Willard's people as He has to the rest of us. There must be a way for us to coexist. Otherwise, we'll destroy each other. And that can't be His will.

How have they avoided the *physiological transformations* bestowed upon us by the spirits? If Willard's people have never been in contact with the new earth, that could explain it. And it could also explain why I haven't been able to sense the spirits' presence since we entered this underground city. Perhaps their influence doesn't extend this far beneath so much concrete and steel.

I stare into the shadows beyond the foot of my bed. Why has this woman been collared? The only female I've seen among these Eden Guards, and she's obviously been beaten, starved, controlled remotely—to what end? What did she try to tell me before she was cut short?

A door creaks open from off to the left, behind my line of sight. White light washes inside before the door slides shut with a solid thud. But in that moment, the shadows beyond the foot of my bed are illuminated, and I see Margo cowering in the corner, her face hidden behind a curtain of matted hair.

"How's our favorite patient?" Willard drags a stool toward my bedside and grins, glancing at the hose between my legs. "Yikes. Be glad you can't feel that one." He chuckles and swivels toward the shadows. "Get up," he barks. "Get over here. I want him to be able to talk some—not a lot, mind you. Just enough for us to have a little conversation."

Her feet shuffle out of the dark as she moves toward the steel cart. She keeps her head down as she removes a hand-held instrument and inserts a cartridge of some kind into its base. Willard watches her closely, his small eyes full of contempt, tracking her every move. She hesitates, standing frozen.

"Give it to 'im already!" he startles her.

She comes around the other side of the bed and applies her instrument to my throat. I feel nothing. Willard fishes a protein pack from his pocket and tosses it into the shadows.

"Eat," he tells her. She drops the instrument onto the cart and dives after her meal. She tears it open and chews noisily, gasping between each bite. "Try to talk a little," he tells me. "Start with a whisper. Your vocal cords have been asleep most of the day now. Don't stress 'em out too much."

I swallow, then attempt, "Where are my friends?" Relief pours through me as a voice similar to my own hoarsely emerges.

Willard shakes his head. "You've got a one-track mind, I'll give you that. Didn't I tell you not to worry about them? You have more than enough going on right here, Luther."

"Who is she?" I turn my eyes to the shadows.

"None of your concern." His expression hardens. "For now

she's your doctor, and she's going to fix you up. That's all you need to know."

"What have you done to her?"

"You name it. She's a real animal in the sack, and that's a fact." He chuckles but seems to catch himself, sobering instantly. "We're taking your seed, Luther. Your sperm cells."

I stare at him.

"Figured you'd want to know what that's for." He shrugs and gestures at my groin. "The others are for blood work, making sure everything checks out. We don't want you to have a relapse or anything." He winks. "Then we'd have to put you down for good."

I swallow again. "Why...my sperm cells?"

"C'mon now. Use that staggering intellect God gave you. Can't you put the pieces together here?" He sighs, squeezing between his eyes. "All right, all right. You've been through a lot today, so I'll go easy on you. Here's the situation: we're fresh out of seed around here. The government bigwigs made sure of it before they sent us below. We're all out of eggs, to boot, so we're stocking up on those as well. We've got all the facilities we need for cold storage, and with her expertise—" He jerks a thumb toward the dark corner. "—we should be able to whip up a batch or two of test-tube babies in no time." He laughs out loud at my expression. "Pretty neat, huh?"

I'm going to be sick.

"So what do you think, Luther my man? Up for becoming Father Abraham to Eden's next generation?"

Are Samson and Shechara in rooms like this one? Has the time finally come for us to fulfill our life's purpose of repopulating the earth—against our will? I close my eyes, unable to look at this man's hideous grin without wanting to tear it off his face. What am I going to do? What can I? I'm completely at his mercy.

"It's a lot to wrap your head around, I'm sure. But believe me, you're doing a good thing here. The survival of the human race—"

"How do you know," I manage in a whisper, "that this generation you plan on creating will not exhibit the same *physiological transformations* you seem to despise so much?"

"Now that's using the ol' noggin. I knew you had it in you." He nods, grinning. "Of course, you're right. We don't know yet. This is the first major step we've been able to take in months. We tried with the mutos, but they're all messed up. You wouldn't believe it. No chance they'll ever be able to reproduce anything but snot. You're the first virile specimens we've come across, so you have the distinction of being our guinea pigs, if you know what I mean." He winks and leans in. "That's what all these tests are for. We're checking every cell to make sure none of 'em are infected."

Is that how he perceives our gifts? "And you, your men... How have you been able to avoid this *infection*?"

He leans back. "Easy. Just stay off the surface, that's the ticket. The demon-dust can't get us down here. We've got the air filtered and purified, pumping throughout all of Eden, and we never need to go topside. The dogs bring down everything we need from the ruins." He catches himself. "Though now we've got a hundred less of 'em, thanks to you and your buddies."

"Dogs?" Does he mean the collared daemons we encountered in the tunnel?

"That's what we call 'em. Because they *fetch* what we need from any storehouses still intact."

"How have you managed to collar so many?"

"I've got a very special helper."

"Like Margo?"

His expression hardens. "That's not who she is anymore."

Have I struck a nerve? "It's her name."

"No. It's not. It hasn't been for a long time now."

I glance at the shadows. "She's infected?"

He clenches his jaw, and a large vein in his temple twitches. For once, he has nothing to say.

"You were unable to reverse her physiological—"

He stands. "Let's hope you're a success, Luther. I don't think you'd much like the alternative."

"You control her...and you abuse her." Is there any humanity left in this man? "Her name is Margo, and she's one of your own. A child of God."

"She's an *animal*." His eyes bulge, the muscles in his neck expanding as he screams, "Nothing more!"

He leaves the room, slamming the door shut behind him. But before it closes, exterior light invades the darkness for a fraction of a second, illuminating the far corner. She crouches on the floor, licking the wrapper of a devoured protein pack, oblivious as shadows consume her.

There's something about her history with Willard, something in their past that caused him to lose control of himself just now. It may be a weakness I can exploit in the future. A very trivial victory in the grand scheme of things, but lying paralyzed in this bed, I can't help but find some measure of satisfaction in getting under his skin for the first time.

Does he feel guilt for what he's done to this woman? If there remains any good in him at all, he would have to. Some part of him must know his treatment of her is demented and wrong. She's no animal.

Or is she? Are we all—those who've been changed by the spirits—more like animals than not? We're more than merely human; that can't be denied.

I glance at my mutilated fingers. What will the tests show? Have I become as I once was, as Willard and his men are: humans left untouched by the spirits? Or will I remain changed on a cellular level and be exterminated because of it? Or worse: will I be collared as one of Willard's *dogs*, forced to do his bidding?

How I wish we'd never come here, that Daiyna had never heard from the spirits in the first place. Why did they lead us to Eden? What was their purpose in all of this?

"You haven't asked how long you've been here."

I look up sharply to find Margo standing over me. I didn't hear her approach.

"Does it matter?" my voice croaks.

Her frail shoulders lift and fall. "They usually ask that, when they come to."

"They?"

"The other subjects. The big man did. And the two women."

Only Shechara was with Samson. "*Two* women?" My heart races. Did they find Daiyna?

She leans forward, adjusting the tubes and hoses attached to me.

"Are they all right?"

She gives me a direct look and touches her collar. "I can't tell you anything. I need to check your samples." Then she mouths silently: *They're alive.* She turns away and faces the machines beside me, her hands moving across each apparatus with familiarity.

What about Milton? Was he too fast for Willard's men? Did he abandon us, or is he even now planning a rescue? A foolish thought. From the moment I first met him, I saw that he cared only for himself. More than likely, he's brushed the dust of the city ruins from the soles of his boots and is racing across the scorched earth on his own, come what may. Very little could possibly harm him, due to his gift.

Daiyna said the spirits of the earth wanted him. For what exactly, she didn't know. Those who spoke to her simply told her she must save him, and they showed her how to do so in a dream.

I too dreamt of Milton. While Perch performed his sadistic extractions, my mind escaped from that violent reality, returning to my family's lake house in the Preserve. I was running along one of the forest roads through the rain, and Milton appeared and warned me of something...

His image is vivid now in my mind, but why can't I remember what he said?

"Everything's looking good. I think we can risk bringing your muscles back to life, as long as you promise to behave. You don't want one of these, trust me." She touches the collar again.

"Agreed." My voice cracks, struggling to return full-strength.

She retrieves the same instrument from the cart and fills it with a fresh cartridge. Hesitating a moment, she surveys my body, perhaps waiting to see if her collar shocks her into a different course of action. Then she moves along my arms and torso, applying the instrument at intervals. Injections of some sort, but I feel nothing.

Without warning, a sudden tingle spreads through my muscles, blossoming into a prickling heat similar to what I've experienced after a limb hasn't received adequate circulation.

"Might feel a little weird at first. You'll probably want to jump out of your skin."

That would be an understatement. I grit my teeth as the sensation crawls through me.

"Don't move around or try to get up yet. You might hurt yourself. You haven't been up and around for a couple days now."

So that's how long I've been here. I jerk involuntarily, tugging against the hoses.

"These can go now. We've got plenty of...what we need." She removes each of the plastic tubes. The one at my groin occupies her longer than the others. "You may notice some discoloration here, bruising. It will fade in time."

Is this the same pitiful creature I saw cowering in the corner? How can it be? Now she displays all the poise and detached expertise of a doctor. My muscles shudder spastically, and I shiver with cold. She quickly unfolds a sheet and covers me in a single movement.

"This has a heating element in it. Should help with the shock of your re-entry."

I nod, now that I'm able. "Thank you."

"Just doing my job. Don't you go and get a crush on me or anything."

I catch her eye and mouth the words, *Where are they?*

She looks down, then meets my gaze briefly. *Next door*, her silent lips reply.

I must see them.

She looks away, shaking her head as she tucks the sheet around me. "Give this a few minutes, and then we'll try propping you up."

Warmth oozes across my skin, and my muscles begin to relax. The prickling sensation gradually fades. She removes my right arm from beneath the sheet and holds my hand cupped in her open palms.

"Try wiggling your fingers." She looks at my ravaged fingertips, her expression vacant.

I must see them, I mouth the words again.

"Nothing, huh?" She shakes her head.

I focus on my hand, and eventually my fingers twitch in her grasp.

"Good. Now I'm going to ask you to flex your claws for me."

What? Doesn't she know? "They...they're gone."

"We have to be sure. Do whatever it is you do to make them appear."

Are they all right? I watch her lips.

She massages my fingertips, one at a time. They've been cleaned, no longer bloody. But the skin looks wrinkled, like the aftermath of an amputation. She doesn't answer me.

Have my friends' gifts been removed as well? What have Willard and Perch done to them?

"I'm waiting." She sounds like a physical therapist.

I grit my teeth and flex my fingers, willing them to move. They respond, stretching outward in five directions. The tendons on the back of my hand rise to the surface. But that's all. It's merely the hand of a natural man.

"Very good," she says quietly. She replaces my arm under the sheet and moves around to the other side of the bed where we repeat the same exercise with my left hand. "Captain Willard will be pleased."

"Oh, I'm sure he will be." The sarcasm in my tone isn't lost on her. She gives me a cautionary glance—the only expression I've seen from her yet.

"Now let's get you sitting up." She reaches under the bed to flip a switch, and the entire frame hums to life. The mattress inclines slowly, propping my torso upright. "How's that?"

A slight vertigo swims through me, but it passes. *What's been done to them?* I mouth the words, but she looks away. "How soon before you let me out of here?" I stretch both my arms out in front of me and clench my fists. It's wonderful to have feeling in them again.

"That will be up to the captain to decide. And of course, it'll depend on your behavior." She fixes me with her blank stare.

What have they done to my friends?

This time, she reads my entire question and shakes her head slowly. *You don't want to know,* she mouths.

A heaviness settles in the pit of my stomach. Willard will pay dearly if they've been harmed in any way.

I swing my legs over the edge of the bed and cast aside the sheet. "Give me something to wear." I glance down at my exposed genitals and wince at the bruising.

"I can't help you!" she hisses, then jerks involuntarily, her hands curling inward. "He's coming back!" she chokes out before collapsing to the floor in convulsions. The red light on her collar flashes angrily.

I push myself off the bed and land on legs that wobble, sending me careening against the machines as I do my best to head straight for the door. I right myself quickly and reach for the handle. Unlocked. I shove it to the side and am met with a blast of white light. I raise an arm to shield my eyes and find that I'm on one of the suspended catwalks along the dome's interior. On the concrete floor below, Willard stands with a dozen of his armed soldiers, their rifles aimed at my head.

"I'll give you an *A* for effort, Luther. You've got some real *cojones*—a little blue, from the looks of 'em, but I'm sure that'll pass." He chuckles, and his men echo, nodding to each other.

"I want to see my friends." I keep my voice level and pray for strength to quell the fury raging within me. "I don't want any trouble."

"Right." Willard nods and smoothes his thin mustache with one hand. Then he cocks his head to one side and points next to me. "You'll find one of 'em in there. The big one." He grins, and the others nod knowingly. "What's left of him, that is."

I turn toward the door beside me, next to the unit where I've spent the past two days. Laughter echoes from below as I lay my hand on the handle and push the door aside. My eyes slowly adjust to the dim light above the bed in the center of the room. The machines look familiar, as do the hoses attached to the torso and groin of my brother, Samson.

But there is nothing familiar about the sight of him.

He lies on his back, unconscious, his broad chest expanding and settling with every thunderous snore, his arms amputated and cauterized at the elbows, his legs at the knees.

I stagger forward.

My rage erupts in a hoarse scream.

12. MILTON

TEN MONTHS AFTER ALL-CLEAR

I have no idea what's going on.

First there was that voice in my head telling me to kill them all. Then it told me to take her, forced me to. I couldn't resist the power inside me; it was overwhelming. So I took her throat in my hand...but that's when everything gets real fuzzy.

I remember squealing tires and white-hot floodlights coming out of nowhere. I wasn't really paying attention. Something came over me as soon as I touched her. A sizzling burst of energy shot through my arm, straight to my head—a rush, that's for sure—and the next thing I knew, I was picking her up and carrying her out of there.

She wasn't conscious anymore. What did I do to her? She was limp, draped over my shoulder like a sack of nourishment packs, and I was running as fast as I could, the concrete walls and abandoned vehicles rushing past the periphery of my vision in a blur, illuminated only by my glowstick.

Then we were out in the middle of the city ruins, tearing through debris-strewn streets under the moon's frosty glow. And that's when things got weirder. I was maybe two or three kilometers into the heart of the city when I stopped and lowered her body to the ground. I watched her lying there on her back. Like she was asleep. But she could have been dead.

"Why?" Why was I doing this?

You do not need her now.

The voice came from inside me, but it wasn't the same one I'd heard before, the one that told me to kill everybody except her. Somehow, it had changed. More subdued, maybe. Not as fierce?

Go.

I broke into a run, leaving her behind, alone in the middle of that street. The city ruins vanished behind me as I tore across the cratered desolation. I glanced back at the giant plume of dust in my wake, remembering the first time I ran like this, when Mother Earth chased me in all her fury. I was in danger then. That's what she told me—Daiyna—and I believed it.

But now things are different. I'm faster than I was by a factor of two, maybe ten. And I'm not alone.

That's the really weird thing.

"I always like this part." Julia hugs my arm, pressing her warm curves against me. We sit on a large boulder overlooking the valley below. The moon has faded away with the approach of dawn, and in a moment the sun's golden orb will make its first appearance of the day, peeking over the horizon before us. "It never gets old."

"For you, maybe." Jackson stands with his boots planted shoulder-width apart, arms crossed over his chest. "I for one would've enjoyed sleeping in today."

"Face shields ready..." Julia holds hers up with a giggle, like it's a game. I get mine out of my jumpsuit pocket. Jackson fastens his on right away. "Party pooper," she chides him.

"I don't fancy scorching my retinas," he grumbles.

"You'll wait with me, won't you, Milton?" She hugs my arm tighter, smiling with full lips and sparkling green eyes, her long blonde hair caught by the morning breeze that wafts up from the valley floor below.

I nod. Of course I will. I'll wait until the last nanosecond with her, and we'll see the sun rise together. Just like we do every morning...that I can remember. It doesn't get old for me either.

Weird, but not old. I would never get tired of doing anything with her.

Am I dead? I know they are. I killed them both.

"Three...two," she counts down. "One!"

The sun breaches the horizon in streams of molten bronze, a glorious sight to behold. And behold it we do—for a few seconds, anyway. Then we fasten our face shields into place before the harsh morning rays can do any permanent damage.

I wish we could hold off a little longer. Now with our features hidden, I can't see Julia's eyes behind that panel of reflective polymer. I see only an image of myself, my own cracked, gravel-pitted face shield and filthy jumpsuit. How have they managed to keep theirs so clean? Pristine, fresh from the bunker.

"Hungry?" she asks me.

"Too bad." Jackson curses, shuffling his boots. "We've got nothing."

"He does." She pats my leg, just above my knee. I stir at her touch. "Samson made sure you had a few packs when he brought your suit to you. Don't you remember? Before you were shot by those mutants."

"He doesn't remember any of that." Jackson faces us. "Doesn't matter anymore. We've got just one thing to agree on here, and we can't keep putting it off. You know as well as I do that he's—"

"You remember, don't you, Milton?" She squeezes my thigh as she leans into me. "Luther, Samson...Daiyna?"

The names are familiar, and I remember who they are. But they're from a long time ago. Before this—here, wherever we are.

"He doesn't know what you're talking about." Jackson scoffs.

"Stop trying to interfere," she warns him.

"I don't have to *try*. His hatred of me is greater than his love for you. The guilt he carries only increases my influence. You should stop trying. You won't be able to bring him back from the edge of the abyss."

What the hell? This has to be a nightmare. I'm asleep, haunted by these voices from my past. Unless they're both ghosts... And I've finally lost it. Completely. Crossed the point of no return to semi-sanity.

"You won't take him," she says in a low tone, as if I'm not supposed to hear. "Not easily."

Jackson shrugs. "I've got time. They're not going anywhere, and neither are we." He turns away, leaning against the boulder as he watches the sun in its sluggish ascent.

"Eat, Milton." She pats my pocket, and a wrapper wrinkles in response.

My stomach gurgles and twists. I didn't realize I was so hungry. I pull out the protein pack and tear it open, pausing only to release the bottom of my face shield so I can slide the flavorless meal toward my teeth. I take a big bite and start chewing it down to a consistency I can swallow.

"Good?" She watches me.

I nod. "Tastes like nothing else." She giggles, and I hand her what's left. "Want some?"

She shakes her head, gently pushing it back. "You need it. You have to keep up your strength."

"We don't eat," Jackson tosses over his shoulder.

Right. Because they're *ghosts*.

"Don't listen to him." She bumps my shoulder with her own. "He's just grumpy that we woke him up. Maybe we should watch the sunrise tomorrow without him."

Jackson laughs out loud. "Good luck with that. You're stuck with me now, sweetheart."

"So..." I swallow another bite and hesitate. "Where are we exactly?"

He sighs and drops his head, muttering something that sounds like, "Again?" But I didn't ask him. I asked Julia.

"We're in the Preserve, Milton." She pauses, weighing her words. "This is what it looks like now."

The Preserve? That's crazy. How many hundreds of kilometers did I run? I couldn't have gone that far. And besides, this place doesn't look any different from the rest of this messed-up planet

—the same endless stretches of lifeless terrain I've seen for months. No trees, no babbling brooks. She can't be right.

"This is all that's left. There is no place on earth left untouched by the cataclysmic actions of your kind. There are survivors on every continent, but their world has changed. It's not as they left it, and it's not as they expected to find it."

That much is obvious.

"You're all going to run out of oxygen and starve to death, eventually," Jackson says. "Unless you take to eating each other like those mutant degenerates. Or you could start eating *them*, I guess. Hunt them down." He laughs without any humor in his tone. "Better to be put out of your misery. Believe me, you don't want to see what's coming. You'll put up a good fight, but in the end, it won't matter any. Futile, when you come right down to it."

"Optimist," she teases him.

"Realist." He glances at me. "Don't let her fill your head with empty hope. She doesn't see the big picture. And she refuses to do what's necessary." He curses quietly and mutters, "All she does is delay the inevitable."

"You don't know any more than I do. You don't have the mind of God." She points at him. "You're as finite as I am."

"It doesn't take the mind of *God* to see the future here. Their world is destroyed. They have no way to grow food for themselves. All they can do is scavenge from what's still viable beneath their own ruins. But that supply is far from inexhaustible, believe me. I've seen it. And I'll give them a year or two at most—if they can survive that long, considering everything else." He shakes his head slowly. "Face it. The time of humankind has come and gone."

He says it like he's not human himself. Because he's not. I've got to remember that. None of this is really happening. It is—but it's not real. They're not really...*real*. It's virtual reality or something, my mind playing tricks on me. Hallucinating.

And I thought that voice in my head was bad. Where's it gone?

"You're wrong," she says. "They've been given a second chance."

"By whom? The *Creator*?" His tone sounds bitter. "You know as well as I do, he left us a long time ago. We haven't been the apple of his eye for centuries. Maybe millennia."

"You don't know that."

"Look at what he allowed to happen to his creation. He made us first, before he made them, and look at what he let them do to us!" He lapses into a string of curses.

Good ol' Jackson with his limited vocabulary.

"They've always had free will. He gave it to them in the beginning. Don't you remember? He may have made us first, but we were never *first* in His sight. They've always held that special place. It's been a great mystery, all along."

Honestly, I have no idea what they're going on about. They were never like this in the bunker. They barely said a word to each other. And this discussion seems pretty deep—philosophical, metaphysical, whatever. Really, really weird.

"So..." I break the awkward silence, stuffing the protein pack's wrapper into my pocket. "Any particular reason we're up here?"

"You brought us," Jackson snorts with a backward glance. "But you probably don't remember that either, right?"

I doubt it was my idea. That voice in my head... "What do you want to do?" I nudge Julia and her face shield turns toward me.

"Up for some flying lessons?" Her voice bubbles with sudden excitement.

"Huh?"

"When was it—only yesterday?" Jackson grumbles. "And he's already forgotten."

What happened yesterday? Why can't I remember anything before the sunrise? The most recent memory I have is running up here through the dead of night and—

"Cut him some slack. He's been through a lot, thanks to you." She rubs my leg tenderly with her gloved hand.

Cut me some slack. Right. And then hang me with it.

I squeeze my eyes shut and take a deep breath. I killed them both, along with everybody else in the bunker. Will the rest of them be visiting me too? Is this my punishment, my hell? God knows, I deserve it.

God?

I glance over at Jackson. It was all his fault, and I killed him for it. Do I have it in me to do it again? I don't know if I can, or even if I'd be able to. How do you kill a ghost, anyway? Make it say its true name backwards? Something like that, I bet.

"I'm not finished with him. We're not finished." Jackson shakes his head slowly. "You two can go and play house all you like, but you'll get the idea eventually. There's only one thing for him to do, and you've given him the ability to do it. You can't take it back now."

"C'mon." She tugs at my sleeve as she slides off the boulder, ignoring Jackson. "We'll leave him here and go have our own fun."

She's just like I remember her, so full of life. She loved me for *me*, not anything I could do for her, and I never understood it. How does anyone love like that? But I loved her back because of it, or regardless of it. All we ever had was each other, all the way to the end.

Her end. At my hands.

Yet here she is again, coaxing me off the boulder, giggling at my reluctance. I wish I could see her smile, her sparkling eyes, those thick locks of golden hair, smooth as silk. Her skin, firm but soft, and delicious. I swell as scenes of our love-making play through my mind.

Apparition or not, I'll go with her wherever she leads me, even if it's to my death. That would only be fair, right?

"Don't wander off too far," Jackson mutters, rooted.

"This way, Milton." She leads me by the hand, our gloved fingers intertwined. We climb up the grade toward the plateau above, the gravel shifting beneath our boots. "You're going to love this!"

I love her. More than anything. I always have. I don't care if she's dead or if I am or if none of this is really real. It doesn't matter right now. We're together again.

I glance back at Jackson, his broad figure a dark, motionless silhouette against the rising sun. Why is he here? I don't want him to be. I thought I was finally rid of him.

"Here we are." She sighs, releasing me as we reach the top. Hands on her shapely hips, she turns and tilts her head, her face shield glinting. "Want me to go first?" Another giggle, one that makes her shoulders bounce a little.

"Where?" I step toward her.

She points, and I follow her finger aimed across this barren plateau to its abrupt end, maybe fifty meters ahead of us.

"Off the edge?" I sound like a stupid kid.

She spreads her arms out from her sides and backs away from me. "Watch and learn."

She runs away, her laughter filling the moment. I watch her backside as she takes off, faster, gaining momentum. A grin stretches my face. I'll let her have a head start, but I'll overtake her easily. With each stride she takes, I feel a tug, a yearning for her. I can't let her go.

I dash after her, coming abreast of her in an instant.

"What took you so long?" she says.

"Had to make it seem fair."

"What?" She tilts her head.

"Aren't we racing?"

"Are we?" She reaches out to touch my shoulder. "Look down."

I don't know how or when it happened, but the ground has disappeared. It's still there, but it's not where I left it. Now it's hundreds of meters below us. We're soaring...through the air.

Flying?

"Ho!" My stomach seizes up, and my limbs flail wildly.

"Relax, you're doing great." She pats my shoulder. Her movements are effortless, like an angel, a dove. "You'll get the hang of it again."

Again? I beat the air with my arms and pump my legs, fighting to stay afloat. Being up here is a fluke. I'm going to fall at any moment, plummet back to the earth and break every bone in my body. My heart pounds crazily as adrenaline floods my system. How is this happening?

"Try to float, like you would in a pool. You don't have to fight to stay in the air. Just let it happen naturally."

Easy for her to say. It's obvious she's done this before. "H-how...?" I manage.

She giggles. "Close your eyes. Imagine yourself drifting on a cloud. You wouldn't punch your way through a cloud, would you?"

Point taken—not that I've handled many clouds in my day. Gritting my teeth, I force myself to stop thrashing my limbs.

"Take a deep breath now. Just relax, Milton. It's not about effort." She turns over onto her back and stretches out her arms and legs. "Enjoy it."

I try letting my limbs go limp. Oddly enough, I don't drop instantly. I don't sense any change in altitude at all. She's still beside me.

We're not floating on air here. The wind rushes against us, flapping the baggier portions of our jumpsuits. We're moving, flying fast. But where to?

I swallow, then lick my dry lips. "How is this possible?"

"Doubts from the fastest man on earth?"

"That's a...gift." It's what they told me. From who? No idea, but they had gifts, too—special abilities. Luther, Daiyna, Plato. So long ago and far away from here.

I used to want to fly, back when I was a kid. I had recurring dreams where I could swoop over the heads of crowds, and they'd look up and gasp, amazed at my superhuman ability. Some kind of psychological complex, probably. But I never made it this high, and never this fast.

"I...always wanted to do this." My voice is barely audible.

She nods. "I know."

"How?" I never told her. I'm sure of it.

"I know you, Milton. I was with Daiyna for a time, but now I'm with you, and I know all about you. Everything, both good and bad. I know the burden you carry. You blame yourself for the evil you were forced to do. But you need to let it go. You need to release yourself."

"I killed you." My throat closes up. My eyes sting. "I killed all of you."

"You were in a horrible place. There was nothing you could do—"

"I should have killed him sooner." I was a coward. So weak.

"You can't wallow in regret, Milton. You can't change the past, and you can't let it control you. If you do, he wins."

Jackson? "Why is he here?"

"Why am I here?"

"Because I love you."

She giggles and dips her chin. "I love you too, Milton."

My insides fill with warmth, and tears trail down my cheeks. I'm glad my face shield hides them.

"No matter what, remember that I love you. And that you love me. Let go of the past, Milton. Embrace this moment, right now." She takes my hand and squeezes it. "With me."

We pick up speed then, diving headfirst through the blue, the wind flattening our suits against us and tugging at my hood, rattling my face shield. I can't tell where we're going, but the landscape below is passing faster than I could have imagined possible, so much faster than during my superspeedy sprints.

"Do you know where we are?" she asks.

Everything down there looks the same. She points, and as she does, we angle our trajectory and begin to descend, closing in on a deformed mountain range. My stomach sinks. She's taking me back...where I left them all to die. Why?

I try to pull away from her, but she tightens her grip on my hand, and we plunge toward the foothills.

"Why here?" my voice cracks.

Her face shield turns toward me. "You'll see."

"I don't want to."

"You can't keep running away, Milton."

What's she talking about? How's she even *talking*? I left her body wrapped in a tarp back in the bunker storeroom. With all the others. At All-Clear, I shut that giant door behind me and never looked back. I couldn't.

The earth looms before us now and we shift our postures, rotating backward so the ground meets our boots as we land. Julia does so with practiced ease. I hit the gravel and sprawl forward, rolling a few times before I'm able to stagger to my feet, covered in dust.

"You okay?" She jogs my way.

"Yeah," I manage, stretching my sore back. "I'll have to practice that."

"You're doing better each time."

I've flown before? Why can't I remember? Something like that should stand out.

I glance around us. Then I stare. This is it, where the mutants came en masse with all their jeeps and rifles and rocket launchers. Where I ran past them and left the survivors to their fate up in the caves. Where I paused to turn a few of the mutants' weapons on each other before I raced off.

I remember running away like it was yesterday. But I remember something else, too: the voice in my head telling me what to do, where to go. Why did I listen, obeying without question? Was it controlling me?

"Does this look familiar?" she asks quietly.

I nod. But there are some things here I don't remember from before—mounds of different shapes and sizes in the sand. Of course the vehicles and hungry cannibals are gone. That battle's been over for who knows how long. But what are these strange sand formations?

I point out the closest one and step toward it. "They weren't here before."

She walks beside me as I approach the mound protruding a

meter from the earth. I poke it with my gloved finger. It gives slightly, soft like a hydropack, the ashen sand on the surface shifting, sliding to the ground. Whatever's underneath is covered in a thick layer of the stuff. I stare at it for a moment like I'm waiting for it to reveal itself to me. Then I wipe with both hands, shoving the sand aside.

What emerges is the head of a mutant, buried waist-deep and frozen, jaw locked open in horror.

"Okay then." I drop back a step, my adrenaline surging. "Didn't expect that."

"It's dead."

"Right."

"They all are." She gestures at the sand sculptures around us. "He buried them."

"Who?"

"Once they did what he wanted them to, he drowned them in the dust of the earth. He didn't need them anymore. He'll do the same to you, if you do as he asks."

"Hold on now." I raise both hands. "Who the hell are you talking about?"

She grasps my arm, squeezing it as she implores me, "He'll try to use your past against you, make you think you're something you're not. You can't listen to him. You've got to let go of the past—"

"Right. I get it. Forgive myself, warm fuzzies and all that." I take her by the shoulders. "But who are you talking about?"

"You already know."

The gravel shifts next to us as the dust begins to swirl upward and outward, seeming to come alive. At the same time, the dry earth gives a low rumble and breaks open, the clay below spreading apart to release the figure of a man who erupts headfirst from the ground. He leaps to stand before us, his jumpsuit and face shield covered in dirt.

"How was your flight?" Jackson's voice emerges as he brushes himself off with his gloved hands.

"Exhilarating." Julia crosses her arms. "You should try it."

"No thanks."

"What are you doing here?" I blurt out.

His face shield tilts toward me. "Now that's a multifaceted question, to be sure. Were you enjoying your one-on-one time with her, and my presence here is both unexpected and unwelcome? Or do you think I'm dead, and I should be back in that bunker where you left me, a corpse festering in my own blood? Or could it be that you know none of this is real—we're not really here—but you're okay with it, as long as it's her you see and not me?"

"I thought we left you at the Preserve—or wherever we were."

"Oh." He returns to dusting himself off. "Well, you're gonna find you can't leave me behind anywhere, not anymore. Not for long. I'm with you for the long haul, Milton ol' buddy."

"We were just admiring your handiwork." Julia glances back at the uncovered cannibal.

"Not bad, eh? They never saw it coming." He slaps at his pant legs and returns to his full height, as tall as ever. "So you haven't been up into the caves yet?"

Why would I want to? "I have a pretty good idea what's in there."

"Probably looks a lot like what you'd find in the Sector 43 bunker. Only these corpses are a bit fresher. What's left of 'em, anyway." He chuckles and clears his throat. "But let's take a look-see. You never know. One or two might've made it. And you could redeem yourself, be the big hero come to the rescue!"

I turn to Julia. "Did any of them make it?"

She shakes her head. Her shoulders rise and fall. "I don't know, Milton."

"Of course she does!" Jackson guffaws. "Why else would she bring you way out here? She wants you to let go of the past, right? Isn't that her mantra? Well, what better way than to make up for what you did?" He backs away, beckoning me to follow. "C'mon, let's go take a look around."

Julia stands rooted, her posture unchanged as I take a step after him.

"Aren't you coming?"

"You don't have to go with him, Milton. You have a choice." Then she's quiet, subdued like she used to get in the bunker when she thought about home and her family.

"I have to know." If there's even one who's made it, who's still alive up there—

"You're not going to like what you see. He'll use it against you."

"Let's cut the melodrama. I don't have all day, and I'm pretty sure they don't, either." Jackson starts climbing the steep grade. "How long is a human able to go without water?"

I feel my pocket. There's a hydropack in it, maybe two.

"You'll...still be here." I watch Julia as I follow Jackson.

"I'm not going anywhere, Milton. You're stuck with me, too."

I look back at her as I trudge away. She watches me go. But as the climb becomes more arduous, I have to focus on the shifting gravel beneath me.

"If you want to *fly* on up, I'll meet you there," Jackson tosses over his shoulder.

"I'm fine."

He chuckles. "Avoid doing it whenever you can. Next thing you know, she'll be giving you a harp and a halo. And we both know they wouldn't suit you."

"Am I dead?"

He glances back, his face shield glinting in the sun. "Are you?"

"You are."

"True enough. You laid me out straight and cut me open real good, from what I recall. A little overkill, but I'll chalk that up to years of repressed emotions." He pauses. "If I'm dead, how the hell am I here now?"

"You're not." I nearly slip but catch myself with one hand. "I'm imagining you."

He laughs out loud. "Then you've sure got one hell of an imagination! Wow, I'm just a hallucination, huh?" His laughter subsides. "You're okay with that?"

"With what?"

"Being out of your freakin' mind!"

I hate him. I killed him once, and I'll do it again. Then it'll be just Julia and me, and we'll do whatever we want without his interference. He'll never come between us again.

"Sorry, Milton." He regains his composure. "It's just ironic, that's all. You spent all those months after All-Clear afraid you were going crazy. And now, despite your best efforts, you're completely insane. Spending your last days with a couple of dead ol' pals!"

"We were never friends. Not you and me."

"Oh yeah? Who was it that kept you alive? All those years in the bunker, who kept your name out of the lottery?"

I clench my teeth together. "There was never a food shortage. You lied to us. You made me *kill* them!"

"Don't kid yourself, Milton. You knew what you were doing. You liked the fact that you were making it to the very end with more than enough to keep your belly full—before and after All-Clear. Nobody forced you to do anything. You did it because you knew it had to be done. And you never had a problem with it—not until Julia."

"You knew I loved her. You couldn't stand it."

"She makes you weak, Milton. She'll lead you to your own ruin."

I shouldn't be talking to him. I need to think, to figure out a way to kill him. But what *is* he?

I keep quiet for the rest of our climb, and he does the same. Eventually, we reach the open mouth to the caves, a rock ledge with foul-smelling darkness beyond. Bodies everywhere. Some of them partially intact. Most have limbs missing and half-devoured entrails spilling from their open bellies. A layer of dust covers them all.

I can't go in there.

Jackson navigates his course around the bloody remains, careful not to step on anything but blood and rock. He stops and half-turns toward me, the sunlight still on him for the moment, shining from his face shield.

"You owe it to them," he says.

I could have saved them all. There are mutant corpses here too, gutted and skewered on spears. I wouldn't have saved them. Only the friends of Daiyna, Luther...and Samson. But Samson was Jackson, wasn't he? And wasn't Daiyna really Julia? Maybe I got confused. Maybe nobody's who they say they are. Or no one's who I think they are, because I hear voices and see ghosts.

I should stop trying to figure things out and just accept that I'm messed up.

"I could've stopped them." The mutant cannibals, the *demons*.

"But you wanted these people to die, didn't you?"

That voice in my head—it wanted me to leave them, not interfere, not intervene.

"We should split up, cover more ground." The caves are extensive through these mountains. I was left here in the dark once, lost and alone. "If there are any survivors..."

"We stay together." His tone leaves no room for debate. "Got a glowstick? Pitch black up ahead."

I pull the last stick out of my cargo pocket and toss it to him. He cracks it in one of his big hands. Instantly, the darkness is chased away by a sickening green light that illuminates more bodies to sidestep...so many. Men, women, mutants. A hideous massacre.

"What a mess," he mutters, cursing.

No one could have survived this. What was it—two days ago? A week? They said I was in a coma, that I'd been shot. My hand drifts to my chest. I feel fine now. Maybe I do heal faster now with my superspeed.

I unfasten my face shield and pocket it once I'm out of the sun's reach. Jackson does the same, covering his nose and mouth by reflex. It's bad in here, but I deserve to smell it. I should have to suffer for this.

"Which way?" He glances at me.

"Straight. There's another cavern, larger. Through that passage." Where they slept, where I woke up when they were under attack. When Plato thought I'd help defend their home. "I thought there was an avalanche, that there was no way in or out."

"There was." Jackson winks at me. "I have a way with rocks."

We pass beneath the earthen archway and into the large cavern strewn with bloodstained mattresses and more bodies, too many to count. They must have dragged their dying in here. But from the looks of things, they were feasted upon shortly after.

I choke down the bile in my throat.

"Recognize any of 'em?"

I shake my head. I can't identify the remains. I didn't know them. But I could have... They wanted me to help them, to use my *gift* for good. But I used it to run away instead.

Have I mentioned that I hate myself?

"Any other passages?" He pans the glowstick around and the light sweeps away the shadows. I'm sure there are, but I don't know how to find them.

"Nobody's in here. They're all dead." I turn away to face the black, to find my way out. "I'm done."

"Giving up so soon? Now that's not like you at all. I seem to remember you walking endless kilometers after All-Clear, hoping to find another living soul. You didn't give up then. Why should you now?"

"I don't want—I don't need to be here. There's nothing I can do. They're—"

"Dead. Right. I can see that. But why are you so sure there isn't even *one* sole survivor?"

I stare at his green-lit face. "Is there?" I step toward him and stop. "Is somebody still alive in here?"

He regards me for a moment. "What if there was? Would you be so hasty to leave?"

"If you know something I don't—"

He chuckles. "Don't get me started, Milton."

I curse him, my mind suddenly filled with images of his murder and my blood-covered hands. "Just tell me! Is someone here?"

"Yes."

My heart skips a beat. "Where?"

Without a word, he swings the light toward a cleft a meter up the earthen wall. I take off running and leap into the gap, just as he tosses the glowstick to me. I duck my head and crawl deep inside the crevice.

"Hello?" My voice doesn't echo in the stale air of this confined space. "Is anyone there?"

Silence answers me, interrupted only by the sounds of my shuffling boots. The green light of the glowstick extends a few meters before darkness overwhelms it. I wait, listening. If anyone's in here, I should be able to hear them breathing.

Was Jackson just screwing with me? I curse him under my breath and keep crawling, refusing to turn back until I see how far this passage goes.

Maybe I'll stay in here. If Jackson gets curious, he can join me, and I'll wring his thick neck. But I don't think he'd fit. I barely do, shoulders sliding across unyielding rock cool to the touch. Regardless, I finally have some breathing room. No voice in my head, no ghosts to haunt me. Too bad the air's so unsavory. Otherwise, I'd consider living out the rest of my days in here until I starve to death.

Fitting. I'd die among the remains of the people I killed. Will they call it the *Milton Massacre* someday? Probably not. Nobody survived to tell the tale. I can write history the way I like it: *The mutants outnumbered them ten to one. They never had a chance. It was fate, survival of the fittest. The mutants were stronger, and they easily dominated the humans with superior weapons of warfare.*

It wasn't fair, but that's life. It wasn't fair before D-Day, and it wasn't fair in the bunker. Why should it be any different now?

A dry cough barks ahead of me. I freeze for a second, then double my pace on hands and knees.

"Are you all right?" Stupid question.

Another cough replies, louder, as I draw near. The crawlspace opens into a cave the size of a small storeroom, every corner illuminated in green—including the one where a man's body lies curled on his side, facing away from me.

"Don't be afraid." I drop inside and reach for the hydropack in my pocket. "I'm not—"

"A killer?" Jackson rolls over and grins up at me.

I jump backward, my heart lurching.

"Milton, save me..." he whimpers. "Please Milton, use your *gift*. Help me!" He kicks his feet like an infant. Then he curses, sneering, "You're no hero. Only one thing you're good at: killing. Face it. The sooner you do, the sooner you'll realize your true purpose in this world. You're the Grim Reaper!"

"How the hell did you get in here?"

"I'm your imaginary friend, Milton. You tell me." He laughs and rolls over, raising an eyebrow at my silence. "What? Did you really think anybody survived that mess out there? Not a chance. I mean, they *could* have, if...you know. But that's not what you do. You don't save lives. You take them. That's how it was in the bunker, and that's how it was here." He rises to his feet, his dark eyes fixed on me. "That's how it's going to be in Eden."

She warned me, told me I had to let go of the past. She told me something else, too... Something about those mounds of sand outside.

"What happened to the mutants out there, at the bottom of the grade?"

A grin spreads across his bearded face. "You like it?"

She said he didn't *need them anymore*. "How'd you pull that off?"

"It's amazing what a freak sandstorm can do."

That's when it hits me, a sudden realization that would have come sooner if I was thinking clearly. "You're not Jackson." He's not a figment of my imagination, either. He chuckles and then stares as if he's waiting for me to think things through—or as far as I can take them. "You're something else."

"Thank you." He nods graciously. "And you are very astute, albeit excruciatingly slow."

"You covered those mutants out there in the sand, after they had their fill of these people." How did she say it? "You *drowned* them in it."

"Guilty as charged." He folds his arms and keeps grinning, patiently watching me. "Go on. You're doing great."

"You—" Was it possible? "You made it chase after me, the rocks and sand—when I ran toward these mountains."

"You're finally catching on."

"You wanted to kill me."

"Not exactly. We wanted to see how fast you were. Think of it as your first test—one you passed with flying colors. We had to know the ability she gave you was just what we needed in order to deal with Eden."

I don't know what he's talking about. "So what are you?"

"We are many things, Milton. And we were once much more than we are now. We were the voice that was in your head for a while, if that's any help." He leans in, his tone dropping near a whisper. "We're still in your head, by the way. If anybody came in on us right now, they'd see you talking to yourself in here."

So I really am crazy. I'm not just hearing things, but I'm seeing them as well. And who knows where I am, really? I'm probably not even in this alcove of rock and earth, not standing here holding this glowstick. I could be lying somewhere, out cold for all I know, dreaming all this.

"Do you control me?" Am I possessed?

"I wish," he mutters. "It would've made things a whole lot easier. We got close, but then they—*she*—had to go and muck things up. We thought we could take over the one she was working with too, use you to get to her." He shakes his head. "No dice. You've got that vestigial reminder of the creator's adoration: *free will*. It's a curse on your kind, really. You all used it to the fullest degree, destroying everything he made. Nearly annihilating yourselves in the process."

"Creator? You mean...*God*?"

He shrugs. "At one time, your kind thought of him that way. Before you killed him."

How is that possible?

"We've done our best to try to persuade you, Milton. We came close to dominating your mind, but you're stronger than we expected. We didn't foresee that, not after all you've been through. You've led a real messed-up life. And her influence hasn't helped matters any."

Julia? But no, she's not Julia, not really, just like he's not Jackson.

"What is she?"

"She's like me in many ways—a more *domesticated* version, if you will. We're polar opposites when it comes to our views on humankind. What's left of it, anyway. She thinks you have a chance at survival on this rock, that somehow, maybe with her help, you'll be able to make it. She's an optimist." He sighs, sounding like he pities her. "I'm a realist, Milton. I've seen your future. Yes, you'll survive—for a time. But you'll suffer incredibly in the end, and you'll die. All of you. Your species will be wiped out completely. In time, there won't be a trace left on the earth. You'll destroy yourselves all over again. It's what you do best."

I don't believe it. They had it all planned out for us, those government geniuses. They kept us alive, and we made it. There are enough of us now to start over. I just have to find them, the other survivors like Daiyna and Luther and Samson. They can reproduce, and there must be others like them somewhere. None of them seemed like the type to give up on the future.

The Preserve may be gone, but there have to be other areas that weren't affected on D-Day. Maybe on other continents—Eurasia, or Africa. What about the seas? We could live on boats and fish with nets and poles. Seafood used to be illegal, but those laws don't apply to us anymore. We're in charge now. We can fish—unless the nuclear winters killed all the fish.

"You're having a tough time accepting it," he breaks the silence. "Understandable."

I glare at him. "You don't know the future. You're not *God*. I don't know what you are exactly, but you don't know what we're capable of."

"Unfortunately, I do," he says, his features sagging. "All too well." He stares at me until I drop my gaze. "While the worst of it came twenty of your years ago, by no means is it over. There will be more death and bloodshed. It's the way of your accursed kind. As long as you roam this earth, you'll wreak havoc on it and on each other."

I don't have to listen to this. He's not real. I should just ignore him, pretend he's not there. Because he's not, not really.

I turn away and climb back into the crevice, then race through it and out of the cave, passing swiftly over the bodies without even touching down. I half-run, half-fly over them, the green glowstick guiding me until I'm outside in the blinding sunlight. I snap on my face shield quickly and pocket the glowstick. A moment later, I'm back with Julia—or whatever she is—right where I left her.

"No one?" She rests her hand on my chest.

"Who are you? *What* are you?"

"I think he's waking up." Jackson suddenly appears beside me, sprouting up out of the ground again. That trick is already old.

I focus only on Julia, taking her by the shoulders. "I know you're not her—not really—"

"Figured that out all by himself." Jackson snickers.

"You're not like him. You're different somehow. You want us to survive on what's left of this messed-up planet."

She nods. "Yes, Milton. Of course I do."

"That's why you gave us these *abilities*, right?" She nods again, so I plunge onward, "So tell me who you are. What do you want with me? Why me? What do you want me to do? Why am I seeing and hearing you like this?"

The warmth from her hand is unmistakable—through the glove, through my jumpsuit, straight to my chest. It slows my racing heart. She comforts me like she did in the bunker when I was afraid of the dark. I would hold her close, and we'd lie together that way for hours. But this isn't Julia.

I don't care. I still love her.

"You're approaching a very important choice, Milton. One that only you can make. It will affect many lives and will change the course of the earth's future." She takes my hand and squeezes it. "But you don't have to be afraid. I sense the fear in you, and I know where it comes from. It comes from a lie. You don't have to believe it."

I'm a killer.

"It's the truth." Jackson pats me on the back. "The past speaks for itself. Survival of the fittest, as nature intended. Survivor's guilt is a natural part of it. But you can make amends."

How can I? I let them all die.

She squeezes my hand, brings my attention back to her. "Stay with me, Milton. Live *now*, not in the past. This is who you are, and you want to live. You want to survive."

"You want to pay for what you've done." He pats my shoulder with his heavy paw. "It's only right. Why should you live free and easy on this rock after you killed so many people? You'd hate yourself every day—more than you do already. You'd be miserable."

What's the alternative? I'm miserable enough as it is. Except when I'm with her. With Julia here, I could be happy. But this isn't real. She isn't Julia.

What's she saying now?

"—need your help, Milton. Bad things are happening. Evil men are hurting your friends. Luther and Daiyna—"

"They're not your friends. They never trusted you. You were an outsider."

"She saved you, Milton. From *him*." She faces Jackson.

"What?" He snorts. "I wasn't going to kill him!"

"You tell so many lies, you start believing them yourself." She turns back to me. "Daiyna rescued you, don't you remember? And when the mutants shot you, it was Samson and Plato who carried you deep into the cavern to tend to your wound. Rip watched over you. Luther prayed for you." She takes me by the shoulders now. "They are your *friends*, Milton. And they need you now more than ever before."

They needed me. I remember that clearly. They tried to convince me to join them, to help them fight the cannibals, to disarm the freaks with my superspeed and hand over all the weapons. To even the odds. But I refused.

My eyes drift to the sand formations around us. What would I find if I brushed away the layers of sand and ash? More mutants frozen in death? Jeeps without hope of ever running again?

"Why didn't you take them out before?" I face Jackson. "Why did *you* let those people die?"

"Who said I had anything to do with it?" he retorts.

"You did." Didn't he? Or was it Julia who said he did? Everything was becoming clearer for a moment there.

"Have you ever happened to look over your shoulder when you've taken off, Mr. Speedy?" He chuckles. "You kick up quite a wake."

Does he mean I smothered all the freaks when I passed through?

"He doesn't want you to survive—any of you, human or *daemon*." She shakes her head at him. "He would be just as content if you all killed each other."

"Not true," Jackson counters. "It doesn't make me happy at all. But that doesn't change the way things are. It's human nature. They can't be changed, no matter how many special abilities you give them. They're still cursed, doomed to repeat the past."

She squeezes my shoulders with surprising strength. "You can save them, Milton. Only you. There's no one else."

"Or you can put them out of their misery," Jackson says. "You'd be doing them a favor. Believe me, when you see what's going down in Eden, you'll want to put an end to it once and for all."

"I know you want to live, Milton," she implores me.

"But you can't live with guilt. Better to go out in a blaze of glory, save the world from itself." He squeezes my shoulder and steps away.

She presses herself against me, and I hold her feebly. "Regain what you've lost," she whispers. "Be the man I know you are!"

She breaks away. My arms are empty without her. I don't know what they're talking about; most of it makes no sense at all. But I get the idea she wants me to rescue the others while he wants me to blow them up. Something like that.

"So…" I shrug. "Where are they?"

They look at each other. Then in unison they say, "We'll lead the way."

Weird.

But it gets worse. At the same moment that he dives out of sight into the ground and races away to the northeast, she shoots up into the sky, flying as fast as a rocket, almost out of sight before I know what they're doing.

They're giving me a choice to follow one or the other.

It's a no-brainer. I keep my eyes on Julia and take off running after the crack that splits the earth in Jackson's wake. I put out my arms and will myself upward, and for a moment or two my trajectory changes. My boots leave the ground mid-stride and drift through the air.

But then I land—very hard. I flip forward and tumble five or six times, cursing with every somersault across the unforgiving ground until my momentum finally dies out.

I get up and try again, but the results are the same. And the pain is worse this time. Now Julia's out of sight. But I can catch up, I know I can.

I break into another run at superspeed and veer to the right, up a rocky knoll and off the peak of it, launching myself into the air. This time when my boots leave the earth, they don't come crashing back down.

Now I'm flying.

And it is awesome.

The ground below drops away, but I can still see the jagged crack that Jackson—or whatever he is—makes across the surface from underneath. I follow, glancing above me, hoping to spot Julia. But she's gone.

For good? I sure hope not. I can't lose her again.

I reach forward into the air that whips past me, flattening my suit against my body, cold despite the sun's scorching rays. In a burst of speed, I fly faster in the direction of my outstretched arm. I try my other arm and achieve the same result.

So this is how I change direction... And this is how I increase my speed. Wow. She was right. It's exhilarating.

But this can't really be happening. I've dreamed of flying all my life—and now I am? It's got to be a dream. My unconscious subconscious or something is exerting itself in strange new ways, manifesting repressed desires.

Julia and Jackson have been in my head all this time. None of it was real.

He's waking up, Jackson said. What if I'm asleep somewhere—or still in that coma?

Below, the split in the earth reaches what looks like the sprawling remains of a large city, and there it stops. At the same time, a shape passes through the air in the distance, descending rapidly. Julia.

I reach after her, and within moments I'm right behind her, blasting through the sky. She doesn't glance back, doesn't acknowledge me. Maybe she's concentrating. Maybe I should, too. I didn't land so well the last time, and I'm going ten times faster now.

What's that up ahead? Twisted steel in the middle of the air? She catches onto it and lands with ease like a bird touching down, both boots making contact. Then she looks back at me and holds out her hand.

"Slow down!"

How? I take her forearm, and she clasps onto mine as I whip past. Her grip is strong, but not strong enough to keep me from swinging sideways and pulling her with me. She falls off the mangled steel, but quickly rights herself in mid-air, holding onto me with both hands like a life guard rescuing someone from the deep end of a pool. I feel myself slow as we whirl around and around, and she guides me onto another length of dust-caked steel a few meters lower than where she originally landed. She keeps a tight hold on me as I find my bearings.

"You caught up." She giggles.

"Yeah..." I nod, sucking down air. "I really need to work on the landing."

"This wasn't the easiest spot to touch down."

She's right. We're sitting on what's left of a skyscraper. Jackson stands with his hands on his hips, head thrown back to face us from the ground below. We're at least thirty meters above him.

"All done showing off?" he calls. "You kill yourself, you're no good to either of us!"

She pats me on the thigh and calls down, "I think he did well."

Sure I did. Without her, I probably would have slammed into one of the steel supports and plummeted to my death like a bird shot down from the sky.

"So now what?" I wish I could see her eyes. I have a feeling I won't be seeing them again anytime soon.

She nods slowly, like she knows what I'm thinking. She hugs my arm and points down to where Jackson stands. Beside him, what looks like an open manhole gapes in the middle of the dusty street. The heavy cover has already been slid aside.

"He'll show you how to get—"

"Where am I going?"

"To Eden, Milton."

They mentioned that before, but I didn't understand. The

word sounds familiar, from an old bedtime story maybe, long before D-Day.

"He'll tell you where to go, as far as he knows. We've never been there ourselves."

"Why not?"

"We can't." She pauses. "We move through air, Milton, through earth. Eden... It's encased in concrete and steel, human-made materials, and the air has been altered. It's unnatural." She squeezes my arm. "That's why you never met us while you were in the bunker."

"And that's why you need me to go to this place. Because you can't." I would be the astute one, that's for sure.

She giggles again, and I don't ever want to forget the sound. "You're catching on." Then her tone changes. "But you have to hurry. We don't know exactly what's going on down there, but it's not good. The *daemon* minds are difficult to read, yet we've been able to learn enough. Your friends are in grave danger, and you're the only one who can save them. You must go. Now."

She steps off the beam and glides down toward Jackson. Without taking the time to think better of it, I follow. That's when my stomach seizes up and my heart lurches. But instead of falling to my death, I manage to float after her like a bird, soaring to the ground where I land with only a slight stumble this time.

"Quick learner," Jackson mutters. He points into the manhole. "Down you go."

I face Julia. "Will I see you again—ever?"

Her face shield mirrors my own. "That will depend on the choice you make."

Haven't I already made my choice—to go to this Eden place? What other choice is there? What's she talking about?

"You'll know it when you see it," Jackson says, seeming to read my mind. "A nuclear reactor has a way of standing out like a sore thumb." He chuckles mildly. "Rigging it to blow should be easy enough. Just think of it as the ultimate reset button."

PART VI
REVELATIONS

13. WILLARD

SIX MONTHS AFTER ALL-CLEAR

How I Learned to Stop Worrying and Love the Bomb. It could be the title of my memoir—or my epistle. I listen to the hum of the reactor below us, vibrating the steel beneath my boots. Then I toss the book back onto the stack. "Is this all they found?"

Jamison nods, glancing down at the crate of green hardbounds on the floor between us. "Want them to keep looking?"

War and Peace. I trace the embossed title with my finger and can't help but smile. It's fitting. Apropos.

I hear one of them grunt—or snort—from across the main floor. Four of them stand just inside the south tunnel, their heads hanging low to shield their lidless eyes from Eden's lights. The small red bulbs on their collars blink intermittently, pulsing with the programmed setting that holds them in a catatonic state.

Perch and two others stand by with weapons drawn, leveled on the mutos. Perch carries the remote, but he favors the shock prod dangling from his belt. He enjoys it maybe a little too much, but he's not hurting anybody.

They're just *dogs*, after all.

"Brand new. Like everything else we've found." Jamison squints at me with a sudden thought. "Why'd those government scientists want us to head up to the Preserve after All-Clear? Everything we need to start over is right here!"

I've trained him well. The others, too. You'd think we have a hive mind or something by the way we all tend to stay on the same page these days.

"Send them out for another run. Have 'em finish off the south sector." I watch them. Stoop-shouldered creatures with deformed, lumpy-muscled arms hanging low at their sides. Like apes. "Let's see what else they find."

It'll be getting dark. While it's bright as day here in Eden, night will be coming on strong out there. But Jamison already knows what to do.

"We'll switch the cameras over to night vision."

Good boy. I nod and he salutes—something new they've started doing. Can't say that I mind it. He takes off in an easy jog, looking like a second-stage student warming up for a track meet. I don't know how he's done it, but Jamison has managed to hang onto a youth that's passed the rest of us by. Maybe it comes from having a clear conscience. Bet he sleeps like a baby every night.

He heads over to Perch and the others, and they quickly adjust the cameras on the mutos' collars, then back away. The freaks don't even seem to notice. The collars are a godsend, and that's a fact. Wish we'd come up with them sooner, but better late than never at all.

Perch activates the remote and whips out his prod, jamming it into each of the dogs' sides with a vengeance. He curses them as they cringe and stagger away, lumbering off into the blackness of the tunnel beyond the reach of Eden's lights. Jamison turns my way once they're gone and gives me a double thumbs-up.

Now we watch and wait.

My attention is drawn back to the box of books. Somebody twenty years ago thought these titles were worth publishing, defying a UW mandate. Brand new, never read. It's like they were made just for us. Printed off in secret probably, then buried beneath the rubble in sublevel storerooms. The food and supplies we've found have made sense. Of course there'd be underground warehouses full of that stuff. But illegal books? What was the point?

I bend down to heave the crate against my chest and feel my back pull, then pop. That can't be good. I'm not like Jamison at all. I've probably aged ten years in the past months since All-Clear. One of the banes of leadership. God knows, it hasn't been easy.

But the Good Lord's blessed us again and again, and by his blessings we know without a doubt that we're his chosen ones. All we have to do is look around: Eden, beauty from ashes. A clean, secure city built beneath the rubble of the past. Powered by the same machines of death used to destroy the old world, sustained by resources that remain on the new. It's been one miracle after another with God doing what he does best: using what was meant for evil for our good. That missile we discovered months ago—the first of many now harnessed for our electricity and power. Finding this subterranean dome in the first place, not to mention the plutonium stores to fuel the reactor—both miracles. The dogs themselves, mutant degenerates who attacked us soon after we began engineering the structural integrity of Eden, now our servants. All things have worked together for good!

I drop the crate onto the conveyor and start up the ladder nearby. We'll both reach the catwalk above us at the same time. Jamison's boots echo as he trots by, headed for the monitoring station. He frowns up at me, confused.

"I'll join you shortly," I toss over my shoulder as I climb.

He pauses to salute again, then resumes his jog toward the north tunnel and the station beyond where he'll see everything the dogs see through the cameras in their collars.

I pull myself over the last rung and reach the steel grate of the catwalk just as the conveyor drops off my parcel. Another book's golden title catches the light: *A Holy Bible*. Banned ever since the UW's zero tolerance laws went into effect. Apparently, religions used to cause wars. You want world peace, you get rid of all the holy books.

Right. And that worked out real well for everybody.

I heft the crate, this time remembering to bend with my knees like my grandfather had to whenever he dropped anything. I'm not an old man, I just have an old soul as any prophet would. I'm sure Moses did. God favors old souls. We ask for wisdom instead of riches, and sometimes we end up with both.

Hands full, I knock with the toe of my boot, striking the solid steel door. Not the most polite way to announce my arrival, but I'm sure she'll understand, considering.

Silence. Is she monitoring one of her patients? She was already on her shift when I woke up this morning. Thought she'd be back by now. Doesn't matter. I'll drop off the books and head down—

Muffled footfalls thump across the carpet on the other side of the door. Then it slides aside.

"I come bearing gifts." I give her a wink.

"Books?" Margo steps back as I pass her, wet from a shower. The scent of extinct flowers drifts from her soggy hair.

"Dogs found 'em today. Thought we might see a few we like." I set them down in the middle of the living room floor, right in front of our two couches.

"Do we have time for reading?" She slides the front door shut and adjusts the thin towel that clings to her curves, barely covering her slick body. Beads of water trickle down her chest, between her breasts.

"We'll make time." I take off my beret and sling it across the room. I charge straight for her as she whips off the towel and tosses it into my face with a laugh. Blinded momentarily, I pull it aside and catch hold of her by the bare midsection. She twists away, laughing as I lose my hold on her.

"Slippery when wet!" She runs off down the hallway, her ripe buttocks jiggling. But I'm hot on her tail, and when she ducks into the first bedroom on the left, I dive and land on top of her on the bed. The mattress springs give beneath us, squeaking as our laughter quickly turns to passionate gasps.

We kiss wildly, like animals in heat—if animals kissed, that is. My uniform's torn off, tossed aside. She climbs on top of me, her dark eyes intense, hungry. How long has it been since our last rendezvous? Maybe twelve hours. We both want it now. So we let nature take its course, and as I watch her ride me, I find that the only thing passing through my mind is...

I can't believe I thought she was one of them.

Couldn't be too careful, not when all our lives depended on it. As things turned out, we ended up losing nearly half our numbers. But now we know without a doubt that the fifty-two of us left are all-natural children of God. No demon-dust passing through any of our lungs, no signs of any mutation for almost four months now.

We're safe, finally safe.

She falls beside me, landing on her back and gasping. "Wow..."

Must've been good for her. "I aim to please." I turn onto my side and face her, tracing her smooth flank with my finger.

"And you succeed," she breathes heavily, "every time." There's a smile on her lips as she recovers. "Being sterile certainly has its benefits."

"Really?" No. It's a curse.

"Nothing to fear."

I wouldn't fear it—impregnating her. I would welcome it, a true miracle. But to bring new life to Eden would take an act of God. As it is, we'll eventually die out here after we've lived the rest of our days. No future generations. The end of the line.

Damn those government scientists. What the hell were they thinking?

"Do you think they made it? The *breeders*?" My voice sounds preoccupied, vulnerable. No one else ever sees me like this, laid bare, inside out.

Only Margo. Her eyelashes flutter like the butterflies I've seen in my dreams, and her large pupils focus on me. "You're worrying again."

The breeders from Sectors 50 and 51 are our only hope for the future. Our species won't survive without them. Humankind, gone forever. Never to be seen again on the planet.

But I nod. I made a deal with her just a couple days ago: I was going to give up worrying and enjoy all that God's blessed us with.

Easier promised than done.

"Right. Stop worrying and love the bomb," I mutter.

"What's that?" She rolls onto her side and brushes my nose with hers. She runs her fingers down through the thick hair on my chest and torso.

"A book. One of the treasures the dogs brought down today."

"I wish you wouldn't call them that."

"What else should we call 'em?"

"Servants, maybe?"

"They're not people. You checked them out yourself."

"The tests were limited, inconclusive. We *don't* know more than we *do*." She shakes her head. "I'm not a doctor, you know."

"You're the best one we've got."

"I'm all we've got."

That's what I meant.

She blows out a sigh. "I think they were human at one point, but something went horribly wrong. They were exposed to something toxic or radioactive, maybe both. Something turned them into what they are now. But deep down, they're still human. I'm sure of it."

"They're animals." I take her hand in mine and interlace our fingers. She meets my gaze. "There's nothing human about them, Margo. Even if there was, once upon a long time ago, it's not what they are anymore. And if we didn't collar 'em, they'd be trying to eat every last one of us. Don't you remember?"

Of course she does. It haunts us all—the first time we encountered them. They poured into Eden from every tunnel, all four sides, like a plague hell-bent on our total destruction. But it wasn't God's will for us to be annihilated by these monsters. Instead, he wanted them to serve us.

"I know..." She shakes her head and bites her lip. "But I wish it didn't have to be this way." Does she feel compassion for them?

It's misplaced, but I can't really fault her for it. I'm sure a few of the Egyptians felt sorry for the minions under the whip who built their pyramids. And on our own continent, before the cold wars and everything in between, there were probably folks who felt compassion for the ones who did all the work nobody else wanted to do: the laborers from Sector 43.

The work had to be done regardless, just like it has to be done now. We can't go topside and risk infection, but we won't survive long without having what we need brought down to us. The farthest we venture are the parking structures to the south and east. But even then, we only go up into the first and second sublevels, and we always wear our O2 masks.

Never onto the surface. Never.

I nudge her and wink. "What if we call 'em *retrievers*?"

She almost smiles. "Still reminds me of golden—"

"Captain Willard?" Perch's throaty voice comes through the radio clipped to my uniform, somewhere on the floor.

With a short sigh, I roll off the bed and sink my bare feet into the thick carpet. The radio chirps from my camouflage pants. Takes me a few seconds to locate them in the tangled mess we threw aside moments ago.

"Captain?"

Margo giggles, watching me struggle. She sits up, uncovered and unashamed. I contemplate dropping the uniform and diving onto her for another round.

"Willard here." This had better be good.

"Am I interrupting anything, sir?"

He knows he is. I'm sure he wants her for himself, wishes he was *captain*. Maybe not. Paranoia—another burden of leadership.

"Not at all. Proceed."

A short pause. "The dogs, they-uh...found somethin' you'll want to see."

His tone makes me glance at Margo apologetically. "I'll be right over."

With my uniform and beret back in place, I shut the door to our apartment and head down the ladder. Margo and I will meet up again later when she makes her rounds. She reminded me yet again how important it is for me to be a visible presence amongst the patients. Whatever makes her happy. I can't afford to lose her.

Not that she'd be stupid enough to leave me, of course. She's a smart girl.

Jamison stands outside the door to the monitoring station, his features guarded. He's already seen what I'm about to; that much is obvious. And he doesn't know how I'm going to react. Should be interesting.

I step inside without a word to him, but he salutes anyway and I return the gesture as I pass. Perch is seated inside the dim room in front of a wall of monitors, each one displaying the viewpoint of a different camera-equipped dog collar. His thick fingers are splayed over the dials on the console before him, increasing and decreasing the settings, guiding the mutos where he wants them to go.

"Captain," he greets me without looking my way, his attention divided between the screens and the controls.

I lean over his shoulder. My eyes rove across the monitors. "What am I supposed to be looking at here?" The images are green and fuzzy, distorted. I thought we'd already made all the needed improvements.

"Coming up," he murmurs, concentrating.

"We're—he's getting them to face it from different angles so we can get a better look. But they're tired, probably hungry. They're not responding as quickly as normal," Jamison explains.

"Increase the settings then." Send a thousand volts through them, I don't care. There's plenty more mutos where they come from.

"That's what we're doing, but they can only take so much before they—"

"Keel over." Perch curses as one of the monitors is seized by static. "Lost that one."

"What did they find?" I assumed it would be ready for me to see, whatever it is.

Jamison points to the third screen from the left, second from the top. "There. You can almost make it out."

I see fuzzy green and black shadows. I squint and lean in closer, but it's no help. "Can't you adjust—?"

"Compensating," Perch mutters, reaching for another dial on the control panel. Gradually, the image resolution clears. "How's that?"

"Better." I see it now. Time slows. I forget to breathe. "Where are they?" I whisper.

"From what we can tell, they're beneath one of the storage facilities to the southeast. Two or three levels down." Jamison clears his throat. "It's a radio. Shortwave, by the looks of it."

Obviously. But why is the light on the receiver blinking? "Power source?"

"None that we can see." Perch sets the dials and leans back, folding his hands behind his head. "Three, four, and six." He gestures to the monitors. "Those are our boys. Got 'em on standby."

One muto's camera faces the radio; the other two are aimed at its sides and just behind it, against a concrete wall. The light next to the receiver blinks steadily, patiently, with an incoming transmission. How long has it been functional? Twenty years?

What kind of battery would last that long?

"So..." Jamison clears his throat, crossing his arms. "You can see our dilemma here."

I glance at him. Of course I do. If we have the mutos fetch it for us, we risk losing the call, whoever it's from. The dogs haven't held the greatest track record with retrieving fragile items. But there's no other option. We can't go and get it for ourselves. It's too far out.

That option better not be crossing their minds.

"No dilemma here." I shake my head and step back. "Have 'em bring it down."

Jamison's mouth drops open and hangs there a moment. "This could be important, sir. Can we really expect the mutos to deliver it in one piece?"

"Important?" I raise an eyebrow at him.

"The incoming transmission... I mean, it could be—"

"Are you expecting a call, Jamison?" I grin, and Perch snickers. "From an old girlfriend, perhaps?"

He looks down, but his eyes rebound quickly. "We could send somebody up—"

"Not happening." He's an idiot even to think it.

"Just hear me out, sir." Jamison steps forward and waits for my reluctant sigh before continuing, "The patients. Couldn't we send one of them? They're already infected, so the harm's been done. We could use a radio to guide them to it, then—"

"Then what?" Perch chuckles. "Have 'em talk to whoever's on the other end? Yeah, that would go over real well. Not the best spokesmen for Eden, that bunch." He laughs out loud.

But I don't. Because young Jamison here has stumbled onto something brilliant. Of course we wouldn't want any of the patients to actually *use* the shortwave radio—but they could bring it to us. And I'm sure they'd do a better job handling this sensitive piece of equipment than the mutos ever could, even on their best days.

"How many of those collars do we have left?"

Both of them look at me quizzically. They have no idea what I'm thinking. Or maybe they do, and they can't be sure I'm serious.

But I am. As serious as I've ever been.

Perch scratches his protruding jaw. "Maybe ten. We're makin' more—"

"Get one and meet me at the recovery rooms." I turn on my heel and leave them to stare, forgetting to salute.

Once outside, I make my way across the main floor, my boots

striking the concrete in a clipped rhythm. Men clear a path, avoiding my direct route as their transport vehicles carry pallets loaded with supplies. They salute me and I return the gesture half-heartedly. At the far end of the dome, along the catwalk suspended in the air, I see my destination: unmarked steel doors lined side by side, so neat and tidy.

My stomach tightens as I approach.

I still have my doubts. I hate the uncertainty. Should we have killed them all? Yes. Do we owe them our lives for helping us fight off the mutos when they first attacked? Probably. But it was never my intention to keep these patients around this long. Margo talked me into it. She has a habit of doing that.

Hope she doesn't catch wind of what I'm about to do here. She wouldn't like it. Not one bit.

She wants to study them, find out how the physiological transformations have affected—or been affected by—their current genetic make-up and whatnot. Maybe learn how to reverse the process. She's so passionate about it.

I'm a structural engineer; give me something to work on that's tangible. None of this DNA crap. That's her area of expertise.

If she wasn't here to convince me, they'd all be dead already. She probably knows that. She's no dummy, and that's a fact. They're her pet project, and she won't take kindly to me using one of them like this. But if I play my cards right, I'll have him back in bed before she starts her evening rounds.

"Hello, Mathis." I slide the door shut quietly behind me and try to catch my breath. You'd think I'd be in better shape with all these ladders around here, but they get me every time.

"Go to hell, Willard."

The body in the elevated medical bed lies still, attached by all manner of tubes and hoses to machines on both sides. They bleep and blink, monitoring his vitals, taking samples, recycling his blood. As far as we can tell, he's recovering. One of the lucky ones, I guess.

"Glad to see you're coherent." I pull a stool up to his bedside and take a seat. "How're you feeling these days?"

"Like you care." Unlike his paralyzed body, his head is able to turn—away from me. "Leave me alone, you son of a bitch."

My mustache itches. I scratch it, smooth it down. My other hand drifts to my sidearm. It would be so easy...

What purpose does it serve, keeping them alive like this? Margo can't believe they'll ever be part of the Eden Guard. Not Mathis, not Catherine, none of them. Ash freaks. Even if she manages to permanently reverse the effects of their infection, they'll still be tainted. They won't ever be like us.

This is better. He'll serve a purpose. He'll serve *us*.

"You're going on a little trip, Mathis."

His head rolls toward me as interest flickers in his eyes, but his brow remains furrowed. "Well, that should be fascinating, seeing how I can't move a muscle. You've got me so pumped full of—."

"Easily remedied. Once you're leashed." I grin.

"What're you talking about?"

I pat his bare chest. "Not to worry. You'll love it. How long have you been cooped up in here? Months, right? A little fresh air will do you good."

"It's fresher in here," he retorts. "Have you already forgotten who programmed the air processors?"

"Of course not. You did a great job. All of you. But I was referring to the air your kind prefers."

His severe gaze narrows. "Thought you didn't want anybody going topside."

I can't restrain the chuckle that rocks my shoulders. "Well, you're special, Mathis. And we've got a very *special* assignment, just for you."

He glares at me.

"On our way, Captain," Jamison's voice crackles from my radio.

I raise it to reply, but I pause. There's something strange about Mathis's eyes. He stares straight through me, his corneas glassy, his chapped lips stretching into a gruesome smile. He's quiet for a few moments. Then he chuckles, sounding like he's regurgitating a recent meal.

"Somebody to see you, Willard," he hisses.

"Recovery room eight," I respond to Jamison, keeping my gaze on Mathis as I return the radio to my belt.

"Not them." Mathis rolls his head side to side on his pillow. "Somebody else. He's at the door. Watching you."

I glance over my shoulder. The door's shut, just like I left it.

I don't have time for this crap. I squeeze my temples. Might as well humor the freak. Soon as Perch and Jamison arrive, playtime's over anyway.

"Who do you see, Mathis?"

"Tucker."

The stool skids, screeching out from under me as I get to my feet. Adrenaline courses through my veins, my heart pumping double time. I whip out the Colt holstered at my side and grip it in both hands.

"Never seen you so scared, Willard!" Mathis wheezes.

"Where is he?" I demand, panning the small room with my gun muzzle.

"Can't you see him? Something wrong with your eyes?" he mocks me. "I thought he *died*, Captain. That's what you told us. Remember way back when? You said Sharon and the girls got him when they turned into crazy cannibals."

"They did." Didn't they? They must have. Or something else killed him. When those fools went topside and retrieved the guns, all they found were bloody remains. There's no way Tucker could've survived on the surface. Not all this time, not all alone. "No one survived."

"Well, that's not what he says." There's an edge to Mathis's voice. He thinks he has something on me even as he lies there impotent, paralyzed from the neck down. "He tells me you left him to die. Even though he came to your rescue."

"Why doesn't he speak for himself?" I shout.

"Hey, Willard." The deep voice nearly stops my heart. Familiar. Too familiar. But up to now, I thought I was the only one who could hear it.

"Tucker..." His ghost has haunted me ever since I took the elevator down and disabled it, leaving him to his fate.

But it had to be done. I had no idea he'd make it, and there were ninety-odd other lives to consider. The good of the many!

"Sorry I haven't been around lately. Been busy up there with the mutos and all." Tucker sniffs—his annoying little tick.

I force a smile, feel it stretch my face. "I was starting to think you were just a figment of my imagination." I lower the gun. No use shooting a ghost. "What's it been? A week or so?"

If Mathis can see him, then maybe he's not an apparition at all. Could he be an invisible ash freak instead, and it's taken the eyes of a fellow freak to see him? That would mean these past months of *hauntings* have been actual visits.

It means he's really here.

"You've already talked to Willard?" Mathis's big reveal has fallen flat, and he looks deflated.

Tucker's chuckle emanates from the far corner of the room now. "Scared the living crap out of 'im is more like it. Been a real hoot!" He laughs out loud. "He's thought for sure I'm some kind of spook!"

Not anymore.

I bring up the Colt and pull the trigger. For a split second after the gunshot—loud as a bomb going off in here—Tucker becomes visible as the round meets its mark. Just like I remember him. Same bright eyes, sandy hair and beard, muscular build. He wears an old standard-issue jumpsuit. Couldn't he have found something else? His eyes are wide, his mouth thrown open in total surprise. But then he's invisible again, groaning, stumbling against one of the medical machines and causing it to flicker, vanishing and reappearing. It wobbles as he collapses to the floor.

That'll teach him to screw with me.

"Captain—everything all right up there?" Jamison's on the radio again. "Shots fired?"

"Just one." I keep the gun barrel aimed at Tucker's corner of the room and listen. If he tries to leave, I'll shoot him again. I should've known better. There's no such thing as spirits of the dead. "Make that *two* collars," I order. "We have another volunteer."

Mathis stares at me, eyes unblinking. "What are you going to do?"

I chuckle as I pick up the muscle stimulator from the foot of his bed. "I told you already. Something real special."

Perch and Jamison show up with the collars and a medkit. Tucker being invisible and *alive* throws them for a loop at first, but I explain he's just another one of our infected ash freaks. Why didn't I tell them sooner? Because I was protecting them, of course. He was one of us, close to the inner circle. It would've been more than they could bear to know he'd been turned muto by the demon-dust.

"I can't even see him," Jamison murmurs, kneeling down in the corner where Tucker fell, probably passed out by now. Jamison swings his hand side to side in the air. Then he blinks out of sight, vanishing completely.

"What the—!" Perch jumps back.

Jamison must've bumped into Tucker. His invisibility is transferable by touch. Fascinating.

"Part of the mutation," I explain. "Anything that comes in contact with him disappears." Except for the floor, apparently. What rules govern this bizarre abnormality?

"You mean—I'm..." Jamison gasps.

"You're an invisible man." But we don't have time for show and tell. "Patch him up quick and collar 'im. I want that shortwave down here within the hour."

They work quickly. As soon as Perch has the collar on Mathis and the remote online, I apply the stimulant to each of his major muscle groups. He gets all jittery and starts crying out as his body reacts in violent spasms. I don't know what to do about it; I don't have Margo's bedside manner, and that's a fact. We'll have to wait it out.

Once he's lying still again, heaving one strained gasp after the next, I nod to Perch.

"Up and at 'em." Perch activates the remote.

The light on the collar flares red, and Mathis screams, clutching at his throat as he's thrown from the bed to the floor like a crash test dummy. Perch curses, shaking the remote at him uselessly, trying to make him stand up.

"What's wrong?" I snap.

"His muscles—they're not cooperating." Perch activates the remote again and Mathis flips over onto his arched back, limbs flailing.

"Damn you!" he screams hoarsely. "What have you done to me?"

I blow out a sigh and shake my head. His body must've been sedated for too long. This isn't going to work. "What about the other one?"

Jamison nods, now visible as he backs away from Tucker. "I patched up his wound, and the collar's on, good to go." But he hesitates. "We won't be able to see him—but we'll see everything he sees." He stands at attention. "Permission to return to—"

"Go."

He'll need to be in the monitoring station before Perch activates Tucker's collar. Jamison salutes crisply and leaves, shutting the door.

"What about this one?" Perch curses, gesturing at the writhing Mathis.

"Get him back into bed." Tucker showing up now is a real godsend. This way, I won't have to use any of Margo's pets for my project. "Sedate him completely. And get that collar off 'im." I don't want her knowing what we were up to in here.

Perch nods, but he makes no move to follow orders. Instead,

he fixes me with his steely gaze and sucks on his teeth. "Permission to speak freely, sir?"

"Always."

"I don't like her. Don't trust her one bit. And I don't like the way you take orders from her."

"I don't take orders from anyone but God Almighty."

He nods slowly. "So why does she call the shots where these freaks are concerned?"

"It's her area of expertise. She advises me."

"Maybe so. Or maybe she's one of 'em. She could be, you know."

How dare he? The fool—he wants her for himself, can't stand it that I have the only woman left in Eden. My *Eve*. Since he knows he can't have her and never will, he doesn't want me to enjoy her. He's nothing but an overgrown child.

"And how'd you arrive at this great epiphany?" I raise an eyebrow.

He shakes his head, taking a step toward me. "You're in it too deep, sir—in *her* way too deep to see things clearly."

"Careful, soldier," I warn him.

He apologizes. "But think about it. How many women were in the bunker with us? Near forty, yeah? And how many of them were infected?" He waits, eyes locked with mine. "*All* of 'em, because they went topside. So damn curious. But she's the only one not affected? What are the odds?"

I grin at him. "I'd say it qualifies as a bona fide miracle. Wouldn't you?"

He shakes his head vehemently. "She's hiding it somehow. Her infection. Meanwhile she's convinced you to keep these freaks—her *patients*—alive when they should be shot down like rabid dogs!"

"You've made your point." I nod toward Mathis. "Now take care of this one like I said, and meet us in the monitoring station. On the double."

He stands rigid as I leave the room. On the catwalk outside, I blink beneath Eden's lights and glance down the line of steel doors. Twelve recovery rooms, each with an infected freak inside, hooked up to all manner of machines that drain our power, use up our resources. For what purpose?

It makes her happy, I suppose. Keeps her happy. And she makes me happy. A vicious cycle of happiness is what it is.

I couldn't tell Perch that. Not that I should have. I don't answer to him. But I don't answer to her, either. I'm Captain of the Eden Guard, and if I decide at some point that these ash freaks should be put down, so be it.

She won't stand against me. She'll be standing alone. She knows better. She needs me as much as I need her.

Regardless, there's only one priority right now: get Tucker up on the surface and have him bring down that shortwave radio. Where could the transmission be coming from? The breeders in Sector 50? 51? Eden needs some baby-makers pronto, and that's a fact. Sector 43? We could definitely use some relief around here from all the grunt work. Or maybe trade workers, trapped somewhere beneath the rubble of their own city—all-natural children of God in need of a savior? We could send a Hummer out to them, one of the old gas-powered models we found in that parking garage at the end of the south tunnel. Send Tucker to chauffeur them right here where they belong. We'll welcome them with open arms.

Tucker. What the hell's happened to him? What kind of genetic transmutation makes a body go *invisible*?

When we returned from our first excursion through the tunnels—Jamison, Perch, Margo, and I—we found that Catherine and Mathis had fixed the elevator and gotten the guns from up top. They'd also gotten everybody all riled up about the supposed lies I told. While they'd come across what was left of the infected women's remains, there'd been no sign of Tucker. They hadn't opened the bunker door—hadn't dared to, obviously. They could tell by the fangs and claws on the corpses that I hadn't lied about the mutations. Who knew what might be lurking outside?

Of course I had to talk fast, make them think I'd been protecting them from the awful truth, et cetera. I did pretty well; I usually do. Told them Tucker had been hauled out by the freaks before I could shut the bunker door. Told them nobody had been trying to get down the elevator, every time the DOWN arrow lit up with a ding. Nope, that was just a knee-jerk type response from me cutting the hard lines. Then why'd I tell them something topside was trying to come down? To protect them, of course. Everything was dead up there, I knew that. I just wanted to spare them the gruesome particulars.

That was the official story, and it just about saved my neck. Most of them gobbled it up. Made sense to them, surprisingly. But I kept my eye on the riot instigators, watched them close from then on for any signs of mutation. Didn't take long.

But what really happened? Sometimes even I believe the lies I tell. Not now. I have to figure out how Tucker managed to survive out there.

After that she-cat attacked me and left me bleeding out, I made it to the elevator. I heard shots fired—must've been Tucker with the gun, taking out the last of the ash freaks. I rode the elevator down and left him, and he tried to follow me. Ding. Ding. Maybe thirty-six hours went by. We broke through the southwest tunnel and ran into the nuke. Meanwhile, Mathis fixed the elevator, and he and Catherine went up top. By then, Tucker must've managed to get outside and shut the bunker door behind him.

During the days that followed, he somehow survived in the desolation outside and found the city ruins to the southwest while we were relocating through the tunnels underground. As we dismantled that first nuke we found, he was inhaling the demon-dust. When we came upon the subterranean dome and started building Eden, he was scavenging through the ruins above us. And he was as invisible as the air.

Tucker's *hauntings* began almost as soon as we had Eden's bare necessities up and running: filtered air cycle, reclaimed water—

recycled from our hydropacks and from our own bodies, purified for drinking and showering. While we made a new life for ourselves, he played *ghost*, trying to scare the hell out of me.

Did I think I'd killed him? Of course. Maybe I even felt a little guilty about it.

But not anymore. Now I've got the prankster freak right where I want him. He's going to make up for all those months of screwing around. I'll work him harder than he's ever worked in his life. Getting the shortwave radio is just his first chore on a very long list that'll keep him busy from now till his dying breath —whenever I decide that's to be.

"Well?" I step into the monitoring station.

Jamison starts, salutes, and returns to the screens. "This one's Tucker." He points. "The camera's online, so we're seeing what he sees. Right now...not much."

The screen shows a lopsided view of the recovery room's medical machines and the bed where Perch has replaced Mathis, as limp as a fresh corpse.

"Still out cold?"

Jamison nods. "For now. Soon as Perch comes down, we'll activate Tucker and send him on his way."

I glance at the other three monitors where the mutos remain right where we left them, facing the shortwave radio. The light on the receiver continues to blink. Could it be some kind of automated distress call from D-Day? I can't get my hopes up that it's anything more.

The door creaks open, then shuts. Perch silently takes his post at the control panel. "Showtime," he mutters.

I focus on Tucker's monitor. At first nothing happens, no change at all. It's the same view from the floor where he fell when I shot him. But then there's a jerk, and the image bounces. Tucker groans.

Jamison punches a pad on the console and leans in. "Can you hear me, Tucker?" Another groan. "This is Jamison. You remember me?"

What's he doing? Just send the freak after the radio, for crying out loud!

"I'll wake 'im up," Perch growls.

"No—wait." Jamison holds out his hand. "He's not a muto. We can communicate with him."

"That's what I'm doing." Perch spins a dial and the image on the screen goes haywire. Tucker's agonized scream comes through loud and clear.

Jamison looks back at me, his eyes pleading in the dim light.

"Get on with it," I order, folding my arms.

Perch chuckles at the controls as more screams erupt from the speaker. Jamison leans in again, keeps his voice calm.

"Stand up, Tucker. Get on your feet, and the pain will stop."

"Maybe." Perch snickers.

Good cop, bad cop. I lean back against the wall to watch. This ought to be good.

Hard to tell which gets the most results—Jamison's encouraging words or Perch's jolts of electricity. But they manage to get Tucker out of the recovery room, down the ladder, across the main floor, and into the south tunnel without him running into anything or anybody. Of course, nobody sees him.

"He's on his way," Jamison reports. He glances up at the screen, dark now that Tucker's in the tunnel. "Switching to night vision."

The green, fuzzy image doesn't change for close to half an hour, not until Tucker reaches the uppermost level of the parking garage. All that time, he doesn't say a single word.

"You'll need to take the stairs to the top, out to the surface," Jamison tells him. He releases the audio pad on the panel. "So far so good."

"We should put cameras in there," I muse aloud. "Thermoptic, infrared. See the mutos before they get close to Eden."

"Good idea, sir." Perch glances back at me and grins. "Tucker's next assignment?"

Glad to see he's on board. I'm willing to forgive and forget the stupid things he said up in the recovery room. He's a good soldier. I'd hate to have to put him down.

"We'll make a list." I chuckle, smoothing my mustache. Almost time for a trim.

Tucker takes the stairs one at a time with excruciating deliberation. That bullet to the chest could be slowing him down. Can't be comfortable. Jamison said it was just a flesh wound and that he stopped the bleeding, so Tucker should be fine. But will he be able to lift the radio? He sure had better. He botches this, Perch won't have to handle the shock collar. I'll crank it up myself and blow Tucker's head clean off.

The image on the screen pans left to right as Tucker walks through the uppermost level of the garage, passing by one derelict vehicle after the next. Their solar panels have been stripped by the mutos—not the ones we've managed to collar, the wild ones. Doesn't seem like they'd be able to figure out how to use them, but those freaks do surprise us on occasion.

"Now what?" Tucker speaks for the first time, his voice a monotone as he steps out of the garage and into the empty night.

"It talks." Perch guffaws.

Jamison leans in again, pressing the same audio pad on the console. "You're going to turn to the southeast—thirty degrees to your left."

"Any hint what I'm looking for?" Tucker sniffs, sounding dejected. No fun being our remote-controlled dog?

"We'll guide you to it."

"I'm just saying, you tell me what it is, I'll find it easy enough. I know where all the good stuff's at around here."

Excellent. He's a real godsend, and that's a fact.

Jamison looks back at me. "Sir?"

"Go ahead." There's no harm in it. Perch has him wired in case he tries anything funny.

"All right, Tucker." Jamison nods. "It's a shortwave radio. Should be located beneath what's left of a storage facility on the—"

"I know where it is," Tucker cuts him off. The image on the screen starts moving. He's heading out. "I replaced the batteries last week."

Half a smile creeps up the side of my face. Good ol' Tucker. But I have to catch myself. He's not Tucker, not anymore. He's an abomination. Only a means to an end.

We watch the screen as Tucker finds the sublevels and makes his way with obvious familiarity. Down another flight of steps, then through a long hallway where at the end three mutos stand staring at a fixed point between them.

"Our loyal hounds," Perch mutters. "On standby."

They look like they're asleep on their feet, swaying as they stare at the shortwave radio. Tucker slows his approach.

"Yours?" he makes sure, coming to a standstill.

"They won't hurt you," Jamison assures him.

"Move 'em," Tucker says.

Perch glances back at me and I nod. "Bring 'em home," I say. "They need their beauty sleep."

Perch chuckles as his hands glide over the controls. The three dogs stir, jerking awkwardly, stepping away from the radio and reeling to face Tucker. Their bulging eyes focus on him as they stagger his way.

"Hey now..." Tucker backs up.

"There's only one way in and out. Stand still, and they won't notice you." Jamison releases the pad and faces Perch. "Right?"

He shrugs. "They're awful hungry."

"He's invisible," I retort. "They won't even know he's there."

"Might be able to sniff 'im out. Invisible or not, he smells like food to them."

"You just make sure they don't try anything."

We watch the screen from Tucker's point of view as the three mutos approach one step at a time, grunting and drooling. The stuff of nightmares, really—even more horrific in the night vision's negative light. Their glowing white eyes seem to stare straight at Tucker, even though they can't see him.

Or can they? Like Mathis, are they able to see what we can't? Regardless, I'm sure they reek in that confined space. All that foul mucus oozing out of them. Nasty. I almost feel sorry for Tucker.

They come upon him and brush past. One turns and snorts suddenly, fangs flashing hungrily—but Perch is right on it, sending a jolt of electricity through its collar. It falls backward, flailing, then scrambles away. The other two stagger on, oblivious.

Without a word, Tucker heaves a deep breath and turns toward the radio. The screen focuses on the blinking light—that incoming transmission.

"Well, what d'you know," he muses, cursing softly. "Looks like we've got something."

"We need you to bring it back to us," Jamison tells him, in case it isn't obvious.

"How about I see who's calling first?" Tucker reaches forward, his hand emerging from the bottom of the screen.

"No." Jamison glances back at me. "Just bring it back, Tucker. Be careful. We need it in one piece."

I nod. Only one person's going to answer that transmission. Me.

"Bring it back the way you came...and Perch won't have to hurt you again." Jamison swallows, staring at the screen.

Tucker's hand remains poised in mid-air. He sniffs. "Didn't hurt all that much."

He flips the switch on the receiver. Instantly the blinking light dims, and a deep voice speaks loud and clear in the Common language of the UW, but with a thick Eurasian accent:

"—physical mutations. Consider them hostile, armed and dangerous. Repeat: What remains of the North American Sectors is a forbidden zone. Off limits entirely. Do not venture within fifty nautical miles of the coastline. Proceed, and you will be fired upon. Search and rescue teams have not returned. It is believed they were infected and have suffered severe physical mutations. Consider them hostile, armed and dangerous.

Repeat: What remains of the North American Sectors is a forbidden zone..."

"They're on a loop." Jamison frowns. "A recorded message?"

"Then nobody will hear 'im scream." Perch spins the dial under his left hand and the voice on the radio is drowned out by Tucker's sudden shriek. The image on the screen goes berserk. "Didn't hurt that much, huh?" Perch grins. "How about *this?*" He twists the dial 360 degrees, and our speakers crackle with a guttural roar.

"He's no good to us dead." Jamison scowls.

"Just showing 'im who's boss."

That would be me. I'm the boss. "Stop it."

Perch doesn't look back. He's enjoying this too much. The sadist.

"I said stop!" I clench my fists.

He shrugs with a curse and dials down the settings. The screams subside to groans, then weak whimpers, the kind no man would want anybody to hear. I lean forward and press the audio pad on the console.

"Tucker, you there?" I listen to him gulp and sniff. The image on the screen continues to quake. "Let me know you can hear me."

"Yeah," he manages in a hoarse whisper. "I'm still here."

Good. "Listen, Tucker. We can do this the easy way or the hard way. But you're going to bring that radio back here, regardless. And you're going to do it now. No more fooling around. You hear me?"

Another sniff. "Yes sir."

"Good." I turn to Jamison as I release the pad. "Get him back here on the double. Undamaged."

"We'll contact you as soon as he returns, Captain. As soon as we've got the radio." Jamison salutes as I leave.

I shut the door behind me and stand there a moment, sucking down a deep breath. Too many thoughts crowd my mind. Chiefly: Where's this UW transmission coming from? How long has it been on the air? Is it even current? If so, that would mean the rebels weren't successful in demolishing the United World as we knew it. It would mean there's still a government out there, beyond our *forbidden* shores. A world without demon-dust, ash freaks, and mutos.

A world we could rejoin, eventually.

My pulse quickens at the thought of it. This is the best news we could have gotten. What a morale booster for the Eden Guard, to know exactly what we're fighting for now.

There's still a whole lot to be confirmed, and that'll have to wait until we've got the radio and can make contact with the outside world. But to think... *The outside world.* It's still there. The whole planet isn't an ash-covered wasteland!

Images fly through my mind of UW helicopters landing with rescue teams ready to take us away, the rotors stirring up demon-dust and infecting the crews as they land—

No. No, I can't. The glass if half-full here, half-full. Our salvation is near. I know it, I can feel it. It's no time for pessimism. We *will* be saved.

"A credit for your thoughts."

Margo smiles as she steps close for a brief embrace. She retreats a step and salutes. "Ready for my rounds, Captain." She's wearing her white medical coat, the one our dogs found for her. Makes her look so official.

"Right." I nod as if remembering something from a lifetime ago. "And I'm riding along."

"That you are, sir. As a man true to his word."

I've got to stop making her so many promises. She slips her arm around mine and guides me toward the ladder at the other end of the main floor. Might look like I'm the one escorting her, but it's the other way around. She's in charge right now. Just like Perch said.

"They're really starting to make progress. I think you'll be impressed by what you see. It shouldn't be long until we're able to start acclimating them back to life as we know it—as they used to know it."

Not an option. Keeping them in the recovery rooms is one thing. Sedated. Away from us. Out of mind, out of sight. We never agreed on them joining the Eden Guard.

We walk a ways before she hugs my arm. "You're awful quiet."

"Sorry. Got a lot on my mind is all."

"Tell me about it."

Should I? Is it too soon to share the hope welling up inside me? "We found a shortwave radio on the surface. The dogs are bringing it down now."

"Does it work? Too early to tell?" She starts up the ladder as soon as we reach it.

I can't stop myself. I tell her about the transmission, what it could mean for us. For the all-natural children of God who survived the end of the world. I tell her everything, and it spills out of me like an oil gusher.

"Willard, that's incredible!" She stares at me as we stand on the catwalk beside the row of recovery rooms. "I never expected..." She shakes her head and smiles. "I've always thought we were on our own down here. All alone. I never considered that there could be survivors on other continents. It makes sense, though. If they just bombed our sectors, where the rebel uprising began, there would've been no need for the rest of the world to share our fate."

"From the sound of things, they're more than just survivors. Sounds like the UW is strong as ever out there, patrolling our shores to keep anybody from joining us."

"Do you think they'll allow us off the continent?"

"We're still the way God made us." Except for our missing gonads. "No genetic abnormalities rearing their ugly heads. I'll make 'em understand. Soon as we get the radio, we'll transmit our own message, tell 'em where we are. They'll figure out some way to rescue us, I guarantee it."

I look across Eden, taking in all the progress we've made in the past months. But this was never meant to be our home. There is a bigger world waiting for us.

"We'll figure it out. That's what we do." I wink at her, but she doesn't respond.

Instead, she slides open the first door she comes to—one I've already visited today. Inside, Mathis lies dead to the world. Good to see Perch got him back into his bed where he belongs. Otherwise, I would've had some explaining to do.

"Mathis, right?" She likes it when I use their names.

She glances at me and nods, concern arching her brow. She checks the monitors beside the bed, examines each of the hoses connecting him to the machines that feed him while they feed on our power supply. She stares at him like something's wrong.

"What is it?"

"He's been over-sedated." She turns her gaze to me. "He's in a coma."

"That can't be right. You're the only one authorized to be up here, and you'd never make a mistake like that."

"I know." Her dark eyes remain on me. "I wouldn't."

"Who then?"

"You tell me."

"How would I know?" Why are her eyes boring into me like this? Is she trying to read my mind?

A ridiculous thought.

"Have any of the men expressed an interest in pulling the plug on my patients?"

"No." I frown, shaking my head. "None of 'em. They know what you're doing here is important."

If it wasn't for her, I'd pull the plug myself.

"What about Perch?"

What about him? Yes, he hates your guts, thinks you're a muto-lover and probably one yourself. Yes, he over-sedated this patient because he didn't know what the hell he was doing. And yes, it's my fault for having him do it. So blame me, if you're looking to blame somebody.

"You think he did this?"

"He's never supported my efforts here."

"He just has a crush on you is all, and he doesn't know how to express himself." I squeeze her shoulders and whisper into her ear, "There's not enough of you to go around." I nibble on her ear lobe until the hint of a smile breaks across her lips. "Wouldn't have it any other way."

She pulls away from me, concentrating on her patient now.

"Anything you can do?" I lean on the railing at the foot of the bed and glance down. The muscle stimulator is where we left it...but it's not how we found it. The cartridge is almost empty. I turn, blocking her view of the device.

"Not much at this point." She touches Mathis's brow tenderly. Her gaze roves along the blinking lights on the machines beside her. "He's stable for now, but this could be a major setback in the progress we've made."

"He'll pull through. He's strong. Always has been." The platitudes just roll off my tongue. But she didn't see him earlier, flailing around like a fish with too much air in its gills.

She clenches her jaw, the muscle twitching as her eyes lose focus. Then she looks up at me with a forced smile. "On to the next?"

Of course. The rounds. We have eleven more recovering ash freaks to visit. With a slight bow, I slide open the door and hold it for her. "After you, Doc."

In the next room, we find Catherine looking more fragile than I remember, plugged into more of the same medical machines. But unlike Mathis, she's wide awake, paralyzed from the neck down. If only we could paralyze her mouth. Permanently.

"Hey Catherine." Margo comes around the side of her bed to kiss her forehead like she would an ailing sister. "How are you feeling today?"

"Brought Captain Prick, I see." The freak fixes me with a withering look. "Figure you'd finally stop by and finish me off, eh Willard?"

"Didn't even cross my mind." I fold my arms.

"I'll be the judge of that." She closes her eyes, squeezing them tight and scowling. The muscles in her neck tighten. Her face flushes like she's constipated. Then she relaxes all of a sudden, sighing with a curse. "Can't...not anymore. Thanks to you." She glares at me. "The new world gives us these special abilities, and you can't stand to see us with 'em. The good Lord gives, and Willard takes away. God damn you!"

"Your telepathy didn't come from God. It was an abomination."

"*You're* the abomination!" she screams, eyes wild with rage.

Margo tries to calm her down.

"Go to hell, Willard!" Catherine shrieks. "You bastard!"

I glance at Margo as I turn away. "I'll wait outside."

The door slides shut behind me—but not before I hear Catherine whisper hoarsely to Margo between coughs, "He doesn't know about you, does he? He has no idea!"

Only a steel door separates us now, yet I suddenly feel a thousand kilometers away. I could go back inside, demand to know what she meant by that. But I don't. I don't need to.

A part of me always knew, I suppose.

I watch the men hauling pallets of supplies to and fro on the main floor. I listen to the steady hum of the air purifiers, feel the constant vibration in the catwalk from the nuclear reactor far below us. Across the floor, I notice Perch. He's carrying the shortwave radio into the monitoring station.

Things around here are about to change in a big way.

14. DAIYNA

TEN MONTHS AFTER ALL-CLEAR

I can't feel anything. My body is numb, curled inward on itself like a fetus, twitching involuntarily. What did they hit me with? All of them, all at once. Some kind of electric shock rounds. Enough to drop me convulsing to the floor.

I'm going to be sick.

"Fall back." A voice of authority from far away. Boots shuffle back from me, all but one pair. "You'll have to forgive my men." The same voice. A face with a thin mustache and a tight-lipped grin makes eye contact. "We don't get many visitors down here."

Someone sniffs. "So what do you say, Captain?"

Tucker. He betrayed me. I never should have trusted him.

"We'll have to see about that. From what I recall, you've still got plenty left on your to-do list." A pause. "So quit standing around and get back at it!"

Someone starts up the ladder. I hear the contact against each rung as it's made to disappear by invisible hands and feet.

"All of you—back at it!" Boots scurry away. In their absence, I hear the machines humming nearby, a throbbing between my ears. A chill spreads down my side. The slick concrete floor is cold beneath me. "Can you stand?" A hand touches my shoulder tentatively.

"Who—?" My lungs shudder.

"Plenty of time to get ourselves acquainted. You just try and relax now. I'm real sorry about my men—they can get a little trigger-happy from time to time, and that's a fact. But the effects will pass. No permanent damage done." Something clicks, hisses static. "Jamison. Meet me in the east tunnel, out by the air processors." Another click. "Deep breaths, if you can," he tells me. "Try and steady your nerves. I'm sure they're going haywire right now." His fingers gently tug at my head covering. "Let's get this out of the way a bit so you can breathe easier."

I let him uncover my face.

"Well now." He sits back on his haunches. "Ain't you a sight for sore eyes." He grins again, but his eyes stare at me hard.

I try to move, to uncurl myself as my muscles tremble.

"Captain?" Boots approach, striking the pavement in an easy jog.

"Help me get her to her feet."

"Who's—?"

"Guest quarters. We'll give her some time to get over the shock."

They haul me up off the floor and carry me between them like so much dead weight. My head swims crazily at the sudden altitude, and I fight to stay conscious. But it's futile. My head drops forward, and darkness swallows my senses.

The night doesn't last long. My eyes open wide, and my head jerks upward.

I'm sitting in a large bed, enveloped by a mound of plush blankets. A small bedroom with painted walls—mustard-colored. Artwork mounted in rustic frames. Soft ambient light.

Is this a dream?

Milton sits at my bedside.

I nearly jump out of my skin at the sight of him.

"Hello Daiyna." He smiles sheepishly. The layer of grime on his face cracks at the corners of his mouth.

"What are you doing here?" I gasp, clutching at my covers. Underneath, I'm naked.

He still wears his filthy urine suit, and it reeks. The scarred face shield dangles idly from his fingers, swaying to and fro, as he reclines in an overstuffed armchair. He parts his lips, takes a breath to answer me, but shrugs instead.

"I'm going to rescue you," he says.

What's that mean? The last time I saw him... My hand drifts to my throat.

"Yeah. About that." He leans forward, biting his lip with a sudden frown. "I'm sorry." He meets my gaze, his eyes clear and earnest. "I think I might've been possessed or something."

I nod slowly. "Right..." I remember seeing the evil spirit inside him, fighting against his will. "Not anymore?"

"I don't think so. Some weird stuff's been going on, but I feel like myself again—more or less." Another shrug.

I don't sense the spirit of the earth in him, but I don't sense anything in myself, either. The voice of the spirits remains silent.

I glance quickly around the room. "How did you—?" I was going to ask how he found me, how he got in here, but I'm not even sure where *here* is.

"I found a way in." He watches me. "They don't know I'm here yet. So far, I've managed to stay under their radar. I think."

"How long?" My head swims again. I hold it with one hand, keeping the covers in place with the other. Where are my clothes?

"An hour or so. The others—"

"An *hour*?" I've been here that long?

"I've been keeping an eye on you. Wasn't easy finding you. This place is a crazy maze."

Does he mean *he's* been here for an hour? "How long have *I* been here?" The words barely escape my lips. I've never felt so exhausted.

"Uh—you don't remember?"

"Remember what?" My head aches now. Something isn't right.

He hesitates. "They brought you in here—into this room—on a stretcher. Like you'd been in surgery...or something."

"When?" My abdomen tightens.

He bites his lip again. "Hard to keep track of the time without sunlight."

Surgery. Why don't I remember it? They shot me, knocked me off that ladder, helped me to my feet. I must have blacked out. Then here. How much time passed in between?

"The others are across the way, on the other side. I found them yesterday." He blows out a short sigh and shakes his head. "They're in pretty bad shape, but they're alive."

The others. "Shechara? Luther and—"

"Samson, yeah." He nods grimly. "They've...done stuff to them. Bad stuff."

They who? Wait. I remember. Tucker told me about them. He called them *naturals*.

"Can you walk?" He rises. "I didn't want to wake you, figured you could use the sleep after whatever they did..." His gaze drifts down the blankets. "But we should go. Before they come back."

"Right." Of course. I can't stay here, wherever we are. We have to find the others, get back to the caves. That's why we came here in the first place.

But what is this itching sensation along the middle of my belly? I reach down to scratch it...and find a rough row of stitches.

My blood runs cold. I throw aside the covers.

"Turning away now." Milton shuffles quickly.

Whoever sewed me up did a good job. The two centimeters of black thread below my navel are tight and even. Why did I need this? I gingerly touch the smooth skin around the wound and press on it. Why did they cut me open? Did I injure myself when I fell from the ladder? But no...there are other scars here, smaller, only millimeters in length. One in my navel, too.

"I'll find you some clothes." Milton leaves the bedroom. Closet doors slide with a thud outside.

Why can't I remember what happened? Tucker said these naturals tried to *cure* others gifted by the spirits. Is that what they did to me? But why these stitched incisions? Why would they need to see inside me?

Amnesia is infuriating.

"These might work. Just guessing your size here—not that I saw anything." He drops some colorful women's apparel onto the foot of the bed. "I'll be out front. Let me know when you're ready." He leaves without a backward glance.

I catch myself staring at the clothes. Floral patterns take me back to another life. It's been so long without color...

But there's no time to lose. I slide off the side of the bed and sink into thick carpet. I close my eyes at the memory of home—my real home, long before All-Clear, before the bunker, before D-Day. My room, my dollhouse, the one we made from a blueprint we found on the web, my mother, my sister, my dog—

Now the only family I have left is here, somewhere. I need to find them.

I reach for the dress Milton found for me. Wasn't there anything more practical? Pulling it on, I step outside into a short hallway.

A sudden spasm of pain rocks me. I clutch my stomach and lean against the wall. I grit my teeth to keep from crying out. Eventually the pain subsides, releasing its grip on my abdominal muscles. My fingers brush the stitches beneath the fabric of the dress.

What did they do to me?

Milton looks up as I enter the front room, a spacious area with couches and bookshelves and a fireplace. It's a living room, so much like the home I remember from long ago. What is this place?

"It fits? Good."

I glance down at the dress and pluck at it self-consciously. It leaves my shoulders and arms bare and ends just below my knees —legs exposed that haven't been shaved in who knows how long. Good thing the hair down there is so fine, barely noticeable. I hope.

A strange thing to focus on right now.

"Couldn't find anything else?" The pattern is full of red roses and purple lilacs. I remember them both from another world.

"That's all there is in the closet—dresses, that sort of thing. Looks like somebody's already been through them. A few hangers are empty."

I try to maintain what dignity I can muster. "No undergarments?"

"Uh..."

The front door rattles. Unlike the rest of this comfortable living space, it's solid steel and formidable, like something on a warehouse. Or a prison. Locked from the outside.

Milton disappears at superspeed, passing me with a blast of air and a whisper, "I'm not here."

He's left me. Again.

The door slides to the side as two men enter. They both wear blue camouflage uniforms and black berets. Guns holstered at their sides. *Soldiers?*

"Up so soon?" asks the one with a thin mustache. His beady eyes rove up and down the dress I'm wearing, and he grins with appreciation. "You look great, Daiyna."

I step back reflexively. How does he know my name?

"Lock the door on your way out," Mustache orders his partner.

"Sir?"

Mustache's eyes remain on my dress. "You heard me, Jamison."

Jamison glances from him to me. Then he salutes awkwardly. "Yes sir." He steps out and hauls the door shut. The bolt reverberates as it's locked in place.

"Now then." Mustache moves toward one of the couches and sits carefully, as though he doesn't want to wrinkle his uniform. He gestures toward the cushion beside him. "Won't you join me, Daiyna?"

I watch him. I listen for Milton. Where's he hiding?

"Please." The grin remains, stretching Mustache's gaunt face.

I sit down on the cushion farthest from him, careful to keep my knees together. Strange how old habits return unbidden.

"I'm sure you're feeling a bit out of sorts right now, Daiyna. One of the side effects of the drugs we gave you, I'm afraid. All of them necessary, of course. But you should be—"

"Who are you?" I demand.

He chuckles. "Believe it or not, we've already had this conversation. Two days ago." He waves a slight hand through the air. "Never mind. My name is Captain Arthur Willard, and you're currently in the tender loving care of the Eden Guard. We're doing our damnedest to make sure you're comfortable during your stay with us, and I hope we're succeeding." He winks.

I keep anything worth reading out of my expression. "You're the naturals."

His eyebrows lift. "Wow. No beating around the bush with you!" His gaze wanders down my dress again. "Well, if by that you mean we're all-natural children of God, then yes. We're guilty as charged."

"Where are my friends?" My abdomen cramps up. I bite my lip.

His grin fades. He raises his chin, sweeping the room with a steely gaze. Then he fixes me with a sidelong look. "I'm pretty sure one of them is in here."

How does he know? My guard falters.

Willard chuckles again and lifts a finger toward the ceiling. "Daiyna, Daiyna. We're always watching. We've got cameras in every room. Had 'em installed back when I suspected my old squeeze of being an ash freak. Boy, have they come in handy!" He leans toward me and rests his hand on my bare knee. "That one, she could move things with her mind and get inside your head. Telepathy, telekinesis. God-awful stuff." He squeezes my knee. I cringe inwardly. "But boy oh boy, was she good in the sack." He licks his lips. "Just like an *animal*."

I grab hold of his wrist and jerk his hand into the air between us. "Don't touch me."

I release him, and he leans back.

"All right then. We can either do this the easy way—" He winks at my figure with appreciation. Then he sighs reluctantly and draws his handgun, pointing it at my face. "—or the hard way."

A rush of air whips past, and Milton stands between me and Willard's gun. No, Milton now holds Willard's gun, aimed at the floor.

"Howdy."

Willard stares up at him, speechless.

"You're the guy in charge down here. Right?"

"Yes..." Willard finds his voice, his thin lips parted but no other words emerge.

"Thought I've seen you around, telling people what to do." There's an easy confidence about Milton. He doesn't seem afraid at all. "I've been waiting to get you alone. So I can tell *you* what to do."

Willard blinks, snatching the radio off his belt. He has it halfway to his mouth—but in a blur of speed, so fast he's almost invisible, Milton's other hand reaches out and tugs it away.

"Nope. You're on your own now, *Captain*."

Willard curses him, glancing at his gun and radio in Milton's hands. "They'll be here in no time. They're watching us as we speak! My men are well-trained, armed to the teeth—"

"And s-l-o-w. I'll knock them out before they even know what hit them. Probably with their own guns." It's a statement of fact, not arrogance.

"You won't make it out of here alive," Willard counters, licking his lips. "I don't care how fast you are. We'll loose the dogs on you."

"Now I know you're bluffing." Milton grins. "There aren't any dogs, not anymore." He points the gun between Willard's dumbfounded eyes and cocks the hammer with his thumb. The resounding clink holds the moment. "Now I'm going to give you back this radio, and you're going to call one of your men. That brown-noser who was here before. Jamison. Got it?"

Willard's eyes dart to the radio.

"Nothing funny, or I blow off one of your ears. Okay?"

Willard keeps his mouth shut as Milton hands him the radio. Then he mutters, "What do you expect me to say?"

Milton glances at me. His eyes hold a sadness I haven't seen in them before. "Tell him to bring Luther over here."

"Under what pretense?" Willard scoffs. "We keep them separated—"

"I don't care. Tell him it's mating season and you want to watch." Milton cringes at me apologetically. Then to Willard, "He won't question it, probably knows you're a little kinky."

Willard curses him, fuming, gripping the radio with white knuckles.

"Make the call." Milton presses the gun muzzle hard into Willard's left ear.

The radio clicks on with static.

"Jamison..." Willard clears his throat, seething.

"Sir?"

"Bring Luther over here."

A pregnant pause. "Sir?"

"You heard me. On the double." Willard leans sideways to wink at me. "Daiyna's feeling extra frisky today."

Milton snatches the radio and shuts it off, tossing it onto the couch.

"Now what?" Willard smirks. "Torture? Death?"

"Soon," Milton mutters.

"What did you do to me?" I rise, fists clenched.

"When?" He winks again, suggestively.

I punch him in the face, sending him over onto his side.

Willard grins with blood in his teeth. "You mutant *freaks*!" He laughs as he sits up, wiping his mouth on his sleeve. "Where do you think you'll go? How will you survive? There's no place on this earth for the likes of you."

"Answer her." Milton's tone is cold.

Willard sniffs and feels his nose with bloodied fingers. "I think you broke it," he mutters. Then he fixes his eyes on me. "We harvested your eggs. You were quite the fertile specimen, and that's a fact. Took some doing, but we managed to get them all. And now we have what we need to start up Eden's first generation of test-tubers!"

The room spins as I drop back onto the couch. My hand slides toward the stitches under my dress. The cramping pain blossoms again. I grit my teeth to keep from making a sound.

"How about you, soldier?" Willard's eyes drift down Milton's filthy jumpsuit. "Got any seed in there to donate to the cause?"

"Not even if I could."

"Sterile too, huh? Yeah." Willard stares at nothing in particular. "Ain't it a bitch."

Their voices fade as reality hits me hard. I look down at the roses and lilacs, dizzying in their random pattern, swirling wildly without purpose. Like me. What they took... How is it possible?

A void has opened deep inside me, one that won't be filled again.

Rehana would laugh. *Now you'll never be their cow*, she'd say. *You never wanted to be—or did you?*

I don't know. Luther and I agreed that our brothers and sisters should wait until later, when we reach the Preserve. Then, when the daemons can no longer find us, when we're safe, we'll finally fulfill our purpose and repopulate this new earth.

But now? What will Luther think?

Why do I care?

The lock rattles. The door slides open to reveal not only Luther—wearing only a pair of white undershorts—but at least twenty armed soldiers packed close around them, weapons trained on Milton and me.

"Just give the word, Captain," growls one with a protruding jaw, his weapon aimed at Luther's head.

Luther... Our eyes meet as I stand. My lips part. He smiles

with relief. I want to run to him, throw my arms around him and weep into his chest. His arms hang limply, palms tilted toward me. He doesn't look away, not for a second. Neither do I.

"You want to tell them, or you want me to?" Milton glances at Willard.

"Of course." He turns on the couch to face his men. "Thanks for coming, boys, but the situation here is under control. Just send Luther inside and shut the door. Everything's fine." He wipes at a fresh trail of blood issuing from his nose. "We're good."

The stocky soldier looks skeptical. "Doesn't look *good*, Captain. Give the word, and we'll blow these freaks to hell."

"You heard me, Perch," Willard says.

With obvious reluctance, they shove Luther inside and heave the door shut, locking it behind him. I run to him, and he meets me after my second step, pulling me into his strong arms and holding me tight. I throw my arms around his neck and press my face against his cheek. It's rough with stubble and wet with tears. Mine? His?

"You're all right," he gasps, squeezing me.

"Yes...And you—"

He draws back, cupping my face in his hands. "Your eyes—your *eyes*..." He smiles, looking from my right eye to my left. Then he hugs me close. "Thank God!"

I tremble in his arms, my lungs shuddering as I allow the tears to fall. I cling to him, even as pain throbs in my hollow abdomen. It doesn't matter now. Not right now. Nothing else does.

He kisses my forehead, and a warm sensation floods through me. My heart pounds, my breath catches. I look into his eyes as he touches my face. I take his strong hand and kiss it. Tentative? Maybe. I smile at his smile.

Then I see his fingers.

"Luther?"

I take his hand in mine and cradle it like a wounded bird. Each finger has been mutilated, bruised and bloodied. Where the nails—his claws—should be...they're mangled beyond recognition. He lifts my chin gently with his other hand. I meet his gaze.

"I'm fine, Daiyna." He kisses my cheek tenderly.

I want to kiss him.

"Nothing like two mutos in love," Willard remarks with a vulgar curse.

I want to kill him.

"What should I do with this one?" Milton asks.

Luther half-turns, his arm around me, keeping me close to his side. His jaw muscle twitches as he regards Willard with a steely gaze. "What I want you to do is not necessarily what should be done."

"Oh, have at it, Luther." Willard chuckles, rising to his feet. "She's already busted up my nose. There's plenty of me left to go around. What do you want? C'mon, let me have it. Bust my balls, really give it to me. You know you want to!"

I can tell Luther's tempted. But he doesn't give in. "Sit down."

Willard almost replies, but he sees something in Luther's eyes that makes him keep his mouth shut. Muttering a curse, he slumps onto the couch and stares at the carpet.

"We need him—for now," Luther says. "His men listen to him. We'll need them to follow his orders if we're to make it out of here alive."

Milton nods. "So...stage two?"

Willard can't contain himself. He laughs out loud. "*Stage Two?*" he mocks. "What? You've got some kind of operation all planned out?"

Milton and Luther nod.

Willard's grin freezes on his face, then fades. He stares hard at Milton. "How long have you been down here?"

Milton shrugs. "Long enough."

"Agreed." Luther squeezes me once more and breaks away, moving back toward the hallway with familiarity. The closet doors slam side to side, and he returns with a few items of men's clothing. He hands me a pair of jeans—coarse and blue. "If you'd like."

I definitely would. I pull them on under my dress.

"When would you like me to start?" Milton stretches his back as though he's warming up for a track meet.

Luther buttons his jeans and tugs on a form-fitting black short-sleeve. His toned arm muscles ripple. "Whenever you'd like. Let us know if we're in the way."

"Shouldn't be a problem." Milton swings the handgun mid-stretch to point at Willard's face. "Have your men open the door now."

"Sure you want that? They've got you outnumbered twenty to one."

"I hope they're all out there chomping at the bit." He retrieves the radio and clicks it on with another static hiss, handing it to Willard. "Tell them to come on in."

"Stage Two, huh?" Willard smirks, shaking his head. "Boy, are you in for some real trouble. And too stupid even to know it. Death's at the door, you damn freak." He barks into the radio, "Jamison, Perch: get the hell in here! Code red!"

As soon as the door's unlocked and shoved open, a horde of Willard's troops charges in, heeding his shrill command to fire at will. Bullets pock the ceiling and the far wall and shatter one of the framed paintings. I hit the floor and cry out. It feels like something has torn inside my abdomen. Luther falls beside me, shielding me with his body. Would he sacrifice himself like this if he knew I could no longer fulfill my purpose?

The air in the room rushes wildly like a mini-tornado's roving around. I spot just a blur here and there as Milton slows down long enough to drop one of the unconscious soldiers against the wall. Willard stares, wide-eyed, as his men are piled on top of each other like sandbags, unarmed, dead to the world. The stack rises, spilling across the couch and against Willard himself, pinning him where he sits. The bodies come too fast for him to avoid the onslaught.

As suddenly as the mayhem began, it's over. Milton stands in the middle of the room. On one side of him sits a pile of countless firearms. On the other side are the unconscious soldiers, stacked around Willard. The steel door yawns open, allowing harsh white light from outside to flood in.

"So, what were you saying?" Not even the least bit out of breath, Milton turns to wink at Willard.

"I think he's speechless." Luther rises and offers me a hand. I take it. "A welcome change, I must say."

Willard squirms, struggling against the bodies that wedge him in tightly where he sits. He curses and fumes but eventually grates out, "You have nowhere to go. Why are you so hell-bent on leaving? You're safe here, for God's sake."

"Safe?" I step toward him with fury boiling in my belly. I pull up the dress to expose my stitched abdomen, just above the waistline of the jeans Luther gave me. "How *dare* you?"

"You're the first virile survivors we've come across, in all this time. We built Eden for you—to protect the future. Our future!"

"You built this place for yourself." Luther picks up a rifle and jams a handgun into the waist of his pants. He beckons me to join him at the pile of weapons.

"I know all about you. You and your *naturals*." I lean in closer so Willard can see the hate burning in my eyes. But he doesn't look up. "Look at me!"

Slowly his eyes rotate upward. "From Tucker, right? Everything you think you know, you heard from half-baked ol' Tucker."

Luther steps toward me. "Don't listen to this man."

Milton glances outside. "We should get going."

Blood oozes from Willard's nose into his mustache. Arms pinned to his sides by the weight of his own men, he's unable to wipe it. "Tucker told you only half the story. It's all he knows."

I'm listening, but I don't know why. I shouldn't be.

"He's a lunatic. Been alone too long up there on the surface. My fault, truth be told. I left 'im…for the good of the many."

"Are we leaving him here?" Milton glances at Luther, who nods.

"Daiyna." Luther's voice is quiet. He touches my arm.

"You're not safe. You have no idea. It's not just the mutos and the demon-dust anymore." Willard licks his lips as the blood dribbles across them. "They know what you are. And they're coming for you. Just like they've done everywhere else." His eyes implore me.

I frown at him. What's he talking about? *They* who?

Luther takes my arm gently but firmly. He tells me we have to get Shechara, Samson, and another one whose name I don't recognize. He hands me a rifle. I take it, but I watch Willard. A tear leaves his eye as we step outside onto a steel catwalk suspended over an expanse of concrete littered with crates.

"I'm sorry," he calls after us. "I tried to fix you, but it's too late. God have mercy on you—on us all!"

Milton heaves the steel door shut and locks it. "Wacko," he mutters.

We're inside an enormous dome, lit by bright lights mounted at intervals high above us. I blink in the glare. The steel beneath my bare feet vibrates with the low hum of distant machinery.

"How many remain?" Luther scans the vacant floor below us, his weapon at the ready.

Milton jerks a thumb toward the steel door behind him. "Close to forty in there...so that should leave less than a dozen. Probably hiding out somewhere, waiting to ambush us." He grins.

I glance at the large bolt on the door. "Shouldn't we take their weapons?"

Milton pats the pockets of his jumpsuit, which I notice are bulging beyond capacity. "Got all the ammo."

Luther moves toward the ladder. "Margo should be finished with Samson soon." He slings the rifle across his back and heads quickly down the steel rungs.

"Margo?" I watch him go.

"Another gifted type." Milton sweeps the floor below us with his rifle as Luther descends. "She was their doctor here. More like their slave. But she's with us now."

Us. I watch him, this man who wanted to kill me. This man I

saved from the spirits of the earth when they intended to drown him in sand and dust, stone him to death as he ran. He who was possessed by evil...who now has been set free. To set us free.

Was this the spirits' purpose all along?

"What is it?" He catches me looking at him.

"It's good to see you, Milton."

He almost smiles. "Good to see you too."

Luther beckons us to follow. I leap over the railing and plummet to the ground, landing in a crouched position at his side. Milton does the same, but instead of falling as I do and landing cat-like, he seems to glide, floating down the twenty meters to the floor.

I can only stare.

"Something new he's picked up," Luther says with half a grin.

"He's certainly full of surprises." I press a hand against my sore abdomen.

"Meet you guys at the recovery rooms, after I take a quick look around." Milton turns away.

"God's speed," Luther says.

Milton glances at him. "Maybe." Then he's off in a blur of speed with a blast of air in his wake.

"This way." Luther touches my side and jogs across the dome's main floor.

I do my best to keep up, but my stomach cramps immediately, and I have to slow down.

"Are you all right?" He stops.

"Fine," I gasp. "How did he find us?"

"Milton? The spirits told him. They...appeared to him as people from his past, from his sector. Good and evil, as he puts it. They showed him a way into the tunnels from the east, and he was able to enter Eden without Willard's men or cameras seeing him. He visited my room yesterday—startled me quite a bit, I assure you."

I can relate. "Eden?"

"This place." He gestures at the arched ceiling above us.

"Willard's paradise beneath the earth, away from the spirits' influence."

Should I tell him I can't hear their voice anymore? Does it matter?

"Where were they keeping you?" I glance at his hands.

A somber look fills his eyes. "The recovery rooms, where we're headed. They held us there for days, ran tests on us...attempted to change us. Permanently."

I force myself to say it: "They took your gift."

He raises a hand and flexes his fingers. No miraculous talons extend outward. His eyes hold a deep sorrow.

"Luther..." Tears blur my vision.

He shakes his head. "Samson and Shechara had the worst of it." He pauses. His lips part to speak, but no words come.

We continue on in silence. Eventually, we reach another catwalk suspended above us with a ladder leading up to a row of identical steel doors. Luther starts up the ladder and I follow close behind, the throbbing pain in my abdomen keeping me from launching upward on my own.

Milton joins us as we climb off the last rung and onto the steel grate.

"Nobody." He emerges from a gliding blur of speed. "If they're hiding out, I can't find them. Maybe I spooked 'em."

"Let's hope they remain hidden until after we're well on our way." Luther steps toward the first door and knocks twice, then waits. He looks at me. "Brace yourself," he warns.

What's happened to my sister? What have these *naturals* done to Shechara? To Samson? If they're hurt in any way, I'll go back to that Captain Willard and rip out his throat. Why did we leave him and his men alive?

The door slides open. "Luther?" a quiet voice emerges from the darkness inside.

Shechara.

I rush forward crying her name and embrace her, folding her in my arms, pulling her close. She responds weakly, saying my name, but it sounds like a foreign word on her lips. I take her face in my hands.

Her eye sockets are empty.

I choke. "Shechara..."

"Daiyna—" She smiles suddenly. "You're here! You're *alive*!"

What have they *done*? My sister, my dear Shechara, blessed with far-sight, able to see what no one else can...

They will pay for this dearly. I'll kill every last one of them.

She touches my face. "They took my eyes, Daiyna. I don't know why they needed them. And they took..." Her fingers slide across my dress and find the stitches beneath the thin fabric. "You too?"

"Yes, my sister," I manage, fighting back tears. "Me too."

Luther touches us both on the shoulder. "Are you ready, Shechara?"

She nods bravely. "Yes, Luther." She slips her arm around mine. "I'll follow you."

I turn to Luther. He must see the questions in my eyes. The rage. But all he says is "This way." He leads us down the catwalk to the door at the end, the last room. Again, he knocks twice and waits.

This time, no one opens the door. Instead, Samson's voice thunders from the other side, reverberating the steel, "Enter!"

Luther glances at me, then slides the door open, stepping into the darkness beyond. Shechara and I follow, but Milton remains outside on the catwalk, keeping watch.

"Come one, come all!" Samson booms from the bed in the middle of the small room. On both sides are medical machines, blinking, bleeping. "Come and see the one, the only Samson—the human cyborg!"

He raises both arms over his head in a gesture of strength—but from the elbows onward, his arms are made of steel and hydraulics. Mechanical fingers curled into fists gleam in the fluorescent light above his bed. One of his legs is also robotic from the knee down, solid steel with bolted joints and exposed biofluid tubes. His other leg is missing, but a small-framed woman in a white lab jacket assists him, struggling to fit his second leg apparatus into place.

"You'll be a one-legged cyborg if you don't lend me a hand here," she says.

I stare, unable to comprehend what I'm seeing.

"This is Margo," Luther introduces her. "She's been a godsend."

Samson heaves one of his mechanical arms and awkwardly assists with the placement of his artificial leg. His fingers splay and curl, twitching as though he's not in complete control of them.

Rage boils to the surface within me.

"If you don't do something, I will," I grate out through clenched teeth.

Luther turns to meet my gaze. "I know what you're feeling, Daiyna. Believe me. We've all lost..." He rests his hand on my shoulder. "But we're not here to repay evil with evil. We need to leave as soon as we possibly can. That's our priority."

Samson grunts, scowling with determination as he swings his artificial legs over the side of the bed and positions himself with his arms. The one named Margo cautions us to stay back. Samson agrees with a short chuckle. Then he shoves himself forward onto his robotic legs and wobbles, waving his mechanical arms to steady himself. He grins at us briefly, then frowns at his legs, shifting one hip upward to take a full step forward and stomping down with a heavy metallic thud.

"All right!" he booms triumphantly.

"Shechara—" Margo approaches us. "I have something for you as well."

"Yes?" Shechara leans blindly toward the woman's voice.

Margo reaches into the pocket of her lab coat and removes two small metal spheres, holding them out in her palm.

"Artificial eyes." I fix her with a cool stare.

Margo returns my direct look. "Yes, Daiyna. Cybernetic." She's haggard, malnourished, unkempt. But there's sincerity in her eyes. "Would you please escort Shechara over here to take a seat? We'll get her seeing again. I know time is a factor."

I touch my sister's forehead with my own. "Do you want this?" I whisper.

She hesitates. Then she squeezes my arm. "I want to see. Will you stay with me?"

"I'm not going anywhere."

Samson stomps around, rattling everything in the room and knocking over a few of the machines with his flailing arms. Luther suggests they go outside and ready a vehicle. Samson agrees, pausing at the door to bellow, "You may not like what you're going to see, Small Fry."

He winks at me, and I can't help but smile. I don't understand his good spirits, considering all that's happened to him. But his joviality is oddly contagious.

A broad smile spreads across Shechara's lips. "Maybe I'll have X-ray vision."

His expression clouds. "No. That wouldn't be good." He stomps away, thundering out onto the steel catwalk one metallic thump at a time until he comes to an abrupt halt. "Hmmm," he murmurs, loud enough for us to hear. "Ladder, huh?"

"We could put you on the conveyor," Milton suggests.

"Don't push it, kid," Samson growls. "You're all right. But don't push it."

Margo tells Shechara to lay her head back, to relax. I hold my sister's hand, and by the strength of her grip I can tell she's far from relaxed.

"These should work fine, but if they don't, or if you want them out for any reason, we can remove them even faster than we install them." Margo applies a muscle relaxant to Shechara's left eye socket. "They'll take some getting used to, though. You'll suffer from some bad headaches at first. But you will see again."

"How did you get them—the prosthetic limbs, the eyes?" I watch her work.

She remains focused on every move she makes, but she speaks

to me as if we're having a friendly conversation. Are we? She's one of them, Willard's people—or she was. I don't trust her. I won't make the mistake of trusting a stranger ever again.

"Well, we're located beneath a trade sector. It's amazing what we've been able to lay our hands on."

"Like incubation equipment." My tone is spiteful.

She carefully clamps Shechara's eyelids open. "Yes," she replies. "Your eggs are in cold storage, along with Shechara's. The men's sperm is on ice as well."

She's so matter-of-fact about it. I would punch her right now if she wasn't in the middle of a delicate procedure.

"Why?" I demand.

She sanitizes the first metal orb with a clear lubricant. "Well, it all goes back to the shortwave radio. Everything changed after that. Willard had originally wanted to exterminate everyone who came into contact with the ash on the surface—the *infected*. But I was able to convince him we could change them back, reverse the process of their physiological transmutations. At the time, he didn't know I was one of them. An *ash freak*."

Where is this going? I asked a simple question. But I bite my tongue and watch as she places the first artificial eye into Shechara's gaping socket.

"You're doing great," I tell my sister, squeezing her hand.

She squeezes mine in return. "I don't feel anything."

"That's a good thing." Margo's hands are steady. Her head tilts toward me, but her eyes remain fixed on her work as she continues, "Willard was always concerned about our future, about Eden's next generation. We were sterile, of course. The government scientists didn't want us reproducing in the bunker, using up all of the food reserves. We knew you *breeders* would find us, eventually. We just had to be patient. Together, we would rebuild our species and its future. That was the plan, anyway." She sanitizes the second metal orb and glances at me. "But then Willard found the radio. He learned that the hope of this world's future didn't rest on his shoulders alone, that Eden wasn't the last bastion for humanity. He didn't have to keep the next generation safe from the surface and its *demon-dust*. Because the world—the rest of it, all we thought had been annihilated on D-Day—is still out there." She glances at me again. "Or so he thought."

"What do you mean?"

She goes on as if she didn't hear me, leaning toward Shechara to slip the second eye into place. "The North American Sectors are now a UW Forbidden Zone. Search and rescue teams were sent in at one point, years ago, but they became infected. The origin of the mutos, we assume. Willard was determined to let them know—whoever was still out there beyond our *verboten* shores—that we were safe and sound in Eden, uninfected. He wanted to figure out a way for the UW to rescue us and bring us back into the world."

"But the UW no longer exists," I murmur, noticing a ring of raw flesh around her neck, close to her throat, as if something she once wore had been too tight or had melted onto her skin and been torn away.

"We thought the same. And they don't, not to the extent they did prior to D-Day. The rebels didn't destroy them entirely, but they made a valiant effort and achieved some impressive results. Regardless, the United World—more or less—is still out there. Willard found this out when he made the mistake of contacting them, using a frequency adjacent to the looped quarantine message they'd been broadcasting for years." She activates one of Shechara's eyes, then the other. "Tell me what you see."

The metallic corneas stare blankly from behind Shechara's open eyelids. No iris, no pupil. She blinks once, twice, shifts in her seat, rocks her head to one side, then the other. She frowns, seeming to see something in a dark corner of the room.

"Who are you?" she asks.

"You...can see me?" A familiar voice—unfortunately—emerges from the shadows.

"Tucker?" Margo turns sharply. "How long have you been standing there?" She sounds perturbed, not startled.

I squeeze Shechara's hand and stare into the empty corner. "What do *you* want?"

He sniffs, shuffles an invisible step forward.

"Everything all right?" Milton leans in the open doorway.

"Is he armed?" I ask Shechara. She shakes her head.

"I was just wondering—" Tucker sniffs again. "How you managed to get your collar off, Margo. And if you could maybe..."

She blinks into the dark. Then she nods, reaching for an instrument on the cart at the foot of the bed. "Come here. Let's see what we can do about that."

Tucker's invisible feet move toward her. She reaches for him blindly. As soon as they make contact, she blinks out of my sight, vanishing. I remember being on the receiving end of that trick not too long ago.

"What do you see?" I ask Shechara.

"She's helping him take off his collar. Willard's men use them to control the daemons."

"They control the daemons?" I exclaim too loud as fury burns through me.

Another reason to wipe out these *naturals*!

"I was getting to that," Margo murmurs. "Hold still, Tucker! This laser will cut straight through you if we're not careful." He mumbles something in apology. She continues, "Willard figured out a way to remote-control some of the mutos so they could gather what we needed from the surface. He and Perch had maybe a dozen of them fitted, with more collars in production. Originally, that's all they were meant for. But when it became clear the UW didn't plan on rescuing us any time soon, that they were planning something else entirely—our *extermination*—he started raising up his own little army of collared mutos to protect Eden."

My simple question now seems insignificant, dwarfed by the crazy things she's saying. More conspiracy theories? Is she insane like Tucker? She sounds completely rational, matter-of-fact, even as she relates a story that's far too bizarre to believe.

"But what does any of this have to do with..." I trail off.

"Everything." She pauses. "You see, Willard and I were once in love. He allowed me to keep the infected alive, to study them, try to cure them. But he found out I was one of them around the same time as his first contact with the UW. He thought I had lied to him, betrayed him. He nearly fell apart, regressing beyond the point of simply wanting to kill off the infected. With the eager assistance of Perch, he started to reverse engineer them—taking them apart piece by piece without the proper use of sedatives—to find out how the physiological transmutations worked on a subatomic level. Of course they were unsuccessful and ended up killing all their subjects. Willard thought he could ingratiate himself with the UW leaders by studying a contagious phenomenon they didn't fully understand, one they couldn't allow themselves to come near enough to study. He hoped he could delay their plans to exterminate us." She pauses. "Then we found you."

She reappears suddenly with a thin strip of steel in her hand and sets it on the cart.

"Thanks, Margo," Tucker says.

"How about you go help Luther and Samson. They're getting a Hummer ready."

He sniffs and shuffles away, past me. Then he stops. His breath is warm and sour as he leans close. I have to restrain myself from slapping him as hard as I can.

"I'm sorry," he says quietly.

I don't know where to look in the empty space before me, just like when we first met. And I don't know what to say. I can't forgive him. He sniffs again and his footsteps exit the room, passing Milton as they step across the catwalk outside.

Margo faces Shechara. "Needless to say, you're able to see more than a mere mortal with these new eyes. It will take some time to adjust to the way they perceive the spectrum. They give you infrared thermoptic and night vision perception." She almost smiles, an awkward twitch of her lips. "But no X-ray, I'm afraid."

Shechara nods. "Thank you."

Margo turns away quickly. "Back to what we were saying."

What *she* was saying. I've never heard anyone so long-winded—besides Mother Lairen, maybe. Margo busies herself cleaning up, moving instruments, replacing used cartridges.

"When he found you, Willard thought he'd been given another chance to forestall the inevitable. He believed if he could prove to the UW that a new generation was going to be born in Eden, that they would postpone the *end of days* they had in store for us." She turns to fix me with her unblinking stare. "So yes, we took your eggs and sperm. And yes, we have all of the equipment and resources necessary to create new life from what we've taken. The first generation since All-Clear."

Is she proud of herself? "What's to keep us from smashing everything you have and leaving you with *nothing*?"

Milton leans in again. "Uh...because that's not the deal Luther made."

What? He made a *deal* with these people? Why? We have the upper hand here. We can destroy what they took from us and blow them all to hell!

"But you won't," Margo says, her deep-set eyes boring into me.

Did she just read my mind?

"Why won't we? You mean nothing to us, and after all you've done—!"

"Daiyna." Shechara squeezes my hand tightly, her gleaming eyes rotating toward me. "Daiyna, listen to her."

"I have. She's said more than enough."

"Then you won't mind if I add something else." Margo pauses. "The UW knows about you. Us. Our abilities. When Willard told them, their first inclination was to shower us with another Destruction-Day of nukes, wipe us out along with the hundreds of deformed soldiers they abandoned here years ago. But Willard assured them he had things under control. And while they may still risk sending over a team to assess the situation themselves, they will not destroy us while we have a new generation down here in the making. You see, from the sound of things, repopulation has been a global priority for years. But it hasn't been met with success. The UW is concerned the bioweapons and airborne toxins released by the rebels two decades ago may have rendered the rest of the world...infertile. An unexpected result of the plagues." She lets those words sink in. "The deal I made with Luther is simple. You are free to go, and we will give you a vehicle, weapons, fuel and supplies. Whatever you need. But you will not retaliate against us in any way. Go, and leave us far behind. Forget about us. But know that because of you, because of what we took from you... The world will live."

I stare at her. I don't know what to say. I sway on my feet, unable to sort out my thoughts. But one question arcs through my mind: "They would have to know the eggs and sperm came from us. Wouldn't our...children be like us? *Infected*?"

Her frail shoulders lift and fall. "From what we can tell, our superhuman abilities are the result of contact with the surface. The dust enters our lungs, spreads through our system, and we're changed. Willard and his soldiers have never ventured out onto the surface, and they remain unaffected. So, we're almost certain these gametes and the fetuses they will become won't be at risk, as long as we keep them in Eden during their gestation, growth, and development."

All so very scientific. Nothing supernatural about it.

"You can't know for sure."

"Of course not." She pauses. "What matters is the UW thinks we do. And they'll have to wait nine months to see if we're wrong."

A sudden blast shatters the moment as Milton fires his weapon.

"Sneaky devils. There you are." He fires again. I let go of Shechara and join him at the doorway. "See?" He points across to the catwalk at the other side of the dome where the steel door of that strange apartment remains locked from the outside. Half a dozen soldiers ride up the conveyor, crouching with wide pallets held up as shields. "Probably planning to unlock the door and let their boss out. Where have they been hiding?"

He fires again, obviously a warning shot. But the soldiers dive off the conveyor in all directions and scramble for cover. Milton will make sure none of them get close to that door.

A loud horn honks below. Luther and Samson climb out of a black armored vehicle.

"All aboard!" Samson grins up at me.

Shechara takes my hand. "Time to go, Daiyna."

I turn and look back at Margo. Who is this woman? Ally? Enemy?

"God be with you," she says with that twitch of a smile. "Though I'm not sure whose side he's on anymore."

"You don't belong here. You're not one of them."

She nods slowly, eyes unblinking. "They need me."

I can soften his heart, she places the thought into my mind. Does she mean Willard? Right. Good luck with that.

She smiles.

"You two go ahead." Milton stands rooted, covering the main floor with his rifle. "I'll catch up."

"I'm sure you will." I pat his shoulder.

I look Shechara in the eye. It'll take a while to get used to the new additions. "Ready?"

She nods, squeezing my hand. "Yes, Daiyna."

We jump up onto the railing and leap down from it, plunging to the concrete floor below and landing on all-fours.

"Good to see you still have it in you," Samson rumbles, balancing awkwardly on his new legs. He winks at me.

"Good to see your spirits are still up."

"And that's not all." He thrusts his pelvis forward suggestively and nearly topples over.

Luther chuckles. "Let's get out of here, shall we?" He raises his hand in farewell, his fingers wounded, his eyes full of gratitude.

Margo stares down at him. Slowly she raises her hand in return.

We file into the large vehicle, Samson taking the seat next to the driver while Luther, Shechara and I slide into the seats behind. The doors close automatically, and the engine roars to life. But the driver's seat is absent, as is the steering wheel.

"Ready folks?" Tucker says.

He's not coming with us. He can't be.

"Take us out, Mr. Tucker," Luther tells him. "Thank you. We'd be lost without your help."

"I know these tunnels like the back of my invisible hand," he says with a sniff. We roll forward, then surge across the main floor with a sudden burst of speed, heading toward what looks like the open mouth of a cave. Shots echo outside, the rounds pinging across the vehicle's surface. "Damn fools," Tucker mutters, flooring the gas pedal.

I look out the window just as five of the armed soldiers rush our way, firing wildly. I cringe as the shots bounce off the pane of tinted glass. Bullet-proof, apparently.

A moment later, we're in the tunnel, and all I see is the glow of the headlights against the curved concrete ahead of us. I glance back as the half-circle of light behind us recedes in the distance along with the small silhouettes of soldiers halting their pursuit and shaking their weapons in frustration.

Eden. I hope I never see that place again.

My mind feels heavy, overloaded as I try to process everything that whirls through it like a tornado. An impossible task. Some things I'm able to catch and tie down: We have a vehicle. Our original task is finally complete. Now we can go back to the caves and see if anyone survived the daemons' attack.

Margo said Willard controlled the daemons. Did he send them after us? He's still alive back there with everything they took from us. Will he send the daemons after us again?

And what's all this about the United World still being alive and well, out there somewhere? How many continents survived D-Day? Why didn't the spirits tell me?

The spirits. I can't even tackle that one right now. Where have they been? Why haven't they spoken to me? Was I possessed like Milton all that time? Milton's spirit has left him. Has mine done the same?

Before I realize it, we're in the underground parking structure at the south end of the city ruins, back where this ordeal began. Our invisible chauffeur takes us up through the sublevels and eventually out into the light of the morning sun.

I have no idea what day it is.

Tucker doesn't stop once we're out on one of the rubble-strewn streets. He takes us through the city and into the desert beyond, across barren terrain that rocks the vehicle with every ditch we cross.

Is he actually coming with us? A sinking feeling hits the pit of my stomach. He can't be trusted. The others need to know.

He brakes once we're over a kilometer outside the ruins.

"This should do it. Give you a head start on the hungriest of the mutos." The steering wheel materializes and the driver's door swings open automatically.

"Thanks again." Luther steps out and strides around the front of the vehicle. He holds his hand in the air as if he's expecting a handshake. Then he disappears. Samson curses softly to himself at the sight. I can't hear what Luther and Tucker say to each other. Moments later, Luther reappears and climbs into the driver's seat, leaving the door to shut automatically behind him.

"You're sure you don't want to give it a try," he asks Samson, nodding toward the steering wheel.

"Tempting." Samson shakes his massive head. "You go ahead. I'd probably kill us all with these things." He wobbles one arm.

"Where's Milton?" I ask.

Luther glances back with half a smile, then leans forward, squinting through the windshield. He points up at the sky. "There he is."

"Flying again?" Samson mutters. "Yeah, I won't be getting used to that anytime soon."

Milton can *fly*?

"He wants us to follow him." Tentative—but trying not to look it—Luther shifts the vehicle into drive and steps on the gas pedal. "Let's hope we have enough fuel to reach wherever he leads us."

Aren't we going back to the caves?

"We've got a few reserve tanks and some solar panels in back. We can install them if we need to." Samson chuckles and rotates his left wrist. Instantly, his fingers flip out of socket and spin to transform into various tools—screwdrivers, crescent wrenches and the like. "A dream come true."

Shechara giggles—something I haven't heard her do since we were down in the bunker years ago, playing practical jokes on our sisters. I catch her eye and reach up toward the dark stubble on her head, almost a centimeter long now. I run my fingers through it.

"You need a haircut," I tease.

"So do you!"

I glance into the rear-view mirror. "I'm thinking of growing it out."

She giggles again. "Me too."

"I don't know, Luther," Samson cautions. "We won't know what to do with *two* beautiful women."

Luther looks at me in the mirror. "They've always been beautiful, my friend."

I smile and look away, out the window. That's when I see it. We're going the wrong way—north instead of southeast.

"Where's Milton taking us?" I frown.

"He's been fairly enigmatic about it." Luther shakes his head.

"What about the caves?"

Luther glances at me in the mirror. "He said…no one's left."

"But that was before, when he was possessed—"

"When he came for us in Eden, he said he'd gone back there already. To see…" Luther shakes his head again, resolutely, his voice grim. "No one survived."

Why would Milton have gone back there alone?

We ride on in silence, crossing kilometer after kilometer of desolation, rocking through ditches, plunging down craters only to climb up the other sides and tear across the cracked hardpan beyond. Luther is a capable driver. Not as fast or as reckless as Samson, but we'll get there in one piece—wherever *there* is.

It's past noon, the sun high in the sky, when Luther slows to a stop on a flat plateau of hard-packed earth, hot beneath the scorching rays of the sun. He reaches back to hand us jumpsuits, boots, gloves, and face shields in neat stacks.

I wrinkle my nose at the sight. *Urine suits.*

"It's all we could find," he apologizes.

Outside, maybe thirty or more meters beyond the front of our vehicle, Milton has touched down and now stands with two other figures wearing the same suits and face shields. Who are they? Where have they come from? One of them hugs him close, and he returns the embrace. The other one stands off with arms crossed and chin raised. I watch them through the windshield as I pull the jumpsuit on over my clothes.

"Who are they?" I ask Luther.

He pauses, hesitating before he meets my gaze. "Milton said you'd be able to see them."

What does he mean? "You don't?"

He shakes his head.

"I'll stay put if it's alright with you," Samson growls. "I'd probably destroy any jumpsuit I tried climbing into." He wobbles both his arms and chuckles.

Luther reaches over to squeeze his bulky shoulder with obvious affection and steps out, snapping his face shield into place as the doors swing open. Shechara and I follow. The sun's heat is a strong presence, beating down on us and baking everything it touches. Luther steps toward Milton, and they confer quietly. Shechara walks toward the end of the plateau, probably to test the range of her new eyes. I hang back, feeling awkward and out of place as the two strangers stare at me, their face shields glinting in the sunlight.

Who the hell are they?

Suddenly a wall of sand flies up on one side, then the other, rushing into the sky. I whirl around as sand behind me does the same, trapping me where I stand. I turn to face the two strangers. I know better than to break through the rushing sand. I remember what happened to Rehana when she did, so long ago. It ripped her skin off.

One of the strangers moves toward me, cutting the distance between us in half as the sand arches over us now, blocking out the sun and casting a shadow across the ground. As the stranger approaches, the sand encircles us both, whirling around, shooting up into the sky where it creates a rushing canopy in motion. The other stranger stands just inside this perimeter of thrashing sand, rooted with arms crossed. Watching me.

Just the three of us. Luther and the others—will they try to break through and pull me out? Should I call to them, warn them to stay back? Would they even hear me?

The closer of the two strangers stands a few meters away. My hands have curled into fists, muscles tight. I'll fight them if I have to.

The stranger takes a step toward me and stops. The opaque polymer of the face shield holds no expression. Slowly, both of the stranger's gloved hands reach up. The clasp snaps open, and the face shield comes off.

"Hello, Daiyna." Rehana grins.

It can't be.

I stumble backward, muscles suddenly loose, my lips parting without sound. I stare, but I know she can't possibly be here. I saw them kill her.

"Surprised?" Her teeth flash white against flawless olive skin.

"How?" I manage weakly, my throat dry. "You're...*dead*!"

"Really? I look that bad?" She curses, then frowns with half a smile. "Thanks. You look good, too—from what I can tell."

I release my face shield and drop it to the ground. I stare at her.

"That's better." She winks. "Growing out your hair, or just lazy?"

How can this be? "How did you get here?"

The other one speaks. The voice is familiar but unwelcome. My abdomen tightens.

"We're here to send you off, Daiyna." She steps forward, beside Rehana, and takes off her face shield. Her fiery red hair billows around her pale, pinched face. "You have a long journey ahead."

Mother Lairen. This can't be real. I must've passed out. I'm dreaming this nightmare.

"He told you, didn't he?" Rehana raises an eyebrow.

Told me? Who? I shake my head sluggishly.

"You will go west," Mother Lairen says.

What about the Preserve? Aren't we going north?

"You will go to the coast. The path will be difficult. There will be others like you that you will meet along the way, and you will convince them to join you. It will not be easy." Mother Lairen casts a sidelong look at Rehana, one of both disapproval and resignation. "But it is the choice he made for you."

"He chose life over death, Daiyna." Rehana grins again. "So you will live. All of you."

"For now." Mother Lairen's eyes are cold as they glare at me. "Your days are numbered. The age of humans has come and gone. You will not last long on this New Earth."

Rehana frowns at her. "Doomsayer."

"Realist," Mother Lairen retorts, folding her arms.

This is so bizarre.

Rehana approaches me, and my first instinct is to draw back. But I don't. She wraps her arms around me and squeezes. I can't fight it. I melt into her embrace as tears sting my eyes, spilling down my cheeks. I've missed her so much.

"I will go before you, my sister," she whispers into my ear. "You have nothing to fear."

Nothing to fear...

I gasp. The voice of the spirits—

The sun blinds me, burning my wet cheeks. The sand canopy has vanished. Barely a breeze stirs now. I replace my face shield as fast as I can in the sudden absence of any shade.

Milton stands in front of me. "Weird, huh?"

"You saw them too?" I stare at my reflection in his cracked face shield.

"Sort of. They looked like...people I used to know."

"The spirits?"

He shrugs. "Yeah."

But they were *real*. They had substance. Some kind of physical manifestation, taking the form of people from our past... Copied from our own memories, stolen from our minds?

"Only we can see them?"

"I guess we're special, you and me."

The spirit manifesting itself as Rehana said *he chose life*. Did she mean Milton?

"They gave you a choice." What could it have been?

He looks away. "I hope I made the right one." He doesn't elaborate.

I nod slowly and look around, look for them—Rehana, Mother Lairen. But they're gone. Samson sits in the vehicle where we left him. Luther and Shechara stand a short distance away, their backs to us as they gaze into the west. No swirling sand. No spirits of the earth.

"So now what?" I feel empty inside, weightless...and yet something stirs deep within me, something I haven't felt for a very long time. Is it *hope*?

"The sky's the limit." He stretches his back, looking ready to return to the clouds.

I almost smile. "And after the sky?"

He nods, and the sun shines from his face shield. He watches Shechara and Luther.

"That'll be tomorrow."

FROM THE PUBLISHER

Thank you for reading *After the Sky,* book one in Spirits of the Earth.

We hope you enjoyed it as much as we enjoyed bringing it to you. We just wanted to take a moment to encourage you to review the book on Amazon and Goodreads. Every review helps further the author's reach and, ultimately, helps them continue writing fantastic books for us all to enjoy.

If you liked this book, check out the rest of our catalogue at www.aethonbooks.com. To sign up to receive a FREE collection from some of our best authors as well as updates regarding all new releases, visit www.aethonbooks.com/sign-up.

JOIN THE STREET TEAM! Get advanced copies of all our books, plus other free stuff and help us put out hit after hit.

SEARCH ON FACEBOOK:
AETHON STREET TEAM

ALSO IN THE SERIES

You just read: ***After the Sky***
Tomorrow's Children
City of Glass

Printed in Great Britain
by Amazon